SCATTERGOOD BAINES

Clarence Budington Kelland

Contents

SCATTERGOOD BAINES

BY

Clarence Budington Kelland

CHAPTER I
HE INVADES COLDRIVER

The entrance of Scattergood Baines into Coldriver Valley, and the manner of his first taking root in its soil, are legendary. This much is clear past even disputing in the post office at mail time, or evenings in the grocery-- he walked in, perspiring profusely, for he was very fat.

It is asserted that he walked the full twenty-four miles from the railroad, sub- sisting on the country, as it were, and sagged down on the porch of Locker's grocery just before sundown. It is not implied that he walked all of the twenty-four miles in that single day. Huge bodies move deliberately.

He sagged down on Locker's porch, and it is reported the corner of the porch sagged with him. George Peddie has it from his grandfather, who was an eyewit- ness, that Scattergood did not so much as turn his head to look at the assembled manhood of the vicinity, but with infinite pains and audible grunts, succeeded in bringing first one foot, then the other, within reach of his hands, and removed his shoes. Following this he sighed with a great contentment and twiddled his bare toes openly and flagrantly in the eyes of all Coldriver. He is said now to have uttered the first words to fall from his mouth in the town where were to lie his life's unfoldings and fulfillments. They were significant--in the light of subsequent activities.

"One of them railroads runnin' up here," said he to the mountain just across the road from him, "would have spared me close to a dozen blisters."

Conversation had expired on Scattergood's arrival, and the group on the porch converted itself into an audience. It was an audience that got its money's worth. Not for an instant did the attention of a single member of it stray away from this God- send come to furnish them with their first real topic of conversation since Crazy French stole a box of Paris green, mistaking it for a new sort of pancake flour.

Scattergood arose ponderously and limped out into the middle of the dusty road. From this vantage point he slowly and conscientiously studied the village.

"Uh-huh!" he said. "'Twouldn't pay to do all that walkin' just for a visit. Calc'late I'll have to settle."

He walked directly back to the absorbed group of leading citizens, his shoes dangling, one in each hand, and addressed them genially.

"Your town," said he, "is growin'. Its population jest increased by me."

"Sizable growth," said Old Man Penny, dryly, letting his eye rove over Scattergood's bulk.

"My line," said Scattergood, "is anythin' needful. Outside of a railroad, what you figger you need most?"

Nobody answered.

"Is it a grocery store?" asked Scattergood.

Locker stiffened in his chair. "Me and Sam Kittleman calc'lates to sell all the groceries this town needs," he said.

"How about dry goods?" said Scattergood.

Old Man Penny and Wade Lumley stirred to life at this.

"Lumley and me takes care of the dry goods," said the old man.

"Uh-huh! How about a clothin' store?"

"We got all the clothin' stores there's room for," said Lafe Atwell. "I run it."

"Kind of got the business of this town sewed up, hain't you?" Scattergood asked, admiringly. "Wouldn't look with favor on any more stores?"

"We calculate to keep what business we got," said Old Man Penny. "A outsider would have a hard time makin' a go of it here."

"Quite likely," said Scattergood. "Still, you never can tell. Let some feller come in here with a gen'ral store, sellin' for cash--and cuttin' prices, eh? How would an outsider git along if he done that? Up-to-date store. Fresh goods. Low prices. Eh? Calc'late some of you fellers would have to discharge a clerk."

"You hain't got money enough to start a store," Old Man Penny squawked. "Why, you hain't even got a satchel! You come walkin' in like a tramp."

"There's tramps--and tramps," said Scattergood, placidly. He reached far down into a trousers pocket and tugged to the light of day a roll that his fingers could not encircle. He looked at it fondly, tossed it up in the air a couple of times and caught it, and then held it between thumb and forefinger until the eyes of his audience had assured themselves that the outside bill was yellow and its denomination twenty dollars.... The audience gulped.

"Meals to the tavern perty good?" Coldriver's new citizen asked.

"Say," demanded Locker, "be you really thinkin' about startin' a cash store here?"

"Neighbor," said Scattergood, "never give up valuable information without gittin' somethin' for it. How much money would a complete and careful account of my intentions be worth to you?"

Locker snorted. "Bet that wad of bills is a dummy with a counterfeit twenty outside of it," he said.

Scattergood smiled tantalizingly. Locker had not, fortunately for Scattergood, the least idea how close to the truth he had been. On one point only had he been mistaken. The twenty outside was not counterfeit. However, except for three fives, four twos, and ninety cents in silver, it represented Scattergood's total cash capital.

"I'm goin'," said Scattergood, "to order me two suppers. Two! From bean soup to apple pie. It's my birthday. Twenty-six to-day, and I always eat two suppers on my birthdays.... Glad you leadin' citizens see fit to give me such a hearty welcome to your town. Right kind and generous of you."

He turned and ambled down the road toward the tavern, planting his bare feet with evident pleasure in the deepest of the warm sand, and flirting up little clouds of it behind him. The audience saw him seat himself on the tavern steps and pull on his shoes. They were too far to hear him say speculatively to himself: "I never heard tell of a man gittin' a start in life jest that way--but that hain't any reason it can't be done. I'm goin' to do this town good, and this valley. Hain't no more 'n fair them leadin' citizens should give me what help they feel they kin."

Scattergood ate with ease and pleasure two complete suppers--to the openly expressed admiration of Emma, the waitress. Very shortly afterward he retired to his room, where, not trusting to the sturdiness of the bed-slats provided, he dragged mattress and bedding to the floor and was soon emitting snores that Landlord Coombs assured his wife was the beat of anybody ever slept in the house not countin' that travelin' man from Boston. Next morning Scattergood was about early, padding slowly up and down the crossed streets which made up the village.

He was studying the ground for immediate strategic purposes, just as he had been studying the valley on his long trudge up from the railroad for purposes related to distant campaigns. Though Scattergood's arrival in Coldriver may have seemed impromptu, as his adoption of the town for a permanent location seemed abrupt, not to say impulsive, neither really was so. Scattergood rarely acted without reason and after reflection.

True, he had but a moment's glimpse of Coldriver before he decided he had moved there, but the glimpse showed him the location was the one he had been searching for.... Scattergood's specialty, his hobby, was valleys. Valleys down which splashed and roared sizable streams, whose mountain sides were covered with timber, and whose flats were comfortable farms--such valleys interested him with an especial interest. But the valley he had been looking for was one with but a single possible outlet. He wanted a valley whose timber and produce and products could not go climbing off across the hills, over a number of easy roads, to market. His valley must be hemmed in. The only way to market must lie down the valley, with the river. And the river that flowed down his valley must be swift, with sufficient volume all twelve months of the year to turn possible mill wheels.... As yet he thought only of the direct application of power. He had not dreamed yet of great turbine generators which should transport thousands of horse power, written in terms of electricity, hundreds of miles across country, there to light cities and turn the wheels of huge manufactories....

Coldriver Valley was that valley! He felt it as soon as he turned into it; certainty increased as he progressed between those gigantic walls black with tall, straight, beautiful spruce. So, when he sat shoeless, resting his blistered feet on Locker's porch, he was ready to make his decision. The mere making of it was a negligible detail.

So Scattergood Baines found his valley. He entered it consciously as an invader, determined to conquer. Pitiful as were the resources of Cortez as he adventured against the power of Montezuma, or of Pizarro as he clambered over the Peruvian Andes, they were gigantic compared with Scattergood's. He was starting to make his conquest backed by one twenty, three fives, four twos, and ninety cents in silver. It was obvious to him the country to be conquered must supply the sinews of war for its own conquest.

Every village has its ramshackle, disused store building. Coldriver had one, especially well located, and not so ramshackle as it might have been. It was big; its front was crossed by a broad porch; its show windows were not show windows at all, but were put there solely to give light. Coldriver did not know there was such a thing as inviting patronage by skillful display.

"Sonny," said Scattergood to a boy digging worms in the shade of the building, "who owns this here ruin?"

"Old Tom Plummer," said the boy, and was even able to disclose where old Tom was to be found. Scattergood found him feeding a dozen White Orpingtons.

"Best layers a man can keep," said Scattergood, sincerely. "Man's got to have brains to even raise chickens."

"I git more eggs to the hen than anybody else in town," said old Tom, "but nobody listens to me."

"Own a store buildin' downtown, don't you?"

"Calc'late to."

"If you was to git a chance to rent it, how much would it be a month?"

"Repairs or no repairs?"

"No repairs."

"Twenty dollars."

"G'mornin'," said Scattergood, and turned toward the gate.

"What's your hurry, mister?"

"Can't bear to stay near a man that mentions so much money in a breath," said Scattergood, with his most ingratiating grin.

"How much could you stay and hear?"

"Not over ten."

"Huh!... Seein' the buildin's in poor shape, I'll call it fifteen."

"Twelve-fifty's as far's I'll go--on a five-year lease," said Scattergood. It will be seen he fully intended to become permanent.

"What you figger on usin' it fur?"

"Maybe a opry house, maybe a dime museum, maybe a carpenter shop, and maybe somethin' else. I hain't mentionin' jest what, but it's law-abidin' and respectable."

"Five-year lease, eh? Twelve-fifty."

"Two months' rent in advance," said Scattergood.

"Squire Hastings'll draw the papers," said old Tom, heading for the gate. Scattergood followed, and in half an hour was the lessee of a store building, bound to pay rent for five years, with more than half his capital vanished--with no stock of goods or wherewith to procure one, with not even a day's experience in any sort of merchandising to his credit.

His next step was to buy ten yards of white cloth, a small paint brush, and a can of paint. Ostentatiously he borrowed a stepladder and stretched the cloth across the front of his store, from post to post. Then, equally ostentatiously, he mounted the stepladder and began to paint a sign. He was not unskilled in the business of lettering. The sign, when completed, read:

CASH AND CUT PRICES IS MY MOTTO

Having completed this, he bought a pail, a mop, and a broom, and proceeded to a thorough housecleaning of his premises.

Old Man Penny and Locker and the rest of the merchants were far from oblivious to Scattergood's movements. No sooner had his sign appeared than every merchant in town--excepting Junkin, the druggist, who sold wall paper and farm machinery as side lines--went into executive session in the back room of Locker's store.

"He means business," said Locker.

"Leased that store for five year," said Old Man Penny.

"Cash, and Cut Prices," quoted Atwell, "and you fellers know our folks would pass by their own brothers to save a penny. He'll force us to cut, too."

"Me--I won't do it," asserted Kettleman.

"Then you'll eat your stock," growled Locker.

"Fellers," said Atwell, "if this man gits started it's goin' to cost all of us money. He'll draw some trade, even if he don't cut prices. Safe to figger he'll git a sixth of it. And a sixth of the business in this region is a pretty fair livin'. If he goes slashin' right and left, nobody kin tell how much trade he'll draw."

"We should 'a' leased that store between us. Then nobody could 'a' come in."

"But we didn't. And it's goin' to cost us money. If he puts in clothing it'll cost me five hundred dollars a year in profits, anyhow. Maybe more. And you other fellers clost to as much."

"But we can't do nothin'."

"We can buy him off," said Atwell.

The meeting at that moment became noisy. Epithets were applied with freedom to Scattergood, and even to Atwell, for these were not men who loved to part with their money. However, Atwell showed them the economy of it. It was either for them to suffer one sharp pang now, or to endure a greater dragging misery. They went in a body to call upon Scattergood.

"Howdy, neighbors!" Scattergood said, genially.

"We're the merchants of this town," said Old Man Penny, shortly.

"So I judged," said Scattergood.

"There's merchants enough here," the old man roared on. "Too many. We don't want any more. We don't want you should start up any business here."

"You're too late. It's started. I've leased these premises."

"But you hain't no stock in."

"I calc'late on havin' one shortly," said Scattergood, with a twinkle in his eye, whose meaning was kindly concealed from the five.

"What'll you take not to order any stock?" asked Atwell, abruptly.

"Figger on buyin' me off, eh? Now, neighbors, I've been lookin' for a place like this, and I calc'late on stayin'. I'm goin' to become all-fired permanent here."

"Give you a hundred dollars," said Old Man Penny.

"Apiece?" asked Scattergood, and laughed jovially. "It's my busy day, neighbors. Better call in again."

"What's your figger to pull out now--'fore you're started?"

"Hain't got no figger, but if I had I calc'late it would be about a thousand dollars."

"Give you two hundred," said Old Man Penny.

Scattergood picked up his mop. "If you fellers really mean business, talk business. I've figgered my profits in this store, countin' in low prices, wouldn't be a cent under a couple of thousand the first year.... And you know it. That's what you're fussin' around here for. Now fish or git to bait cuttin'."

"Five hundred dollars," said Atwell, and Old Man Penny moaned.

"Tell you what I'll do," said Scattergood. "You men git back here inside of an hour with seven hundred and fifty cash, and lay it in my hand, and I'll agree not to sell groceries, dry goods, notions, millinery, or men or women's clothes in this town for a term of twenty year."

They drew off and scolded one another, and glowered at Scattergood, but came to scratch. "It's jest like robbery," said Old Man Penny, tremulously.

"Keep your money," retorted Scattergood. "I'm satisfied the way things is at present."

Within the hour they were back with seven hundred and fifty dollars in bills, a lawyer, and an agreement, which Scattergood read with minute attention. It bound him not to sell, barter, trade, exchange, deal, or in any way to derive a profit from the handling of groceries, dry goods, notions, millinery, clothing, and gent's furnishings. It contained no hidden pitfalls, and Scattergood was satisfied. He signed his name and thrust the roll of bills into his pocket.... Then he picked up his mop and went to work as hard as ever.

"Say," Old Man Penny said, "what you goin' ahead for? You jest agreed not to."

"There wasn't nothin' said about moppin'," grinned Scattergood, "and there wasn't nothin' said about hardware and harness and farm implements, neither. If you don't b'lieve me, jest read the agreement. What I'm doin', neighbors, is git this place cleaned out to put in the finest cash, cut-price, up-to-date hardware store in the state. And thank you, neighbors. You've done right kindly by a stranger...."

To this point the history of Scattergood Baines has been for the most part legendary; now we begin to encounter him in the public records, for deeds, mortgages, and the like begin to appear with his name upon them. His history becomes authentic.

Seven hundred and fifty dollars is not much when put into hardware, but Scattergood had no intention of putting even that into a stock of goods. He had a notion that the right kind of man, with five hundred dollars, could get credit to twice that amount, and as for farm machinery, he could sell by catalogue or on commission. His suspicion was proven to be fact.

But it was not in Scattergood to sit idle while he waited for his stock to arrive. Coldriver doubtless thought him idle, but he was studying the locality and the river with the eye of a commander who knew this was to be his battlefield. What Scattergood wanted now was to place himself astride Coldriver Valley, somewhere below the village, so that he could control the upper reaches of the stream. It was not difficult to find such a location. It lay three miles below town, at the junction of the north and south branches of Coldriver. The juncture was in a big, marshy, untillable flat, from which hills rose abruptly. From the easterly end of the flat the augmented river squeezed in a roaring rapids through a sort of bottle neck.

Scattergood stood on the hillside and looked upon this with satisfied eye.

"A dam across that bottle neck," he said to himself, "will flood that flat. Reg'lar reservoy. Millpond. Git a twenty-foot fall here easy, maybe more. Calc'late that'll run about any mill folks'll want to build. And," he scratched his head as a sort of congratulation to it for its efficiency, "I can't study out how anybody's agoin' to git logs past here without dickerin' with the man who owns the dam...." Plenty of water twelve months a year to give free power; a flat made to order for reservoir or log pond; a complete and effective blockade of both branches of the river which came down from a country richly timbered! It was one of the spots Scattergood had dreamed of.

Scattergood knew perfectly well he could not stop a log from passing his dam. Nor could he shut off the stream. Any dam he built must have a sluice which could be opened for the passage of timber, and all timber was entitled to "natural water." But, as he well knew, "natural water" was not always enough. A dam at this point would raise the level on the bars of the flat so that logs would not jam, and a log which used the high water caused by the dam must pay for it. What Scattergood had in mind was a dam and boom company. It was his project to improve the river, to boom backwaters, to dynamite ledges, to make the river passable to logs in spring and fall. It was his idea that such a company, in addition to demanding pay for the use of "improvements," could contract with lumbermen up the river to drive their logs.... And a mill at this point! Scattergood fairly licked his lips as he thought of the millions upon millions of feet of spruce to be sawed into lumber.

The firm foundation that Scattergood's strategy rested upon was that lumbering had not really started in the valley. The valley had not opened up, but lay undeveloped, waiting to be stirred to life. Scattergood's strength lay in that he could see ahead of to-day, and was patient to wait for the developments that to-morrow must bring. To-day his foresight could get for him what would be impossible to-morrow. If he stepped softly he could obtain a charter from the state to develop that river, which, when lumbering interests became actually engaged, would be fought by them to the last penny.... And he felt in his bones that day would not long be delayed.

The land Scattergood required was owned by three individuals. All of it was worthless--except to a man of vision--so, treading lightly, Scattergood went about acquiring what he needed. His method was not direct approach. He went to the owners of that land with proffers to sell, not to buy. To Landers, who owned the marsh on both shores of the river, he tried to sell the newest development in mowing machines, and his manner of doing so was to hitch to the newly arrived machine, haul it to Landers's meadow--where the owner was haying--drag it through the gate, and unhitch.

"Here," he said, "try this here machine. Won't cost you nothin' to try it, and I'm curious to see if it works as good as they say."

Landers was willing. It worked better. Landers regarded the machine longingly, and spoke of price. Scattergood disclosed it.

"Hain't got it and can't afford it," said Landers.

"Might afford a swap?"

"Might. What you got in mind?"

"Say," said Scattergood, changing the subject, "ever try drainin' that marsh in the fork? Looks like it could be done. Might make a good medder."

Landers laughed. "If you want to try," he chuckled, "I'll trade it to you for this here mowin' machine."

"Hum!..." grunted Scattergood, and higgled and argued, but ended by accepting a deed for the land and turning over the machine to Landers. Scattergood himself had sixty days to pay for it. It cost him something like half a dollar an acre, and Landers considered he had robbed the hardware merchant of a machine.

One side of the bottle neck Scattergood took in exchange for a kitchen stove and a double harness; the third parcel of land came to him for a keg of nails, five gallons of paint, sundry kitchen utensils, and twelve dollars and fifty cents in money.... And when Coldriver heard of the deals it chuckled derisively and regarded its hardware merchant with pitying scorn.

Then Scattergood left a youth in charge of his store and went softly to the state capital. In after years his skill in handling legislatures was often remarked upon with displeasure. His young manhood held prophecy of this future ability, for he came home acquainted with nine tenths of the legislators, laughed at by half of them as a harmless oddity, and with a state charter for his river company in his pocket.... When folks heard of that charter they held their sides and roared.

Scattergood returned to selling hardware, and waited. He had an idea he would hear something stirring on his trail before long, and he fancied he could guess who and what that something would be. He judged he would hear from two gentlemen named Crane and Keith. Crane owned some twenty thousand acres of timber along the North Branch; Keith owned slightly lesser limits along the South Branch. Both gentlemen were lumbering and operating mills in another state; their Coldriver holdings they had acquired, and, as the saying is, forgotten, until the time should come when they would desire to move into Coldriver Valley.

Now these holdings were recalled sharply to memory, and both of them took train to Coldriver.

Scattergood had not worried about it. He had simply gone along selling hardware in his own way--and selling a good deal of it. His store had a new front, his stock was augmented. It was his business to sell goods, and he sold them.

For instance, Lem Jones stopped and hitched his team before the store, one chilly day. His horses he covered with old burlap, lacking blankets. While Lem was buying groceries, Scattergood selected two excellent blankets, carried them out, and put them on the horses. Then he went back into the store to attend to other matters. Presently Lem came in.

"Where'd them blankets come from?" he asked.

"Hosses looked a mite chilly," said Scattergood, without interest, "so I covered 'em."

"Bleeged," said Lem. Then, awkwardly, "I calc'late I need a pair of blankets, but I can't afford 'em this year. Wife's been sick--"

"Sure," said Scattergood, "I know. If you want them blankets take 'em along. Pay me when you kin.... Jest give me a sort of note for a memorandum. Glad to accommodate you."

So Scattergood marketed his blankets, taking in exchange a perfectly good, interest-bearing note. Also, he made a friend, for Lem could not be convinced but Scattergood had done him a notable favor.

Scattergood now had money in the bank. No longer did he have to stretch his credit for stock. He was established--and all in less than a year. Hardware, it seemed, had been a commodity much needed in that locality, yet no one had handled it in sufficient stock because of the twenty-four-mile haul. That had been too costly. It cost Scattergood just as much, but his customers paid for it.... The difference between him and the other merchants was that he sold goods while they allowed folks to buy.

So, wisely, he kept on building up in a small way, while waiting for bigger things to develop. And as he waited he studied the valley until he could recite every inch of it, and he studied the future until he knew what the future would require of that valley. He knew it before the future knew it and before the valley knew it, and was laying his plans to be ready with pails to catch the sap when others, taken by surprise, would be running wildly about seeking for buckets.

Then Crane and Keith arrived in Coldriver.... That day marked Scattergood's emergence from the ranks of country merchants, though he retained his hardware store to the last. That day marked distinctly Scattergood's launching on a greater body of water. For forty years he sailed it with varying success, meeting failures sometimes, scoring victories; but interesting, characteristic in every phase--a genius in his way and a man who never took the commonplace course when the unusual was open to him.

"I suppose you've looked this man Baines up," said Crane to Keith when they met in the Coldriver tavern.

"I know how much he weighs and how many teeth he's had filled," Keith replied.

"He ought not to be so difficult to handle. He hasn't capital enough to put this company of his through and his business experience don't amount to much."

"For monkeying with our buzz saw," said Keith, "we ought to let him lose a couple of fingers."

"How's this for an idea, then?" Crane said, and for fifteen minutes he outlined his theory of how best to eliminate Scattergood Baines from being an obstruction to the free flowage of their schemes for Coldriver Valley.

"It's got others by the hundred, in one form or another," agreed Keith. "This jayhawker'll welcome it with tears of joy."

Whereupon they went gladly on their way to Scattergood's store, not as enemies, but as business men who recognized his abilities and preferred to have him with them from the start, that they might profit by his canniness and energy, rather than to array themselves against him in an effort to take away from him what he had obtained.

Only by the exercise of notable will power could Crane keep his face straight as he shook hands with ungainly Scattergood and saw with his own eyes what a perfect bumpkin he had to deal with.

"I suppose you thought we fellows would be sore," he said, genially.

"Dunno's I thought about you at all," said Scattergood. "I was thinkin' mainly about me."

"Well, we're not. You caught us napping, of course. We should have grabbed off that dam location long ago--but we weren't expecting anybody to stray in with his eyes open--like yourself.... Of course your property and charter aren't worth a great deal till we start lumbering."

"Not to anybody but me," said Scattergood.

"Well, we expect to begin operations in a year or so. We'll build a mill on the railroad, and drive our logs down the river."

"Givin' my company the drivin' contracts?"

"Looks like we'd have to--if you get in your dam and improvements. But that'll take money. We've looked you up, of course, and we know you haven't it--nor any backing.... That's why we've come to see you."

"To be sure," said Scattergood. "Goin' to drive 'way to the railroad, eh? How if there was a mill right at my dam? Shorten your drive twenty mile, wouldn't it, eh?"

"Yes," said Keith, laughing at Scattergood's ignorance; "but how about transportation from your mill to the railroad? We can't drive cut lumber."

"Course not," said Scattergood, "but this valley's goin' to open up. It's startin'. There's only one way to open a valley, and that's to run a railroad up it.... Narrow-gauge 'u'd do here. Carry mostly lumber, but passengers, too."

"Thinking of building one?" asked Crane, almost laughing in Scattergood's face.

"Thinkin' don't cost nobody anythin'," said Scattergood. "Ever take a look at that charter of mine?"

"No."

"I'll let you read it over a bit. Maybe you'll git a idea from it."

He extracted the parchment from his safe, and spread it before them. "Kind of look careful along toward the end--in the tail feathers of it, so to speak," he advised.

They did so, and Crane looked up at the fat hardware man with eyes that were not quite so contemptuous. "By George!" he said, "this thing's a charter for a railroad down the valley, too."

"Uh-huh!" said Scattergood. "Dunno's the boys quite see what it was all about, but they calculated to please me, so they put it through jest as it stood. Mighty nice fellers up to the legislature."

"Pretty far in the future," said Keith, "and mighty expensive."

"Maybe not so far," said Scattergood, "and I could make a darn good start narrow-gaugin' it with a hunderd thousand."

"Which you've got handy for use," said Crane.

"There is that much money," said Scattergood, "and if there is, why, it kin be got."

"Let's get back to the river, now," said Keith. "If we're going to start lumbering in a year, say, we've got to have the river in shape. Take quite some time to get it cleared and dammed and boomed."

"Six months," said Scattergood.

"Cost a right smart pile."

"The work I'm figgerin' on would come to about thirty-odd thousand."

"Which you haven't got."

"Somebody has," said Scattergood.

"We have," said Crane. "That's why we came to you--and with a proposition. You've grabbed this thing off, but you can't hog it, because you haven't the money to put it through. Our offer is this: You put in your locations and your charter against our money. We'll finance it. Your enterprise entitles you to control. We won't dispute that. You can have fifty-one per cent of the stock for what you've contributed. We take the rest for financing. We're known, and can get money."

"How you figger to work it?"

"We'll bond for forty thousand dollars. Keith and I can place the bonds. That'll give us money to go ahead."

Scattergood reached down and took off a huge shoe. Usually he thought more accurately when his feet were unconfined. "That means we'd sort of mortgage the whole thing, eh?"

"That's the idea."

"And if we didn't pay interest on the bonds, why, the fellers that had 'em could foreclose?"

"But we needn't worry about that."

"Not," said Scattergood, "if you fellers sign a contract with the dam and boom company to give them the exclusive job of drivin' all your timber at, say, sixty cents a thousand feet of logs. And if you'd stick a clause in that contract that you'd begin cuttin' within twelve months from date."

"Sure we'd do that," said Keith. "To our advantage as much as to yours."

"To be sure," said Scattergood.

"It's a deal, then?"

"Far's I'm concerned," said Scattergood, slipping his foot inside his shoe, "it is."

That afternoon, the papers having been signed and the deal consummated, Scattergood sat cogitating.

"I've been done," he said to himself, solemnly, "accordin' to them fellers' notion. They come and seen me, and done me. They planned out how they'd do it, and I didn't never suspect a thing. Uh-huh! Seems like I was unfortunate, just gettin' a start in life like I be.... Bonds, says they. Uh-huh! They'll place 'em, and place 'em handy. First int'rest day there won't be no int'rest, and them bonds'll be foreclosed--and where'll I be? Mighty ingenious fellers, Crane and Keith.... And I up and walked right into it like a fly into a molasses barrel. Them fellers," he said, even more somberly, "come here calc'latin' to cheat me out of my river.... Me bein' jest a fat man without no brains...."

Crane and Keith had left Scattergood the executive head of the new dam and boom company, and had confided to him the task of building the dam and improving the river. He approached it sadly.

"Might as well save what I kin out of the wreck," he said to himself, and quietly manufactured a dummy contracting company to whom he let the entire job for a lump sum of thirty-eight thousand seven hundred dollars. The dummy contractor was Scattergood Baines.

The dam was completed, booms and cribbing placed, ledges blasted out well within the six months' period set for those operations. Every thirty days Scattergood, in the name of the dummy contractor, was paid eighty per cent of his estimates, and at the completion of the work he received the remainder of the whole sum.

"I wouldn't 'a' done it to them boys," he said, as he surveyed a deposit of upward of seven thousand dollars, his profit on the transaction, "if it hadn't 'a' been they organized to cheat me out of my river. I calc'late in the circumstances, though, I'm most entitled to what I kin salvage out of the wreck."

Now the Coldriver Dam and Boom Company, Scattergood Baines president and manager, was ready for business, which was to take the logs of Messrs. Crane and Keith and drive them down the river at the rate of sixty cents per thousand feet. It was ready and eager, and so expressed itself in quaintly worded communications from Baines to those gentlemen. But no logs appeared to be driven.

"Jest like I said," Scattergood told himself, and, the day being hot and the road dusty, he removed his shoes and rested his sweltering bulk in the shade to consider it.

"It's a nice river," he said, audibly. "I hate to git done out of it."

After long delays Crane and Keith made pretense of building camps and starting to log. But one difficulty after another descended on their operations. In the spring, when each of them should have had several millions of feet of spruce ready to roll into the water, not a log was on rollways. Not a man was in the camps, for, owing to reasons not to be comprehended by the public, the woodsmen of both operators had struck simultaneously and left the woods.

Presently the first interest day arrived, with not even a hope of being able to meet the required payment at a future date. Bondholders--dummies, just as Scattergood's contractor was a dummy--met. Their deliberations were brief. Foreclose with all promptitude was their word, and foreclose they did. With the result that legal notices were published to the effect that on the sixteenth day of June the dam, booms, cribbing, improvements, charter, contracts, and property of whatsoever nature belonging to the Coldriver Dam and Boom Company were to be sold at public auction on the steps of the county courthouse. Scattergood had lost his river....

"Terms of the sale are cash with the bid," said Crane to Keith. "I saw to that."

"Good. Wasn't necessary, I guess. There hasn't been even a wriggle out of Baines."

"Won't be. We'll have to send somebody up to bid it in. It's just taking money out of one pocket to put it into the other, but we've got to go through the motions."

"Anyhow, let's get credit for grabbing a bargain," said Keith. "Bid her in cheap. No use taking a big wad of money out of circulation even for a few days."

"Ten thousand'll be enough. Say ten thousand six hundred, just to make it sound better. Have to have two bidders there."

"Sure," agreed Keith. "I guess this'll teach our fat dreamer of dreams not to get in the way of the cars."

Scattergood's stock had gone down in Coldriver. True, his hardware store was thriving. In the two years his stock had increased from what his seven hundred and fifty dollars, with credit added, would buy, to an inventory of better than five thousand dollars, free of debt. It is true also that with the last winter coming on he had looked about for a chance to keep his small surplus at work for him, and his eyes had fallen upon the item of firewood. In Coldriver were a matter of sixty houses and a hotel, all of which derived their heat from hardwood chunks, and cooked their meals on range fires with sixteen-inch split wood. The houses were mostly of that large, comfortable, country variety which could not be kept warm with one fire. Scattergood figured they would burn on an average of fifteen cords of wood.

Now stove wood, to be really useful, must have seasoned a year. It is not pleasant to build fires with green wood. Appreciating this, Scattergood ambled about the countryside and bought up every available stick of wood at prices of the day--and under, for he was a good buyer. He secured a matter of a thousand cords--and then waited hopefully.

It was a small transaction, promising no great profits, but Scattergood Baines was never, even when a rich man, one to scorn a small deal.... Within sixty days he turned over his corner in wood, realizing a profit of something over four hundred dollars.... This is merely to illustrate how Scattergood's capital grew.

On June 16th Scattergood drove to the county seat. He now owned a horse, and a buggy whose seat he more than comfortably filled. In the county seat Scattergood was not unknown, for various county officers had been helped to their place by his growing influence in his town--notably the sheriff.

There was little interest in the sale, and what interest there was Scattergood caused by his unexpected appearance. Nobody had imagined he would be present. Now that he was there, nobody could imagine why. He did not enlighten them, though he was delighted to sit in the sun on the courthouse steps, waiting for the hour of the sale, and to chat. He loved to chat, especially if he could get off his shoes and wriggle his toes in the sunshine. And so he sat, bare of foot, when the sheriff appeared and made his announcement of the approaching sale. Scattergood chatted on, apparently not interested.

"All the dams, booms, cribbings, improvements, and property of the Coldriver Dam and Boom Company ..." the sheriff read.

"Including contracts and charter," amended Scattergood.

"Including contracts and charter," agreed the sheriff, and Scattergood continued his chat.

Bidding began. It was not brisk or exciting. Five thousand was the first offer, from a young man appertaining to Crane. Keith's young man raised him five hundred. Back and forth they tossed it, carrying on the pretense, until Keith's young man reached the sum of ten thousand six hundred dollars.... A silence followed.

"Ten thousand six hundred I'm offered," said the sheriff, loudly, and repeated it. He had been a licensed auctioneer in his day. "Do I hear seven hundred? Seven hundred ... Six fifty ..." A portentous pause. "Going at ten thousand six hundred, once. Going at ten thousand six hundred, twice ..."

"Ten thousand seven hunderd," said Scattergood, casually.

Crane's young man looked at Keith's young man in a panic. They had only the sum they had bid upon them.... Cash with bid were the terms of sale. Scattergood, out of the corner of his eye, saw them rush together and confer frenziedly. His eye glinted.

"Ten thousand eight hundred," Crane's youth bid, desperately.

"Cash with bid is terms of sale," said Scattergood. "I object to listenin' to that bid without the young man perduces." He smiled at the sheriff.

"Mr. Baines is right," said the sheriff. "Protect your bid with the cash or I cannot receive it."

"Make him protect his bid!" shouted Crane's young man.

"Certain," said Scattergood, approaching the sheriff and drawing a huge roll of bills from his sagging trousers pocket. "Calc'late you'll find her there, Mr. Sheriff, and some besides. Make your change and gimme back the rest."

"I'm waitin' on you, young feller," said the sheriff, eying the young men.... "Ten thousand seven hundred I hear. Going at ten thousand seven hundred-- once.... Twice.... Three times!... Sold to Mr. Baines for ten thousand seven hundred dollars...."

So ends the first epoch of Scattergood Baines's career in Coldriver Valley. Here he emerges as a personage. From this point his fame began to spread, and legend grew. Had he not, in two brief years, after arriving with less than fifty dollars as a total capital, acquired a profitable hardware store--donated in the beginning by competitors? Had he not now, for the most part with money wrenched from Crane and Keith by his dummy contracting, been enabled to bid in for ten thousand seven hundred dollars a new property worth nearly four times that much? He was a man into whose band wagon all were eager to clamber.

But Scattergood did not change. He went back to his hardware store and waited--waited for Crane and Keith to start their inevitable logging operations. For in his safe reposed ironclad contracts with those gentlemen, covering the future for a decade, compelling them to pay him sixty cents for every thousand feet of timber that floated down his river. It was a good two years' work. He could well afford to wait....

Scattergood sat on the porch of his store, in the sunniest spot, twiddling his bare toes.

"The way to make money," he said to the mountain opposite, "is to let smarter folks 'n you be make it for you ... like I done."

CHAPTER II
SCATTERGOOD KICKS UP THE DUST

Scattergood Baines sat on the porch of his hardware store and looked down Coldriver Valley. It was very beautiful, even under the hot summer sun of the second anniversary of Scattergood's arrival in that part of the world, but he was not seeing it as it was--mountainous, green, with untouched forests, quickened to life and sound by the swift, rushing, splashing downrush of a tireless mountain river. Scattergood saw the valley as he was going to make it, for he was a specialist in valleys.

For years he had searched for an undeveloped valley--for the sort of valley it would be worth his while to take in hand, and two years ago he had found it and invaded it. His equipment for its conquest had been meager--some fifty dollars in money and a head filled from ear to ear and from eyebrows to scalp lock with shrewdness. His progress in twenty-four months had been notable, for he was sole proprietor of a profitable hardware store in Coldriver village, and controlled the upper stretches of Coldriver by virtue of a certain dam and boom company built with other men's capital for Scattergood's benefit and behoof.

Now, in the eye of his mind, he could see the whole twenty-odd miles of his valley. Along the left bank, hanging perilously to the slope of the mountain, he saw the rails of a narrow-gauge railroad reaching from Coldriver Valley to the main line that passed the valley's mouth. He saw sturdy, snorting little engines drawing logs to sawmills of a magnitude not dreamed of by any other man in the locality, and he saw other engines hauling out lumber to the southward. He saw villages where no villages existed that day, and villages meaning more traffic for his railroad, more trade for the stores he had it in his thought to establish. Something else he saw, but more dimly. This vision took the shape of a gigantic dam far back in the mountains, behind which should be stored the waters from the melting snows and from the spring rains, so that they might be released at will to insure a uniform flow throughout the year, wet months and dry months, as he desired. He saw this water pouring over other dams, turning water wheels, giving power to mills and factories. More than that, in the remotest and dimmest recess of his brain he saw not sharply, not with full comprehension, this tremendous water power converted into electricity and transported mile upon mile over far-reaching wires, to give light and energy to distant communities.

But all that was remote; it lay in the years to come. For the present smaller affairs must content him. Even the matter of the narrow-gauge railroad was beyond his grasp.

Scattergood reached down mechanically and removed his huge shoes; then, stretching out his fat legs gratefully, he twiddled his toes in the sunlight and gave himself up to practical thought. He controlled the tail of the valley with his dam and boom company; he must control its mouth. He must have command over the exit from the valley so that every individual, every log, every article of merchandise that entered or left the valley, should pass through his hands. That was to be the next step. He must straddle the mouth of the valley like the fat colossus he was.

Scattergood was placid and patient. He knew what he wanted to do with his valley, and had perfect confidence he should accomplish it. But he had no disposition to hasten matters unwisely. It was better, as he told Sam Kettleman, the grocer, "to let an apple fall in your lap instead of skinnin' your shins goin' up the tree after it--and then findin' it was green."

So, though he wanted the mouth of his river, and wanted it badly, he did not rush off, advertising his need, and try brashly to grab the forty or fifty acres of granite and scrub and steep mountain wall that his heart desired. Instead, he basked in the sunshine, twiddling his bare toes ecstatically, and let the huge bulk of him sink more contentedly into the well-reinforced armchair which creaked under his slightest motion.

Scattergood glanced across the dusty square to the post office. The mail was in, and possibly there were letters there for him. He thought it very likely, and he wanted to see them--but movement was repulsive to his bulging body. He sighed and closed his eyes. A shrill whistle attempting the national anthem, with certain liberties of variation, caused him to open them again, and he saw, passing him, a small boy, apparently without an object in life.

"A-hum!" said Scattergood.

The boy stopped and looked inquiringly.

"If I knew," said Scattergood to his bare feet, "where there was a boy that could find his way across to the post office and back without gittin' sunstroke or stone bruise, I dunno but I'd give him a penny to fetch my mail."

"It's worth a nickel," said the boy.

"Give you two cents," said Scattergood.

"Nickel or nothin'," said the boy.

Scattergood scrutinized the boy a moment, then surrendered.

"Bargain," said he, but as the boy hustled across the square Scattergood heaved himself out of his chair and padded inside the store. He stood scratching his head a moment and then removed a tin object from a card holding eleven more of its like. With it in his hand, he returned to his chair and resettled himself cautiously, for to apply his weight suddenly might have resulted in disaster.

The boy was returning. Scattergood placed the tin object to his lips and puffed out his bulging cheeks. A sound resulted such as the ears of Coldriver had seldom suffered. It was shrill, it was penetrating, it rose and fell with a sort of ripping, tearing slash. The boy stopped in front of Scattergood and stared. Without a word Scattergood held out his hand for his mail, and, receiving it, placed a nickel in the grimy palm that remained extended. Then, apparently oblivious to the boy's existence, he applied himself again to the whistle.

"Say," said the boy, "what's that?"

"Patent whistle," said Scattergood, without interest.

"Is it your'n, or is it for sale?"

"Calculate I might sell."

"How much?"

"Nickel."

"Gimme it," said the boy, and Scattergood gravely received back his coin.

"Might tell the kids I got more," said Scattergood, and watched the boy trot down the street, entranced by the horrid sound he was fathering.

This transaction from beginning to end was eloquent of Scattergood Baines's character. He had been obliged to pay more than he regarded a service as worth, but had not protested vainly. Instead he had set about recouping himself as best he could. The whistle cost him two cents and a half. Therefore the boy had come closer to working for Scattergood's figure than for his own demanded price. In addition, Scattergood's wares were to receive free and valuable advertising, as was proven by the fact that before night he had sold ten more whistles at a profit of twenty-five cents! No deal was too small to receive Scattergood's best and most skillful attention.

Now he opened his letters, one of which was worthy of attention, for it was from a friend in the office of the Secretary of State for that commonwealth--a friend who owed his position there in great measure to Scattergood's influence. The letter gave the information that two gentlemen named Crane and Keith had pooled their timber holdings on the east and west branches of Coldriver, and had filed papers for the incorporation of the Coldriver Lumber Company.

This was important. First, the gentlemen named were no friends of Scattergood's by reason of having underestimated that fleshy individual to their financial detriment in the matter of a certain dam and boom company, of which Scattergood was now sole owner. Second, because it presaged active lumbering operations. Third, because, in Scattergood's safe were ironclad contracts with both of them whereby the said dam and boom company should receive sixty cents a thousand feet for driving their logs down the improved river.

And fourth--the fourth brought Scattergood's active toes to a rest. Fourth, it meant that Crane and Keith would be building the largest sawmill--the only sawmill of consequence--that the valley had seen.

It was an attribute of Scattergood's peculiar genius that even after you had encountered him once, and come out the worse for it, you still rated him as a fatuous, guileless mound of flesh. You did not credit his successes to astuteness, but to blundering luck. Another point also should be noted: If Scattergood were hunting bear he gave it out that his game was partridge. He would hunt partridge industriously and conspicuously until men's minds were turned quite away from the subject of bear. Then suddenly he would shift shotgun for rifle and come home with a bearskin in the wagon. Probably he would bring partridge, too, for he never neglected by-products.

"Them fellows," said he to himself, referring to Messrs. Crane and Keith, "hain't aimin' nor wishin' to pay me no sixty cents a thousand for drivin' their logs.... I figger they calculate to cut about ten million feet. That'll be six thousand dollars. Profit maybe two thousand. Don't see as I kin afford to lose it, seems as though."

On the river below Coldriver village were three hamlets each consisting of a general store, a church, and a few scattered dwellings. These villages were the supply centers for the mountain farms that lay behind them. Necessity had located them, for nowhere else along the valley was there flat land upon which even the tiniest village could find a resting place. These were Bailey, Tupper Falls, and Higgins's Bridge. In common with Coldriver village their communication with the world was by means of a stage line consisting of two so-called stages, one of which left Coldriver in the morning on the downward trip, the other of which left the mouth of the valley on the upward trip. There was also one freight wagon.

The morning following Scattergood's second anniversary in the region, he boarded the stage, occupying so much space therein that a single fare failed utterly to show a profit to the stage line, and alighted at Bailey. He went directly to the store, where no one was to be found save sharp-featured Mrs. Bailey, wife of the proprietor.

"Mornin', ma'am," said Scattergood, politely. "Husband hain't in?"

"Up the brook, catchin' a mess of trout," she responded, shortly. "He's always catchin' a mess of trout, or huntin' a deer or a partridge or somethin'. If you're ever aimin' to see Jim Bailey here, you want to git around afore daylight or after dark."

"Hain't it lucky," said Scattergood, "that some men manages to marry wimmin that kin look after their business?"

"Not for the wimmin," said Mrs. Bailey, shortly.

"My name's Baines," said Scattergood.

"I calculate to know that."

"Like livin' here, ma'am?"

"Not so but what I could bear a change."

"Um!... Mis' Bailey, I calc'late you'd hate to see Jim make a little money so's to be able to git away from here if he wanted to."

"Him? Only way hell ever make money is to ketch a solid-gold trout."

"Maybe I'm the solid-gold trout you're speakin' about," said Scattergood.

She regarded him sharply a moment. "Set," she said. "Looks like you got somethin' on your mind."

There were times when Scattergood could be direct and succinct. He perceived it was best to be so with this woman.

"I might want to buy this here store--under certain conditions."

"How much?"

"Inventory, and a share in the profits of a deal I got in mind."

"What's them conditions you mentioned?"

"That you and Jim don't mention the sale to anybody, and keep on runnin' the place--for wages--until I'm ready for you to quit."

"What's the deal them profits is comin' from, and how much you figger they'll be?"

"The deal's feedin' about five hunderd men, and the profits'll be plenty. I furnish the capital and show you how it's to be done. All Jim'll have to do is foller directions."

Then, lowering his voice, Scattergood went farther into particulars. Suddenly Mrs. Bailey arose, and screamed shrilly to an urchin playing in the road, "You, Jimmy, go up the brook and fetch your pa." Scattergood knew his deal was as good as closed. Before the up-bound stage arrived it was closed. The Baileys had cash in hand for their store and Scattergood carried away a duly executed bill of sale.

The following day, for fifteen hundred dollars cash, he acquired all the property of the stage line--and when the news became public it was believed that Scattergood had departed from his wits, for the line was notoriously unprofitable and an aching worry to its owners. But the commotion the transfer of the stage line created was as nothing to the news that Scattergood had bought a strip of land along the railroad at the mouth of the river, and was erecting a large wooden building upon it. When asked concerning this and its purpose, Scattergood replied that he wasn't made up in his mind what he would use it for, but likely it would be an "opry" house.

Following this, Scattergood went to the city, where he spent much valuable time interviewing gentlemen in wholesale grocery and provision houses....

Jim Bailey liked to fish--which is not an attribute to create scandal. He was not ambitious, nor was he endowed with a full reservoir of initiative, but he was a shrewd customer and seldom got the worst of it. One virtue he possessed, and that was an ability to follow directions--and to keep his mouth shut.

Not many days after Scattergood became the owner of the store at Bailey, Jim was a caller at the new offices of the lumber company, formed when Crane and Keith pooled their interests.

"I come to see you," he told Crane, "because it seemed like you got to feed your lumberjacks, and I want to git the contract for furnishin' and deliverin' the provisions."

"We've sure got to feed 'em," said Crane. "But five hundred men eat a lot of grub. Can you swing it if we give you a chance at it?"

Bailey produced a letter from the Coldriver bank which stated the bank was willing to stand behind any contract made by the Bailey Provision Company, up to a certain substantial amount.

"Who's the Bailey Provision Company?"

"Me 'n' my wife mostly holds the stock."

"Huh!... You'll handle the stuff, deliver it, and all that? What's your proposition?"

"Well, havin' been in business twenty-odd year, I kin buy mighty favorable. More so 'n you fellers. All I want's a livin' profit. Tell you what I'll do. I'll take this here contract like this: Goods to be delivered in your camps at actual cost of the stuff and freighting plus ten per cent. We'll keep stock on hand in depots, and deliver as needed. It'll save you all the trouble of handlin'. We'll carry the stock, and you pay once a month for what's delivered."

Crane called in Keith, and they discussed the proposition. It presented distinct advantages; might, indeed, save them money in addition to trouble. Bailey clinched the thing by showing an agreement with the stage line to transport the provisions at a price per hundred pounds notably lower than Crane and Keith imagined could be obtained, and went home carrying the contract Scattergood had sent him to get.

Scattergood put the paper away in his safe and sat back in his reinforced armchair, with placid satisfaction making benignant his face. "I calc'late," he said to himself, "that this here dicker'll keep Crane and Keith gropin' and wonderin' and scrutinizin' more or less--when it gits to their ears. Shouldn't be s'prised if it come to worry 'em a mite."

So, having created a diversion to conceal the movements of his main attack, Scattergood got out his maps and began scientifically to plan his fall and winter campaign.

Timber was his objective. Not a hundred acres of it, nor a thousand, but tens of thousands, even a hundred thousand acres of spruce-covered hills was the goal he had set. To control his valley he must have money; to get money for his developments he must have timber. Also, ownership of vast limits of growing spruce was necessary to the control of the valley. He must own more timber thereabouts than anybody else. He must dominate the timber situation. To a man whose total resources totaled a matter of fifty thousand dollars--the bulk of which was tied up in a dam and boom company as yet unproductive--this looked like a mouthful beyond his capacity to bite off. Even with timber in the back reaches selling at sixty-six cents an acre, a hundred thousand acres meant an investment of sixty-six thousand dollars. True, Scattergood could look forward to the day when that same timberland would be worth ten dollars an acre--a million dollars--but looking ahead would not produce a cent to-day.

Of timberlands, whose cut logs must go down Coldriver Valley to reach a market, Scattergood's maps showed him there were probably a quarter of a million acres--mostly spruce. Estimating with rigid conservatism, this would run eight thousand feet to the acre, or twenty billion feet of timber--and this did not take into consideration hardwood. In Scattergood's secret heart he wanted it all. All he might not be able to get, but he must have more than half--and that half distributed strategically.

It will be seen that Scattergood was content to wait. His motto was, "Grab a dollar to-day--but don't meddle with it if it interferes with a thousand dollars in ten years."

Scattergood's maps had been the work of two years. That they were accurate he knew, because he had set down on them most of the facts they showed. They were valuable, for, in Scattergood's rude printing, one could read upon them the owner of every piece of timber, every farm, the acreage in each piece of timber, with a careful estimate of the amount of timber to the acre--also its proportions of spruce, beech, birch, maple, ash.

Toward the head of the valley, where good timber was thickest, Scattergood's map showed how it spread out like a fan, with the two main branches of Coldriver and numerous brooks as the ribs. Then, down the length of the stream, were parallel bands of it. On the map one could see what this timber could be bought for; prices ranging from two dollars and a half an acre down the main river to sixty-six cents at the extremity of the fan.

As Scattergood studied his maps he saw, far in the future, perhaps, but clearly and distinctly and certainly, two parallel lines running up the river to his village; he saw, branching off from a spot below the village, where East and West Branches joined to pour over a certain dam owned by him, other narrower parallel lines following river and brooks back and back into the mountains, the spruce-clad mountains. These parallel lines were rails. The ones which ran close together were narrow-gauge--logging roads to bring logs to the big mill which Scattergood planned to build beside his dam. The broader lines were a standard-gauge road to carry the cut lumber to the outside world, and not only the cut lumber, but all the traffic of the valley, all the freight, the manufactured products of other mills and factories which were to come along the banks of his river. Here, in black and white, was set down Scattergood's life plan. When it was accomplished he would be through. He would be willing to have his maps rolled up and himself to be laid on the shelf, for he would have done the thing he set out to do.... For, strange as it may seem, Scattergood was not pursuing money for money itself--his objective was achievement.

Scattergood was not the only man to own or to study maps. Crane and Keith were at the same interesting employment, but on a lesser scale.

"Here's your stuff," said Keith, "over here on the East Branch--thirty thousand acres. Here's mine, on the West Branch--close to thirty thousand acres. We don't touch anywhere."

"But our locations put us in the driver's seat so far as the timber up here is concerned. We're in control. There are sixty thousand acres of mighty good spruce in that triangle between us, and it's as good as ours. It's there for us when we need it. All we got to do is reach out our hand for it. The folks that own it haven't got the money to go ahead with it. Pretty sweet for us--with sixty thousand acres in the palm of our hand and not a cent invested in it."

"Sweet is the word. But what if somebody grabbed it off?"

"Who'll grab?"

"I think we ought to tie it up somehow. If we owned the whole thing we could work a heap more profitably. Now we've got to divide camps, or else cut off one slice or the other at a time. If we owned the whole thing we could make our cut where it would be easiest handled--and leave the rest till things develop."

"It's safe. And we can make it mighty unpleasant for anybody who comes ramming into this region in a small way. Which reminds me of that Baines--our friend Scattergood. Are we going to let him get away with that dam and boom company we made him a present of?"

"I can't see ourselves digging down for sixty cents a thousand for driving our logs--contracts or no contracts."

"Maybe we can buy him off."

"Hanged if I'll do that--we'll chase him off. Look here--he's got to handle our logs. If he can't handle them we've got a right to put on our own crew and drive them down--and charge back to him what it costs us. Get the idea?"

"Not exactly."

"We deliver the logs as specified in the spring. Let him start his drive. Then, I figure, he'll have some trouble with his men, and most likely men he don't have trouble with will get into a row with lumberjacks going out of camp. See? Men of his that we can't handle we'll pitch into the river. Then we'll take charge with our men and make the drive. On top of that we'll sue Scattergood for thirty or forty cents a thousand--extra cost we've been put to by his inability to handle the drive. That'll put a crimp in him--and if we keep after him hot and heavy it won't take long to drive him out of the valley."

"Don't believe he's dangerous, anyhow. That last deal was bullhead luck."

"Yes, but he's stirring around. We don't want anybody poking in. There's a heap of money in this valley for us, if we can keep it to ourselves, and the sooner the idea gets abroad that it isn't healthful to butt in, the better."

"Guess you're right."

If Scattergood could have heard this conversation perhaps he would not have been so gayly partaking of the softer joys of life. For that is what Scattergood was doing. He had polished up his buggy, put his new harness on his horse, and was driving out to make a social call. Not only that, but it was a social call upon a lady!

Scattergood was lonely sometimes. In one of his moments of loneliness it had occurred to him that a great many men had wives, and that wives were, undoubtedly, a remarkably effective insurance against that ailment.

"I gather," he said, in the course of a casual conversation with Sam Kettleman, the grocer, "that wives is sometimes inconvenient and sometimes tryin' on the temper, but on the whole they're returnin' income on the investment."

"Some does and some doesn't," said Kettleman, lugubriously.

"Hotel grub," said Scattergood, "gets mighty similar. Roast beef and roast pork! Roast pork and roast beef! Then cold roast pork and beef for supper.... And me obliged, by the way I'm built, to pay extry board. Sundays I always order me two dinners. Seems like a wife 'u'd act as a benefit there."

"But there's drawbacks," said Sam, "and there's mother-in-laws, and there's lendin' a dollar to your brother-in-law."

"The thing to do," said Scattergood, "is to pick one without them impediments. I also figger," he added, wriggling his bare toes, "that a feller ought to pick one that could lend a dollar to your brother in case he needed one."

"Hain't none sich to be found," said Sam.

"I calc'late to look," Scattergood replied.

He had already done his looking. The lady of his choice, tradition says, was older than he, but this is a base libel. She was not older. She had not yet reached thirty. Scattergood had first encountered her when she came to his hardware store to buy a plow. On that occasion her excellent business judgment and her powers of barter had attracted him strongly. As a matter of fact, he was a bit in doubt if she hadn't the best of him on the deal.... Her name was Amanda Randle.

Scattergood gave the matter his best thought, then polished the buggy as aforesaid, and called.

"Howdy, Miss Randle?" said he, tying to her hitching post.

"Howdy, Mr. Baines?"

"I calculated," said he, "that, bein' as it's a hot night, a buggy ride might sort of cool you off, after a way of speakin'."

Amanda blushed, for the proffer of a buggy ride was not without definite significance in that region.

"I'll git my shawl and bonnet," she said.

To the casual eye it would have appeared that Scattergood's summer was de-

voted wholly to running his hardware store and to paying court to Mandy Randle....
But this would not have been so. He was making ready for the winter--and for the
spring that came after it. For in the spring came the drive, and with the coming of
the drive Scattergood foresaw the coming of trouble. He was not a man to dodge
trouble that might bring profit dangling to the fringe of her skirt.

Coldriver watched with deep interest the progress of Scattergood's suit. It had
figured Mandy as an old maid--for, as has been mentioned, she was close upon her
thirtieth year, which, in a village where eighteen is the general age for taking a husband, is well along in spinsterhood. It was late in October when Scattergood "came
to scratch," as the local saying is.

"Mandy," said he, "I calc'late you noticed I been comin' around here
consid'able."

"You have--seems as though," she said, and blushed. It was coming. She recognized the signs.

"I been a-comin' on purpose," said Scattergood.

"Do tell," said Mandy.

"Yes, ma'am. It's like this: I own a hardware store and some other prop'ty; not
a heap, ma'am, but some . It's gittin' to be more. I calculate, some day, to be wuth
consid'able. When a man gits to this p'int, he ought to have him a wife, eh?"

Mandy made no reply.

"So," said Scattergood, "I took to lookin' around a bit, and of all the girls there
was, Mandy, it looked to me like you would be the only one to make the kind of a
wife I want. That's honest. Yes, sir. Says I to myself, 'Mandy Randle's the one for
me.' So I washed up the buggy and hitched up the horse and come right out. I been
comin' ever since, because that there first impression of mine has been bore out by
facts.... I'm askin' you, Mandy, will you be Missis Baines?"

"You're stiddy and savin'--and makin'," said Mandy. "Add what you got to
what I got, and we'll be pretty well off. And I aim to help take care of it."

"I aim to have you help," said Scattergood. "But, Mandy, I don't want you
scrimpin' and savin' too much. I want my wife should have as good as the best,
and be looked up to by the best. The day'll come, Mandy, when we'll keep a hired
girl!"

"No extravagances, Scattergood, till I say we kin afford it.... And, Scattergood, you got to promise not to make no important move without consultin' me. I got a head for business."

"Mandy," said Scattergood, "you and me is equal partners."

Which, say both tradition and history, is how the arrangement worked out. Mandy and Scattergood were *equal partners. Scattergood was to learn through the years that Mandy's* was a good head for business, and, though business men who came to deal with Scattergood in the future sometimes laughed when they found Mandy present at their conferences, they never laughed but once.... And, though Scattergood's proffer of marriage had not been couched in fervent terms of love, nor had Mandy fallen on his overbroad bosom with rapture, theirs was a married life to be envied by most, for there was between them perfect trust, sincere affection, and wisest forbearance. For forty years Scattergood and Mandy lived together as man and wife, and at the end both could look back through the intimate years and say of the other that he had chosen well his mate.

It may be thought that this bit of romance is dropped in here by legend and history merely to amuse, or as a side light on the character of Scattergood Baines. This is not so. We are forced by the facts to regard the matter as an integral part of the business transaction related in this narrative. Not a minor part, not an important part, but perhaps the deciding factor....

John Bones, lawyer, age twenty-six, was a recent acquisition to Coldriver village. Scattergood had watched the young man's comings and goings, and had listened to his conversation. Early in November he went to his bank and drew from deposit two hundred and fifty dollars.... Then he went to call on Bones.

"Mr. Bones," he said, "folks says old Clayt Mosier's a client of your'n."

"He's given me some business, Mr. Baines."

"Uh-huh!... Somethin' to do with title to a piece of timber over Higgins's Bridge way, wa'n't it?"

"I'm sorry, Mr. Baines, but I guess you'll have to ask Mr. Mosier about that."

"Huh!... Mosier hain't apt to tell me. Seems like I was sort of int'rested in that thing. I can't manage nohow to git the facts, so I thought I'd talk to you."

"I can't help you. I have no right to talk about a client's confidential matters."

"To be sure.... How's business?"

"Not very good."

"Not gittin' rich, eh?"

Young Bones looked unhappy, for making both ends meet was a problem he had not mastered as yet.

Scattergood got up, closed the door, and walked softly back to the desk. He drew from his pocket the roll of bills, and spread them out in alluring pattern.

"Them's your'n," said he.

"Mine? How? What for?"

"I'm swappin' with you."

"For what, Mr. Baines?" A slight perspiration was noticeable on young Lawyer Bones's brow.

"Information," said Scattergood, looking him in the eye. As the young man did not speak, Scattergood continued, "about Mosier's title matter."

For an instant the young man stood irresolute; then he reached slowly over, gathered up the money into a neat roll--while Scattergood watched him intently-- and then, with suddenly set teeth, hurled the roll into Scattergood's face, and leaped around the desk.

"You git!" he said, between his teeth. "Git, and take your filthy money with you...."

Scattergood, who did not in the least look it, could move swiftly. The young lawyer was abruptly interrupted in his pastime of ejecting Scattergood forcibly. He found himself seized by his wrists and held as if he had shoved his arms into steel clamps.

"Set," said Scattergood, "and be sociable.... And keep the money. It's your'n. You're hired. I guess you're the feller I'm aimin' to use."

He forced the struggling young man back into his chair, and released him-- grinning broadly, and not at all as a tempter should grin. "If it'll relieve your con- science," he said, "I hain't got no more int'rest in Mosier's affairs than I have in the emperor of the heathen Chinee.... But I have got a heap of int'rest in a young feller that kin refuse a wad of money when he can't pay his board bill. Maybe 'twan't jest a nice way, but I had to find out. The man I'm needin' has to have a clost mouth-- and somethin' a mite better 'n that--gumption not to sell out.... Git the idee?"

"I--yes, I guess I do--but--"

"Any objections to workin' for me?"

"None."

"All right. Keep the money. When you've worked it up come for more. And, young feller, if things turns out for me like I think they will, you're goin' to quit bein' a lawyer one of these days. I'm a-goin' to need you in my business. Come over to my store."

At the store Scattergood spread his maps before the young man, and pointed to a certain spot. "There's about fifty different passels of timber in that crotch. I don't aim to need 'em all to-day, but I calc'late on gittin' a sort of fringe around the edge." He drew his finger down the East Branch and up the West Branch in a sort of horse-shoe. "Your job's to git options on the fringe--in your own name. Git the idee?"

"Yes."

"Git 'em cheap."

"Yes, sir."

"There's five thousand dollars on deposit in the bank in your name. Use it." When Scattergood trusted a man he trusted him. "And now," he said, "I calc'late to raise a little dust, so's you won't be noticed."

Scattergood's little dust consisted of allowing to be inserted in the local paper an item announcing that Scattergood Baines had bought all the stock and contracts of the Bailey Provision Company, which concern was purveying food supplies to all the camps of Messrs. Crane and Keith.... Then Scattergood settled back to watch the dust rise.

The dust arose, and filled the eyes and noses of Messrs. Crane and Keith, as Scattergood expected, with the result that Mr. Crane was a passenger on Scatter-good's stage to Coldriver village.

"Howdy, Mr. Crane?" said Scattergood, as that gentleman belligerently entered the hardware store. "I was sort of lookin' forward to seein' some of you folks."

"Look here, Baines," said Crane, "what are you butting into our game for? We let you get away with that other thing, but this last deal of yours makes it look as if you were hunting trouble. You bought that provision company to get a lever on us."

"Maybe so.... Maybe so, but I wouldn't get het up about it.... You see, it's like this: you folks kind of did what I expected you'd do on that dam and boom deal, and come pretty close to doin' me out of some valuable property. I didn't get het up, though, I jest sort of sat around and waited.... And it come out all right. Now, didn't it?"

"Bullhead luck."

"Maybe so.... Maybe so. Now, here's how I figger things to-day. You and Keith hain't amiable about that deal, and you don't aim to let my dam and boom company make any money out of you. I expect you can manage it. If I was in your shoes, and was the kind of a man I judge you folks be, I'd fix it so's the dam and boom company couldn't handle the drive. Buy up the men, maybe, and start fights, and be sort of forced to take charge so's to get my drive through. And then I'd sue for damages.... That's how I'd do. I calc'late that's about what you and Keith has in mind, hain't it?"

Crane was purple with rage, but underneath his rage was a clammy layer of unpleasant surprise that this mound of flabby fat should have had such uncanny vision into his hardly creditable plans.

"You're crazy, man," he blustered.

"Maybe so.... Maybe so. Anyhow, I took out a mite of insurance ag'in' sich a happenin'. I got me this here provision company to feed your men.... Ever happen to think what would happen in the woods if your lumberjacks run short of grub? Eh?... And suppose it happened, and your men come bilin' out of camp, sore as bears with bee stings. What then, eh? Couldn't git another crew this winter, maybe. Eh?"

Crane blustered. He threatened legal measures, but Scattergood pointed out no legal measures could be taken until he failed to deliver supplies. Also, he directed Crane's attention to the fact that the provision company was a corporation, and liable only to the extent of its assets. "So, even if you got a judgment, you wouldn't collect enough to make no profit. And your winter's cut would be off, and what logs you got cut would rot in the woods. I calc'late you'd stand to git damaged consid'able."

"What's your proposition?" spluttered Crane.

"Hain't got none.... You jest run back to Keith and repeat as much of this here talk as you can remember. I'm goin' to be busy now. Afternoon."

For two weeks Scattergood disappeared, and though Crane and Keith sought him with fever in their blood, he was not to be found. He filled their minds; he dominated their conversation; he gave them sleepless nights and unpleasant days....

Their attention was effectively focused on the emergency he had presented to them. Scattergood had kicked up an effective dust.

At the end of two weeks Scattergood appeared again in town, and went directly to Johnnie Bones's office. Scattergood now called his lawyer Johnnie.

"Got 'em?" he asked.

"Not all. There's a fifteen-thousand-acre strip cutting right across your horseshoe, from East to West Branch, and I couldn't touch it. I got all the rest. That one belongs to a woman, and a more unreasonable woman to try to do business with I never saw."

"Um!" said Scattergood. "Know where I been, Johnnie?"

"No, sir."

"Gittin' married."

"What?"

"Yes. Me 'n' the lady, we met by arrangement in Boston and got us a preacher and done the job. Marriage, Johnnie, is a doggone solemn matter."

"I've heard so," said the young man.

"Some day," said Scattergood, "I'm a-goin' to marry you off. Calculate I got the girl in my eye now."

"I hope," Johnnie said, "that you'll be--er--very happy."

"Guess we'll manage so-so.... Now about them options, Johnnie. You make tracks for the city and sort of edge up to Crane and Keith. Might start by showin' 'em a deed for a mill site down across from theirs at the railroad. Then you might start askin' questions like you was lookin' for information. Guess that'll git up their curiosity some. Then you kin spring your options on 'em.... When you've done that, come off and leave 'em sweatin'. And don't mention me. I hain't in this deal a-tall."

But before Johnnie could get to Crane and Keith, Crane and Keith came to Scattergood.

"You've got some kind of a proposition in mind," said Keith, who did the talking because he could keep his temper better than Crane. "What do you want?"

"Make me an offer," said Scattergood.

"We'll buy your provision company--and give you a decent profit."

"Don't sound enticin'," said Scattergood, reaching down and loosening his shoe.

It was too cold to omit the wearing of heavy woolen socks, so he could not twiddle his toes with perfect freedom, but he could twiddle them some, and that helped his mental processes.

"Well, what do you want?"

"I'll sell the provision company's stock of provisions--and nothin' more.... At a profit. You got to buy, 'cause you can't make arrangements to git in grub before I bring on a famine for you.... And I got the grub stored in warehouses. That's part of it. Second, I'll lease you my river for three years. You wasn't calc'latin' to pay for the use of it. So you be obleeged to pay in advance. I figgered my profits on drivin' at about two thousand this year. Give you a three-year lease for five thousand. I hain't no hog.... Yes or no."

There was a brief conference. "Yes," was the answer.

"Cash," said Scattergood.

"You'll have to come to the city for it," Keith said, which Scattergood was not unwilling to do. He returned with a certified check for twenty-six thousand five hundred and twenty-four dollars and nineteen cents, of which five thousand was rental of his river, and four thousand and odd dollars were his profits on his provisions. Not a bad profit from a dust-throwing project!

Meantime Johnnie paid his visit to Crane and Keith, and came home to report.

"It hit them between wind and water," he said.

"Uh-huh!... What did you judge they had in mind?"

"They wanted to buy me out.... Of course I wouldn't sell. My clients wanted that timber, and were going to work to build their mill.... The last they said was that they were coming up to see me."

"Uh-huh! When they come, you mention about that strip of fifteen thousand acres you couldn't buy, eh? Let on you couldn't get it."

Johnnie held Scattergood as he was going out. "I want to account for that five thousand dollars you placed in my name."

"Go ahead. I hain't perventin' you."

"I got options on eighteen thousand six hundred acres of timber. The options cost me twenty-one hundred and seventy dollars, and my expenses were sixty-one dollars and a half."

"Um!... Cheap enough. What did the land cost an acre?"

"Averaged a dollar and seventy-five cents."

"Huh!... Not so bad. Now tend to Crane and his quiet friend."

They arrived in due time, accompanied by their lawyer.

"Mr. Bones," said the lawyer, "you have certain options that my clients wish to purchase. Undoubtedly they were taken in good faith, but we would like, before going farther, to know whom you are acting for."

"You can deal with me. I have full powers."

"You decline to disclose your principal?"

"Absolutely."

"Do I understand the project is to build a mill at once and start to cut this timber?"

"That is my information."

"Aha!... May I ask how much land you have?"

Johnnie exhibited a map, on which was blocked off the timber in question. "You see," he said, "there's one fifteen-thousand-acre strip I couldn't get hold of. It cuts right across the triangle from river to river."

Crane looked at Keith and Keith looked at Crane.

"It belongs to a woman who wouldn't do business," Johnnie added.

"What figure did you pay for the land?"

"That is hardly a fair question."

"What do you ask for your options? That's a fair question, isn't it?" "They're not for sale."

"But we may make an offer. It might be profitable for your principals to sell. My clients feel they need this property, lying as it does between their holdings."

"I'll listen."

There followed whispered arguments among the three, resulting in an offer of a dollar and seventy-five cents an acre for the whole tract--exactly what Johnnie had agreed to pay.

"I said I'd listen," said Johnnie, "but I don't seem to hear anything."

Another conference and a bid of two dollars. Johnnie shrugged his shoulders. Two dollars and a half an acre was finally offered, and then Johnnie leaned forward and tapped with his finger on his desk. "If you gentlemen mean business, let's talk business. I've got what you want. You can't get it unless I want to sell, and I don't want to sell. I and my clients know what that timber is worth to us, but any business man will consider a quick profit if it is enough profit. In five years that timber will be worth five or six dollars standing; in fifteen years it will be worth fifteen to twenty.... But if you want to buy to-day you can have it for three dollars through and through."

"We've got to have it," said Crane, and Keith nodded.

"Cash," said Johnnie, for cash was a hobby of Scattergood's.

"Our bank has made arrangements with your local bank to give us what money we need," said Keith.

And then, clattering upstairs, came a small boy. Without ceremony he burst into the room. "Mr. Bones," he shouted, "I was sent to tell you that strip of timber you tried to buy from the lady is for sale." Then he whisked out of sight.

Johnnie shrugged his shoulders. "Costs me some profit," he said. "Confound that woman!... Well, we can go to the bank and close this up. Then you fellows can finish up by buying that last fifteen thousand acres."

"You bet we will," said Crane, savagely.

At the bank fifty-five thousand eight hundred dollars in the form of a certified check was deposited in the hands of the cashier to be paid to Johnnie when he should deliver proper deeds to the property sold.... It represented a profit of twenty-three thousand two hundred and fifty dollars.

"Now for the other parcel," said Crane, and getting the information as to ownership, he and his companions took buggy to the spot. It was a comfortable farmhouse, white painted and agreeable to look upon, but the pleasure of the view was ruined for Crane and Keith by reason of a bulky figure standing on the porch in conversation with a woman.

"Baines!" ejaculated Crane. It sounded like a swear word as he said it.

The three rushed the piazza.

"Madam," said Crane, not deigning to recognize Scattergood's presence, "you own a tract of timber--fifteen thousand acres. We hear it is for sale. We want to buy it."

"This gentleman was just making me an offer for it," she said, pointing to Scattergood.

"We raise his offer twenty-five cents an acre," said Crane, and drew from his-pocket a huge roll of bills--it being his idea of the psychology of women that the sight of actual money would have a favorable effect.

"That makes two dollars an acre," said she, and looked at Scattergood.

"Two and a quarter," said he.

"Two and a half," roared Crane.

"Two seventy-five," said Scattergood. "Three dollars."

"Three ten," said Scattergood.

"Three and a quarter" said Crane. He glared at Scattergood. "If you want it worse than that," he shouted, "why, confound you, you can have it!"

"I don't," said Scattergood, placidly.

The woman figured a moment. "That makes forty-eight thousand seven hundred and fifty dollars," she said. "I kind of like even money. You can have it for an even fifty thousand."

Scattergood looked at her and grinned. One might have detected admiration in his eyes.

"Done," said Crane. "We'll get into town and close the deal, ma'am, if you don't mind."

"Your buggy seems to be crowded," said Scattergood. "I'll drive the lady in, if you want I should."

"We want nothing from you at all, Baines."

"All right," said Scattergood, placidly, and, getting into his buggy, he drove away. He drove rapidly, and alighted at Johnnie Bones's office. Presently he emerged, carrying a legal-appearing document in his hand, and went across to the bank, where he handed the document to the cashier.

Presently the parties appeared, entered the bank, and the cashier, upon being directed, executed a certified check to the lady for fifty thousand dollars. Then he handed it to her, and the deed to Mr. Crane. "You see," said he, "we have the deed all ready for you."

"Yes," said Scattergood, stepping through the door. "I had it fixed up for you. I aim to be prompt when I'm tendin' to my wife's business matters. Gentlemen, I guess you hain't met Mrs. Baines real proper yet...."

It was not a happy moment for Messrs. Crane and Keith, but they weathered it, not suavely, not with complete dignity, but after a fashion.... Their departure might, perhaps, have been termed brusque.

"Well, Scattergood," said Mandy, "it was a real good deal."

"The way you h'isted 'em to fifty thousand was what got my eye," he said, proudly. "I wouldn't 'a' had the nerve."

"I knew they'd pay it," she said. "Seems like a reasonable profit, though the land's been a-layin' there unproductive for thirty year. Father, he give a thousand dollars for it, and the taxes must 'a' been a couple of thousand more. Say forty-seven thousand dollars profit...."

"And I come out of the other deals perty fair. Made twenty-three thousand off of the options, and nine or ten off of the other things. Guess the Baines family's a matter of seventy-five thousand dollars richer by a good day's work."

"But it can't lay idle," she said.

"Not a minnit. We'll buy that sixty thousand acres 'way back up the river for sixty-six cents, like we planned, and have some workin' capital.... And, Mandy, Crane and Keith hain't got that timber for keeps. It's comin' back to us some of these days. I feel it in my bones...."

"Kind of a nice wind-up for our honeymoon," said Mrs. Baines, practically.

CHAPTER III
THE MOUNTAIN COMES TO SCATTERGOOD

Scattergood Baines was on his way to the city! An exclamation point deserves to be placed after this because it rightly belongs in a class with the statement that the mountain was coming to Mohammed. Scattergood had fully as much in common with cities as eels with the Desert of Sahara.

He had not started the journey brashly, on impulse, but after debate and discussion with Mandy, his wife. Mandy's conclusion was that if Scattergood had *to go to the city he might as well get at it and have it over, exercising the care of an exceedingly prudent man in the circumstances, and following minutely advice that would be forthcoming from* her. Undoubtedly, she thought, he could manage the matter and return to Coldriver unscathed.

So Scattergood was clambering into the stage--his stage that plied between Coldriver village and the railroad, twenty-four miles distant. When he settled in his seat the stage sagged noticeably on that side, for Scattergood added to his weight yearly as he added to his other possessions. Mandy stood by, watching anxiously.

"Remember," said she, "I pinned your money in the right leg of your pants, clost to the knee."

"Mandy," said he, confidentially, "I feel the lump of it. I hope I don't have to git after it sudden. Dunno but I should have fetched along a ferret to send up after it."

"Don't git friendly with no strangers--dressed-up ones, especial. And never set down your valise. There's a white shirt and a collar and two pairs of sox, and what not, in there. Make quite an object for some sharper."

He nodded solemnly.

"If you git invited out to his house," she said, "it'll save you a dollar hotel bill, anyhow, and be a heap sight safer."

"You're right, Mandy, as usual," he agreed. "G'by, Mandy. I calculate you won't have no trouble mindin' the store."

"G'by, Scattergood," she said, dabbing at her eyes. "I'll be relieved to see you gittin' back."

There seemed to be little sentiment in these, their words of parting, but in reality it was an exceedingly sentimental passage for them. Between Scattergood and his wife there was a deep, true, abiding affection. Folks who regarded it as a business partnership--and there were many of them--lacked the seeing eye.

The stage rattled off down the valley--Scattergood's valley. He had invaded it some years before because valleys were his hobby and because this valley offered him the opportunity he had been searching for. Scattergood knew what could be done with a valley, and he was busy doing it, but he was only at the beginning. As he bumped along he could see busy villages where only hamlets rested; he could see mills turning timber into finished products; he could see business and life and activity where there were only silence and rocks and trees. And where ran the rutted mountain road, over which his stage was carrying him uncomfortably, he could see the railroad that was to make his dream a reality. He could see a railroad stretching all the way from Coldriver village to the main line, and by virtue of this railroad Scattergood would rule the valley.

He had arrived with forty-odd dollars in his pocket. His few years of labor there, assisted by a wise and business-like marriage, had increased that forty dollars to what some folks would call wealth. First, he owned a prosperous hardware store. This was his business. It netted him a couple of thousand dollars a year. The valley was his avocation. It had netted him well over a hundred thousand dollars, most of which was growing on the mountain sides in straight, clear spruce, in birch, beech, and maple. It had netted him certain strategic holdings of land along Coldriver itself, sites for future dams, for mills yet to be built--for railroad yards, depots, and terminals. Quietly, almost stealthily, he had gotten a hold on the valley. Now he was ready to grip it with both hands and to make it his own.... That is why he journeyed to the city.

He put his canvas telescope between his feet so that he could feel it. It was as well, he determined, to practice caution where none was needed, so he would be letter perfect in the art when he reached the dangers of the city. Between Scattergood's shoes and the feet they inclosed, were sox. Before his union with Mandy he had been a stranger to such effeteness. Even now he was prone to discard them as soon as he was out of range of her vision. To-day he had not escaped, for, warm as the day was, heavy white woolen sox folded and festooned themselves modishly over the tops of his shoes. He could not wriggle a toe, which made his mental processes difficult, for his toes were first aids to his brain.

However, he was going to visit a railroad president, and railroad presidents were said by Mandy to go in for style. Scattergood mournfully arose to the necessities of the situation.

The twenty-four-mile ride was not long to Scattergood, for he occupied it by studying again every inch of his valley. He never tired of studying it. As the law book to the lawyer so the valley was to Scattergood--something never to be laid aside, something to be kept fresh in mind and never neglected. He never passed the length of it without seeing a new possibility.

Scattergood flagged the train. The four-hour ride to the city he occupied in talking to the conductor or brake-man or any member of the train's crew he could engage in conversation. He was asking them about their jobs, what they did, and why. He was asking question after question about railroads and railroading, in his quaint, characteristic manner. It was his intention to own a railroad, and he was at work finding out how the thing was done.

Next morning at seven he was on hand at the terminal offices of the G. and B. An hour later minor employees began to arrive.

"Young feller," he said, accosting a pleasant-faced boy, "where d'you calc'late I'll find Mr. Castle?"

"President Castle?" asked the boy.

"That's the feller," said Scattergood.

"About now he'll be eating grapefruit and poached egg," said the boy.

"Don't he work none durin' the day?"

The boy laughed good-humoredly. "He gets down about nine thirty, and when he don't go off somewheres he's mostly here till four--except between one and two, when he's at lunch."

"Gosh!" said Scattergood. "Must be wearin' him to the bone. 'Most five hours a day he sticks to it. Bear up under it perty well, young feller, does he? Keep his health and strength?"

"He works enough to get paid fifty thousand a year for it," said the boy.

"That settles it," said Scattergood. "I've picked my job. I'm a-goin' to be a railroad president." He put his canvas telescope down, and placed a heavy foot on it for safety. "Calc'late I kin sit here and wait, can't I?"

The boy nodded and went on. During the next hour more than one dozen young men and women passed that spot to eye with appreciation the caller who waited for Mr. Castle. Scattergood was unaware of their scrutiny, for he was building a railroad down his valley--a railroad of which he was the president.

Scattergood looked frequently at a big, open-faced, silver watch which was connected to his vest in pickpocket-proof fashion with a braided leather thong. When it told him nine thirty had arrived, he got up, his telescope in his hand, and ambled heavily down the corridor. He poked his head in at an open door, and called, amiably, "Kin anybody tell me where to find Mr. Castle?"

He was directed, and presently opened a door marked "President's Office." The room within did not contain the president. It was crossed by a railing, behind which sat an office boy. Behind him was a stenographer.

"President in?" asked Scattergood.

The boy looked at him severely, and replied, shortly, that the president was busy.

"Havin' only five hours to do all his work," said Scattergood, "I calc'lated he would be some took up. Tell him Scattergood Baines wants to have a talk to him, sonny."

"Have an appointment?"

"No, sonny," said Scattergood, "but if you don't scamper into his room fairly spry, the seat of your pants is goin' to have an appointment with my hand." He leaned over the railing as he said it, and the boy, regarding Scattergood's face a moment, arose and whisked into the next room.

Shortly there appeared a youngish man, constructed by nature to adorn wearing apparel.

"Be you Mr. Castle?" asked Scattergood.

"I'm his secretary. What do you want?"

"Young man, I'm disapp'inted. When I see you I figgered you must be president of the railroad or the Queen of Sheeby. I want to see Mr. Castle."

"What is your business with him?"

"'Tain't fit for young ears to listen to," said Scattergood.

"If you have any business with Mr. Castle, state it to me."

"Um!... I come quite consid'able of a distance to see him--which I calc'late to do." He reached over, with astonishing suddenness in one so bulky, and twirled the secretary about with his ham of a hand. At the same time he leaned against the gate, which was not fastened to restrain such a weight. "Now, forrard march, young feller. Lead the way. I'm follerin' you." And thus Scattergood entered the presence.

He saw behind a huge, flat desk a very thin man, who leaned forward, clutching his temples as though to restrain within bounds the machinery of the brain inside. It was President Castle's habitual posture when working. The temples and dome of the head seemed to bulge, as if there was too much inside for the strength of the restraining walls. The president looked up and fastened eyes that themselves bulged from hollowed sockets. It was the face of a man who ran his mental dynamo at top speed in defiance of nature's laws against speeding.

"Well?" he snapped. "Well--well?"

"Name's Scattergood Baines. Figger to build a railroad. Want to see you about it," said Scattergood, succinctly.

"Not interested. Busy. Get out," said Castle.

Scattergood dropped the secretary, and lumbered up to the president's desk. He leaned over it heavily. "I've come to see you about this here thing," he said, quietly. "Either you'll talk to me about it now, or I'll have to sort of arrange so that you'll come to me, askin' to talk about it, later. Now you kin save both our time."

Castle regarded Scattergood with eyes that seemed to burn with unnatural nervous energy--it was a brief scrutiny. "Clear out," he said to his secretary. "Sit down," to Scattergood.

"Obleeged," said Scattergood. "I'm figgerin' on buildin' a railroad down Coldriver Valley from Coldriver to connect with the G. and B. narrow gauge. Carry freight and passengers. Want you to agree about train service, freight transfer, buildin' a station, and sich matters."

Here was a man who could get down to business, President Castle perceived, and who could state his business clearly and to the point.

"I know the valley. Been talking about it. Where do you come in?"

"I calculate to build the road."

"For Crane and Keith?"

"Eh?"

"They're the men backing it, aren't they? In to see me about it last week."

Crane and Keith! Scattergood's career in the valley had been one of warfare with Crane and Keith. He had beaten them with his dam and boom company; he had beaten them in certain stumpage operations. Now they were after his railroad and his valley.

"Um!..." he said, and reached down mechanically to loosen his shoe. Here was need for careful thought.

"I gave them all necessary information," said the president.

"Don't concern me none," said Scattergood. "This here is to be my railroad, and I'm the feller that's goin' to own and run it. Crane and Keith hain't in it at all."

"You're too late. The G. and B. has agreed to handle their freight and to stop passengers at their station. Tentatively agreed to lease and operate the road when built.... Good morning." "I calculate there's room for argument," said Scattergood. "I own right consid'able of that right of way."

"Railroad can take it under the right of eminent domain," said the president.

"Kin one railroad take from another one?" asked Scattergood, a bit anxiously.

"No."

"Um!... Wa-al, you see, Mr. Castle, I got me a charter to build this railroad. Legislature up and give me one."

"Makes no difference. We've made an agreement with Crane and Keith which stands. You can't build your road, whatever you've got. Frankly, we won't tolerate a road there that we don't control. Good morning."

"That final, Mr. President?"

"Absolutely."

"If I was to build in spite of you I calc'late you'd fix things so's runnin' it wouldn't do much good to me, eh? Stop no trains for me, and sich like?"

"Exactly."

"Um!... Mornin', Mr. President. If you ever git up to Coldriver don't go to the hotel. Come right to my house. Mandy'll be glad to see you. Mornin'."

Scattergood and Johnnie Bones, the young lawyer whom Scattergood had taken to his heart, were studying a railway map of the state with special reference to the G. & B. It showed them that the G. & B. traversed a southerly corner of the state and had within its boundaries some forty miles of track.

"The idee," said Scattergood, "is to make that forty mile of track consid'able more of a worry to Castle than all the rest of his railroad."

"Meddling with the railroads is a dangerous pastime," said Johnnie. "Besides, how can you manage it?"

"We got a legislature, hain't we?"

"Yes, but the boys feel pretty friendly to the railroads, I understand."

"Feel perty friendly to me, too," said Scattergood.

"I doubt if you could pass any legislation they wanted to fight hard."

"Um!... I'll look out for that end, Johnnie. Now what I want is for you to draw up a bill for me that'll sort of irritate 'em where irritation does the most hurt--which, I calc'late, is in the pocketbook. Here's my notion: To make a pop'lar measure of it; somethin' that'll appeal to the folks. We kin git the papers to start a holler and have folks demandin' action of their representatives, and sich like. Taxes! That'll fetch 'em every time."

"Yes," said Johnnie, dubiously, "but--"

"You listen" said Scattergood. "It stands to reason that the state don't realize much out of that there forty mile of track. The G. and B. gits the use of the state, so to speak, without payin' a fair rent for it. You draw up a bill pervidin' that the railroad has got to pay a fee of, say a dollar, for every passenger car it runs over them forty miles, and fifty cents for every freight car. That'll mount to a consid'able sum every year, eh?"

"It'll amount to so much," said Johnnie, gazing ruefully at his client, "that there'll be the devil to pay. You'll pull every railroad in the state down around your ears."

"Let 'em drop."

"And I don't know if the law'll hold water--even if you got it passed. It's darn-fool legislation, Mr. Baines--but some darn-fool legislation sticks. I don't believe this would, but it might ."

"That's plenty to suit me," said Scattergood, slipping on his shoes and standing up. "You git at it.... And say," he said, as a sort of afterthought, "I want to git through a leetle bill for my stage line. Here's about it. Won't take more'n fifty words." He handed Johnnie a slip, crumpled and grimy, with lead-pencil notes on. "This won't cause no trouble, anyhow."

Scattergood went back to his hardware store and sat down in his reinforced armchair on the piazza. As he sat there young Jim Hands drove up with his girl, alighted, and went into the ice-cream parlor for refreshment. Scattergood studied the rig. It lacked something to give it the final touch of style dear to the country youth.

Scattergood got up, and ambled into his store, returning with a resplendent buggy whip--one with a white silk bow tied above its handle. This he placed in the socket on the dashboard. Then he resumed his chair. Presently Jim emerged with his girl and helped her into the rig. He noticed the whip, took it out of its place, and examined it; swished it through the air to try its excellence.

"Mighty nice gad," said Scattergood.

"Where in tunket did it come from?" asked Jim.

"I stuck it there. Looked to me like a rig sich as your'n needed a good whip to set it off. I jest put it there to see how it looked."

Jim glanced at his girl, scratched the back of his suntanned neck, and felt in his pocket.

"Calc'late I did need a whip," he said. "How much is sich whips fetchin'?"

"I kin give you that one a might lower 'n usual. It'll be two dollars to you, seem's you got sich a purty girl in the buggy."

The girl giggled, Jim flushed, and fished out two one-dollar bills, which he passed over to Scattergood. Then, whip in hand, he drove off with a flourish. Scattergood pocketed the money serenely. It was by methods such as this that he did, in his hardware store, double the business such a store in such a locality normally accounted for. Scattergood's most outstanding quality was that he never let a business opportunity slip--large or small--and that he manufactured for himself fully half of his business opportunities. He had lifted retail salesmanship to the rank of an art.

Again he got up and went inside, where he wrote a letter to a certain wholesale house with whom his account was large. The letter said he had pressing need for half a dozen railroad rails of certain size and weight, and didn't know where to get them, and would the recipient find them and ship them at once.

Presently Tim Plant, teamster, drove by, and Scattergood hailed him.

"Tim," he said, "you owe me a leetle bill. This hain't a dun, but I got a mite of work to be done, and seein' things wasn't brisk with you, I figgered you might want to work it out--jest to keep busy."

"Sure," said Tim.

Whereupon Scattergood elevated himself to the seat beside Tim, and was driven to the spot he had selected for the Coldriver terminal of his railroad.

"I want about a hunderd feet graded along here," he said, "to lay rails on."

"Rails!... Gosh! Scattergood, you hain't thinkin' of buildin' a railroad, be you?"

"Shucks!" said Scattergood. "I jest got a half dozen rails comin', and I figgered I'd like to see how they'd look all laid down on the spot. Give folks an idee how a railroad 'u'd look if there was one."

In which manner Scattergood collected a doubtful bill, obtained a quantity of labor at what might be called wholesale rates--and actually started work on his railroad. Actual, patent for the world to see. The railroad was begun. Not Crane & Keith, not President Castle, not a court in the world could deny that actual construction had begun. Scattergood was insuring himself against possible steps by the enemy to nullify his charter.

"What's this here eminent domain?" Scattergood asked Johnnie Bones.

"It's a legal thing that allows railroads to take land necessary to its operation-- paying for it, of course."

"Anybody's land?"

"Yes."

"Crane and Keith, f'r instance?"

"Yes."

"Um!... Have to be right of way, or jest land for railroad yards, or to build railroad buildin's on?"

"Any land necessary to a railroad."

"Um!... Who says if it's necessary?"

"The courts."

"How'd you git at it?"

"Start what are called condemnation proceedings."

"All right, Johnnie, start me some."

"Against whom, and for what, Mr. Baines?"

"Against Crane and Keith, to git their land down at the G. and B. All their mill yards, you know. Don't want the mill buildin'. They're welcome to that. Jest their yards."

"But they can't run the mill without the log yard and the yard to pile out their lumber."

"Be too bad, wouldn't it? Calc'late I'm a heap sorry for Crane and Keith. Them fellers arouses my sympathy mighty frequent."

"But you're not a railroad, Mr. Baines."

"Yes I be, Johnnie. To-morrow I'll be layin' rails to prove it."

"But you own land right adjoining Crane and Keith's yards. Plenty of it."

"Not plenty, Johnnie.... Not plenty. As long as Crane and Keith owns anything in this neighborhood I hain't got plenty of it. Get the idee?"

"You want to run them out?"

"Wa-al, they hain't been exactly friendly to me. I like to dwell among friends, Johnnie. Lately they been makin' a sight of trouble for me. Seems like I ought to sort of return the favor. 'Tain't jest spite, Johnnie. Spite's a luxury I can't afford if there hain't a money profit in it. Seems like there might be a dollar or two in this here proceedin'--if handled jest right."

Johnnie didn't see it, but then he failed to see the profitable object in a great many things that Scattergood undertook. It was not his business to see, but to carry out promptly and efficiently Scattergood's directions. The time had not yet arrived when Johnnie was Scattergood's right hand, as in the bigger days that lay ahead.

"Didn't know Crane's sister married President Castle of the G. and B., did you, Johnnie?"

"No. What has that to do with it?"

"Consid'able.... Consid'able. Goes some ways toward provin' to me I was expected to call on Castle and that things was arranged on purpose. Proves to my satisfaction that Crane and Keith went out of their way to start this rumpus with me.... You start them condemnation proceedin's as quick as you kin."

Johnnie started them. Scattergood waited a few days; watched with interest the laying of the first rails of the Coldriver Railroad, and then made the day's drive to the state capital with drafts of his pair of bills in his pocket. He hunted up the representative from his town--Amri Striker by name.

"Amri," said he, "how's your disposition these days, eh? Feel like doin' favors?"

"Guess a lot of us boys feel like doin' favors for you, Scattergood." Which was not short of the truth, for Scattergood had been studying the science of politics as it was practiced in his state and putting to practical use his education. Indeed, he added to the science not a few contrivances characteristic of himself, which made the old-timers scratch their heads and admit that a new man had arisen who must be reckoned with. Not yet did Scattergood hold the state in the hollow of his hand, naming governors, senators, directing legislation, as he did when his years were heavier on his shoulders. Probably, however, there was no single individual in the commonwealth who could exert as much influence as he. If there was a single man to compare with him it was Lafe Siggins, from the northern part of the state. All men admitted that a partnership between Scattergood and Lafe would be unbeatable.

"Got a bill I want introduced, Amri," said Scattergood.

"Let's see her, Scattergood."

Amri read the bill; then he turned around in his chair and looked out of the window. Then he walked to the door and opened it suddenly, and peered up and down the hall.

"The dum thing's loaded with dynamite," he said, when he came back.

"Calc'lated on some explosion," said Scattergood. "But I calc'late the folks'll be for it. Shouldn't be s'prised if the feller who introduced it and made a fight for it would stand mighty well, back home. Might git to be Senator, Amri. No tellin'."

"Can't no sich bill be passed. The boys likes their passes, and I guess there's some that gits more than passes out of the railroads."

"If this bill's introduced, Amri," said Scattergood, solemnly, "there'll be a chance for some of the boys to fat up their savings' account--pervidin' there's a good chance of its passin'. The railroads'll git scairt and send quite a bank roll up this way."

"You bet," said Amri, with watering mouth.

"Lafe in town?"

"Come in last week."

"Lafe, I understand, hain't in politics for fun."

"Lafe's in right where he kin git the most the quickest."

"Run out and git him to step up here," said Scattergood.

In half an hour Lafe Siggins, tall, bony, long, and solemn of face, stepped into the room, and closed the door after him cautiously.

"Howdy, Scattergood!" he said.

"Howdy, Lafe!... Want your backin' for a pop'lar measure. I've up and invented a new way of taxin' a railroad."

Lafe started for the door. "Afternoon," he said, with a tone of finality.

"But," said Scattergood, "I figger you to do the fightin' for the railroads--reapin' whatever benefits you can figger out of it for yourself."

Lafe paused, considered, and returned. "What's the idee?" he asked.

"I jest don't want this bill to pass too easy," said Scattergood, soberly, but with a twinkle in his eye.

"It wouldn't," said Lafe.

"Um!... Railroads is more liberal, hain't they, when there's a good chance of their gittin' licked? Suppose this come to a fight, and it looked like they was goin' to git the worst of it. Supposin' the outcome hung on two or three votes, eh? And them votes looked dubious."

Lafe pressed his thin lips together.

"I guess I kin account for near half of the boys, Lafe, and I guess you kin line up clost to half with the railroads, can't you? Well, you don't stand to lose nothin', do you? All we got to do is keep them decidin' votes where we want 'em." Then he leaned over and whispered in Lafe's ear briefly.

Lafe's thin lips curved upward a trifle at the ends. "Scattergood," said he, "this here's an idee. Never recollect nothin' resemblin' it since I been in politics. What you after?"

"Jest pleasure, Lafe.... Jest pleasure. Is it a deal?"

"It's a deal."

"Amri outside?"

"Standin' guard, Scattergood."

"When you go out send him in."

Amri opened the door that Lafe closed behind him.

"All fixed," said Scattergood. "I want to see these boys to-night." Scattergood handed Amri a list of names. "And say, Amri, here's a leetle bill you might jest slip along quick. Don't amount to nothin', but it might help me some. Like to git the Governor's signature to it as soon as it kin be done."

Amri read it cautiously. It was just a harmless little measure having to do with stage lines. "All right," he said, carelessly.

Crane was in President Castle's office, and his demeanor was that of a man who has heard disquieting news.

"I told you," he said, in tones of reproach, "that he wasn't safe to monkey with. Keith and I thought he was just a fat, backwoods rube, but we got burnt, and burnt good. We were going to let him alone, but you got us into this--and now you've got to get us out again. Know what he's done? Nothing much but start condemnation proceedings against us to take our mill yards down on the railroad for a site for a depot and freight sheds. That's all. And us with close to a hundred thousand tied up in that mill. If he puts it through ..."

"He won't," snapped Castle.

"He's started to build his railroad. Actually laying rails."

"So I heard. That's to hold his charter.... Don't you worry. He can't build that road, and you men will. As soon as I found out he had that charter, and saw the possibilities of that valley, I made up my mind he had to be eliminated. And he will be."

"Keith and I tried that."

"I saw him," said Castle. "He's no fool. You thought he was. I'm not making any such mistake. Going after you the way he has proves it."

"And he'll be going after you, too. You want to mind your eye."

"It's a little different tackling the G. and B., don't you think? And I doubt if he figures we're really backing you."

"What he figures and what you think he figures are mighty wide apart some-times. It cost me money to find that out."

The telephone interrupted. Castle answered: "Yes, Hammond, I can see you now. What is it?... All right. Come right up." Hammond was the railroad's general counsel.

He appeared presently.

"I thought we had the legislature up yonder tamed," he said, angrily, as he entered the office.

"We have."

"Huh!... Take a look at this." He handed to the president Scattergood's novel taxation, measure. "What you make of that? Who's behind it? What's the game?"

Castle read it carefully; then he turned to Crane. "You win," he said, succinctly. "Your friend Scattergood has brought the fight right on to our front porch.... What about it, Hammond? Will such a tom-fool law stand water?"

"Can't tell. My judgment is that it wouldn't, but it's such a fool law that nobody can tell. And if it stuck--" He sucked in his breath. "It would give every jay legisature a show to rough the railroads beautifully."

"It would hurt.... Of course it mustn't pass. Get after it and don't let any grass grow. Kill it in committee. That's the safest way.... Have Lafe Siggins look after it."

Hammond bustled out, and Castle turned to his brother-in-law. "I underestimated this Scattergood some," he said. "Now I'll go after him.... For reasons of necessity we will discontinue all train service at the flag station at the mouth of Coldriver Valley. That'll leave his stage line dangling in the air. Just for a taste of what we can do.... I'll have Hammond look after that condemnation matter for you."

"He'll be coming around to offer to sidetrack that legislation if you'll let him build his railroad."

"Probably. I guess we won't trade."

But Scattergood did not come around to offer a compromise. He seemed to have lost interest in the matter wholly and to give his time solely to his hardware store. But the Transient Car bill, as it came to be called, began mysteriously to attract unprecedented attention. The press of the state showed unusual interest in it. In short, it became the one big measure of the legislative session. Everything else was secondary to it. When a railroad measure is hotly discussed in every loafing place in a state there is a measure that legislators handle with gloves. It is loaded. When the home folks get really interested in a thing they are apt to demand explanations. Wherefore it was but natural that President Castle's experts found it impossible to strangle the bill in committee. It was reported out, and then Hammond found it wise to journey to the capital to take charge of things himself.

At the end of a week, Mr. Hammond, general counsel for the G. & B. and expert handler of legislatures, was forced to write President Castle that he faced a condition new in his broad experience.

"The chances," he said, "are more than even that this bill passes. Men we have been able to depend on are refractory. Siggins is doing his best, but so far he has been able to account for only forty-five per cent of the votes. The strange thing about it," he finished, with genuine amazement, "is that the other side doesn't seem to be spending a penny."

Which was perfectly true. Neither in that fight nor in any of the scores of legislative battles in which Scattergood took part in his after life did he spend a dollar to buy a vote or to influence legislation. Perhaps it was scruple on his part; perhaps economy; perhaps he felt that his own peculiar methods were more efficacious than mere barter and sale.

From end to end, the state was in excitement over the measure. Skillful work had made it seem a vital thing to the people, and hundreds of letters and telegrams poured in to representatives. It looked as if public opinion were overwhelmingly with the bill. It was Scattergood's first use of the weapon of public opinion. In this battle he learned its potentialities. Men who knew him well and were close to him in political matters declare he became the most skillful creator of a fictitious public opinion that ever lived in the state. It was in keeping with his methods that he always seemed to be acting in response to a demand from the public rather than that he excited the public to demand what Scattergood wanted. But that was when Scattergood's hair was touched with gray and his girth had increased by twoscore pounds.

"I can't find any trace of Scattergood Baines in this matter," Hammond reported to President Castle.

That was true. Scattergood stayed at home, tending vigorously to his hardware business. Representatives did not call on him; he did not call on them. No trails led to his door.

President Castle had expected overtures from Scattergood, but none materialized. To a man of Castle's experience this was more than strange; it was uncanny. He began to consider the situation really serious. Was the man so confident as his silence indicated?

"Get the votes," he wired succinctly to Hammond, and Hammond, reading the message correctly, dipped into the emergency barrel of the railroad with generous hands. Prosperity had come to that legislature. Yet he was able, at the end of another two weeks, to guarantee six votes less than a majority. The opposition had captured one more vote than he, and needed but five to pass their measure. Hammond faced the task of acquiring those five unplaced legislators, and of weaning one away from Scattergood--and the bill was due to come up in the House in two days.

That day President Castle himself arrived in the capital, and, after discussing the situation with Hammond, wired Scattergood, asking for an appointment. The mountain was going to Mohammed. Scattergood replied not a word.

"I calc'late," he said to Mandy, "that President Castle's raisin' him a blister."

On the morning of the day on which the bill was to come to a vote Scattergood appeared unostentatiously in the capital, but word of his presence flashed from tongue to tongue with miraculous speed. Word of it came to President Castle, who pocketed his pride for excellent business reasons, and sent up his card to Scattergood's room.

"Guess I kin see him a minute," said Scattergood, and the president ascended with thoughts in his heart which Scattergood was well able to lead.

"Baines," said Castle, without preface, "what do you want?"

"Nothin' you've got, I calc'late," said Scattergood, serenely.

"You're back of this infernal bill. The railroads can't permit it to pass. It won't pass."

"Then what you wastin' your time on me for?" Scattergood asked.

"If we let you build your infernal little railroad will you drop out of this?"

"Hain't in it to speak of."

"Will you take your hands off--if we give you your railroad and guarantee train service?"

"Can't seem to see my way clear."

"What do you gain by passing this bill? You're nothing ahead. It won't give you your railroad. It won't give you anything."

"Calc'late you're right."

"Listen to reason, man. You want something. What is it?"

"Me?... Um!... I'm a plain kind of a man, Mr. President, with a plain kind of a wife. Hain't never met Mandy, have you? Wa-al, her and me is perty contented with life. We got a good hardware store ..."

"Rot! What do you want?"

Scattergood leaned forward, his round face, with its bulging cheeks, as expressionless as some particularly big and ruddy apple.

"If you're achin' to do favors for me, Mr. President you kin drop in along about supper time. Right now can't think of a thing you kin do for me. But I'll try ... I'll spend the afternoon thinkin' over all the things you might be able to do, and I'll try to pick one of 'em out.... I got to see a hardware salesman now. Afternoon Mr. President."

"Baines," said Castle, losing his temper for the first time in a dozen years, "we'll smash you for this. We'll drive you out of the state. Well--"

"Don't slam the door," said Scattergood, placidly; "it might disturb the other folks in the hotel."

That afternoon the galleries of the House were jammed. Below, in their seats, the legislators sat uncomfortably. There was a tenseness in the air which made men's skin tingle. The Transient Car bill was about to come to a vote. Everything had been done by both sides that could be done. There could be no more outside interference; no more money influence. It was all over. Now the matter was in the hands of those uneasy men, who, even now, might hold steadfast to their principles or to the money that had bought them or to the power that had compelled them-- or who might, for reasons secret to their several souls, change sides with astonishing suddenness, upsetting all calculations. Such things have been done.... But, even without the happening of the unexpected, no man could say how the votes would fall. Neither side had obtained a sure majority.

The preliminary formalities went forward. Then began the roll call, and from his place in the gallery Hammond shecked off on his list name after name, as they voted yea or nay--and President Castle watched and kept mental count. Scattergood was not present. The thing was even, dangerously even. For every yea there sounded a balancing nay. The count stood sixty-one for, sixty against ... with ten more votes to call.... With six votes to call the count was even.

"Whittaker," called the clerk's monotonous voice.

"Nay."

"Robbins."

"Nay."

"Baker."

"Nay."

"Hooper."

"Nay."

"Bolger."

"Nay."

"Brock."

"Nay."

The six final votes had been cast--and cast solidly against Scattergood's bill. Scattergood was beaten, decisively, destructively beaten. Not only was he defeated here, but he was smashed where the damage was even more destructive--in his prestige. He was a discredited political leader.... Lafe Siggins could not restrain a chuckle, for Scattergood had played into his hands. Scattergood had allowed himself to be eliminated from calculation in the state, leaving Siggins as sole, undisputed, victorious boss. It had been a clever scheme that Scattergood had outlined to Lafe--so clever that Lafe hadn't seen the great good that lay in it for himself--until days later. He shrugged his shoulders. It was just another case of a man unfamiliar with the game overplaying his hand.

President Castle shook hands openly with Hammond. True, there was a demonstration of disapproval from the gallery--but that was only the people! It did not signify.

"We got him," said Castle.

"But it was a close squeak."

Castle looked grimly down on the representatives, now huddled together in whispering groups.

"I don't often have the impulse to crow over a man," he said, "but this Baines was so infernally cocky. He told me I might see him at six o'clock and he'd tell me what I could do for him. Well, I'm going to see him." His voice was grim and forbidding.

On the way they picked up Siggins and invited him to dinner. The three went to the hotel, where, sitting calmly, placidly in the lobby, was Scattergood.

Castle walked directly to him. "You were going to tell me what I could do for you--at this hour, I believe."

"Did say somethin' like that."

Castle eyed Scattergood venomously, found him a hard man to crow over. He admitted Scattergood to be a good loser.

"I expect you'll be asking favors for some time," Castle said, "and not getting them. I told you we'd lick you--and we have. I told you we'd smash you and drive you out of the state. We'll do that just as surely ..."

"Maybe so," said Scattergood, phlegmatically. "Maybe so. Nobody kin tell.... Howdy, Siggins! Lookin' mighty jubilant about somethin'. Glad to see it.... And Mr. Hammond seems pleased, too. Done a good job of work, didn't you? Bet your boss is pleased with you, eh?"

"When you're ready to turn your chunks of right of way over to Crane and Keith, let them know," said Castle. "I guess the G. and B. loses interest in you from this on--or it will presently."

"Jest a jiffy," said Scattergood, as the trio turned away. "Seems like you was goin' to do a favor for me. Well, you hain't done it yet.... Guess I need a favor perty bad at this minute, eh? Wa-al, 'tain't a big one. Jest sort of cast your eye over this here." Scattergood handed Castle a folded paper of documentary appearance.

Castle snatched it and read it. It was brief. Not more than fifty words. It was a copy of a bill having to do with stage lines, passed by both Houses and signed by the Governor. It provided that wherever any stage line or other transportation company of whatsoever nature intersected the line of a railroad or terminated on such line, the railroad should be compelled to establish a regular station on demand, for the handling of passengers and freight, and should stop all trains except through trains, and should establish sidetracks for the handling and transfer of freight.

A few formal words, backed by the authority of the state, compelling the G. & B. to do all, and more than all, that Scattergood had requested of them! A few words making possible Scattergood's railroad more surely than agreement with President Castle could have made it!

"While you folks was busy with the Transient Car bill," Scattergood said, amiably, "the boys sort of tended to this for me. If I'd thought Hammond was int'rested

I might have called it to his attention. But I figgered he was paid to watch out for sich things, and I didn't want to interfere none. Jest as well, I take it."

Castle was scowling at Hammond, momentarily at a loss for words. Siggins was gazing at Scattergood with thin lips parted a trifle. His joy was blanketed.

"Somethin' else," said Scattergood, looking from one to another, and finally at Lafe. "Siggins figgered that my gittin' a beatin' on this bill would sort of make him boss of the state. You see, Mr. President, this here bill wasn't meant *to pass.* *It was fixed up for a couple of reasons. One was to git something which I'll tell you about in a second. Another was to make the boys in the House sort of prosperous like, and grateful to me for gittin' 'em the prosperity--with the railroads payin' for it. The last was to settle things between Lafe and me. I sort of wanted Lafe and the boys in politics to understand which was which.... And they'll understand.... Now, Mr. President, the thing I wanted to git was in two parts. First one was to git your attention on this here bill so's you wouldn't notice my little stage-line thing. The other was pretty nigh as valuable. I got it. It's a list of every man in this legislature that took money for a vote on this thing, with how much money he took and the hour and minute it was paid him--and* who by. Seems like I managed to git your *name, Mr. President, connected with them last six votes that you took over body and britches this noon. And I kin* prove every item of it.... With the folks around the state feelin' like they do, I shouldn't be s'prised if I could make a heap of trouble."

President Castle was a big man or he would not hold the position that was his. He knew when a fight was over. "You win," he said, tersely. "Name it."

"Two things. First off I want an agreement with your road, made by a full vote of the board of directors, agreein' to do jest what this bill pervides--in case of emergencies. And second, I want your folks should handle the bonds of my railroad--construction bonds. Guess I could manage it without, but I need my money for somethin' else. About two hunderd thousand dollars' worth of bonds'll do it."

Castle shrugged his shoulders--seeing possibilities for the future. However, he knew Scattergood had weighed those possibilities himself.

"Agreed," he said. There was a moment's silence. "By the way," he asked, "what was the idea of the condemnation proceedings against Crane and Keith?"

"Jest a mite of business. With the railroad goin', I need a good mill up on a site I got below Coldriver. Seems like Crane and Keith got a might timid, and yestiddy they up and sold out that mill to a friend of mine--actin' for me--for fifty-five thousand dollars. Figger I got it dirt cheap. Wuth close to a hunderd thousand, hain't it?... I'm goin' to move it to Coldriver, lock, stock, and barrel."

"Baines," said Castle, presently, "the G. and B. will keep hands off your valley. It will be better for us to work together than at odds. Suppose we bury the hatchet and work for each other's interest.... I'm paid to know a coming man when I see one."

"Was hopin' you'd see it that way, Mr. President. I hain't one that hankers for strife ... not even with Lafe, here, if he can figger he's willin' to admit what he's got to admit."

"I take my orders from you," said Lafe.

In which authentic manner Scattergood Baines, in one transaction, made possible and financed his railroad, obtained his first mill, and became undisputed political dictator of his state. Characteristically, there was charged to expense for the whole transaction a sum that a very ordinary man could earn in a week. Scattergood loved cheap results.

CHAPTER IV
HE DEALS IN MATCHMAKING

It is known to all the world that Scattergood came to own the stage line that plied down the valley to the railroad, but minute research and a sifting of dubious testimony was required to unearth the true details of that transaction in which the peg leg of Deacon Pettybone figured in a dominant manner.

Scattergood had long had his eye on the stage line, because his valley, the Coldriver Valley, was dominated by it. Transportation was king, and Scattergood knew that if his vision of developing that valley and of acquiring riches for himself out of the development were ever to become actuality, he must first control the means of transporting passengers and commodities. But the stage line was not to be acquired, because Deacon Pettybone and Elder Hooper, who owned it in partnership, had not been on speaking terms for twenty years. So bitter was the feud that either would have borne cheerfully a loss to prevent the other from making a profit. The stage line was a worry and an annoyance to both of them, but neither of them would sell, because he was afraid his enemy might derive some advantage.

As Scattergood well knew, the feud had its inception in religion as religion is practiced in that community. Deacon Pettybone had been born a Congregationalist. Elder Hooper was the sturdiest pillar of the Congregationalist church. They had grown up together from boyhood, as chums, and later as business partners, but at the mature age of forty Deacon Pettybone had attended a revival service in the Baptist church. When he came out of that service the mischief was done--he had been converted to the tenets of immersion and straightway withdrew from the church of his birth to enter the fold of its bitterest rival in Coldriver, if it were possible for the Baptists to be bitterer rivals of the Congregationalist than the Methodists and Universalists were. Coldriver's population was less than four hundred. It required a great deal of religion to get that four hundred safely past the snares and pitfalls of Coldriver, for there were no fewer than five full-grown churches, of which the Roman Catholic was the fifth, and a body of folks who met in one another's houses of a Sabbath under the denomination of the United Brethren. Five churches worshiped God through the crackling parchment of their mortgages, when one, or at most two, might have pointed the way to heaven free and clear, and with no worries over semiannual interest.

When Pettybone turned apostate there was such a commotion as had never before disturbed Coldriver; it subsided, and was forgotten as the years dragged on, by all but Pettybone and Hooper, who continued tenaciously to hate each other with a bitter hatred--and the more so that their financial affairs were so inextricably mingled.

Even when Pettybone's leg was mashed by a log, and he lay between life and death, there was no hint of a reconciliation; and when Pettybone appeared again on Coldriver's streets, hobbling on a peg leg of his own fashioning, the fires of vindictiveness burned higher and hotter than ever.

The situation would have been hopeless to anybody not possessed of Scattergood's optimism and resource. It is reported that Scattergood propounded a saying early in his career at Coldriver, to this effect:

"Anybody kin git anythin' done if he wants it hard enough. Trouble is, most folks hain't got a sufficient capacity for wantin'."

Scattergood's capacity for wanting was abnormal, and his ability to want until he got was what made him the remarkable figure in the life of his state that he was destined to become.

Scattergood was sitting on the piazza of his hardware store, basking in the sunshine, and gazing up the dusty road which passed between Coldriver's business structures, and disappeared over the hill. His eyes were half closed, and his bulk, which later became phenomenal, filled comfortably the specially reinforced chair which came to be called his throne. Pliny Pickett slouched around the corner, and, as he approached, the unmistakable odor of horses became noticeable. Inhabitants of Coldriver knew when Pliny came into a room even if their backs were turned.

"Mornin', Pliny," said Scattergood.

"Mornin', Scattergood."

"Fetch any passengers?"

"Drummer 'n' a fat woman to visit the Bogles. Say, Scattergood, looks like you're goin' to have competition."

"Um!... Don't say."

"Hardware," said Pliny, nasally. "Station's heaped with it. Every merchant in town's layin' in a stock."

"Do tell," said Scattergood, without emotion. "Kettleman and Locker?" They were the grocers.

Pliny nodded. "An' Lumley and Penny mixin' it in with dry goods, and Atwell minglin' it with clothin'."

Scattergood reached down and unlaced his shoes. His mind worked more freely when his toes were unconfined, so that he might wriggle them as he reasoned. Pliny knew the sign and grinned.

"Much 'bleeged," said Scattergood, and Pliny moved off.

"Pliny," said Scattergood.

"Eh?"

"Was you thinkin' of buyin' a stove?"

"No."

"Could think about it, couldn't you?"

"Might manage it."

"Folks thinkin' of buyin' stoves gits prices, don't they? Kind of inquires around to see where they kin buy cheapest?"

"Most does."

"G'-by, Pliny."

"G'-by, Scattergood."

Something of the sort was not unanticipated by Scattergood. He knew the merchants of the town had not forgiven him for once getting decidedly the better of them in a certain transaction, and he knew now that they had combined against him. Their idea was transparent to him. It was their hope to put him out of business by adding hardware to their stocks and to sell it at cost, until he gave up the ship. They could afford it. It would not interfere with their normal profits.

Scattergood wriggled his toes furiously and squinted his eyes. They alighted on a young man in clerical black, who crossed the square from the post office. It was no other than Jason Hooper, son of Elder Hooper, who had been educated to the ministry and had recently come to occupy the pulpit of his father's church--a pleasant and worthy young man. Almost simultaneously Scattergood's eyes perceived Selina Pettybone, daughter of Deacon Pettybone, just entering the post office.

"Purty as a picture," said Scattergood to himself, and then he chuckled.

The young minister nodded to Scattergood, and Scattergood spoke in return. "Mornin', Parson," he said. "How d'you find business?"

"Business?" The young man looked a bit startled.

"Oh, how's the marryin' industry, f'r instance? Brisk?"

Jason smiled. "It might be brisker."

"Um!... Maybe folks figgers you hain't had enough experience to do their marryin' jest accordin' to rule--seein' 's you hain't married yourself."

Jason blushed and frowned. This was a subject that had been brought to his attention insistently; he had been informed that a minister should marry, and there were several marriageable daughters in his church.

"You aren't going to pick a wife for me, too?" he said, with a rueful smile.

"Dunno but I might," said Scattergood. "Got any preferences as to weight and color?"

"My only preference is to have them all--a long way off," said the young minister.

"Some day you'll have opposite leanin's. There'll be a girl you'll want to snuggle right clost to.... G'-by, Parson, I'll keep my eyes open for you."

A few days later consignments of hardware began to arrive, and Scattergood, sitting on the piazza of his store, watched them carried with much ostentation into the stores of his rivals. It was noticed that he scarcely had his shoes on during this week and that he even walked to the post office barefooted, squirming his delighted toes into the warm sand with apparent enjoyment. Immediately Locker and Kettleman and Lumley and the rest made it known to Coldriver and environs that they were dealing in hardware and not for profit, but merely as a convenience to their patrons. They emphasized the fact that they would sell hardware at cost, and exhibited prices which Scattergood studied and saw that he could not meet.

The town watched the affair, expecting much of Scattergood, but he made no move. Apparently he was contented to sit on his piazza and see customers passing him by for the alluring bargains offered beyond. Coldriver was disappointed in Scattergood, and it said so, much as a disgruntled critic will speak of an actor who has made a flat failure in a favorite piece.

On a certain afternoon Scattergood was seen to accost Selina Pettybone, who paused, and drew nearer, showing signs of regret and interest.

"Seliny," said Scattergood, "you're one of them Daughters of Dorcas, or half sisters of Mehitable, or somethin' religious and charitable, hain't you?"

"Yes," said Selina, with a smile.

"What does sich folks do when they git to hear of a case of misery and distress?"

"They do what they can, Mr. Baines," said Selina.

"Um!... If you heard Xenophon Banks was took sick of a busted leg, and his wife was dead these two year, and a 'leven-year-old girl was tryin' to nuss her pa and look after four more, what d'ye calc'late you'd calc'late?"

"I'd calculate," said Selina, "that I ought to go out there to the farm and see about it at once."

"Usin' your buggy or mine?"

"Mine, thank you."

"G'-by, Selina."

"G'-by, Mr. Baines," she said, and laughed.

Scattergood watched her disappear in the direction of her home and then got up leisurely and ambled toward the Congregational parsonage, in which young Jason Hooper lived in solitary dignity. Mr. Hooper was in his study.

"Howdy, Parson?" said Scattergood.

"How do you do, Mr. Baines?"

"Bible say anythin' regardin' visitin' the sick an' ministerin' to the oppressed?"

"A great deal, Mr. Baines."

"Think it's meant, eh? Or was it put there jest to preach about?"

"It is meant, undoubtedly."

"For ministers?"

"Yes."

"Um!... Xenophon Banks busted his leg. 'Leven-year-old daughter's tryin' to carry him and four other childern on to her back, so to speak."

"I'll go at once, Mr. Baines."

Scattergood fidgeted. "Calculate Xenophon wasn't forehanded. Six mouths to feed. More mealtimes than meals," he said, and fumbled in his pocket. He was visibly embarrassed. "Here's ten dollars that was give me to be used for sich a purpose. The feller that give it let on he wanted it to come like it was give by the church, and him not mentioned. Git the idee?"

"I get the idea perfectly," said young Mr. Hooper, his face lighting as he surveyed Scattergood with a whimsical twinkle--and as he saw this scheming, money-hungry, power-hungry man in a new light. "The man may feel confident I shall not betray him."

"If I was a minister in sich a case I wouldn't forgit some stick candy for them five childern. Seems like candy's 'most necessary for sich. Dum foolishness, but keeps 'em quiet.... Git a big bag of candy.... And, if I was doin' this, I wouldn't let no grass grow under my feet."

So it happened that Selina Pettybone and the Rev. Jason Hooper, respectively, daughter of the leading deacon of the Baptist church, and parson of the Congregational church, arrived at Xenophon Banks's little house within ten minutes of each other, and each was greatly embarrassed by the other's presence, for the family feud had compelled them to be coldly distant to each other all of their short lives.... But there was much to do, and embarrassment of such kind between an unusually pretty and wholesome girl, and a reasonably well-looking and kindly young man, is not an emotion that cannot be easily dissipated.

About a week later Scattergood chanced to pass Deacon Pettybone's house, and saw the old gentleman sitting on the front porch, shaping a large piece of wood with a draw-shave.

"Afternoon, Deacon," said Scattergood.

"Set and rest your legs," said the deacon. "Jest puttin' the finishin' touches on this timber leg of mine."

"Sturdy-lookin' leg, Deacon."

"Best I ever made. Always calc'late to keep one ahead. Soon's one leg wears out and I put on the spare one, I set to work fashionin' another, to have by me. Always manage to figger some improvement."

"More int'restin' than cuttin' out ax handles," said Scattergood.

The deacon looked his scorn. "Anybody kin cut an ax handle, but lemme tell you it takes study and figgerin' and brains to turn out a timber leg that's full as good if not better 'n a real one.... I aim to varnish this here leg and hang it in the harness room. Wisht I could keep it by me in the kitchen, but the ol' woman says it sp'iles her appetite. Wimmin is full of notions. Claims she'd go crazy with a leg a-hangin' back of the stove, and some day she'd up and slam it in the oven and serve it up for a roast. You kin thank your stars you hain't got wimmin's notions to worry you, Scattergood."

"How d'ye stand on the proposition to have the town build a sidewalk up the hill apast the Congregational church, Deacon?"

The deacon pounded on the porch with his nearly finished leg, and grew red in the face. "All the doin's of ol' man Hooper. Connivin' and squillickin' around for his own ends. Lemme tell you, Scattergood, no town meetin' of Coldriver'll ever vote sich a steal only over my dead body. Jest you tell that far and wide."

Business had been almost at a standstill for Scattergood. The only sales he made were of small articles his competitors had forgotten or neglected to stock. He had not taken in enough money for a month to pay for the wear and tear on his fixtures. Coldriver was coming to set him down as a failure and a black disappointment; but it marveled that he took no action whatever and showed no signs of worry. His eyes were as blue and his manner as humorous as it had ever been. Most of his conversation seemed to be on the subject of the sidewalk past the Congregational church, and it was carried on in low tones, and never to more than one individual at a time. If those individuals had compared notes they would have been astonished. Scattergood's attitude on the matter was widely different, depending on whether he talked with Baptist or Congregationalist. One might almost say that both sides were coming to him for advice on how to conduct its campaign to carry the town meeting--and one would have been right.

The matter had developed into the hottest political issue Coldriver had ever seen. No presidential election had come near to rivaling it, and the local-option issue had stirred up fewer heartburnings and given rise to less bellowing and to fewer hard words. The town meeting was less than a month away.

But even in the heat of the campaign Scattergood found time to drive out to Xenophon Banks's. The road to Banks's was fairly well traveled these days, for there was hardly a day that did not see either Selina Pettybone or Parson Hooper driving out to the little house, and, strangely enough, the days on which both were present appeared to be in the majority. Scattergood dropped out now and then with pockets full of stick candy, which he never delivered himself, but which he always handed to the minister or to Selina to be given anonymously after he was gone. He seemed as much interested in watching Selina and Jason as he was in talking with Xenophon, and he might have been perceived frequently to nod his head with satisfaction--especially on the day when he heard Jason call Selina by her first name, and on the other day when he saw the young minister retaining Selina's hand longer than he should have done in saying good afternoon. That day Jason drove back to town with Scattergood.

"Likely-lookin' girl--Seliny," observed Scattergood.

"Beautiful," said the parson, and Scattergood grinned.

"Um!... Single ministers is a menace. Yes, sir, churches has busted up on account of their ministers not bein' married."

There was no reply.

"But I calculate you're different. You're jest made and created to be an old batch. Never seen sich a feller. Couldn't no girl interest you, not if she was the Queen of Sheeby."

"Mr. Baines," said Jason, after a pause, "I'm very miserable. I--I think I shall resign from my church and go away."

"Sandrich Islands or somewheres--missionery feller?" said Scattergood.

"I--why, yes, that's what I'll do.... I wish I'd never seen her." Then he corrected himself sharply. "No, I don't. I'm glad I've seen her. I've got that much, anyhow. I can always remember her and think about how sweet and beautiful she was--"

"And die at the age of eighty with her name comin' from your lips on your last breath. To be sure.... Seems to me, though, it would be a sight more satisfyin' to live them fifty-odd years with her and raise up a fam'ly, and git some benefits out of that sweetness and beauty and sich like, besides mullin' 'em over in your mind. Speakin' of Seliny, wasn't you?"

"Yes."

"Don't hanker to marry her?"

"Mr. Baines--"

"Then why in tunket don't you?"

"She's a Baptist."

"White, hain't she?"

"Yes."

"Respectable?"

"Of course, sir."

"Don't call to mind no state law ag'in' Congregationalists marryin' Baptists."

"My congregation wouldn't allow it."

"Hain't never seen no deed of sale of you to your congregation."

"Her father would never permit it?"

"Huh!..."

"And she's an obedient daughter."

"Has she said so?"

"Y-yes."

"Ho! Kind of human, after all, hain't you? Look pleased when she said it?"

"She cried."

"Comfort her--some."

"I--She--she loves me, Mr. Baines."

"Well, I snum! Kind of disobedient to love you, hain't it? Knows her father 'd be set ag'in' it?"

"Yes, but she can't help that."

"Why?"

"You--why, you fall in love! You don't do it on purpose, Mr. Baines. It just comes to you."

"From where?" said Scattergood, abruptly.

The young minister stared.

"Who's to blame for there bein' love?" Scattergood demanded.

After a pause the young man answered. "God," he said. "Why does He send it?"

"So that people will marry, and the love will keep them together, strong to bear the trials and labors of life. I think love is a kind of wages that God pays to men and women for living on His earth."

"Um!... Does He send love sort of helter-skelter and hit-or-miss, or does He aim it at certain folks?"

"I have often preached that marriages were made in heaven."

"Then it's a kind of a command, hain't it?"

"Yes."

"Which d'ye calculate is the wust disobedience? To refuse to obey an order sich as this, or to disobey a parent that runs counter to the wants of the Almighty?"

The young man's face was alight with happiness. "Mr. Baines," he said, "I'm grateful to you. I shall marry Selina."

"Maybe," said Scattergood. "It runs in my mind you got to have dealin's with Deacon Pettybone, and the deacon always figgers that the news he gits from heaven is fresher and more dependable than what anybody else gits. Might ask him and see."

A few days after that Coldriver knew that Parson Hooper had asked the hand of Selina from her father and had been rejected with language and almost with violence. Then a strange thing took place. If Jason had married Selina without opposition, his congregation would have been enraged. He might have been forced from his pulpit. Now it regarded him as a martyr, and with clacking tongues and singleness of purpose it espoused his cause and declared that their minister was good enough to marry any girl alive, and that Deacon Pettybone was a mean, narrow-minded, bigoted, cantankerous old grampus. The thing became a public question, second in importance only to the sidewalk.

"Hold your hosses," Scattergood advised Jason. "Let's see what a mite of dickerin' and persuasion'll do with the deacon. Then, if measures fails, my advice to you as a human bein' and a citizen is to git Seliny into a buckboard and run off with her. But hold on a spell."

So Jason held on, and the town meeting approached, and Scattergood continued to sit in idleness on the piazza of his store and twiddle his bare toes in the sunshine. Deacon Pettybone was a busy man, organizing the forces of the Baptists, and seeking diligently to round up the votes of neutrals. Elder Hooper, the leader of the Congregationalist party, was equally occupied, and no man might hazard a guess at the outcome of the affair.

"This here is a great principle," said Deacon Pettybone, "and men gives their lives and sacrifices their families for sich. I'm a-goin' to fight to the last gasp."

"Don't blame ye a mite," said Scattergood. "If them Congregationalists rule this town meetin' you might's well throw up your hands. They'll rule the town forever."

"It's got to be pervented."

"And nobody but you kin manage it," said Scattergood. "The hull thing rests with you. Why, if you was sick so's to be absent from that meetin' the Congregationalists 'u'd win, hands down."

"I b'lieve it," said the deacon, "and nothin' on earth'll keep me away--nothin'. If I was a-layin' at my last gasp I'd git myself carried there."

"Deacon," said Scattergood, solemnly, "much is dependin' on you. Coldriver's fort'nit to have sich a man at the helm."

Even the cribbage game under the barber shop was suspended, and the cribbage game was an institution. It was the deacon's one shortcoming, but even there he strove to get the better of the enemy, for the two men who were considered his only worthy antagonists at the game were Congregationalists. The three bickered and quarreled and threatened each other with violence, but they played daily. There were few afternoons when a ring of spectators did not surround the table, breathlessly watching the champions. It was the great local sporting event, and who shall quarrel with the good deacon for touching cards in the innocent game of cribbage? Certainly his pastor did not do so, nor did the fellow members of his congregation. Indeed, there was even pride in his prowess.

But the game was discontinued, and Hamilcar Jones and Tilley Newcamp were loud in their excoriations of their late antagonist. The Congregationalists had no hotter adherents than they, nor none who entered the conflict with more bitterness of spirit. Scattergood saw to it that he encountered them on the evening before the momentous town meeting.

"Evenin', Ham. Evening Tilley."

"Howdy, Scattergood?"

"How's things lookin' for to-morrer?"

"Mighty even, Scattergood. If 'twan't for that ol' gallus Pettybone, we'd git that sidewalk with votes to spare."

"Um!... If he was absent from the meetin' things might git to happen."

"Ho! Tie him to home, and there wouldn't even be a fight."

"Got a wooden leg, hain't he?"

"Wisht he had three."

"Got two, one hangin' in the harness room. Harness room's never locked. If 'twas a boy could squirm through the window."

"What of it?"

"Nothin'. Jest happened to think of it.... Ever stop to think what a comical thing it 'u'd be if somebody was to ketch a wooden-legged man and saw his leg off about halfway up? Jest lay him across a saw buck and saw her off while he hollered and fit. Most comical notion I ever had."

"Would make a feller laugh."

"More 'special if his spare leg was stole away and he didn't have nothin' but the sawed-off one. Sich a man would have difficulty gittin' any place he wanted to git to.... G'-by, Ham. G'-by, Tilley. Hope the meetin' comes out right to-morrer."

Scattergood went inside and looked at his bank book. In two months his deposits from sales had amounted to something like a hundred dollars. The situation spelled nothing less than bankruptcy, but Scattergood replaced the book and waddled out to his piazza, where he sat in the cool of the evening, twiddling his toes and looking from the store of one competitor to the store of another, reflectively.

At a late hour a small boy named Newcamp delivered a bulky package to Scattergood, and vanished into the darkness. The package was about large enough to contain a timber leg.

The town seethed with politics next morning, and the deacon was in the center of it. The meeting was called for ten o'clock. At nine thirty a small boy wriggled up to the deacon and whispered in his ear. The deacon quickly made his way out of the crowd and down the stairs into the basement room under the barber shop--for news had been given him of a chance to swap for votes. He burst into the room, and stopped, frowning, for Tilley Newcamp stood before him. Hamilcar Jones was not at the moment visible, because he was behind the door, which he slammed shut and locked.

No word was uttered, but a Trojan struggle ensued. It was two against one, but even those odds did not daunt the deacon. It was full five minutes before he was flat on his back, panting and uttering such burning and searing words as might properly fall from the lips of a Baptist deacon. Tilley Newcamp, who was heavy, sat on his chest. Hamilcar Jones dragged up a saw buck and laid the deacon's timber leg across it.... The deacon saw and comprehended, and lifted up his voice. Another five minutes were consumed in returning him to quiescence. And then the saw did its work, while the deacon breathed threats of blood and torture, and regretted that his religion prevented him from using language better suited to his purpose. The leg was severed; a fragment full ten inches long fell from the end, and the deacon's assailants drew away, their fell purpose accomplished.

There was a rapping on the door. It was Scattergood Baines, and he was admitted. His face was full of wrath as he gazed within, and he quivered with fury as he ordered the two miscreants out of the place.

"What's this, Deacon, what's this?" he demanded.

The deacon told him at length, and fluently.

"I was jest in time. Now we kin send for that spare leg and you kin git to the meetin'. Lucky you had that spare leg."

The deacon sat on the floor, speechless now, staring down at all that remained to him of his timber leg. Scattergood, with great show of solicitude, dispatched a youngster to the deacon's house for his extra limb. He returned empty-handed.

"This here boy says the leg hain't in the harness room. Sure you left it there?"

Again the deacon found his voice, and his words were to the general effect that the blame swizzled, ornery, ill-sired, and regrettably reared pew-gags had, in defiance of law and order, stolen and made away with his leg--and what was he to do?

"Deacon, you can't go like that. If this story got into the meetin' it would do fer you. You'd git laughed out. Them Congregationalists 'u'd win. You got to have a sound leg to travel on, and I don't see but one way to git it."

"How's that?"

"Call in young Parson Hooper and make him force them adherents of hisn to give it up."

Scattergood did not wait for the permission he surmised would not be given, but sent word for Jason Hooper, who came, saw, and was most remarkably astonished.

"Parson," said Scattergood, "this here outrage is onendurable. Some of you Congregationers done it, and stole his other leg. As leader of your flock and a honest man, it's your bounden duty to git it back."

"But I--I know nothing about it. What can I do? I--There isn't a thing you can do."

"Deacon," said Scattergood, "there hain't a soul in the world can git back your leg in time but this young man. Maybe he don't know he kin do it, but he kin. Hain't you got no offer to make?"

The parson started to say something, but Scattergood silenced him with a waggle of the head.

"I got to git to that meetin'," bellowed the deacon. "There hain't nothin' in the world I wouldn't give to git there, and git there whole and hearty, and so's not to be laughed at."

"Remind you of any leetle want of yourn?" asked Scattergood. He took the young man aside and whispered to him.

"Deacon," he said, presently, "Parson Hooper says as how he don't see no reason for interferin' and helpin' his enemy." The parson had said nothing of the sort. "But I kin see a reason, Deacon. If this here young man was a member of your family, so to speak, and was related to you clost by ties of love and marriage, I don't see how he'd have a right to hold his hand.... Want this man's daughter f'r your wedded wife, don't you?"

"Yes," said the parson, faintly.

"Hear that, Deacon? Hear that?"

"Never, by the hornswoggled whale that swallered Jonah."

"Meetin's about to start," said Scattergood, looking at his watch.

The deacon sweated and bellowed, but Scattergood adroitly waved the red flag of animosity before his eyes, and pictured black ruin and defeat--until the deacon was ready to surrender life itself.

"Git me my leg," he shouted, "and you kin have anythin'.... Git me my leg."

"Is it a promise, Deacon? Calculate it's a promise?"

"I promise. I promise, solemn."

Scattergood whispered again in the pastor's ear, who stuttered and flushed and choked, and hurried out of the room, presently to reappear with the deacon's spare leg.

"Now, young feller, make your preparations for that there weddin'.... Scoot."

It is of record that the deacon arrived, like Sheridan at Winchester, in the nick of time; that he rallied his flustered cohorts and led them to triumph--and then regretted the bargain he had made. But it was too late. He could not draw back. Wife and daughter and townsfolk were all against him, and he could not withstand the pressure.

And then....

"Parson," said Scattergood, "your pa and the deacon ought to make up."

"They'll never do it, Mr. Baines."

"Deacon'll have to let your pa come to the weddin'. There'll be makin' up and reconciliations when there's a grandson, but I can't wait. I'm in a all-fired hurry. You go to the deacon and tell him your pa sent him to say that he's ready to bury the hatchet and begs the deacon's pardon for everythin'--everythin'."

"But it wouldn't be true."

"It's got to be true. Hain't I sayin' it's true? And then you go to your pa and tell him the deacon wants to make up, and begs his pardon out and out. Tell both of 'em to be at my store at three o'clock, but don't tell neither t'other's to be there."

At three o'clock Deacon Pettybone and Elder Hooper came face to face in Scattergood's place of business.

"Howdy, gents?" said Scattergood. "Lookin' forward to bein' mutual grandads, I calc'late. Must be quite a feelin' to know you're in line to be a grandad."

"Huh!" grunted the deacon.

"Wumph!" coughed the elder.

"To think of you old coots dandlin' a baby on your knees--and buyin' it pep'mint candy and the Lord knows what, and walkin' down the street, each of you holdin' one of its hands and it walkin' betwixt you.... Dummed if I don't congratulate you."

The deacon looked at the elder and the elder looked at the deacon. They grinned, frostily at first, then more broadly.

"By hek! Eph," said the deacon.

"I'll be snummed!" said the elder, and they shook hands there and then.

"Step back here a minute. I got a mite of business. You won't want the nuisance of that stage line--with a grandson to fetch up. I'm kinder hankerin' to run the thing--not that it'll be much of an investment."

"What you offerin'?" asked the deacon.

Scattergood mentioned the sum. "Cash," he concluded.

"Calc'late we better sell," said the elder.

An hour later, with the papers in his pocket to prove ownership, Scattergood visited the stores of his rivals, Locker, Kettleman, Lumley, and Penny.

"Gentlemen," he said, "you been a-tryin' to crowd me out of business. I hain't made a cent of profit f'r two months, and I calc'late on a profit of two hunderd and fifty a month. Jest gimme your check for five hunderd dollars and I'll take your stocks of hardware off'n your hands at, say, fifty cents on the dollar, and we'll call it a day."

"Scattergood, we got you where we want you. You can't hold out another sixty days."

"Maybe. But, gentlemen, I guess we kin do business. I jest bought the only means of transportin' goods, wares, and merchandise into Coldriver. Beginnin' now, rates for freight goes up. I've studied the law, and there hain't no way to per- vent me. I kin charge what I want for freighting and what I want will be so much not a one of you kin do business.... And I'll put in groceries and what not, myself. Gittin' my freight free, I calc'late to under-sell you quite consid'able.... Kin we do business?"

The enemy went into executive session. They surrendered. Scattergood pock- eted a check for five hundred dollars, and came into possession of a fine stock of hardware at fifty cents on the dollar. Likewise, he owned the stage line and fran- chise, controlling the only right of way by which a railroad could reach up the valley. It had required politics, marrying and giving in marriage, and patience, to accomplish it, but it was done.

That evening Mrs. Hooper and Mrs. Pettybone, childhood friends, long sepa- rated by the feud, stopped to speak to Scattergood.

"Nobody knows how we appreciate what you done Minnie and me," said Mrs. Pettybone.

"Blessed is the peacemaker," said Mrs. Hooper.

"Thankee, ladies. I don't mind bein' a peacemaker any time--when I kin do it at a profit."

"It's always done at a profit, Mr. Baines, if you read the Good Book. This day you laid up a treasure in heaven."

"Trouble with depositin' profits in heaven," said Scattergood, very soberly, "is that you got to wait so tarnation long to draw your int'rest."

CHAPTER V
HE MAKES IT ROUND NUMBERS

It's a telegram from Johnnie Bones," said Scattergood Baines to his wife, Mandy, as he tore open the yellow envelope and read the brief message it contained. "Telegram!" said Mandy. "Why didn't he write? Them telegrams come high.... Huh! Jest one word--'Come.' Costs as much to send ten as it does one, don't it?"

"Identical," said Scattergood.

"Then," said Mandy, sharply, "if he was bound to telegraph why didn't he git his money's worth?"

"I calc'late he thought he said a plenty," Scattergood replied. "Johnnie he don't like to put no more in writin' that's apt to pass from hand to hand than he's obleeged to.... Mandy, looks like we better start for home."

"What d'you s'pose it kin be?" Mandy asked, already busy laying clothing in their canvas telescope. "Mostly telegrams announces death or sickness."

"I kin think of sixty-nine things it might be," said Scattergood, "but I got a feelin' it hain't none of 'em."

"We shouldn't of come away on this vacation," said Mandy. "Johnnie Bones is too young a boy to leave in charge."

"Johnnie Bones is a dum good lawyer, Mandy, and a dum far-seein' young man. I don't calc'late Johnnie's done us no harm. Hain't no hurry, Mandy. We can't git a train home for five hours."

"We'll be settin' right in the depot waitin' for it," said Mandy, who declined to take chances. "Be sure you keep your money in the pants pocket on the side I'm walkin' on. Pickpockets 'u'd have some difficulty gittin' past me."

"Only thing ag'in' Johnnie Bones," said Scattergood, "is that he hain't a first-rate hardware clerk."

Scattergood, in spite of the ownership of twenty-four miles of narrow-gauge railroad, of a hundred-odd thousand acres of spruce, and of a sawmill whose capacity was thirty thousand feet a day, persisted in regarding these things as side lines, and in looking upon his little hardware store in Coldriver as the vital business of his life. It was now ten years since Scattergood had walked up Coldriver Valley to the village of Coldriver. It was ten years since he had embarked on the conquest of that desirable valley, with a total working capital of forty dollars and some cents--and he not only controlled the valley's business and timber and transportation, but generally supervised the politics of the state. He could have borne up manfully if all of it were taken away from him--excepting the hardware store. To have ill befall that would have been disaster, indeed.

On the train Scattergood turned over a seat to have a resting place for his feet, took off his shoes, displaying white woolen socks, a refinement forced upon him by Mandy, and leaned back to doze and speculate. When Mandy thought him safely asleep she covered his feet with a paper, to conceal from the public view this evidence of a character not overgiven to refinements. It is characteristic of Scattergood that, though wide awake, he gave no sign of knowledge of Mandy's act. Scattergood was thinking, and to think, with him, meant so to unfetter his feet that he could wriggle his toes pleasurably.

Johnnie Bones was waiting for Scattergood at the station.

"Johnnie," said Scattergood, "did you sell that kitchen range to Sam Kettleman?"

"Almost, Mr. Baines, almost. But when it came to unwrapping the weasel skin and laying money on the counter, Sam guessed Mrs. Kettleman could keep on cooking a spell with what she had."

"Johnnie," said Scattergood, "you're dum near perfect; but you got your shortcomings. Hardware's one of 'em.... What about that telegram of yourn?"

"Yes," said Mandy.

"Mr. Castle, president of the G. and B.--"

"I know what job he's holdin' down, Johnnie."

"--came to see you yesterday. I wouldn't tell him where you were, so he had to tell me what he wanted. He wants to buy your railroad. Said to have you wire him right off."

"Um!..." Scattergood walked deliberately, with heavy-footed stride, to the telegraph operator, and wrote a brief but eminently characteristic message. "I might," the telegram said to President Castle.

"Now, folks," he said, "we'll go up to the store and sort of figger on what Castle's got in mind."

They sat down on the veranda, under the wooden awning, and Scattergood's specially reinforced chair creaked under his great weight as he stooped to remove his shoes. For a moment he wriggled his toes, just as a golfer waggles his driver preparatory to the stroke. "Um!..." he said.

"Castle," said he, presently, "works for jest two objects--makin' money and payin' off grudges. Most gen'ally he tries to figger so's to combine 'em."

Johnnie and Mandy waited. They knew better than to interrupt Scattergood's train of thought. Had they done so he would have uttered no rebuke, but would have hoisted himself out of his chair and would have waddled away up the dusty street, and neither of them would ever hear another word of the matter.

"He knows I wouldn't sell this road without gittin' money for it. Therefore he's figgerin' on makin' a lot of money out of it, or payin' off a doggone big grudge.... Somebody we don't know about is calc'latin' on movin' into this valley, Johnnie. Somebody that's goin' to do a heap of shippin'--and that means timber cuttin'.... And it must be settled or Castle wouldn't come out and offer to buy."

Johnnie and Mandy had followed the reasoning and nodded assent.

"What timber be they goin' to cut?" Scattergood poked a chubby finger at Johnnie, who shook his head.

"The Goodhue tract, back of Tupper Falls. Uh-huh! Because there hain't no other sizable tract that I hain't got strings on. And the mills, whatever kind they be, will be at Tupper Falls. Mills got to be there. Can't git timber out to no other place. And, Johnnie, buyin' timber is a heap more important and difficult than buyin' mill sites. Eh?... Johnnie, you ketch the first train for Tupper Falls. I own a mite of land along the railroad, Johnnie, but you buy all the rest from the falls to the station. Not in my name, Johnnie. Git deeds to folks whose names we're entitled to use--and the more deeds the better. Scoot."

"Now, Scattergood, don't go actin' hasty," said Mandy. "You don't know --"

"The only thing I don't know, Mandy, is whether Johnnie 's too late to buy that land. Knowin' nobody else wants it, and it hain't no good for nothin' but what they want it for, these folks may not have bought yit ...."

Scattergood shouted suddenly at the passing drayman. "Hey, Pete.... Come here and git a cookin' range and take it up to Sam Kettleman's house. Git a man to help you. Tell Mis' Kettleman I sent it, and she's to try it a week to see if she likes it. Set it up for her and all."

Scattergood settled back to watch with approval, while two men hoisted the heavy stove on the wagon and drove away with it. Presently Sam Kettleman appeared on the porch of his grocery across the street, and Scattergood called to him: "Well, Sam, glad you decided to git the woman a new stove. Shows you're up an' doin'. It's all set up by this time."

Sam stared a moment; then, smitten speechless, he rushed across the road and stood, a picture of rage, glaring at Scattergood. "I didn't buy no stove. You know dum well I didn't buy no stove. I can't afford no stove. You jest git right up there and haul it back here, d'you hear me?"

"Well, now, Sam, don't it beat all--me makin' a mistake like that? Sure I'll send after it, right off.... Now I won't have to order one special for Locker." Locker was the rival grocer. "I kin haul this one right to his house, and explain to him how he come to git it so soon. I'll say: 'Locker, we jest hauled this stove down from Sam Kettleman's. Had it all set up there and then Sam he figgered it was too expensive a stove for him and he couldn't afford it right now on account of business not bein' brisk.'"

"Eh?" said Kettleman.

"'Twon't cause a mite of talk that anybody'll pay attention to. Everybody knows what Locker's wife is. Tongue wagglin' at both ends. And I'll take pains to conterdict whatever story she goes spreadin' about you bein' too mean to git your wife things to do with in the kitchen, and about how you're 'most bankrupt and ready to give up business. Nobody'll b'lieve her, anyhow, Sam, but if they do I'll explain it to 'em."

"Now--"

"Locker's wife'll be glad to have it, too. She'd have to wait two weeks for hers, and now she'll git it right off. Oven's cracked on hern, and she allows she sp'iles every batch of bread she bakes--and her pledged to furnish six loaves for the Methodist Ladies' Food Sale...."

"Scattergood Baines, if you dast touch my stove I'll have the law onto you. You can't go enterin' my house and removin' things without my permission, I kin tell you. Don't you try to forgit it, neither. If you think you can gouge me out of my stove jest to make it more convenient for Mis' Locker, you're thinkin' wrong...."

"'Tain't your stove till it's paid for, Sam."

"Then, by gum! it'll be mine darn quick. Thirty-eight dollars, was it? Now you gimme a receipt.... Locker!..."

Scattergood waddled into the store, wrote a receipt, and put the money in the safe. When Sam had recrossed the road again he turned to Johnnie Bones. "Sellin' hard-ware's easy if you put your mind to it, Johnnie. Trouble with you is you don't take no int'rest in it.... Next time you'll know better. Train's goin' in fifteen minutes. Better hustle."

Next noon Scattergood was in his usual place on the piazza of his store when the train came in. Presently Mr. Castle, president of the G. & B., came into view, and Scattergood closed his eyes as if enjoying a midday snooze. Mr. Castle approached, stopped, regarded Scattergood with a pucker of his thin lips, and said to himself that the man must be an accident. It was one of Scattergood's most valuable qualities that his appearance and manner gave that opinion to people, even when they had suffered discomfiture at his hands. Mr. Castle coughed, and Scattergood opened his eyes sleepily and peered over the rolls of fat that were his cheeks.

"Howdy?" said Scattergood, not moving.

"Good day, Mr. Baines. You got my message?"

"Seein' as you got my reply to it, I must have," said Scattergood.

"Can we talk here?"

"I kin."

Mr. Castle looked about. No one was within earshot. He occupied a chair at Scattergood's side.

"I understand your message to mean that you are willing to sell your railroad."

"I calculate that message meant jest what it said."

"I know what your railroad cost you--almost to a penny."

"Uh-huh!" said Scattergood, without interest.

"I'll tell you why I want it. My idea is to extend it through to Humboldt--twenty miles. May have to tunnel Hopper Mountain, but it will give me a short line to compete with the V. and M. from Montreal."

"To be sure," said Scattergood, who knew well that such an extension was not only impracticable from the point of view of engineering, but also from the standpoint of traffic to be obtained. "Good idee."

"I'll pay you cost and a profit of twenty-five thousand dollars."

"Hain't interested special," said Scattergood. "I git that much fun out of railroadin'."

"It isn't paying interest on your investment."

"I calculate it's goin' to. I'm aimin' to see it does."

"Set a figure yourself."

"Hain't got no figger in mind."

"Mr. Baines, I'll be frank with you. I want your railroad."

"So I jedged," said Scattergood.

"I need it. I'll pay you a profit of fifty thousand--and that's my last word."

Scattergood closed his eyes, opened them again, and sat erect. "Now that business is over with," he said, "better come up and set down to table with Mandy and me. Mandy's cookin' is considered some better 'n at the hotel."

"You refuse?"

"I was wonderin'," said Scattergood, "if you had any notion if I could buy the Goodhue timber reasonable?"

"Eh?" said Mr. Castle, startled. "The Goodhue timber?"

"Back of Tupper Falls."

"Who told--" Mr. Castle snapped his teeth together sharply.

"Leetle bird," said Scattergood. "Dinner's ready."

"There might come a time when you'd be mighty glad to sell for less than I'm offering."

"Once there was a boy," said Scattergood, "and he up and says to another boy, 'I kin lick you,' The story come to me that the boy sort of overestimated his weight.'"

"I'm not threatening you," said Castle.

"It's a privilege I don't deny to nobody.... Say, Mr. Castle, be you goin' into this deal to make money or to take somebody's scalp?"

"Baines," said Mr. Castle, "I'll buy you the best box of cigars in Boston if you'll tell me where you get your information."

"Hatch it," said Scattergood, gravely. "Jest set patient onto the egg, and perty soon the shell busts and there stands the information all fluffy and wabbly and ready to grow up into a chicken if it's used right."

"Will you answer a fair question?"

"If our idees of the fairness of it agrees with one another."

"Has McKettrick got to you first?"

It was the information Scattergood wanted, but his dumplinglike face showed no sign of satisfaction. As a matter of fact, he did not know who McKettrick was--but he could find out. "Don't seem to recall any conversation with him," he said, cautiously, leaving Castle to believe what he desired--and Castle believed.

"He was keeping his plans almighty dark. I don't understand his spilling them to you. It cost me money to find out."

"Dinner's waitin'," said Scattergood.

"Did he offer to buy your road?"

"If he did," said Scattergood, "it didn't come to nothin'."

It will be observed that Scattergood had obtained important information, though affording none, and in addition had surrounded himself with a haze through which President Castle was unable to see clearly. Castle knew less after the interview than he had known when he came; Scattergood had discovered all he hoped to discover.

Johnnie Bones came home next noon and reported to Scattergood that he had been partially successful.

"I couldn't get all of that flat," he said. "Somebody's been buying on the quiet. Three strips from the river to the hill were not to be had, but I bought four strips, two at the ends and two between the pieces I couldn't get."

"Better call it a side of bacon, Johnnie. Strip of fat and strip of lean. Dunno but it's better as it lays. Hear anythin' about the Goodhue tract?"

"Somebody's been cruising it for a month back--without a brass band."

"Um!... Send a wire, Johnnie. Lumberman's Trust Company, Boston. Set price

Goodhue tract...."

Johnnie telephoned the wire. Two hours later the answer came, "Goodhue tract no longer in our hands."

"Did you ever wonder, Johnnie, why I never got int'rested into that Goodhue timber?"

Johnnie shook his head.

"Because," said Scattergood, "you got to log it by rail. Forty thousand acres of it, and no stream runnin' through it big enough to drive logs down.... But I got an idee, Johnnie, that loggin' by rail can be done economical. Know who bought that timber?"

"No."

"McKettrick of the Seaboard Box and Paper Company, biggest concern of the kind in America. Calc'late they'll be makin' pulp here to ship to their paper mills. Calculate I'll give 'em a commodity rate of around seven cents to the G. and B. Johnnie, our orchard's goin' to begin givin' a crop. That'll give us sixteen dollars and eighty cents for haulin' a minimum car of twenty-four thousand. And this hain't goin' to be any one-car mill, neither. Five cars a day'll be increasin' our revenue twenty-four thousand three hunderd dollars a year--on outgoin' freight. Then there's incomin' freight to figger. All we got to do is set still and take that. Beauty of controllin' the transportation of a region. But it seems like we ought to git more out of it than that--if we stir around some. Especial when you come to consider that McKettrick and Castle is flyin' at each other's throats. It's a situation, Johnnie, that man owes a duty to himself to take advantage of."

Scattergood went back to his hardware store and seated himself on the piazza. Presently a team drove up from down the valley and a tall, gaunt individual, with hair of the color of a dead leaf, alighted.

"I was told I could find a man named Scattergood Baines here," he said.

"You kin," Scattergood replied.

"Where is he?"

"Sich as he is," said Scattergood, "you see him."

The man looked from Scattergood's shoeless feet and white woolen socks to Scattergood's shabby, baggy trousers, and then on upward, by slow and disapproving degrees, to Scattergood's guileless face, and there the scrutiny stopped.

"Some mistake," he said; "I want the owner of the Coldriver Valley Railroad."

"It may be a mistake," said Scattergood. "Calculate it is a mistake to own a railroad. But 'tain't the only mistake I ever made."

"You own the road?"

"Calculate to."

Evidently the stranger was not impressed by Scattergood in a manner to arouse him to a notable exertion of courtesy. He allowed it to appear in his manner that he set a light value on Scattergood; in fact, that it was not exactly pleasant to him to be compelled to do business with such a human being. Scattergood's eyes twinkled and he wriggled his toes.

"Well, Baines," said the stranger, "I want to talk business to you."

"Step into my private office," said Scattergood, motioning to a chair at his side, "and rest your legs."

"I'm thinking of establishing a plant below," said the stranger. "A very considerable plant. In studying the situation it seems as if your railroad might be run as an adjunct to my business. I suppose it can be bought."

"Supposing" said Scattergood, "is free as air."

"I'll take it off your hands at a fair figure."

"'Tain't layin' heavy on my hands," said Scattergood.

"How much did it cost you?"

"A heap less 'n I'll sell for.... You hain't mentioned your name."

"McKettrick."

Scattergood nodded.

"I'd sell to a man of that name."

"How much?"

"One million dollars," said Scattergood.

"You're--you're crazy," said McKettrick. It was an exclamation of disgust, a statement of belief, and a cry of pain. "I might go a quarter of a million."

"This here's a one-price store--marked plain on the goods. Customers is requested not to haggle."

"You're not serious?"

"One million dollars."

"I'll build a road down my side of the river."

"Maybe. Can be done. Twelve mile of tunnel and the rest trestle. Wouldn't cost more 'n fifteen, twenty million--if you're figgerin' on the west side of the stream.... How you figgerin' on gettin' your pulp wood down to Tupper Falls?"

"What?... What's that?"

"Goin' to log, yourself, or job it?"

"Look here, Baines, what do you know?"

"About what's needful. I try to keep posted."

"Tell me what you know. I insist."

Scattergood opened his eyes and peered over his dumpling cheeks at McKettrick, but said nothing.

"And how you found it out."

"I've been figgerin' over your case," said Scattergood. "I'll give you a sidetrack into your yards pervidin' you pay the cost of bridgin' and layin' the track, me to furnish ties and rails. Also, I'll give you a commodity rate of seven cents to the G. and B. As to sellin', I don't calc'late you want to buy at a million. But that hain't no sign you and me can't do business. You got to log by rail. You got to cut consid'able number of cords of pulpwood. I'll build your loggin' road, and I'll contract to cut your pulp and deliver it.... Want to go into it with me?"

McKettrick peered at Scattergood with awakened interest. His scrutiny told him nothing.

"What backing have you?"

"My own."

McKettrick almost sneered.

"Been lookin' me up?" asked Scattergood.

"No."

"Let's step to the bank."

McKettrick followed Scattergood's bulky figure-wondering.

In the bank Scattergood presented the treasurer. "Mr. Noble, meet Mr. McKettrick. He wants you should tell him somethin' about me. For instance, Noble, about how fur you calculate my credit could be stretched."

"Mr. Baines would have no difficulty borrowing from five hundred thousand to three quarters of a million," said Noble.

"How's his reppitation for keepin' his word?" said Scattergood.

"The whole state knows your word is kept to the letter."

"What you calculate I'm wuth--visible prop'ty?"

"I'd say a million and a half to two millions."

"Backin' enough to suit you, Mr. McKettrick?" asked Scattergood.

McKettrick wore a dazed look. Scattergood did not look like two millions; he did not look like ten thousand. His bearing became more respectful.

"I'll listen to any proposition you wish to make," he said.

"Come over to Johnnie Bones's," said Scattergood.

In a moment they were sitting in Johnnie's office, and McKettrick and Johnnie were acquainted.

"Here's my proposition," said Scattergood. "I'll build and equip a loggin' road accordin' to your surveys. You furnish right of way and enough money to give you forty-nine per cent of the stock in the company we'll form. I kin build cheaper 'n you, and I know the country and kin git the labor. You pay the new railroad a set price for haulin' pulpwood--say dollar 'n a quarter to two dollars a cord, as we figger it later.... Then I'll take the job of loggin' for you and layin' down the pulpwood at sidings. It'll save you labor and expense and trouble. I've showed I was responsible. The new railroad company'll put up bonds, and so'll the loggin' company--if you say so."

This was the beginning of some weeks of negotiations, during which Scattergood became convinced that McKettrick was wishful of using him so long as he proved useful; then, when the day arrived for a showing of profit on the profit sheet, the same McKettrick was planning to see that no profit would be there and that Scattergood Baines should be eliminated from consideration--to McKettrick's profit in the sum of whatever amount Scattergood invested in the construction of the railroad. It was a situation that exactly suited Scattergood's love of business excitement.

"If McKettrick had come up here wearin' better manners," said Scattergood to Johnnie, "and if he hadn't got himself all rigged out as little Red Ridin' Hood's grandmother--figgerin' I'd qualify for little Red Ridin' Hood without the eyesight for big ears and big teeth that little girl had--why, I might 'a' give him a reg'lar business deal. But seem's he's as he is, I calc'late I'm privileged to git what I kin git."

Therefore Scattergood made it a clause in the contract that all the stock in the new railroad and construction company should remain in his own name until the road was completed and ready to operate. Then 49 per cent should be transferred to McKettrick. This McKettrick regarded as a harmless eccentricity of the lamb he was about to fleece.

The new company was organized with Johnnie Bones as president, Scattergood as treasurer, an employee of McKettrick's as secretary, and Mandy Baines and another employee of McKettrick's as the remaining two directors.

While the negotiations regarding the railroad were being carried on, another matter arose to irritate Mr. McKettrick, and, in some measure, to take the keen edge off his attention. Scattergood usually endeavored to have some matter arise to irritate and distract when he was engaged on a major operation, and it was for this reason he had bought the four strips of land at Tupper Falls.

McKettrick awoke suddenly to find that his men had not secured the site for his mills, and that, apparently, it could not be secured. He discussed the thing with Scattergood.

"Prob'ly some old scissor bills that got a notion of hangin' on to their land," Scattergood said.

"It can't be that, for the sales to the present owners were recent. The new owners refuse absolutely to sell."

"And pulp mills hain't got no right of eminent domain like railroads."

"All substantial businesses ought to have it," said McKettrick. "You know these folks. I wish you'd see what you can do."

"Glad to," Scattergood promised, and two days later he reported that all four landowners might be brought to terms. Three would sell, surely; one was holding back strangely, but the three had put the matter into the hands of a local real-estate and insurance broker, by name Wangen. "We'll go see him," said Scattergood.

Which they did. "My clients," said Wangen, importantly, "realize the value of their property. That, I may say, is why they bought."

"It cost the three of 'em less 'n three thousand dollars for the three passels," said Scattergood.

"Prices have gone up," said Wangen.

"Give them two hundred dollars profit apiece," said McKettrick.

"Consid'able difference between givin' it and their takin' it," said Scattergood.

"I agree with that," said Wangen.

"Now, Wangen, you and me has done consid'able business," said Scattergood, "and you hain't goin' to hold up a friend of mine."

"If it was a personal thing, Mr. Baines; but I've got to do my best for my clients."

"What's your proposition?"

"Five thousand dollars apiece for the three strips."

"It's an outrage," roared McKettrick. "I'll never be robbed like that."

"Take it," said Wangen, "or leave it."

"You've got to have it," Scattergood whispered.

McKettrick spluttered and stormed and pleaded, but Wangen was firm and gave but one answer. There could be but one result: McKettrick wrote a check for fifteen thousand dollars--and still had one strip to buy--a strip not at an edge of his mill site, but bisecting it.

This strip caused the worry when Scattergood needed attention distracted the most. But Scattergood managed finally to secure it for McKettrick for seventy-five hundred dollars. Thus it will be seen how Scattergood resorted to the law of necessity, and how McKettrick suffered from failure to build securely his commercial structure from its foundation. Twenty-two thousand two hundred and fifty dollars were paid by McKettrick for land that had cost Scattergood exactly three thousand six hundred dollars. Scattergood believed in always paying for services rendered, so Wangen and each of the four ostensible landowners were given a hundred dollars. Net profit to Scattergood, eighteen thousand one hundred and fifty dollars.

"Which it wouldn't 'a' cost him if he hadn't looked sneerin' at my stockin' feet," said Scattergood to Johnnie Bones.

Johnnie Bones prepared the papers for the incorporation of the new railroad, and the organization was perfected. There were two thousand shares of one hundred dollars each. McKettrick put in his right of way at five thousand, an excessive figure, as Scattergood knew well, and gave his check for the balance of his 49 per cent. Scattergood deposited a check for his 51 per cent, or one hundred and two thousand dollars. Work was begun grading the right of way immediately.

McKettrick vanished from the region and did not appear again except for flying visits to his rising plant at Tupper Falls. He never inspected so much as a foot of the new railroad back into the Goodhue tract--and this, Scattergood very correctly took to be suspicious. The work was left utterly in Scattergood's hands, with no check upon him and no inspection. It was not like a man of McKettrick's character--unless there were an object.

Once or twice Scattergood encountered President Castle of the G. & B. while the road was building.

"Hear you're putting in a logging road for McKettrick," he said.

"For me," said Scattergood. "Stock stands in my name. Calculate to operate it myself."

"Oh!" said Castle, and drummed with his fingers on the window ledge. Scattergood said nothing.

"Own the right of way?" asked Castle.

"'Tain't precisely a right of way," said Scattergood. "It's a easement, or property right, or whatever the lawyers would call it, to run tracks over any part of McKettrick's property and operate a loggin' railroad--where McKettrick says he wants to get logs from."

"No definite right of way?"

"Jest what I described."

"Capitalized for two hundred thousand, I see."

"Uh-huh!"

"Any stock for sale?"

"Not at the present writin'."

"At a price?"

"Wa-al, now--"

"Say a profit of twenty dollars a share."

"It'll pay dividends on more 'n that figger," said Scattergood, "which," he added, "you know dum well."

"Yes," said Castle, "but for a quick turnover--and I'm not figuring dividends altogether."

"Kind of got a bone to pick with McKettrick, eh?"

"Maybe."

"Tell you what I'll do," said Scattergood. "I'll sell you forty-nine per cent of the stock at a hunderd and twenty. Stock to stand in my name till the road's ready to operate, I don't want it known I've been sellin' any.... Shouldn't be s'prised if you was able to pick up control one way and another--but I hain't goin' to sell it to you."

"I see," said Castle, closing his eyes and squinting through a slit between the lids. "It's a deal, Mr. Baines," he said, presently.

"Cash," said Scattergood.

"You'll find a certified check in the mail the day after I get the proper papers."

Which transaction gave Scattergood another profit on the whole affair of nineteen thousand six hundred dollars--this time a capitalization of the spite of man toward man. It will be seen that McKettrick owned 49 per cent of the stock, Castle, 49 per cent, and Scattergood, 2 per cent. He was now in a position to await developments.

They arrived as the railway was on the point of running its first train. McKettrick brought them in person. He burst upon Scattergood as Scattergood sat in front of his hardware store, and began to storm.

"What's this? What's this?" he roared. "What's that railroad doing up the easterly side of our timber? It's waste money, lost money. It'll have to be rebuilt. We've made all arrangements to cut off the westerly side. Now we'll have to swamp roads and log by team till the road can be moved."

"Um!..." said Scattergood, "so that's it, eh? I was wonderin' how it would come."

"It was an inexcusable blunder, and it'll cost you money. You know how the railroad's contract with the company reads. Who gave you directions to run up the easterly side?"

"My engineer got 'em in your office."

"Oh, your engineer. He made the mistake, eh? Then the mistake's yours, all right, for every scrap of writing in our office has the word 'westerly' in it, plain and distinct. It means tearing up those rails, grading a new line--and you'll pay for it. I sha'n't stand loss for your mistake. It'll cost you a hundred thousand dollars for that blunder."

"Hain't you discoverin' it a mite late?"

"It was left wholly to you."

"Seems like I noticed it," said Scattergood. "So all that work's lost, eh? Seems a pity, too."

"You don't seem to take it seriously."

"You bet I do, and I calculate to look into it some ."

"It won't do any good. The mistake is plain."

"Shouldn't be s'prised. I git your idee, McKettrick. You've been figgerin' from the start on smougin' me out of what I invested in that road, eh?... By the way, your stock's in your name. I'll git the certificates out of the safe."

McKettrick shoved the envelope in his pocket. "The Seaboard Box and Paper Company will force you to remove your tracks from our land. I'll sue you for damages for your blunder. The Seaboard will sue the new railroad for damages for failure to have the tracks into the cuttings on time. I guess when we begin collecting judgments by levying on the new road, there won't be much of it left. The Seaboard will come pretty close to owning it."

"And you and I will be frozen out, eh?" said Scattergood.

McKettrick purred and smiled. "Exactly," he said. "Now, my advice to you is not to fight the thing. You can't deny the blunder and you'll save cost of litigation."

"What's your proposition?"

"Transfer your stock to the Seaboard."

"And lose a hunderd and two thousand?"

"It's not our fault if you make expensive mistakes."

"Course not," said Scattergood. "I admit I hain't much on litigation. S'posin' you and me meets in Boston to-morrow with our lawyers, and sort of figger this thing out."

"There's nothing to figure out--but I'll meet you to-morrow. You're sensible to settle."

"Calc'late I be," said Scattergood.

That afternoon Johnnie Bones carried President Castle's 49 per cent of the railroad's stock to the G. & B. offices, and gave them into the hands of the railroad's chief executive.

"Mr. Baines will be here to-morrow. There will be a meeting at his hotel at three o'clock. McKettrick will be there."

"I'll come," said President Castle.

The meeting was held in the shabby hotel which Scattergood patronized. McKettrick was there with his attorney, Scattergood was there with Johnnie Bones--and last came President Castle.

At his entrance McKettrick scowled and leaped to his feet.

"What do you want here?" he demanded.

"Well," said Mr. Castle, with a smile which descended into great depths of disagreeability, "I own forty-nine per cent of the stock in this concern. I imagine I have a right to be here."

"What's that? What's that?" McKettrick glared at Scattergood, who sat placidly removing his shoes.

"Calc'late I'll relieve my feet," he said.

"So I got you, too," McKettrick said to Castle. "I didn't figure on that luck."

"Got me? I'm interested."

McKettrick explained at length, and, as he explained, Castle glared at him, and then at Scattergood, with increasing rage. As he saw it there was a plot between Scattergood and McKettrick to get him--and he appeared to have been gotten. He started to speak, but Scattergood stopped him.

"Jest a minute, Mr. Castle," he said. "'Tain't time for you to cuss yet. Maybe you won't git to do no reg'lar cussin' a-tall. You see, McKettrick he up and made a little error himself. Regardin' me makin' an error. Yass.... I don't calc'late to make errors costin' upward of a hunderd thousand. No.... Not," he said, "that I got any doubts about the word 'westerly' appearin' in all the papers McKettrick's got regardin' this enterprise. What I doubt some is whether the word 'westerly' was there right from the start off of the beginnin'. In other words, it looks to me kind of as if McKettrick had done a mite of fixin' up to them documents. Rubbin' out and writin' in, so to speak."

"Fiddlesticks!" said McKettrick. "Of course that is what you would charge."

"McKettrick," said Scattergood, "did you figger I'd take notes in lead pencil on my cuff of where I was to build that railroad? Did you figger I was goin' to lay down a railroad without knowin' the place I put it was where it b'longed? Castle he knows me better 'n you, and he wouldn't guess I'd do sich a thing. No, sir, Mr. McKettrick. I took them original papers out of your office for jest a day, and bein' as they constituted an easement on land, I got 'em recorded in the office of the recorder of deeds.

Paid reg'lar money in fees to have it done. And who you think I got to compare the records with the original in case somethin' come up, eh? Why, the circuit jedge of this county and the prosecutin' attorney--they both bein' personal and political friends of mine.... That's what I done, and if you'll search them records you'll find the word 'easterly' standin' cool and ca'm in every place where it ought to be.... So, if you're figgerin' on litigation, I guess maybe we'll litigate, eh?"

"These are the references to the records," said Johnnie Bones, laying a memorandum on the table. "You'll find them correct."

"Knowing Baines as I do," said President Castle, "I'm satisfied."

McKettrick and his attorney were conversing in hoarse whispers. McKettrick looked like a man who had come out of a warm bath into a cold-storage room. He was speechless, but his lawyer spoke for him.

"You win," he said, succinctly.

"Always calc'late to when I kin," said Scattergood. "Now, don't hurry, gentlemen. I got another leetle matter to call to your attention. McKettrick there's got forty-nine per cent of the stock in the railroad that's built where it ought to be, and Castle's got another forty-nine per cent. That leaves two men with all but two per cent of the stock, and neither of them in control. If I know them men they hain't apt to git together and agree peaceable and reasonable. Therefore, the feller that has the remainin' two per cent of the stock, or forty shares, stands perty clost to controllin' the corporation, eh? Him votin' with either of the forty-nine per cents? Sounds that way, don't it?... And I got that two per cent.... Do I hear any suggestions?"

Castle stood up and bowed. "I take off my hat to you, Baines.... I bid ten thousand."

"Eleven," choked McKettrick.

"This here road's goin' to be mighty profitable. Contract with the Seaboard folks makes it look like it would pay eighteen, twenty per cent on the investment, maybe more. And control--hain't that wuth a figger?"

"Fifteen," said Castle.

"Sixteen."

"Seventeen five hundred."

"That's enough," said Scattergood. "I got a leetle grudge ag'in' McKettrick for havin' bad manners, and for regardin' me as somethin' to pick and eat. It'll hurt him some to have you control this road, Castle, so you git it, at seventeen thousand five hunderd. I don't want to burn you, and I calc'late the figger you're payin' is clost to bein' fair. I'm satisfied. Write a check."

Castle drew out his check book, and in a moment passed the valuable slip across to Scattergood. "Thankee," said Baines, "and good day.... Another time, McKettrick, don't look sneerin' at white woolen socks."

He walked out of the room, followed by Johnnie Bones.

"Perty fair deal for a scissor bill," said Scattergood. "This last check, deductin' four thousand as cost of stock, gives me a profit of twelve thousand two hunderd and fifty for the day. Add that to eighteen thousand one hunderd and fifty on the strips of land, and nineteen thousand six hunderd on the stock I sold Castle first, and what do we git?"

"Even fifty thousand," said Johnnie.

"I always did cotton to round figgers," said Scattergood, comfortably. "Let's git us a meal of vittles."

CHAPTER VI
INSURANCE THAT DID NOT LAPSE

Scattergood Baines was not a man to shingle his roof before he built his foundations. He knew the value of shingles, and was not without some appreciation for frescoes and porticoes and didos, but he liked to reach them in the ordinary course of logical procedure. His completed structure, according to the plans carefully printed on his brain, was the domination of Coldriver Valley through ownership of its means of transportation and of its water power. He wanted to be rich, not for the sake of being rich, but because a great deal of money is, aside from love or hate, the most powerful lever in the world. For five years, now, Scattergood had moved along slowly and irresistibly, buying a bit of timber here, acquiring a dam site there, taking over the stage line to the railroad twenty-four miles away, and establishing a credit and a reputation for shrewdness that were worth much more to him than dollars and cents in the bank.

As a matter of fact, Scattergood had amassed considerable more money than even the gimlet eyes and whispering tongues of Coldriver had been able to credit him with. It is doubtful if anybody realized just how strong a foot-hold Scattergood was getting in that valley, but the men who came closest to it were Messrs. Crane and Keith, lumbermen, who were beginning to experience a feeling of growing irritation toward the fat hardware merchant. They were irritated because, every now and then, they found themselves shut off from the water, or from a bit of timber, or from some other desirable property, by some small holding of Scattergood's which seemed to have dropped into just the right spot to create the maximum amount of trouble for them. It could be nothing but chance, they told each other, for they had sat in judgment on Scattergood, and their judgment had been that he was a lazy lout with more than a fair share of luck.

"It's nothing but luck," Crane told his partner. "The man hasn't a brain in his head--just a big lump of fat."

"But he's always getting in the way--and he does seem to know a water-power site when he sees it."

"Anybody does," said Crane. "He's a doggone nuisance and we might as well settle with him one time as another--and the time to settle is before his luck gives him a genuine strangle hold on this valley. We've got too much timber on these hills to take any risks."

"I leave it with you, Crane. You're the outside man. But when you bust him, bust him good."

Crane retired to his office and devoted his head to the subject exclusively, and because Crane's head was that sort of head he devised an enterprise which, if Scattergood could be made to involve himself in it, would result in the extinction of that gentleman in the Coldriver Valley.

It was a week later that a gentleman, whose clothes and bearing guaranteed him to be a genuine denizen of the city, stopped at Scattergood's store. Scattergood was sitting, as usual, on the piazza, in his especially reinforced chair, laying in wait for somebody to whom he could sell a bit of hardware, no matter how small.

"Good morning," said the gentleman. "Is this Mr. Scattergood Baines?"

"It's Scattergood Baines, all right. Don't call to mind bein' christened Mister."

"My name is Blossom."

"Perty name," said Scattergood, unsmilingly.

"I wonder if I can have a little talk with you, Mr. Baines?"

"Havin' it, hain't you?"

Mr. Blossom smiled appreciatively, and sat down beside Scattergood. "I'm interested in the new Higgins's Bridge Pulp Company. You've heard of it, haven't you?"

"Some," said Scattergood. "Some."

"We are starting to build our mill. It will be the largest in America, with the most modern machinery. Now we're looking about for somebody to supply us spruce cut to the proper length for pulpwood. You own considerable spruce, do you not?"

"Calc'late to have title to a tree or two."

"Good. I came up to find out if you are in a position to swing a rather big contract--to deliver us at the mill a minimum of twenty-five thousand cords of pulpwood?"

"Depends," said Scattergood.

Mr. Blossom drew a jackknife from his pocket and began leisurely to sharpen a pencil. It was a rather battered jackknife, and Scattergood noticed that one blade had been broken off. He stretched out his hand. "Jackknife's kind of lame, hain't it? Don't 'pear to be as stylish as the rest of you?"

"It is a bit dilapidated."

"Got some good ones inside. Fine line of jackknives. Only carry the best. Show 'em to you."

He lifted himself out of the groaning chair and went into the store, to return with a dozen or more knives, which he showed to Mr. Blossom, and Mr. Blossom looked at them gravely. He was smiling to himself. A man who could interrupt a deal involving upward of a hundred thousand dollars to try to sell a jackknife certainly was not of a caliber to give serious worry to an astute business man.

"Recommend the pearl-handled one," said Scattergood. "Two dollars 'n' a half."

"I'll take it," said Mr. Blossom, and he stuck his old knife in a post, replacing it in his pocket with the new purchase.

"Cash," said Scattergood, and Mr. Blossom handed over the currency.

"Speakin' of pulpwood," said Scattergood, "how much you figger on payin'?"

Mr. Blossom named a price, delivered at the mill.

"Pay when?"

"On delivery."

"When want it delivered, eh? What date?"

"Before May first."

"Water power or steam?" said Scattergood, somewhat irrelevantly.

"Both. We're putting in steam engines and boilers, but we're going to depend mostly on water power."

"Goin' to build a dam, eh? Big dam?"

"Yes."

"Um!... Stock company?"

"Yes. We'll be solid. Capitalized for a quarter of a million and bonded for a quarter of a million. Gives us half a million capital to start business."

"Stock all sold?"

"Every share."

"Who to?"

"Mostly in small blocks in Boston."

"Um!... Bonds sold?"

"Yes."

"Who bought 'em?"

"They're underwritten by the Commonwealth Security Trust Company."

"Want to know!... Got authority? Vested with authority to put it in writin'?"

"The contract, you mean?"

"Calculate to mean that."

"Yes."

"Lawyer acrost the street," said Scattergood.

"You can swing it?"

"Calculate to."

"You have the capital to make good?"

"Know I have, don't you? Wouldn't have come to me if you hadn't?"

"You'll have to borrow heavily."

"My lookout, hain't it? Don't need to worry you?"

"Not in the least."

"Lawyer's still across the street."

So Scattergood and Mr. Blossom went across the street and up the narrow stairs to Lawyer Norton's office, where a contract was drafted and signed, obligating Scattergood to deliver to the Higgins's Bridge Pulp Company twenty-five thousand cords of pulp, on or before May 1st, payment to be made on delivery. Mr. Blossom went away wearing a satisfied expression, and in the course of the day sent to Crane & Keith a brief message, a message of two words. "He bit," was the telegram.

Scattergood went back to his chair, and presently might have been seen to unlace his shoes absent-mindedly. For an hour he sat there, twiddling his bare toes. Then he got up, jerked Mr. Blossom's old jackknife from the post where it had been abandoned, and pocketed it.

"If nothin' else happens," he said to himself, "I'm figgered to make a profit of sixty cents and a tradin' knife."

There followed a very busy fall and winter for Scattergood. Not that he neglected his hardware store, but from its porch, and later from a post beside its big stove, he recruited men for his camps and directed the labor of cutting and piling pulpwood along the banks of Coldriver. Also, from time to time, he visited various banks to borrow the money necessary to carry on the operation, sometimes on notes and collateral, sometimes on timber mortgages. The sum of his borrowing mounted and mounted, until, before the arrival of spring, his credit had been strained to the uttermost.

Nor had the pulp company been idle. Its new mills had arisen beside the river at Higgins's Bridge, machinery had been installed, and the little hamlet was beginning to speculate in town lots and to look forward to unexampled prosperity.

But before the ice was out of the river disquieting rumors began to breathe out of Higgins's Bridge. They were the meerest vapor of conjecture at first, apparently based upon no evidence whatever, but friends delighted to convey them to Scattergood, as friends always delight to perform such a disagreeable duty.

"Hear things hain't goin' right down to the new pulp mill," said Deacon Pettybone, one bitterly cold afternoon, when he came into Scattergood's store to thaw the icicles out of his sparse beard.

"Do tell," said Scattergood.

"Be perty bad for you if they was to go wrong, wouldn't it?"

"Perty bad, Deacon."

"'Most ruin you, wouldn't it? Clean you out? Leave you with nothin'?"

"Hain't mortgaged my health. Hain't mortgaged my brains. Have them left, Deacon. Don't figger I'm clean bankrupt till them two is gone."

But it was to be noticed that Scattergood toasted his bare toes a great deal during the ensuing days. He scarcely put on his shoes except when he was going out to wallow through the drifts; and, as Coldriver knew, when Scattergood waggled his bare toes he was struggling with a problem.

Also it might have been noticed that he pored much over the detailed maps in the county atlas, studying the flow of streams and the lie of timber. It might have been seen that several large blocks of timber had been marked by Scattergood with red crosses, and that certain other limits had been blotted out in black. The black pieces were neither numerous nor individually extensive, but they belonged to Scattergood. Those marked with red crosses were the property of Messrs. Crane & Keith.

Now, it may be taken as axiomatic that in those early days the value of a piece of timber depended upon its accessibility to flowing water down which logs might be driven. A medium piece of timber on the banks of a stream which came to plentiful flood in the spring was worth more in hard dollars and cents than a much larger and finer piece back in the hills. A piece of timber which had no access whatever to water approximated worthlessness. On the atlas, the largest pieces of Crane & Keith timber were back from the river--not too far back, but still separated from it by narrow strips which, for the most part, were farms. Some few pieces ran down to the river, but it was apparent that Crane & Keith were looking to the future--buying timber when it was at its lowest, and preparing to hold for a better day. They had bought strategically. More than one tributary valley was in their hands, and, when the day ripened, small land purchases would connect their holdings, bring them to water, and place them in such a commanding position that the valley would be as surely theirs as if they owned every foot of it. Inasmuch as Scattergood planned, himself, to control Coldriver Valley, the prospect was not pleasing to him.

Scattergood closed the atlas and put on his shoes. "Um!..." he said. "Calculate that'll keep their minds off'n other things a spell. If they see me dickerin' there, they won't figger I'm dickerin' some place else."

If Scattergood had been a general, history would have recorded that he won his battles by making feints at some vulnerable point in the enemy's line, and then struck his major blow at a distance where he was not suspected to be operating at all.

It chanced that Crane & Keith were cutting timber from the Bottle--a valley so named. Their rollways were piled high, and it was time for them to team to the river. To reach the river they must pass through the Bottleneck and over the farm belonging to Old Man Plumm. There was another road into the valley--a public road--but it was a fifteen-mile haul. Old Man Plumm was a non-assertive person, and good-natured. His farm was a ramshackle, down-at-heels, worthless place, off which he gleaned the meagerest of livelihoods, so that he had not been averse to permitting Crane & Keith to traverse his land for a nominal consideration. It was cheaper for Crane & Keith than purchase--and so the matter stood.

Scattergood went across the road to Lawyer Norton's office.

"Goin' up Bottleneck way perty soon?" he asked.

"Not that I know of, Scattergood."

"Nice drive. Old Man Plumm's got a farm there."

"I know that, of course."

"Don't figger to visit him?"

"Why--" said Norton, beginning to see that Scattergood had something in view--"I could."

"Wouldn't try to buy the farm, would you?"

Norton hesitated. "I--I might."

"Cash?"

"Why, I suppose so."

"In your own name, eh? Not in anybody else's."

"How much should I pay?"

"Folks always pays what they have to--no more--no less. Immediate possession. Always a good thing. Got any money?"

"No."

"Call at the bank. They'll give you what's needed. Ought to be back with the deed by night. Fast hoss?"

"Fast enough."

"G'-by, Norton."

That night Norton returned with the deed and with Old Man Plumm, who took the morning stage for Connecticut and his youngest daughter.

"Hear folks is trespassin' on your land, Norton. Name of Crane and Keith. Haulin' logs acrost. No contract with you? No contract with Plumm?"

"No contract."

"Hain't got a right to do it, have they?"

"No."

"If I owned that land I'd give 'em notice," said Scattergood. "G'-by, Norton. Goin' to Boston to-day. Set tight, Norton. G'-by."

Twenty-four hours later both Crane and Keith were in Coldriver, storming up to Lawyer Norton's office. Scattergood was in Boston and not visible.

"What does this mean?" blustered Crane, displaying to Norton the notice mailed at Scattergood's direction.

"What it says."

"You can't stop us hauling to the river."

Norton shrugged his shoulders. "You can use the state road."

"Fifteen miles! You know it's impossible. We've got millions of feet on our rollways. It'll doze and spoil if we don't get it out."

"That's your lookout."

"What do you want?"

"Nothing."

"It's some kind of a hold-up. What'll you take for that farm?"

"Not for sale."

"What will it cost us to haul across you?"

"You can't haul across. Not for money, marbles, or chalk. Use the road."

That was the best Crane & Keith could get out of Norton, though they besieged him for a week, though they consulted lawyers, though they made threats, and though they begged and promised. Norton was a stubborn man.

During this week Scattergood had been in Boston. His first visit had been to Linderman, president of the Atlantic Pulp and Paper Company.

"Have you an appointment with Mr. Linderman?" asked a clerk.

"Never heard of me."

"Then I'm afraid you can't see him. He's very busy."

"That his office? That door?"

"Yes."

"He in? Right in there?"

"Yes."

Scattergood walked calmly toward it. The slender clerk interposed. Scattergood picked him up, tucked him under a huge arm, and waddled through the great man's door.

"Howdy, Mr. Linderman? Howdy?"

Linderman looked up and frowned, then his eyes twinkled.

"Who are you? What have you there?"

"Young feller I found outside. 'Fraid of steppin' on him, so I picked him up to save him. You can run along now, sonny," he said to the clerk. "He let on I couldn't see you," Scattergood explained.

"What's your name?"

"Scattergood Baines."

"Of Coldriver?" Scattergood was surprised, but did not show it. "Yes."

"Sit down."

"Thankee.... Come to do a mite of business with you. Interested in pulp, hain't you. Quite consid'able interested?"

"Very much."

"Know the Higgins's Bridge Pulp Company?"

"Of course. Understand they're in difficulties."

"In some, and goin' to be in more. That's why I come down."

Thereupon Scattergood explained in detail his contract with the pulp company, and his theories of what that company was planning to do to him. "Double barreled," he said. "Crane and Keith owns them bonds. Figger on freezin' out the stockholders and buyin' 'em out for a song. Figger on bustin' me. Next we hear the mill'll be in receiver's hands. No money. Can't pay no contracts. My notes'll come due, and I'm done for. Simple. Crane thought it up."

"What do you want of me? So far as I can see, you are up against it. You can't borrow any more, and your notes won't be extended. You're done."

"Hain't started yet--not yet. Figger to start to-day. That's why I come to see you."

"But I can do nothing for you."

"Higgins's Bridge mill's good, hain't it? Logical payin' proposition? Money to be made?"

"Yes."

"Like to own it cheap?"

"Of course."

"Crane and Keith is gittin' ready for a killin'. Own big block of stock. Paid par. Want to sell, I hear ... if anybody's fool enough to buy. Then want to buy back for dum' near nothin' when receivership comes. Good scheme. Money in it. Crane thought it up."

"What's your idea?"

"Buy all they got. Option the rest. Easy.... What happens when a man sells somethin' he hain't got?"

"He has to get it some place."

"If he can't get it, what?"

"Makes it expensive for him."

"Thought so. Figgered that way.... Nobody to interfere. Crane and Keith left orders to sell. They won't be takin' notice. Got 'em worried some place else. Mighty worried." Scattergood recounted the story of Plumm's farm.

Mr. Linderman scrutinized Scattergood intently and nodded his head. "And you want me--"

"Put up the money. Git the stock. Lemme handle it. Gimme twenty per cent."

"In stock?"

"Calc'late so."

"Baines," said Linderman, "I'll go you. Crane and Keith are due for a lesson."

"Ready now?"

"Yes."

"G'-by, Mr. Linderman. Have money when I want it. G'-by."

Scattergood had a list of stockholders in the pulp company and knew they were worried. He spent two days in interviewing a dozen of them, and found little difficulty optioning their stock at a pleasant figure. They imagined he must be crazy, and he did nothing to destroy the belief.

Then he called at the offices of Crane & Keith.

"Want to see the boss man," he said.

"What for?"

"Hear you got stock for sale. Pulp company. Figger to buy."

Here was a lamb ready for the slaughter. Mr. McCann, who received him, could see the delight of his employers, and his own profit, if he should succeed in taking this fat backwoodsman into camp.

"You want to buy stock in the pulp company, I understand?"

"Yes."

"How much?"

"How much you got?"

"Guess we can sell you all you want."

"Money-makin' proposition, hain't it?"

"Of course."

"But you're willin' to sell? Kind of funny, hain't it?"

"Oh no. We have so many enterprises."

"Glad you want to sell. I figger to make money on this stock. Want to buy a lot of it."

"About how many shares?"

"What you askin'?" said Scattergood.

"Par."

"Shucks! Give you thirty."

There was haggling and bickering until a price of sixty was agreed upon, and Mr. McCann's heart expanded with satisfaction.

"Now, how many shares?"

"Want control. Want fifty-one per cent, anyhow. Got 'em?"

"Of course." This was not the fact, but Mr. McCann was not addicted to unnecessary facts. He knew where he could get the rest for less than 60. There would be an additional profit and additional credit coming to him. In cold reality, Crane & Keith owned some 40 per cent of the stock.

"Take all you'll sell."

"I can let you have fifteen hundred shares--for cash." This was an even 60 per cent, but McCann knew where he could get the other 20.

"Come to the bank. Come now. Give you the cash."

"I can't deliver but one thousand shares to-day, but I can give you the other five hundred to-morrow."

"Suits me. Pay for 'em all to-day. Gimme what you got and a receipt for the rest. Comin' to the bank?"

Mr. McCann put on his coat and hat and accompanied Scattergood to the bank, where he received a certified check for the full amount, gave Scattergood in return a thousand shares of stock, and a receipt which recited that Scattergood had paid for five hundred shares more, to be delivered within twenty-four hours.

Scattergood went to see Mr. Linderman; McCann went out to round up five hundred shares of stock. By midnight he was a worried young man. The stock he had thought to pick up so readily was not to be had. Everybody seemed to have disposed of it and nobody seemed to know exactly who had been doing the buying, for the options had been taken in a number of names. Next morning McCann sought diligently until he found Scattergood.

"I've been a bit delayed in the delivery of the rest of the stock," he told Scattergood, and there was cold moisture on his forehead. "Would you mind waiting until to-morrow?"

"Guess I'll have to," said Scattergood. "G'-by. Better be movin' around spry. I want to git back home."

That night McCann wired his employers to get back home as quickly as conveyances would carry them. They did so, and in no happy mood, for Lawyer Norton had remained immovable in his position. Young McCann told his tale hesitatingly.

"Who did you say you sold to?" demanded Crane.

"Fat man by the name of Baines."

"Baines! He's busted. Hasn't a cent."

"Paid cash."

Crane looked at Keith and Keith looked at Crane. Just then the telephone rang. It was Scattergood.

"Want to speak to Mr. Crane," he said.

"Hello!" Crane said, gruffly. "What's this about your buying pulp company stock?"

"Bought some. Bought a little. Called up to see why your young man wasn't deliverin'. Want to git home."

"Where did you get the money?"

"Have to know that? Have to know where it come from before you kin make delivery? Hain't inquisitive, be you?"

Mr. Crane made use of language. "I want to see you--got to have a talk. Come right down here."

"Jest been measurin'," said Scattergood, "and I figger it's a mite longer from here to there than it is from there to here. If you want to see me, here I be."

"Where?"

Scattergood gave an office address and hung up the receiver.

"They'll be here in a minnit," he said to Mr. Linderman, and he was not exaggerating greatly as to the time required to bring the gentlemen to him. "Know Mr.

Linderman--Crane and Keith?" said Scattergood. "Come in and set."

"What do you want with pulp company stock?" Crane demanded.

"Paper the kitchen. Maybe, if I kin git enough, I'll paper the parlor. Lack five hunderd shares for the parlor. Got'em with you?"

"No, and we're not going to get them."

"Um!... Paid for 'em, didn't I? Got a receipt?"

"What's Linderman doing in this?"

Mr. Linderman leaned forward a little. "I'm in a legitimate business transaction--something quite foreign to you gentlemen's notions of doing business. I came into it to make a profit, but mostly to teach you fellows a lesson in decent business methods. I don't like you. I don't like your ways. If you like your ways you must expect to pay for the pleasure you get out of them.... Mr. Baines is waiting for delivery of the stock he bought."

"I suppose you know we haven't got it?"

"I do."

"We can't deliver."

"Yes, you can. Go out in the open market and buy. Now, I own a few shares, for instance. I might sell."

The faces of Messrs. Crane and Keith did not picture lively enjoyment. They were caught. If it had been Scattergood alone they might have wriggled out of it, they thought, for they had scant respect for his sagacity, but Linderman--well, Linderman was not to be trifled with.

"How much?" said Crane.

"You need five hundred shares. Par is a hundred, is it not? I will part with mine for three hundred. First, last, and only offer. In ten minutes the price goes up to three fifty, and fifty for each five minutes after that."

"It's robbery ..." Mr. Crane spluttered, and made uncouth sounds of rage.

"Now you know how the other fellow has been feeling. Seven minutes left...."

Four more minutes sped before the surrender came.

"Certified check," said Mr. Linderman. "My messenger will go to the bank for you."

The check was drawn for a hundred and fifty thousand dollars, and Crane and Keith settled back sullenly.

"You can retain your bonds. I believe you have about a quarter of a million dollars' worth of them. Glad to have you finance the mill for me. It will, of course, go ahead under my direction," said Linderman. "I guess I can iron out the difficulties you gentlemen have arranged for, and there will be no receivership. That will relieve Mr. Baines, who has a considerable contract with the company." Mr. Crane swore softly.

Scattergood heaved himself to his feet. "One other leetle matter, Crane. There's the Plumm farm. Kind of exercised about that, hain't you? Stayed up in the country a week to look after it--while I was dickerin' down here.... Like to buy that farm?"

There was no answer.

"Calculate to take a hint from Mr. Linderman. That farm's mine, and you can't haul a log acrost it. My price is fifteen thousand. Bought it for two. Price goes up hunderd dollars a minute. Cash deal."

That surrender was more prompt, and a second check was sent to the bank to be certified.

"G'-by, gentlemen," said Scattergood, and Messrs. Crane and Keith took their departure in no dignified manner, but with rancor in their hearts, which there was no method of salving.

"Let's take stock," said Scattergood. "Like to know jest how we come out."

"Let's see. We bought the stock at an average of sixty dollars a share. That makes a hundred and fifty thousand dollars in expenses, doesn't it? The five hundred shares just transferred cost thirty thousand dollars and we sold them for a hundred and fifty thousand. Profit on that part of the deal is a hundred and twenty thousand dollars. That made the total capital stock in the mill worth a quarter of a million of anybody's money; cost us exactly thirty thousand dollars, didn't it? Nice deal.... And you cleaned up an extra thirteen thousand on your side issue. Not bad."

"I git five hunderd shares worth fifty thousand dollars, don't I? Then my thirteen. That's sixty-three thousand. Then my profit on twenty-five thousand cords of pulpwood--which is goin' to be paid, I jedge. That'll be anyhow another twenty-five thousand. Calc'late this deal's about fixed me so's I kin go ahead with a number of plans. Much obleeged, Mr. Linderman. You come in handy."

"So did you, Mr. Baines. Mighty handy."

"Oh, me. I had to. I was jest takin' out reasonable insurance ag'in' loss...."

"I guess you have a permanent insurance policy against loss, inside your head."

"Um!..." said Scattergood, slipping his feet into his shoes, preparatory to leaving, "difficulty about that kind of insurance is that most folks lets it lapse 'long about the first week after they're born."

CHAPTER VII
HE BORROWS A GRANDMOTHER

The world has come to think of Scattergood Baines as an astute and perhaps tricky business man, or as the political despot of a state. Because this is so it has overlooked or neglected many stories about the man much more indicative of character, and more fascinating of detail than those well-known and often-repeated tales of his sagacity in trading or his readiness in outwitting a political enemy. To one who makes a careful study of Scattergood's life with a view to writing a truthful biography, he inevitably becomes more interesting and more lovable when seen simply as a neighbor, a fellow townsman of other New Englanders, and as a country hardware merchant. There is a certain charm in the naivete with which he was wont to stick his pudgy finger in the affairs of others with benignant purpose; and it is not easy to believe other tales of hardness, of ruthless beating down of opposition, when one repeatedly comes upon well-authenticated instances in which he has stood quietly hidden behind the scenes to pull the strings and to make his neighbors bow and dance and posture in accordance with some schemes which he has formulated for their greater happiness.

Scattergood loved to meddle. Perhaps that is his dominant trait. He could see nothing moving in the community about him and withhold his hand. If Old Man Bogle set about buying a wheelbarrow, Scattergood would intervene in the transaction; if Pliny Pickett stopped at the Widow Ware's gate to deliver a message, Scattergood saw an opportunity to unite lonely hearts--and set about uniting them forthwith; if little Sam Kettleman, junior, and Wade Lumley's boy, Tom, came to blows, Scattergood became peacemaker or referee, as the needs of the moment seemed to dictate. It would be difficult to find a pie in Coldriver which was not marked by his thumb. So it came about that when he became convinced that Grandmother Penny was unhappy because of various restrictions and inhibitions placed on her by her son, the dry-goods merchant, and by her daughter-in-law, he determined to intervene. Scattergood was partial to old ladies, and this partiality can be traced to his earliest days in Coldriver. He loved white hair and wrinkled cheeks and eyes that had once been youthful and glowing, but were dulled and dimmed by watching the long procession of the years.

Now he sat on the piazza of his hardware store, his shoes on the planking beside him, and his pudgy toes wriggling like the trained fingers of an eminent pianist. It was a knotty problem. An ordinary problem Scattergood could solve with shoes on feet, but let the matter take on eminent difficulty and his toes must be given freedom and elbow room, as one might say. Later in life his wife, Mandy, after he had married her, tried to cure him of this habit, which she considered vulgar, but at this point she failed signally.

The facts about Grandmother Penny were, not that she was consciously ill treated. Her bodily comfort was seen to. She was well fed and reasonably clothed, and had a good bed in which to sleep. Where she was sinned against was in this: that her family looked upon her white hair and her wrinkles and arrived at the erroneous conclusion that her interest in life was gone--in short, that she was content to cumber the earth and to wait for the long sleep. To them she was simply one who tarries and is content. Scattergood looked into her sharp, old eyes, eyes that were capable of sudden gleams of humor or flashes of anger, and he knew. He knew that death seemed as distant to Grandmother Penny as it had seemed fifty years ago. He knew that her interest in life was as keen, her yearning to participate in the affairs of life as strong, as they had been when Grandfather Penny--now long gone to his reward--had driven his horse over the hills with one hand while he utilized the other arm for more important and delightful purposes.

Scattergood was remembering his own grandmother. He had known her as no other living soul had known her, because she had been his boyhood intimate, his defender, always his advocate, and because the boyish love which he had given her had made his eyes keen to perceive. His parents had fancied Grandma Baines to be content when she was in constant revolt. They had supposed that life meant nothing more to her now than to sit in a comfortable rocker and to knit interminable stockings and to remember past years. Scattergood knew that the present compelled her interest and that the future thrilled her. She wanted to participate in life, to be in the midst of events--to continue to live so long as the power of movement and of perception remained to her. He was now able to see that the old lady had done much to mold his character, and as he recalled incident after incident his face wore a softer, more melancholy expression than Coldriver was wont to associate with it. He was regretting that in his thoughtless youth he had failed to accomplish more to make gladder his grandmother's few remaining years.

"I calc'late," said Scattergood to himself--but aloud--"that I'll kind of substitute Grandmother Penny for Grandma Baines--pervidin' Grandma Baines is fixed so's she kin see; more'n likely she'll understand what I'm up to, and it'll tickle her--I'm goin' to up and borrow me a grandmother."

He wriggled his toes and considered. What thing had his grandmother most desired?

"Independence was what she craved," he said, and considered the point. "She didn't want to be beholdin' to folks. She wanted to be fixed so's she could do as she pleased, and nobody to interfere. I calc'late if Grandma Baines 'd 'a' been left alone she'd 'a' found her another husband and they'd 'a' had a home of their own with all the fixin's. It wasn't so much doin' that grandma wanted, it was knowin' she could do if she wanted to."

Scattergood's specially reinforced chair creaked as he strained forward to pick up his shoepacs and draw them on. It required no small exertion, and he straightened up, red of face and panting a trifle. He walked up the street, crossed the bridge, and descended to the little room under the barber shop where the checker or cribbage championship of the state was decided daily. Two ancient citizens were playing checkers, while a third stood over them, watching with that thrilled concentration with which the ordinary person might watch an only son essaying to cross Niagara Falls on a tight rope. Scattergood knew better than to interrupt the game, so he stood by until, by a breath-taking triple jump, Old Man Bogle sent his antagonist down to defeat. Then, and only then, did Scattergood speak to the old gentleman who had been the spectator.

"Morning Mr. Spackles," he said.

"Mornin', Scattergood. See that last jump of Bogle's? I swanny if 'twan't about as clever a move as I see this year."

"Mr. Spackles," said Scattergood, "I come down here to find out could I ask you some advice. You bein' experienced like you be, it 'peared to me like you was the one man that could help me out."

"Um!..." grunted Mr. Spackles, his old blue eyes widening with the distinction of the moment. "If I kin be of any service to you, I calculate I'm willin'. 'Tain't often folks comes to me for advice any more, or anythin' else, for that matter. Guess they figger I'm too old to 'mount to anythin'."

"Feel like takin' a mite of a walk?"

"Who? Me? I'm skittisher'n a colt this mornin'. Bet I kin walk twenty mile 'fore sundown."

They moved toward the door, but there Mr. Spackles paused to look back grandly upon the checker players. "Sorry I can't linger to watch you, boys," he said, loftily, "but they's important matters me and Scattergood got to discuss. Seems like he's feelin' the need of sound advice."

When they were gone the checker players scrutinized each other, and then with one accord scrambled to the door and stared out after Scattergood and Mr. Spackles.

"I swanny!" said Old Man Bogle.

"What d'you figger Scattergood wanted of that ol' coot?" demanded Old Man Peterson.

"Somethin' deep," hazarded Old Man Bogle. "I always did hold Spackles was a brainy cuss. Hain't he 'most as good a checker player as I be? What gits me, though, is how Scattergood come to pick him instid of me."

"Huh!..." grunted Old Man Peterson, and they resumed their game.

Scattergood walked along in silence for a few paces; then he regarded Mr. Spackles appraisingly.

"Mr. Spackles," said he, deferentially, "I dunno when I come acrost a man that holds his years like you do. Mind if I ask you jest how old you be?"

"Sixty-six year," said Spackles.

"Wouldn't never 'a' b'lieved it," marveled Scattergood. "Wouldn't 'a' set you down for a day more 'n fifty-five or six, not with them clear eyes and them ruddy cheeks and the way you step out."

"Calc'late to be nigh as good as I ever was, Scattergood. J'ints creak some, but what I got inside my head it don't never creak none to speak of."

"What I want to ask you, Mr. Spackles," said Scattergood, "is if you calc'late a man that's got to be past sixty and a woman that's got to be past sixty has got any business hitchin' up and marryin' each other."

"Um!... Depends. I'd say it depends. If the feller was perserved like I be, and the woman was his equal in mind and body, I'd say they was no reason ag'in' it--'ceptin' it might be money."

"Ever think of marryin', yourself, Mr. Spackles?"

"Figgered some. Figgered some. But knowed they wasn't no use. Son and daughter wouldn't hear to it. Couldn't support a wife, nohow. Son and daughter calc'lates to be mighty kind to me, Scattergood, and gives me dum near all I kin ask, but both of 'em says I got to the time of life where it hain't becomin' in 'em to allow me to work."

"How much kin sich a couple as I been talkin' about live on?"

"When I married, forty-odd year ago, I was gittin' a dollar a day. Me 'n' Ma we done fine and saved money. Livin's higher now. Calc'late it 'u'd take nigh a dollar 'n' a half to git on comfortable."

"Figger fifty dollars a month 'u'd do it? Think that 'u'd be enough?"

"Scattergood, you listen here to me. I hain't never earned as much as fifty dollar a month reg'lar in my whole life--and I got consid'able pleasure out of livin', too." They had walked up the street until they were passing the Penny residence. Grandmother Penny was sitting on the porch, knitting as usual. She looked very neat and dainty as she sat there in her white lace cap and her lavender dress.

"Fine-lookin' old lady," said Scattergood.

Mr. Spackles regarded Grandmother Penny and nodded with the air of a connoisseur. "Dum'd if she hain't." He lifted his hat and yelled across the road: "Mornin', Ellen."

"Mornin', James," replied Grandmother Penny, and bobbed her head. "Won't you folks stop and set? Sun's a-comin' down powerful hot."

"Don't mind if we do," said Scattergood. He seated himself, and mopped his brow, and fanned himself with his broad straw hat, whose flapping brim was beginning to ravel about the edges. Presently he stood up.

"Got to be movin' along, Mis' Penny. Seems like I'm mighty busy off and on.

But I dunno what I'd do without Mr. Spackles, here, to advise with once in a while. He's jest been givin' me the benefit of his thinkin' this mornin'."

With inward satisfaction Scattergood noticed how the old lady turned a pert, sharp look upon Mr. Spackles, regarding him with awakened interest. To be considered a man of wisdom by Scattergood Baines was a distinction in Coldriver even in those days, and for a man actually to be consulted and asked for advice by the ample hardware merchant was to lift him into an intellectual class to which few could aspire.

"I hope he gin you good advice, Scattergood," said Grandmother Penny.

"Allus does. If ever you're lookin' for level-headedness, and f'r a man you kin depend on, jest send a call for Mr. Spackles. G'-by, ma'am. G'-by, Mr. Spackles, and much 'bleeged to you."

Mr. Spackles was a little bewildered, for he had not the least idea upon what subject he had advised Scattergood, but he was of an acuteness not to pass by any of the advantage that accrued from the situation. He replied, with lofty kindness, "Any time you want for to consult with me, young man, jest come right ahead."

When Scattergood was gone, Mr. Spackles turned to the old lady and waggled his head.

"Ellen, that there's a mighty promisin' young man. Time's comin' when he's a-goin' to amount to suthin'. I'm a-calc'latin' on guidin' him all I kin."

"I want to know," said Grandmother Penny, almost breathless at this new importance of Mr. Spackles's, and Mr. Spackles basked in her admiration, and added to it by apochryphal narratives of his relations with Scattergood.

For a week Scattergood let matters rest. He was content, for more than once he saw Mr. Spackles's faded overalls and ragged hat on the Penny premises, and watched the old gentleman in animated conversation with Grandmother Penny, who seemed to be perter and brighter and handsomer than she had ever seemed before.

On one such day Scattergood crossed the street and entered the gate.

"Howdy, folks?" he said. "Wonder if I kin speak with Mr. Spackles without interferin'?"

"Certain you kin," said Grandmother Penny, cordially.

"Got a important bankin' matter over to the county seat, Mr. Spackles, and I was wonderin' if I could figger on your help?"

"To be sure you kin, Scattergood. To be sure."

"Got to have a brainy man over there day after to-morrer. B'jing! that's circus day, too. Didn't think of that till this minnit. Wonder if you'd drive my boss and buggy over and fix up a deal with the president of the bank?"

"Glad to 'bleege," said the flattered Mr. Spackles.

"Circus day," Scattergood repeated. "Been to a circus lately, Mis' Penny?"

"Hain't seen one for years."

"No?... Mr. Spackles, what be you thinkin' of? To be sure. Why, you kin bundle Mis' Penny into the buggy and take her along with you! Finish the business in no time, bein' spry like you be, and then you and her kin take in the circus and the side show, and stay f'r the concert. How's that?"

Mr. Spackles was suddenly red and embarrassed, but Grandmother Penny beamed.

"Why," says she, "makes me feel like a young girl ag'in. To be sure I'll go. Daughter'll make a fuss, but I jest don't care if she does. I'm a-goin'."

"That's the way to talk," said Scattergood. "Mr. Spackles'll be round f'r you bright and early. Now, if you kin spare him, I calc'late we got to talk business."

When they were in the street Mr. Spackles choked and coughed, and said with some vexation:

"You went and got me in f'r it that time."

"How so, Mr. Spackles? Don't you want to take Mis' Penny to the circus?"

"Course I do, but circuses cost money. I hain't got more 'n a quarter to my name."

"H'm!... Didn't calc'late I was askin' you to take a day of your time for nothin', did you? F'r a trip like this here, with a lot hangin' on to it, I'd say ten dollars was about the fittin' pay. What say?"

Mr. Spackles's beaming face was answer enough.

Grandmother Penny and Mr. Spackles went to the circus in a more or less sur- reptitious manner. It was a wonderful day, a successful day, such a day as neither of them had expected ever to see again, and when they drove home through the moonlight, across the mountains, their souls were no longer the souls of threescore and ten, but of twoscore and one.

"Great day, wa'n't it, Ellen?" said Mr. Spackles, softly.

"Don't call to mind nothin' approachin' it, James."

"You be powerful good company, Ellen."

"So be you, James."

"I calculate to come and set with you, often," said James, diffidently.

"Whenever the notion strikes you, James," replied Grandmother Penny, and she blushed for the first time in a score of years.

Two days later Pliny Pickett stopped to speak to Scattergood in front of the hardware store. Pliny supplemented and amplified the weekly newspaper, and so was very useful to Baines.

"Hear tell Ol' Man Spackles is sparkin' Grandmother Penny," Pliny said, with a grin. "Don't figger nothin' 'll come of it, though. Their childern won't allow it."

"Won't allow it, eh? What's the reason? What business is 't of theirn?"

"Have to support 'em. The ol' folks hain't got no money. Spackles 's got two-three hunderd laid by for to bury him, and so's Grandmother Penny. Seems like ol' folks allus lays by for the funeral, but that's every red cent they got. I hear tell Mis' Penny's son has forbid Spackles's comin' around the house."

This proved to be the fact, as Scattergood learned from no less an authority than Mr. Spackles himself.

"Felt like strikin' him right there 'n' then," said Mr. Spackles, heatedly, "but I seen 'twouldn't do to abuse one of Ellen's childern."

"Um!... Was you and Grandmother Penny figgerin' on hitchin' up?" Scattergood asked.

"I put the question," said Mr. Spackles, with the air of a youth of twenty, "and Ellen up and allowed she'd have me. But I guess 'twon't never come off now. Seems like I'll never be content ag'in, and Ellen's that downcast I shouldn't be a mite s'prised if she jest give up and passed away."

"Difficulty's money, hain't it? Largely financial, eh?"

"Ya-as."

"Folks has got rich before. Maybe somethin' like that'll happen to you."

"Have to happen mighty suddin, Scattergood, if it aims to do any good in this world."

"I've knowed men to invest a couple hunderd dollars into some venture and come out at t'other end with thousands. You got couple hunderd, hain't you?"

"Ellen and me both has--saved up to bury us."

"Um!... Git buried, anyhow. Law compels it. Doggone little pleasure spendin' money f'r your own coffin. More sensible to git some good out of it.... I'm goin' away to the city f'r a week or sich a matter. When I come back we'll kind of thrash things out and see what's to be done. Meantime, don't you and Grandmother Penny up and elope."

In this manner Scattergood planted the get-rich-quick idea in the head of Mr. Spackles, who communicated it to Grandmother Penny in the course of a clandestine meeting. The old folks discussed it, and hope made it seem more and more plausible to them. Realizing the fewness of the days remaining to them, they were anxious to utilize every moment. It was Grandmother Penny who was the daring spirit. She was for drawing their money out of the bank that very day and investing it somehow, somewhere, in the hope of seeing it come back to them a hundred-fold.

Scattergood had neglected to take into consideration Grandmother Penny's adventuresome spirit; he had also neglected to avail himself of the information that a certain Mr. Baxter, registered from Boston, was at the hotel, and that his business was selling shares of stock in a mine which did not exist to gullible folks who wanted to become wealthy without spending any labor in the process. He did a thriving business. It was Coldriver's first experience with this particular method of extracting money from the public, and it came to the front handsomely. Mr. Spackles got wind of the opportunity and told it to Grandmother Penny. She took charge of affairs, compelled her fiance to go with her to the bank, where they withdrew their savings, and then sought for Mr. Baxter, who, in return for a bulk sum of some five hundred dollars, sold them enough stock in the mine to paper the parlor. Also, he promised them enormous returns in an exceedingly brief space of time. Their profit on the transaction would, he assured them, be not less than ten thousand dollars, and might mount to double that sum. They departed in a state of extreme elation, and but for Mr. Spackles's conservatism Grandmother Penny would have eloped with him then and there.

"I'd like to, Ellen. I'd like to, mighty well, but 'tain't safe. Le's git the money fust. The minnit the money comes in, off we mog to the parson. But 'tain't safe yit.

Jest hold your hosses."

When Scattergood returned and was visible again on the piazza of his hardware store, it was not long before the village financiers came to him boasting of their achievement. He, Scattergood, was not the only man in town with the ability to make money. No, indeed, and for proof of it here were the stock certificates, purchased from a deluded young man for a few cents a share, when common sense told you they were worth many, many dollars. Scattergood listened to two or three without a word. Finally he asked:

"How many folks went into this here thing?"

"Sev'ral. Sev'ral. Near's I kin figger, folks here bought nigh five thousand dollars' wuth of stock off'n Baxter. Must 'a' been fifty or sixty went into the deal."

"Dum fools," said Scattergood, with sudden wrath. "Has it got so's I don't dast to leave town without you folks messin' things up? Can't I leave overnight and find things safe in the mornin'?... You hain't got the sense Gawd give field mice--the whole kit and b'ilin' of you. Serves you dum well right, tryin' to git somethin' f'r nothin'. Now git away fr'm here. Don't pester me.... You've been swindled, that's what, and it serves you doggone well right. Now git."

It was one of the few times that Coldriver saw Scattergood in a rage. The rage convinced them. Scattergood said they were swindled and he was in a rage. Therefore he must be right. The news spread, and knots of citizens with lowered heads and anxious eyes gathered on street corners and whispered and nodded toward Scattergood, who sat heavily on his piazza, speaking to nobody. It was Grandmother Penny who dared accost him. She crept up to his place and said, tremulously:

"Be you sure, Scattergood, about that feller bein' a swindler?"

Scattergood looked down at her fiercely. Then his eyes softened and he leaned forward and scrutinized her face.

"Did you git into this mess, too, Grandmother Penny?"

"Both me 'n' James," she said. "You let on that folks got rich quick by investin'. Me 'n' James was powerful anxious to git money so's--so's we could git married on it. So we drawed out our money and--and invested it."

"Come here, Grandmother," said Scattergood, and she stood just before his chair, her head coming very little higher than his own as he sat there, big and ominous. "So the skunk took your money, too. I hain't carin' a whoop for them others.

They got what was comin' to 'em, and I didn't calculate to do nothin'. But you! By crimminy!... Wa-al, Grandmother, you go off home and knit. I'll look into things. It's on your account, and not on theirs." He shook his head fiercely toward the town. "But I calculate I'll have to git theirn back, too.... And, Grandmother--you and James kin rest easy. Hain't sayin' no more. Jest wait, and don't worry, and don't say nothin' to nobody.... G'-by, Grandmother Penny. G'-by."

That evening Scattergood drove out of Coldriver in his rickety buggy. Nobody had dared to speak to him, but, nevertheless, he carried in his pocket a list of the town's investors in mining stock, together with the amounts of their investments. He was not seen again for several days.

Two days later Scattergood appeared in the lobby of the Mansion House, in the county seat. He scrutinized the register, and found, to his satisfaction, that a Mr. Bowman of Boston was occupying room 106. Mr. Bowman had signed the hotel register in Coldriver as Mr. Baxter, also of Boston. Scattergood seated himself in a chair and lighted one of the cigars which made his presence so undesirable in an inclosed space. He appeared to be taking a nap.

Fifteen minutes after Scattergood began to nod, Sam Bangs, a politician with some strength in the rural districts, came down the stairs in company with a young man of prepossessing appearance, and clothing which did not strike the beholder as either too gaudy or too stylish. Indeed the young man impressed the world as being a sober, conservative person in whose judgment it would be well to place confidence.

When Bangs saw Scattergood he stopped and whispered a moment to his companion, who nodded. They approached Scattergood, and Bangs touched him on the shoulder.

"Mr. Baines," he said, "I want you should meet my friend Mr. Bowman. Mr. Bowman's a broker. Been buyin' some stocks off'n him--or calculate to. I knowed you done consid'able investing so I took the liberty."

Scattergood looked drowsily at the young man. "Set," he said. "Set and have a cigar."

The young Mr. Bowman accepted the cigar, but, after a glance at it, thrust it into his mouth unlighted. The conversation began with national politics, swung to crops, and veered finally to the subject of investments. Mr. Bowman, backed in his statements by Mr. Bangs, spoke to Scattergood of a certain mine whose stock could be had for a song, but whose riches in mineral, about to be reached by a certain shaft or drift or tunnel, were fabulous. Scattergood was interested. An appointment was made for further discussion.

The appointment was kept that evening, in the same lobby, and Mr. Bowman, while finding more than ordinary difficulty in convincing this fat country merchant, did eventually succeed in bringing him to a point of enthusiasm.

"Looks good," said Scattergood. "Calc'late a feller could make a killin'. I'm a-goin' into it hair, hide, and hoofs. Figger me f'r not less 'n five thousand dollars' wuth of it. Ought to make me fifty thousand if it makes a cent."

"You're conservative, Mr. Baines, conservative."

"Always calculated to be, Mr. Bowman." He looked up as a middle-aged man with a drooping mustache approached. "Howdy, John? Still workin' f'r the express company, be you?"

"Calc'late to, Mr. Baines. Got charge of the local office. 'Tain't all pleasure, neither. In a sight of trouble this minnit."

"I want to know," said Scattergood. "Stand to lose my job," said John, sadly. "Dunno where I'll find me another."

"What you been doin', eh? What got you in bad?"

"One of them dummed gold shipments from the state bank. Hadn't ought to speak about it, 'cause the comp'ny's bein' awful secret. Hain't lettin' it out." He glanced apprehensively at Mr. Bowman.

"Needn't to be afraid of Mr. Bowman, John. What's the story?"

"Bank shippin' bullion. Three chunks of it. Wuth fifty-odd thousand dollars. I know, 'cause that's the comp'ny's liability wrote in black and white.... Been stole," he said, after a brief pause.

"Where?"

"Out of my office, this mornin'. Not a trace. Jest up and disappeared. Detectives and all can't run on to no clue. Might as well 'a' melted and run through a crack. Jest gone, and that's all anybody kin find."

"Mighty sorry to hear it, John. Hope you wasn't keerless, and don't figger you was. Guess you won't be blamed when the facts comes out."

"If they ever do," said John. "G' night, Mr. Baines. I'm mighty oneasy in my mind."

Scattergood turned the subject back at once to mining stocks.

"You set me down for five thousand dollars. Don't let nobody else have it. Got jest that sum comin' due tomorrer. You and me'll drive over to git it, and you fetch them stock certificates along. Got 'em in that little satchel you're always carryin'?"

"No," smiled Mr. Bowman. "That's my purse. I take no chances on robbers, like your express agent spoke of. I don't mind telling you that I have fifteen thousand dollars in that bag--and I intend to keep it there."

"Do tell!" exclaimed Scattergood. "Wa-al, you know your business. Now, then, if you want to drive over six mile with me to-morrer, well git us that money and I'll take the stock."

"Good," said Mr. Bowman. "An early start. Can I take a train from there? I'll be through here, I think."

"To be sure," said Scattergood. "Mighty funny thing about that gold, now wa'n't it? Three bars. Wuth fifty thousand! Mighty slick work--to spirit it off and nobody never find a trace."

"The criminal classes," said Mr. Bowman, "have produced some remarkable intellects. Good night, Mr. Baines."

"See you early in the mornin'," replied Scattergood.

After a breakfast which Mr. Bowman watched Scattergood dispose of with admiration and astonishment, the pair entered the old buggy and started across the hills. In addition to his small bag Mr. Bowman brought a large suitcase containing his apparel, so it was apparent he was leaving the county seat for good. The morning came off hot and humid. Scattergood kept his eyes open for a spring, but it was not until they had driven some miles that an opportunity to find water appeared.

"Calculate we kin git a drink there," said Scattergood, pointing to a little shanty in a clearing by the roadside. He stopped his horse, and they alighted and knocked. There was no reply. Scattergood pushed open the door and then stepped back suddenly, for within were three individuals of disreputable appearance, and one of them regarded Scattergood over the leveled barrels of a shotgun.

"Come right in and set," invited this individual, and Scattergood, followed by Mr. Bowman, entered. On a table of pine wood, unconcealed, lay three enormous bars of gold.

"Um!..." said Scattergood, faintly, and leaned against the wall. "You would come rammin' in," said the gentleman with the shotgun. "Now I calc'late you got to stay."

Scattergood grinned amiably. "Vallyble loaves of bread you got there," he said.

"Gold," said the man, succinctly.

"Hain't no mines around here, be there?"

"We hain't sayin'. But that there gold come from a mine, all right--sometime."

"Calc'late you been robbin' a train or somethin'," said Scattergood, mildly. "Now don't git het up. 'Tain't none of my business. Doin' robbin' for a reg'lar livin'?" he asked, innocently.

"Hain't never done none before--" began one of the men, but his companion directed him to "shut up and stay shut."

"No harm talkin' 's I kin see. We got these fellers here and here they stay till we git clean off. Kind of like to tell somebody the joke."

"I'm doggone int'rested," said Scattergood.

The rough individual with the gun laughed loudly. "May's well tell you," he said, raucously. "Me and the boys was in town yestiddy, calc'latin' to ship some ferns by express. Went into the office. Agent wa'n't there. Safe was. Open. Ya-as, wide open. We seen three gold chunks inside, and nobody around watchin'. Looked full better 'n ferns, so we jest took a notion to carry 'em out to the wagin and drive off.... Now we got it, I'm dummed if I know what to do with it. Hear tell it's wuth fifty thousand dollars."

Mr. Bowman spoke. "You'll find it mighty hard to dispose of."

"Don't need to worry you."

"Suppose you could sell it for a fair price, cash, and get away with the money?"

"That's our aim."

"Mr. Baines," said Bowman, "there's money in this if you aren't too particular."

"Hain't p'tic'lar a-tall. How you mean?"

"What would you say to buying this gold--at a reasonable price? I can dispose of it--through channels I am acquainted with. You can put in the money we were going for, and I'll put in some more. Ought to show a handsome profit."

"Might nigh double my money, maybe, eh? Figger that? Gimme twict as much to buy stock with."

"Yes, indeed."

"Let's dicker."

"What will you men take to walk away and leave that gold?"

"Forty thousand."

"Fiddlesticks. I'll give you ten--and you're clear of the whole mess."

There was a wrangle. For half an hour the dicker went on, and finally a price of fifteen thousand dollars was agreed upon. Mr. Bowman was to pay over the money, and Scattergood was to contribute his five thousand dollars as soon as they got it. For one third of the profits.

The money was paid over; the three robbers disappeared with alacrity, leaving Scattergood and Bowman with the stolen gold.

"We can take it along in the buggy, covered with ferns," said Bowman. "Nobody'll suspect you."

"Be safe as a church," said Scattergood, boldly. "Lug her out."

So they carried the gold to the buggy, covered it snugly with ferns, and drove toward the next town, Scattergood talking excitedly of profits and of how much mining stock he could purchase with the money received, and of ample wealth from the transaction. Mr. Bowman smiled with the faint, quiet smile of one whose soul is at peace. Just before they got to town Scattergood suggested that they stop to make sure the gold was completely concealed.

They drove into the woods a few rods and uncovered the treasure. Scattergood gloated over it.

"I've heard tell you kin cut real gold like cheese," he said, and opened his jack-knife. With it he hacked off a shaving and held it up to the light.

"Is all gold this here way?" he asked. "Don't look to me to be the same color all the way through. Looks like silver or suthin' inside."

Mr. Bowman snatched the shaving, scrutinized it, and uttered language in a loud voice. He snatched Scattergood's knife and tested all three ingots.

"Lead!" he said, savagely. "Nothing but lead! We've been swindled!"

"You mean it hain't gold a-tall?"

"It's lead, I tell you."

"I vum!... Them fellers stole lead! And they got off with all your money. Gosh! I'm glad I didn't have none along." His eyes were mirthless and his face vacuous. "Beats all. Never heard tell of nothin' sim'lar."

They got into the buggy and drove silently into town. Mr. Bowman tried to recover his spirits, but they were at low ebb. He did manage to hint that Scattergood should stand his share of the loss, but in his heart he knew that to be vain. Still, he could get that five thousand dollars for the mining stock. It would be five thousand dollars.

"Anyhow," he said, "you're fortunate. You still can buy the stock and make your pile."

"This here deal," said Scattergood, "has kind of made me figger. 'Tain't safe to buy gold chunks till you know they're gold. Likewise 'tain't safe to buy mine stock till you know there's a mine. Calc'late I'll do a mite of investigatin' 'fore I pungle over that five thousand.... Where kin I leave you, Mr. Bowman? I'm calc'latin' to drive home from here. Maybe I'll see you later. But I got to investigate."

Mr. Bowman made himself unpleasant for a brief time, but Scattergood was vacuously stubborn. Presently he drove away, leaving Mr. Bowman on the veranda of the hotel, scowling and uttering words of strength and meaning. Mr. Bowman was very unhappy.

Scattergood drove as rapidly as his horse could travel, arriving at Coldriver just after the supper hour. He went directly to his store, which had been left in charge of Mr. Spackles. Three men were waiting there for him. They handed him a leather bag and he satisfied himself that it contained fifteen thousand dollars.

"Much 'bleeged, boys," he said. "Do as much f'r you, some day. G'-by."

"Mr. Spackles," he said, "kin you fetch Grandmother Penny over here--right now?"

"Calculate I kin," said Mr. Spackles, and he proved himself able to keep his word.

"Grandmother Penny," said Scattergood, when she arrived, "you and Mr. Spackles up and made a investment. I been a-lookin' after that investment f'r you--and f'r these other dum fools in town. Best I could do f'r them others was to git their money back--every cent of it. But I took keer to do a mite more f'r you and Mr. Spackles. I got your five hunderd f'r you--and then I seen a way to git ten thousand more. Here she be. Count it.... I don't guess there's any way this here money could be put to better use."

"F'r us? Ten thousand--"

"I'll handle it f'r you. Give you int'rest of six hunderd a year. You kin marry like you planned, and if your childern objects you kin tell 'em to go to blazes.... You'll want a place to live. Wa-al, I got twenty acre back of town and a leetle house and furniture. Took it on a deal. You kin move in and work it on shares. Ought to be able to live blamed well."

Grandmother Penny was crying.

"You done all this f'r us, f'r James and me! There hain't no reason f'r it. 'Tain't believable.... There hain't no way to say thankee."

"I hain't wantin' you to say thankee, Grandmother Penny. Jest mog along and marry this old coot, and git what joy you kin out of livin'."

Mr. Spackles was inquisitive in addition to being grateful.

"What I want to know," he demanded, "is how you managed it?"

"Oh," said Scattergood, "jest made use of the sayin' about curin' with the hair of the dog that bit you. Figgered a swindler wouldn't never suspect nobody of swindlin' him with one of his own tricks. This here Mr. Baxter, or Mr. Bowman, or whatever his name is, used to make a livin' sellin' gold bricks. When I found that there fact out I jest calc'lated he was ripe to do a mite of gold-brick buyin' himself.... Which he done."

"Scattergood," said Grandmother Penny, "I'm a-goin' to kiss you."

Scattergood presented his cheek, and Grandmother Penny threw her arms around his neck and pressed her lips to his weather-beaten face. He smiled, but as if he were smiling at somebody not present. When they had gone their way to find marriage license and parson he went out on to his piazza and looked up at the moonlit sky.

"Grandma Baines," he said, after a moment, "if you kin see down from where you be, I hope you hain't missin' that I done this f'r you. I was pertendin' all the time that you was Grandmother Penny...."

CHAPTER VIII
HE DIPS IN HIS SPOON

Scattergood Baines sat on the piazza of his hardware store and twiddled his bare toes reflectively. He was not thinking of to-day nor of to-morrow, but of days a score of years distant and of plans not to come to maturity for twenty years. That was Scattergood's way. From his history, as it is to be gathered from the ancient gossips of Coldriver, one is forced to the conclusion that few of his acts were performed with reference to the immediate time. If he set on foot some scheme, one learns to study it and to endeavor to see to what outcome it may lead ten years after its inception. He looked always to the future, and more than once one may see where he has forgone immediate profit in order to derive that profit a hundredfold a generation later.

So, as Scattergood twiddled his reflective toes, he looked far ahead into the future of Coldriver Valley; he saw that valley as his own, developed as few mountain valleys are ever developed. Its stage line, already his property, was replaced by a railroad. The waters of its river and tributaries were dammed to give a cheap and constant power which should be connected in some way to this electricity of which he heard so much and about which he always desired to hear more. He saw factories springing up. In short, he saw his valley as the center of the state's commercial life, and himself as the center of the valley.

Scattergood was well aware that there always will exist those who will clog the road of progress and attempt to stem any tide arising for the public good--unless they can see for themselves an individual benefit. He knew that it is not uncommon for those whose business is the common good--such individuals as legislators and governors and judges--to assume some such attitude, and he knew that it was regarded as expensive to win their favor. He did not grow especially angry at this condition, but accepted it as a condition and studied to see what he could do about it--for he knew he must do something about it.

He must take it into consideration, because one does not build railroads without legislative sanction, nor does one dam streams nor carry out wide commercial programs. The consent of the people must be had, and the people had handed over their consent in trust to their elected representatives. Scattergood saw at once that it was preferable to be one from whom governors and legislators and judges asked favors and looked to for guidance, than to be one to come a suppliant before those personages, and as soon as he saw that clearly he reached his determination.

"Calculate," said he, to the shoes which he held in his hand, "that I got to git up and stir around in politics some."

From that moment Scattergood scrutinized the bowl of politics to discover when and where he could dip in his spoon.

The opportunity to dip, it soon became apparent, would be at the time of the fall town meetings, for there was a fight on in the state and its preliminary rumblings were already making themselves audible. Hitherto the state had been held securely by certain political gentlemen, who in turn had been held securely by a certain other and greater political gentleman--Lafe Siggins. Other non-political gentlemen who represented money *and* business had seen, as Scattergood did, the necessity for becoming political, and had chosen their moment to endeavor to take the state away from Messrs. Siggins & Co. and to hold it thereafter for their own benefit and behoof. They were, therefore, laying their plans to win the legislature by winning the town meetings of the fall, and to win they had decided to make their fight upon the total prohibition of liquor in the state. It was not that they cared ethically whether drinks of a spirituous nature were dispensed or not, but it was the best available issue. If it did not work out to their satisfaction they could reverse themselves when they came into power.

So they made an issue of prohibition, and planned astutely to go to the town meetings on that platform, for a majority of the towns voted local option with regularity. The new powers would first sweep the town meetings for local option, and in the wave of enthusiasm put into office at the same time legislators chosen by themselves.

Scattergood saw the trend of affairs early and gave them his earnest consideration. That his ancient ill wishers, Messrs. Crane & Keith, were identified with the new and rising power may not have been the least of the considerations which determined him to dip in his spoon on the side of Siggins and the old order. But there was one obstacle. Scattergood desired local option, for he was now the employer of many men, both in the woods and in other enterprises, and he knew well that labor and hard liquor are disturbing bedfellows.... He considered and reached the conclusion that for this one time, perhaps, he could both have his cake and eat it.

He could have his cake and still eat it only by the results of an election which should not be a victory for the new powers nor for the old, but for another minor power differing from each. In other words, Scattergood saw the wisdom of defeating both the contenders locally, and then of throwing in with Siggins as to the fight for state control.... But of this determination he notified not a soul. Judging from his actions, it may be safely said that he was at some pains to conceal the fact that he was interested in politics in any manner or degree whatever.

But Scattergood was a chatty body, and Coldriver would have been surprised if he did not talk politics, as did all its other male inhabitants. It came about that more politics than hardware was discussed on Scattergood's piazza, but to the casual listener it seemed only purposeless discussion. But Scattergood was a master of purposeless discussion. His methods were his own and worthy of notice.

Marvin Towne and Old Man Bogle sauntered past and paused to mention the weather.

"Goin' to be lots of politics this year," said Scattergood. "Jest got in a line of gardenin' tools, Bogle."

"Town's goin' to be het up for certain," said Mr. Bogle, waggling his ancient head. "Calc'late to have all the tools I need."

"Who's figgerin' on runnin' for legislature, Marvin?"

"Guess Will Pratt's puttin' up Pazzy Cox ag'in." Pratt was postmaster and local party leader.

"Anybody calc'latin' to run ag'in' him, Marvin? Any opposition appearin'?"

"Goin' to be a fight, Scattergood. Big doin's in the state. Tryin' to upset Lafe Siggins. Uh-huh! Wuth watchin', says I."

"I hear tell the lawless elements is puttin' up Jim Allen on a whisky platform," said Old Man Bogle, acidly.

"Them all the candidates, Bogle? Hain't no others?"

"Nary."

"Coldriver's got to take whatever candidates them outsiders chooses, eh? Coldriver hain't got no say who'll represent her in the legislature?"

"Don't 'pear so. All done by party machinery, Scattergood. We got nothin' to do but pick between parties."

"Looks so.... Looks that way," said Scattergood. "Too bad there hain't one more party that hain't controlled so folks could git a chance.... What's this here Prohibition party I been hearin' some of in other parts?"

"'S fur's I know it's all right, only it hain't got no votes, and votes is necessary in politics."

"Licker enters into this here campaign, don't it?"

"Backbone of it."

"Seems like these Prohibition fellers ought to take a hand. Any of 'em in Coldriver?"

"Don't seem like I ever heard speak of one."

"Could be, couldn't there? 'Tain't impossible?"

"S'pose one could be got up--if anybody was int'rested."

"Need a strong candidate, wouldn't they? Have to have a man to head it up that would command respect?"

"Wouldn't git fur with it. Parties too well organized."

"Um!... Lemme show you a new hand seeder I jest got in. Labor savin'. Calc'late it's a bargain."

"Don't hold with them newfangled notions, Scattergood."

"S'prised at you, Marvin. Folks expects progress of you. Look up to you, kind of. Take their idees from you."

"I dunno," said Marvin, visibly pleased, but deprecatory.

"Careful, cautious--but most gen'ally right, that's what I hear folks say. Quite a bit of talk goin' around about you. Politics. Uh-huh! Heard several say it was a pity Marvin Towne couldn't be got to go to the legislature. Heard that, hain't you, Bogle?"

"Don't call it to mind, but maybe I have. Maybe I have. Anyhow, I calc'late it's true."

"There you be, Marvin. Now it behooves a man that's looked up to for to keep in the lead. Ought to look into that seeder, Marvin. Folks'll say: 'Marvin Towne's got him one of them seeders. Darn progressive farmer. Gits him all the modern improvements.'"

"Suthin' in what you say, Scattergood. Calculate I might examine into that tool one of these days."

"Hain't much choice between Pazzy Cox and Jim Allen, eh? Hain't neither of 'em desirable lawmakers, eh? That what you was sayin'?"

"Them's my idees," said Marvin.

"Too bad we're forced to take one or t'other. Now if they was some way for you to step in and run."

"Hain't."

"Sh'u'd think you'd look over them Prohibitionists. Draw all the best citizens after you. Set a example to the state.... Step back and look at that there seeder, Marvin."

Marvin looked at the seeder judicially. "Calc'late to guarantee it, Scattergood?"

"Put it in writin'," said Scattergood.

"Calc'late I'll have to have it. Considerin' everything, guess I'll take it along."

"Knowed you would, Marvin. Sich men as you is to be depended on. Folks realizes it."

"If I thought they was a call for me to go to the legislature--"

"Call?" said Scattergood. "Marvin, I'm tellin' you it's dum near a shout."

"Huh!... Where could I git to find out about this here Prohibitionist party?"

Presently Marvin Towne and Old Man Bogle went along. Scattergood gazed after them speculatively, and as he gazed his hands went automatically to his shoes, which he removed to give play to his reflective toes. "Um!..." he grunted. "If nothin' more comes of it I made a profit of three dollar forty on that seeder."

Pliny Pickett, stage driver, was a frequent caller at Scattergood's store, first as an employee, but more importantly as a dependable representative who could carry out an order without asking questions, especially when no definite order had been given.

"Pliny," said Scattergood, "know Marvin Towne, don't you? Brought up with him, wasn't you?"

"Know him like the palm of my hand."

"Um!... Strange he hain't never been talked up for the legislature, Pliny. Strange there hain't talk about him on the stagecoach. Ever hear any?"

"Some, lately."

"Could hear more, couldn't you? If you listened.... Set around the post office, evenin's, don't you?"

"Some."

"Discussin' topics? Ever discuss this Prohibition party?"

"I could," said Pliny.

"Seems like a shame folks here can't run the man they want for office. Strike you that way?"

"Certain sure. Calc'late they want Marvin bad?"

"They could," said Scattergood. "G'-by, Pliny."

Ten days later a third party made its appearance in the politics of Coldriver, and Marvin Towne was announced as its candidate for the legislature. It seemed a spontaneous excrescence, but, nevertheless, it caused a visit from that great man and citizen, Lafe Siggins, as well as a call from Mr. Crane, of Crane & Keith. Both astute gentlemen viewed the situation, and their alarm subsided. Indeed, both perceived where it could be turned to advantage. A canvass of the situation showed them that the new Prohibitionists, though they talked loud and long, were made up mainly of the discontented and of a few men always ready to join any novel movement, and promised at best to poll not to exceed forty votes of Coldriver's registered three hundred and eighty. It really simplified the situation to Lafe and to Crane, for it removed from circulation forty doubtful votes and left the real battle to be fought between the regulars. Wherefore Messrs. Siggins and Crane departed from the village in satisfied mood.

Scattergood sat on his piazza as usual, the morning after the portentous visit, and called a greeting to Wade Lumley, dry-goods merchant, as that prominent citizen passed to his place of business.

"How's the geldin' this mornin', Wade?" he asked.

"Feelin' his oats. Got to take him out on the road this evenin'. Time to begin shapin' him up for the county fair."

"Three-year-old, hain't he?"

"Best in the state."

"Always figgered that till I heard Ren Green talkin'. Ren calculates he's got a three-year-old that'll make any other boss in these parts look like it was built of pine."

Wade was eager in a moment. "Willin' to back them statements with money, is he?"

"Said somethin' about havin' a hunderd dollars that wasn't workin' otherwise, seems as though," said Scattergood. "Jest half a mile from Pettybone's house to the dam," he continued, with apparent irrelevance. "Level road."

"And my geldin' kin travel that same road spryer 'n Green's hoss--for a hunderd dollars," said Wade, eagerly.

"Dunno," said Scattergood. "Hoss races is uncertain. G'-by, Wade. See you later."

A similar conversation with Ren Green during the day resulted in a meeting between the horsemen, an argument, loud words, and a heated offer to wager money, which was accepted with like heat.

"From Pettybone's to the dam--half a mile," shouted Wade.

"Suits me to a T," bellowed Ren; "and now you kin step across with me and deposit that there hunderd dollars ag'in' mine with Briggs of the hotel."

So, terms and conditions having been arranged, the bets were made, and the money locked in the hotel safe. News of the matter swept through Coldriver, and for the evening politics were forgotten and excitement ran high. Next day it arose to a higher pitch, for Town-marshal Pease had forbidden the race to be run through the public streets of Coldriver, viewing it as a menace to life, limb, and the public peace. Scattergood had conversed sagely with Pease on the duties of a town marshal.

Marvin Towne had formed the habit of stopping to chat with Scattergood daily, totally unconscious that to all intents and purposes he had been ordered by Scattergood to make daily reports to him. He seemed depressed as he leaned against a post of the piazza.

"Lookin' peaked, Marvin. Hain't all goin' well? Gittin' uneasy?"

"It's this dum hoss race," said Marvin. "Everybody's het up over it so's nobody'll talk politics. How's a feller goin' to win votes if he can't git nobody to talk to him, that's what I want to know? Seems like there hain't nothin' in the world but Wade Lumley's geldin' and that hoss of Green's."

"Um!... Sort of distressing hain't it? Know Kent Pilkinton perty well, Marvin?"

"Brother-in-law."

"Holds public office, don't he?"

"Chairman of the Board of Selectmen's what he is."

"Good man fur't," said Scattergood, waggling his head. "Calculate to be on good terms with him, Marvin? Perty good terms?"

"Good enough so's he kin ask me to loan him two thousand dollars he's needin' a'mighty bad."

"Give it to him, Marvin?"

"Huh!" said Marvin, eloquently.

"If I was to indorse his note, think you could see your way clear?"

"Certain sure."

"See him ag'in, won't you? Perty soon?"

"Yes."

"What d'you calc'late to tell him?"

"What you said?"

"Didn't say nothin', did I? Jest asked a question. It was you said something Marvin, wa'n't it? Said you'd lend on my indorsement."

"That what you want me to tell him?"

"Didn't say so, did I? Jest asked a question. G'-by, Marvin. Lemme know what he says."

It was unnecessary for Marvin to report, for early next morning Kent Pilkinton, owner of a hill farm on the out-skirts of a village--a farm on which he succeeded in raising the most ample crop of whiskers in Coldriver, and little else, came diffidently up to Scattergood as he sat in front of his hardware store.

"Morning Kent," said Scattergood. "Come to look at mowin' machines, I calc'late."

"Might look at one," said Kent.

"Need one, don't you?"

"Bad."

"Need quite a mess of implements, don't you?"

"Could do with 'em if I had 'em.... 'Tain't what I come fur, though, Scattergood. Been tryin' to borrow money off of my brother-in-law, but he don't calclate to lend without I git an indorser, and seems like he sets store by your name on a note."

"Does, eh? Any reason I should indorse for you? Know any reason?"

"Nary," said Kent, and started to move off.

"Hold your bosses. What you need the money for?"

"Pay off a thousand-dollar mortgage and another thousand to git the farm in shape to run."

"Calculate you kin run it, then?"

"If I git the tools."

"I figger maybe you kin. Like to see you git ahead. Where d'you calculate to buy them implements?"

"Off of you."

"I got 'em to sell. When you got to have the money?"

"Two weeks to-morrow."

This was the day after the town meeting.

"Come in and pick out your implements," said Scattergood.

"Meanin' you'll indorse?"

"Meanin' that--pervidin' nothin' unforeseen comes up between now and then."

Half a day was spent selecting tools and implements for the farm, and though Pilkinton did not know it, it was Scattergood's selection that was purchased. Scattergood knew what was necessary and what would be economical, and that was what Pilkinton got, and nothing more. It netted Scattergood a pleasant profit, and Kent got the full equivalent of his money.

"Preside at town meetin', don't you?"

"My duty," said Kent.

"Calc'late to do your duty?"

"Always done so."

"Comin' to see you do it," said Scattergood. He paused. "Next mornin' we'll fix up the note. G'-by, Kent." During the fourteen days that followed Coldriver was happy; between politics and the forbidden horse race, it had such food for conversation that even cribbage under the barber shop languished, and one had to walk into the road to pass the crowd at the post office of evenings. As to the horse race, it resembled a boil. Daily it grew more painful. Like a boil, such a horse race as this must burst some day, and it was reaching the acute stage. But Town-marshal Pease was vigilant and spoke sternly of the majesty of the law.

As to the election, it grew even more dubious. Scattergood privately took stock of the situation. Marvin Towne and the Prohibitionists might count now on a vote or two more than fifty. Postmaster Pratt appeared certain of better than a hundred, and so did the opposing party. One or the other of them was certain to win as matters lay, and Marvin's case seemed hopeless. Marvin conceived it so and was for withdrawing, but Scattergood saw to it that he did not withdraw.

"Keep your votes together," he said. "Stiffen 'em." It was his first direct order. "Fetch 'em to the meetin' and be sure of every one."

On town-meeting day Coldriver filled with rigs from the surrounding township. Every rail and post was utilized for hitching, and Town-marshal Pease, his star displayed, patrolled the town to avert disorder. He patrolled until the meeting went into session, and then he took his chair just under the platform, and, as was his duty, guarded the sacredness of the ballot.

Scattergood was present, sitting in a corner under the overhang of the balcony, watching, but discouraging conversation. If one had studied his face during the early proceedings he would have read nothing except a genial interest, which was the thing Coldriver expected to see on Scattergood's face. Town questions were decided, matters of sidewalks, of road building, of schools, and every instance Marvin Towne's fifty-two voted as a unit, swinging from one side to the other as their peculiar interest dictated. On all minor questions it was Marvin Towne's Prohibitionists who decided, because they carried the volume of votes necessary to control. But when it came to major affairs, such as the election of officers, there would be a different story. Then they could join with neither party, but must stand alone as a unit, far outvoted.

So the regulars disregarded them, or if they gave them any attention it was jocular. Even Marvin viewed the day as lost, but Scattergood held him to the mark with a word passed now and then. It came three o'clock of the afternoon before nominations for the high office of legislator were the order of proceeding. Jim Allen and Pazzy Cox were placed before the meeting as candidates amid the stimulated applause of their adherents. Marvin Towne's name was received with laughter and such jeers as the New England breed of farmer and townsman has rendered his own, and at which he is a genius surpassed by none.

Chairman Pilkinton arose, as befitted the moment.

"Feller townsmen, we will now proceed to cast our ballots for the office of representative in the legislature. The polls is open, and overlooked by Town-marshal Pease. The ballotin' will begin."

And then....

At that instant there was an uproar on the stairs. Pliny Pickett burst into the room, his hat missing, his eyes gleaming with excitement.

"It's a-comin' off. They've stole a march. Hoss race!... Hoss race!... Ren Green and Wade Lumley's got their bosses up to Deacon Pettybone's and they're goin' to race to the dam. Everybody out. Hoss race!... Hoss race!..." He turned and ran frantically down the stairs, and on his heels followed the voters of Coldriver. But one or two remained; men too rheumatic to chance rapid movement, or those whose positions compelled them to consider as non-existent such a matter as a race between quadrupeds.

But no sooner had the hall cleared than men began to return, in couples, in squads, and to take their seats. Scattergood was standing up now, counting. Fifty-two he counted, and remained standing.

"Polls is open, Mr. Chairman," says he.

"They was declared so, but--er--the voters has gone. I hain't clear how to perceed."

"Do your duty, chairman, like you said. Town meetings don't calculate to take account of hoss races, do they? Eh?... None of your affair, is it?"

Pilkinton looked at Scattergood, who smiled genially and said: "Duty's duty, Pilkinton. If you was to fail in your duty as a public officer, folks might git to think you wasn't the sort of citizen that could be trusted. Might even affect sich things as credit and promissory notes."

Mr. Pilkinton no longer hesitated.

"The polls is open," he said.

The fifty-two, ballots ready in their hands, started for the box, but Town-marshal Pease, awakened from his astonishment, lifted his voice.

"I got to stop that hoss race. Stop the votin' till I git back. That hoss race has got to be stopped."

"Seems to me like votes was more important than hoss races," said Scattergood.

"The town marshal will stay right where he is, and guard the ballot box," said the chairman.

The voters moved to the front, and as they deposited their ballots, sounds from without, indicating excitement and delight, were carried through the windows to their ears. The fifty-two voted and returned to their seats.

"If everybody present and desirin' to vote has done so," said Scattergood, "I move you them polls be closed."

Mr. Pilkinton put the motion, and it was carried with enthusiasm.

"Tellers," suggested Scattergood.

As was the custom, the votes were counted immediately. The result stood, Marvin Towne: fifty-three votes; Jim Allen, two votes; Pazzy Cox, four votes.

"I declare Marvin Towne elected our representative to the legislature," said Chairman Pilkinton, weakly, and sat down, mopping his brow.

"That bein' the final business of this meetin'," said Scattergood, "I move we adjourn."

The story swept the state. Twenty-four hours later Lafe Siggins visited Coldriver and was driven to Scattergood Baines's hardware store. Scattergood sat on the piazza, and as soon as the visitor was identified the male inhabitants of the village began to gather.

"Kin we talk in private?" said Mr. Siggins.

"Hain't got no need for privacy. Folks is welcome to listen to all I got to say."

Mr. Siggins frowned, but, being a politician and partially estimating the quality of his man, he did not protest.

"You beat us clever," said he.

"Calculated to," said Scattergood.

"In politics for good?"

"Calculate to be."

"What you aim to do?"

"Kind of look after the politics in Coldriver."

"Be you fur me or ag'in' me?"

"I'm fur you till my mind changes."

"How about this here Prohibition party?"

"Don't figger it's necessary after this."

"Guess we kin agree," said Siggins. "You can figger the party machinery's behind you. So fur's we're *concerned*, you're Coldriver."

"Calc'lated to be," said Scattergood.

"Some day," said Siggins, in not willing admiration, "you're goin' to run the state."

"Calc'late to," said Scattergood, and thereby rather took Mr. Siggins's breath. "Figger on makin' politics kind of a side issue to the hardware business. Find it mighty stimilatin'. Politics took in moderation, follerin' a meal of business, makes an all-fired tasty dessert.... G'-by, Siggins, g'-by."

CHAPTER IX
HE ADMINISTERS SOOTHING SYRUP

Calc'late both them young folks was guilty of an error of jedgment when they up and married each other," said Will Pratt, postmaster of Coldriver, in the judicial tone which he had affected since his elevation to office. "Mean Marthy Norton and Jed Lewis, Will? Referrin' to them especial?" Scattergood peered after the young couple who had the moment before passed his hardware store, not walking jovially in the enjoyment of each other's presence as young married folks should walk, but sullenly and in silence.

"They be the i-dentical ones," Will declared. "Naggin' and quarrelin' and bick-erin' from sunup to milkin' time. Used to do it private like, but it's been gittin' so lately you can't pass the house without hearin' 'em referrin' to each other mighty sharp and searchin'."

"Um!... Difficulty appears to be what, Will? Got any idee where lies the seat of the trouble?"

"They jest hain't habitually suited to one another," said Will. "Whatever one of 'em is fur the tother's ag'in'. Looks like they go to bed spiteful and wake up acr'monious. 'Tain't like as if Jed was the breed of feller that beats his wife, or that Marthy was the kind that looks out of the corner of her eye at drummers stoppin' to the hotel."

"Jest kind of irritate one another, eh?" said Scattergood, thoughtfully. "Kind of git on each other's nerves, you might say. Um!... I call to mind when they was married, five year ago. 'Twan't indicated them days. Jed he couldn't set easy if Marthy wasn't nigh, and Marthy went around lookin' as if she'd swallered a pin and it hurt if Jed was more 'n forty rod off. If ever two young folks was all het up over each other, Jed and Marthy was them young folks.... And 'twan't but five year ago...."

"End by separating" said the postmaster.

"There's the stage a-rattlin' in," Scattergood said, suddenly. "Better git ready f'r distributin' the mail, Will. G'-by, Will; and, Will, if 'twas me I dunno but what I'd kind of keep my mouth shet about Marthy and Jed. Outside gabblin' hain't calc'lated to help matters none. G'-by, Will."

The postmaster recognized his dismissal; he knew that the manner which had fallen upon Scattergood portended that something was on his mind and that he wanted to be alone and think, so he withdrew hastily and plodded across the dusty road to the office of which he was the executive head.

As for Scattergood, he pressed his double chin down upon his bulging chest, closed his eyes, and gave himself up enthusiastically to looking like a gigantic figure of discouragement. He waggled his head dubiously.

"Wonder if it kin be laid to my door," he said to himself. "I figgered they was about made f'r each other, and I brung 'em together.... Somethin's got crossways. Um!... Take them young folks separate, and you couldn't ask for nothin' better.... Don't understand it a mite.... Anyhow, things has turned out as they be, and what kin I do about it?"

His reinforced chair creaked under the shifting of his great weight as he bent mechanically to remove his shoes. With his toes imprisoned in leather, Scattergood's brain refused to function, a characteristic which greatly chagrined his wife, Mandy--so much so that she had considered sewing him up in his footwear, as certain mothers in the community sewed their children in their underwear for the winter.

Scattergood had amassed a fortune that might be called handsome, but it had not made him effete. His income had never warranted him in purchasing a pair of socks, so now, upon the removal of his shoepacs, his toes were fully at liberty to squirm and wriggle in the most soul-satisfying manner. He sat thus, battling with his problem, until Pliny Pickett, driver of the stage, and Scattergood's man, rattled up to the store in his dust-whitened conveyance.

"Afternoon, Scattergood," he said, in a manner which he endeavored to make as like his employer's as possible.

"Afternoon, Pliny. Successful trip, Pliny? Plenty of passengers? Eh? Any news down the valley?"

"Done middlin' well. Hain't much news, 'ceptin' that young Widder Conroy down to Tupper Falls died of somethin' the matter with her stummick and folks is wonderin' what'll become of her baby."

"Baby? What kind of a baby did she calc'late to have?"

"A he one--nigh onto two year old. Neighbors is lookin' after him."

"Got relatives?"

"Not that anybody knows of."

"Um!... Wasn't passin' Jed Lewis's house, was you?"

"Didn't figger to."

"Wasn't passin' Jed Lewis's, was you?" Scattergood repeated, insistently.

"I could."

"Um!... If you was to, and if you seen Jed, what was you figgerin' on sayin' to him?"

Pliny scratched his head and pondered.

"Calculate I'd mention the heat some, and maybe I might say suthin' about national politics."

"Wouldn't mention me, would you, Pliny? Don't figger my name might come up?"

"It might."

"If it did, what 'u'd you say, eh? Hain't no reason for mentionin' that I might want to talk to him, is there? Hain't said so, have I?"

"You hain't," said Pliny, at last enlightened as to Scattergood's desire in the matter.

"G'-by, Pliny."

"G'-by, Scattergood."

An hour later Jed Lewis sauntered past the store and stopped. "Pliny Pickett says you want to see me, Scattergood."

"Said that, did he? Told you I said I wanted to see you?"

"Wa-al, maybe not exactly. Not in so many words. But he kind of hinted around and pecked around till I figgered that was what the ol' coot was gittin' at."

"Um!... Didn't tell him nothin' of the kind, but as long's you're here you might as well set. Hain't seen much of you lately. How's the hayin'?"

"Too much rain. Got her cocked twice and had to spread her ag'in to dry."

"Hear any politics talked around, Jed?"

"Nothin' special."

Jed was brief in his answers. He seemed depressed, and conducted himself like a man who had something on his mind.

"Any fresh news from anywheres?"

"Hain't heard none."

"Hear about the Packinses down to Bailey?"

"Never heard tell of 'em." There was excellent reason for this, because no such family as the Packinses existed in Bailey or anywhere else, to Scattergood's knowledge.

"Goin' to separate," said Scattergood.

Jed looked up quickly, bit his lip, and looked down again.

"What fur?" he asked.

"Nobody kin figger out. Jest agreein' to disagree. Can't git along, nohow. Always naggin' at each other and squabblin' and hectorin'.... Nice young folks, too. Used to set a heap of store by one another. Can't figger how they come to disagree like they do!"

"Nobody kin figger it out," said Jed, with sudden vehemence. "All to once you wake up and things is that way, and you dunno how they come to be. It jest drifts along. Fust you know things has went all to smash."

"Um!... You talk like you knowed somethin' about it."

"Nobody knows more," said the young man, bitterly. He was suddenly conscious that he wanted to talk about his domestic affairs; that he wanted to loose the story of his troubles and dwell upon them in all their ramifications.

"Do tell," said Scattergood, with an inflection of astonishment.

"Marthy and me has about come to the partin' of our roads," said Jed. "It's come gradual, without our noticin' it, but it's here at last. Seems like we can't bear the sight of each other--when we git together. And yit--sounds mighty funny, too--I calc'late to be as fond of Marthy as ever I was. But the minute we git together we bicker and quarrel till there hain't no pleasure into life at all."

"All Marthy's fault, hain't it? Kind of a mean disposition, hain't she?"

"No sich thing, Scattergood, and you know it dum well. There didn't use to be a sweeter-dispositioned girl in the state than Marthy.... Somethin's jest went wrong.

They's times when I git mad and it all looks to be her fault, and then I ketch my own self startin' some hectorin' meanness. 'Tain't all her fault, and 'tain't all my fault. The whole sum and substance of it is that we can't git along with each other no more."

"So you calc'late to separate?"

"Been talkin' it up some."

"Marthy willin'?"

"Hain't neither of us willin'. We fix it up and agree to try over ag'in, and then, fust thing we know, we're right into the middle of another squabble. I want Marthy, and I guess Marthy wants me, but we want each other like we was five year back and not like we be now."

"Been married five year, hain't you?"

"Five year last April."

"Um!... Wa-al, I hope nothin' comes of it, Jed. But if it has to it will. Better live happy separate than unhappy together.... G'-by, Jed."

Scattergood did not discuss this problem with Mandy, his wife, as it was his custom to discuss business problems. He did not mention the young Lewises because the first rule of Mandy's life was "Mind your own business," and it irritated her beyond measure to see Scattergood poking his finger into every dish that offered. He did talk the matter over with Deacon Pettybone, but got little enlightenment for his pains.

"Don't seem natteral," Scattergood said, "f'r young folks to git to quarrelin' and bickerin' ontil life hain't endurable no longer. 'Tain't natteral a-tall. Somethin' must be all-fired wrong somewheres."

"It's human nature to quarrel," said the deacon, gloomily. "Nothin' onusual about it."

"Human nature," said Scattergood, "gits blamed f'r a heap of things that ought to be laid at the door of human cussedness."

"Same thing," said the deacon. "If you're human you're cussed. Used to be so in the Garden of Eden, and it'll keep on bein' so till Gabriel blows his final trump."

"'Tain't no more natteral to bicker than 'tis to have dispepsy. Quarrelin' and hectorin' hain't nothin' but a kind of dispepsy that attacks families instid of stummicks. In both cases it means somethin' is wrong."

"Can't cure a unhappy family with a dose of calomel," said the deacon, acidly.

"Hain't so sure. Bet that identical remedy' u'd fix up three out of ten. But somethin' else is wrong with them young Lewises. A dose of somethin' 'u'd cure 'em, if only a feller could figger out what 'twas."

"Might try soothin' syrup," said the deacon, with an ironic grin. "Sounds like it ought to git results.... Soothin' syrup--eh? Have to tell the boys that one. Soothin' syrup. Perty good f'r an old man. Don't call to mind makin' no joke like that f'r twenty year."

"Do it often, Deacon," said Scattergood, gravely. "You won't have to take so much sody followin' meals to sweeten you up.... G'-by, Deacon.... Soothin' syrup. Um!... I swanny...."

He looked across the square and saw that Pliny Pickett was delighting an audience with apochryphal reminiscences, doubtless of a gallant and spicy character. It is characteristic of Scattergood that he waited until Pliny had reached his climax, shot it off, and was doubled up with laughter at his own narration, before he lifted up his voice and summoned the stage driver.

"Hey, Pliny! Step over here a minute."

"Comin'," said Pliny, with alacrity. Then in an aside to his audience: "See that? Can't let an evenin' pass without a conference with me. Sets a heap of store by my judgment."

"Sets more store by your laigs," said Old Man Bogle. "They kin run errants, anyhow."

Pliny hastened across the square, and in careful imitation of Scattergood said, "Evening Scattergood."

"Evening Pliny. Flow of language good as usual to-night? Didn't meet with no trouble sayin' what you had to say?"

"Not a mite, Scattergood."

"Come through Bailey to-day?"

"Calculated to."

"Any news?"

"Nary."

"What's become of that What's-his-name baby you was a-tellin' about? The one that lost his ma and was bein' cared for by neighbors?"

"Nothin' hain't become of him. Calc'late he'll be took to a institution."

"Um! Likely-lookin' two-year-old, was he? Take note of any blemishes?"

"I hear tell by them that knows as how he was sound in wind and limb."

"Who's keepin' him, Pliny?"

"Mis' Patterson's sort of shuffled him in with her seven. Says she don't notice no difference to speak of. Claims 'tain't possible f'r eight childern to be no noisier 'n what seven be."

"Um!... G'-by, Pliny. Ever deal in facts over there to the post office? Ever have occasion to mention facts?"

"Er--not reg'lar facts, Scattergood. You needn't to worry about my talkin' too free."

"Seems like a feller that talks as much as you do would have to mention a fact once in a while. G'-by, Pliny."

It was two or three days later that Postmaster Pratt alluded again to Martha and Jed Lewis.

"They're gittin' wuss and wuss," he said, with some gratification. "Last night they was a rumpus you could 'a' heard forty mile. Ended up by him threatenin' to leave her, and by her tellin' him that if he didn't she'd lock him out of the house. Looks to me like that family fracas was about ripe to bust."

"Signs all p'int that way, Will. Too bad, hain't it? There's a reason f'r it, I calculate. Ever look f'r the reason, Will? Ever think about it at all?"

"Hain't had no time. Post office keeps me thinkin' night and day."

"Well, I have. Figgered a heap."

"Any results, Scattergood?"

"Some--some."

"What be they?"

Scattergood's eyes twinkled in the darkness. "I got it all figgered out," he said, "that them young folks needs a dose of soothin' syrup."

"I want to know," said the postmaster, breathlessly and with bewilderment. "Soothin' syrup! I swan to man!... Hain't been out in the heat, have you, Scattergood?"

Scattergood made no reply to this question. He merely waggled his head and said: "G'-by, Will. G'-by."

Next morning Scattergood walked past the Lewis place. He passed it three times before he made up his mind whether to go in or not, but finally he turned through the gate and walked around to the kitchen door. Inside he saw Martha ridding up the kitchen, not with a morning song on her lips, but wearing a sullen expression which sat ill on her fine New England face.

"Mornin', Marthy," he called.

She looked up and smiled suddenly. The change in her face was astonishing.

"Mornin', Mr. Baines. Set right down on the porch. ... Let me fetch you a hot cup of coffee. 'Twon't take but a minute to make."

"Can't stop," said Scattergood. "I was lookin' for Jed."

"Jed's gone," she replied, shortly, the sullen expression returning to her face. "'He won't be back 'fore noon."

"Uh-huh!... Wa-al, I calc'late I kin keep on drawin' my breath till then--if you kin. I call to mind the time when you was all-fired oneasy if Jed got away from you for six hours in a stretch."

"Them times is gone," she said, shortly.

"Shucks!" said Scattergood.

"They be," she said, fiercely. "Hain't no use tryin' to hide it. Jed and me is about through. Nothin' but fussin' and backbitin' and maneuvering'. He don't care f'r me no more like he used to, and--"

"You don't set sich a heap of store by him," Scattergood interrupted.

Martha hesitated. "I do," she said, slowly. "But I can't put up with it no more."

"Jed's fault--mostly," said Scattergood, as one speaks who utters an accepted fact.

"No more 'n mine," she said, with a sudden flash. "I dunno what's got into us, Mr. Baines, but we no sooner git into the same room than it commences. 'Tain't nobody's fault--it jest is ."

"Um!... Kinder like to have things the way they used to be?"

"Oh, Mr. Baines!" Her eyes filled. "Them first two-three years! Jed was the best man a woman ever had."

"Hain't drinkin', is he?"

"Never touches a drop."

"Jest his nasty temper," said Scattergood, casually.

"No sich thing…. It's jest happened so. We can't git on, and I'm through tryin'. One of us is gain' to git out of this house. I've made up my mind." She started untying her apron. "I'm a-goin' right now. It'll be off'n my mind then, and I kin sort of git a fresh start. I'm goin' right now and pack."

"Kind of hasty, hain't you?… Now, Marthy, as a special favor to me I wish you'd stay, maybe two days more. I got a special reason. If you was to go this mornin' it 'u'd upset my plans. After Sattidy you kin do as you like, and maybe it's best you should part. But I do wisht you could see your way to stayin' till Sattidy."

"I don't see why, Mr. Baines, but if it'll be any good to you, I'll do it. But not a minute after Sattidy--now mind that!"

"Much 'bleeged, Marthy. G'-by, Marthy. G'-by."

On Friday Scattergood was invisible in Coldriver village, for he had started away before dawn, driving his sway-backed horse over the mountain roads to the southward. He notified nobody of his going, unless it was Mandy, his wife, and even to her he did not make apparent his errand.

Before noon he was in Bailey and stopping before the small white house in which Mrs. Patterson managed by ingenuity to fit in a husband, a mother-in-law, an aged father, seven children of her own, the Conroy orphan, and a constantly changing number of cats. Nobody could have done it but Mrs. Patterson. The house resembled one of those puzzle boxes containing a number of curiously sawn pieces of wood, which, once removed, can be returned and fitted into place again only by some one who knows the secret.

Scattergood entered the house, remained upward of an hour, and then reappeared, followed by Mrs. Patterson, seven children, an old man, and an old woman-and in his arms was a baby whose lungs gave promise of a healthy manhood.

"Do this much, does he?" Scattergood asked, uneasily.

"Not more 'n most," said Mrs. Patterson.

"Um!… If he lets on to be hungry, what's the best thing to feed him up on? I got a bag of doughnuts and five-six sandriches and nigh on to half a apple pie in the buggy."

"Feed him them," said Mrs. Patterson, "and you'll be like to hear some real yellin'. What he's doin' now hain't nothin' but his objectin' to you a-carryin' him like he was a horse blanket…. You wait right there till I git a bottle of milk. And I'll fix you some sugar in a rag that you kin put into his mouth if he acts uneasy. It'll quiet him right off."

"Much 'bleeged. Hain't had much experience with young uns. Might's well start now. Bet me 'n this here one gits well acquainted 'fore we reach Coldriver."

"'Twouldn't s'prise me a mite," replied Mrs. Patterson, with something that might have been a twinkle in her tired eyes. "I almost feel I should go along with you."

"G'-by, Mrs. Patterson," said Scattergood, hastily, and he climbed into his buggy clumsily, placing the baby on the seat beside him, and holding it in place with his left arm. "G'-by."

The buggy rattled off. The baby hushed suddenly and began to look at the horse.

"Kind of come to your senses, eh?" said Scattergood. "Now you and me's goin' to git on fine if you jest keep your mouth shet. If you behave yourself proper I dunno but what I kin find a stick of candy f'r you when we git there."

Presently Scattergood looked down to find the baby asleep. He drove slowly and cautiously, whispering what commands he felt were indispensable to his horse. This delightful situation continued for upward of two hours, and Scattergood said to himself that folks who bothered about traveling with infants must be very easily worried.

"Jest as soon ride with this one clean to the Pacific coast," he said.

And then the baby awoke. It blinked and looked about it; it rubbed its eyes; it stared severely up at Scattergood; it opened its mouth tentatively, closed it again, and then--and then it uttered such an ear-piercing, long-drawn shriek that the old horse jumped with fright.

"Hey, there!" said the startled Scattergood. "Hey! what's ailin' you now?"

The baby closed his eyes, clenched his fists, kicked out with his legs, and gave himself up whole-heartedly to the exercise of his voice.

"Quit that," said Scattergood. "Now listen here; that hain't no way to behave. You won't git that candy--"

Louder and more piercing arose the baby's cries. Scattergood dropped the reins, lifted the baby to his knee, and jounced it up and down furiously, performing an act which he imagined to be singing, a thing he had heard was interesting and soothing to babies. It did not even attract this one's attention.

"Sufferin' heathen!" Scattergood said. "What in tunket was it that woman said I sh'u'd do? Hain't they no way of shuttin' him off? Look-ee here, young feller, you jest quit it.... B'jing! here's my watch. You kin listen to it tick."

The baby tried the watch on his toothless gums, found it not to his taste, and flung it from him with such vehemence that it would have suffered permanent injury but for the size and strength of the silver chain which attached it to Scattergood. The cries became more maddening. Scattergood was not hungry, so it did not occur to him that the infant might be thinking of food. He dandled it, he whistled, he sang, he pointed out the interesting attributes of his horse, and promised to direct attention to a rabbit or even a deer in a moment, but nothing availed. Perspiration was pouring down Scattergood's face, and his expression was that of a man who devoutly wishes he were far otherwise than he is.

Half an hour of this seemed to Scattergood like the length of a sizable day--and then he remembered the milk. Frantically he fished it out of the basket and thrust it toward the young person, who did with it what seemed right to him, and, with a gurgle of satisfaction, settled down to business. Scattergood sighed, wiped his forehead, and revised his opinion of folks who were worried at the prospect of travel with an infant.

The rest of that drive was a nightmare to Scattergood. When the baby yelled he was in torment. When the baby slept he was in torment lest he wake it, so that it would commence again to cry. He sweat cold and he sweat hot, and he wished wishes in his secret heart and blamed himself for many things--chief of which was that he had not brought Mandy along to bear the brunt of the adventure.

But at last, long after nightfall, with baby fast asleep, Scattergood drove into Coldriver by deserted and circuitous roads. He stopped his horse in a dark spot on the edge of the village, and, with the baby cautiously held in his arms, he slunk through back ways and short cuts to the house where Jed and Martha Lewis made their home. With meticulous stealth he passed through the gate, laid the baby on the doorstep, rang the bell long and determinedly, and then, with astonishing quiet and agility, hid himself in the midst of a clump of lilacs.

The door opened, and a light shone through upon the squirming bundle that lay upon the step. A tentative cry issued from the baby; a bass exclamation issued from Jed Lewis. "My Gawd! Marthy, somebody's left a baby here!"

Martha pushed past her husband and lifted the baby in her arms. She said no word, but Scattergood could see her press it close, and, in the light that came through the door, could see the expression of her face. It satisfied him.

"What we goin' to do with the doggone thing?" Jed demanded.

Martha pushed past him into the house, and he followed, wordless, closing the door after them.... Scattergood remained for some time, and then slunk away....

Postmaster Pratt gave the news to Scattergood in the morning.

"Somebody went and left a baby on to Jed Lewis's stoop last night," he declared. "Hain't nobody been able to identify it. Nary a mark nor a sign on to it no place. ... Whatever possessed anybody to leave a baby there of all places?"

"I want to know!" exclaimed Scattergood. "Girl er boy?"

"Boy, I'm told."

"What's Jed say?"

"Hain't sayin' much. Jest sets and kind of hangs on to his head, and every once in a while he gits up and looks at the baby and then goes back to holdin' his head."

"How about Marthy?"

"Marthy," said Postmaster Pratt. "I can't make out about Marthy, but I heard her a-singin' this mornin' 'fore breakfast. Fust time I heard her sing for more 'n a year."

"Might 'a' been singin' to the baby," Scattergood suggested.

"Naw, it was while she was gittin' breakfast. Jest the time she and Jed quarrels most powerful."

During the day all of Coldriver called to see the mysterious infant. Nobody could give a clue to its identity, and it was decided unanimously that it had been brought from a distance. As to the intentions of the Lewises regarding its disposition, they were noncommittal. It was universally accepted as fact, however, that the baby would be sent to an institution.

Thereupon Scattergood called upon the First Selectman.

"What's the town goin' to do about that baby?" he demanded. "Taxpayers'll be wantin' to know. Seems like the town's liable f'r its support."

"Calculate we be.... Calculate we be. I been figgerin' on what steps to take."

"Better go across to Jed's and notify 'em," said Scattergood. "They'll be expectin' you to take action prompt. I'll go 'long with you."

They walked down the street and rapped at the Lewises' door.

"Come on official business," said the First Selectman, pompously, to Jed, "connected with that there foundlin'."

Martha came hastily into the room. "What you want?" she demanded, in a dangerous voice.

"Come to tell you we would take that baby off'n your hands and send it to a institution. Git it ready, and we'll take it to-morrer."

"Take that baby!... Did you hear him, Jed Lewis? Did you hear that man say as how he was goin' to take away my baby?" She stumbled across the room to Jed and clutched the lapels of his coat. Scattergood noticed with some pleasure that Jed's arm went automatically about her waist. "Make 'em git out, Jed. Tell 'em they can't take this baby.... You want we should keep it, don't you, Jed?... We wanted one. You know how we wanted one.... You're goin' to let us keep it, hain't you, Jed?"

Jed put Martha aside gently and walked over to a makeshift crib in the corner, where the baby was asleep, where he stood for a moment looking down at it with a curious expression. Then he turned suddenly, strode to the door, opened it, and pointed. "Git!" he said to the First Selectman and Scattergood.

"Jed ... Jed ... darlin'," Martha cried, and as Scattergood passed out he saw from the corner of his eye that she was sobbing on her husband's hickory shirt and that he was patting her back with awkward gentleness.

"Looked a mite like Jed wanted we should go," said Scattergood.

"I'll have the law on to him. He'll be showed that he can't stand up to the First Selectman of this here town, I'll--"

"You'll go home and set down in the shade and cool off," said Scattergood, merrily, "and while you're a-coolin' you might sort of thank Gawd that there's sich things as human bein's with human feelin's, and that there's sich things as babies ...that sometimes gits themselves left on the right doorstep.... G'-by, Selectman. G'-by."

A week later Scattergood was passing the Lewis home early in the evening. In the side yard was a hammock under the trees which had been unoccupied this year past, but to-night it was occupied again. Martha was there with the baby against her breast, and Jed was there, his arm tightly about his wife, and one of the baby's hands lying on his calloused palm…. As Scattergood watched he saw Jed bend clumsily and kiss the tiny fingers … and Martha turned a trifle and smiled up into her husband's eyes.

Scattergood passed on, blinking, perhaps because dust had gotten in his eyes. He stopped at the post office and spoke to Postmaster Pratt.

"Call to mind my speakin' of soothin' syrup and Jed Lewis and his wife?" he asked.

"Seems like I mind it, Scattergood."

"Jest walk past their house, Postmaster. Calc'late you'll see I figgered clost to right…. Marthy's a-sittin' there with Jed in the hammick, and they're a-holdin' on their lap the doggondest best soothin' syrup f'r man and wife that any doctor c'u'd perscribe…. Calculate it's one of them nature's remedies…. Go take a look, Postmaster…. G'-by."

CHAPTER X
HE HELPS WITH THE ROUGH WORK

Scattergood Baines, as he sat with shirt open at the throat, his huge body sagged down in the chair that had been especially reinforced to sustain his weight, seemed to passing Coldriver village to be drowsing. Many people suspected Scattergood of drowsing when he was exceedingly wide awake and observant of events. It was part of his stock in trade.

At this moment he was looking across the square toward the post office. A large, broad-shouldered young man, with hair sun-bleached to a ruddy yellow, had alighted from a buggy and entered the office. He was a fine, bulky, upstanding farmer, built for enduring much hard labor in times of peace and for performing feats of arms in time of war. He looked like a fighter; he was a fighter--a willing fighter, and folks up and down the valley stepped aside if it was noised about that Abner Levens had broken loose. It was not that Abner delighted in the fruit of the vine nor the essence of the maize; he was a teetotaler. But it did seem as if nature had overdone the matter of providing him with the machinery for creating energy and had overlooked the safety valve. Wherefore Abner, once or twice a year, lost his temper.

Now, losing his temper was not for Abner a matter of uttering a couple of oaths and of wrapping a hoe handle around a tree. He lost his temper thoroughly and seemed unable to locate it again for days. He rampaged. He roared up and down the valley, inviting one and all to step up and be demolished, which the inhabitants were very reluctant to do, for Abner worked upon his victims with thoroughness and enthusiasm.

When Abner was in his normal humor he was a jovial, noisily jovial young man, who would dance with the girls until the cock tired of crowing; who would give a day's work to a friend; who performed his civic and religious duties punctiliously, if gayly; who was honest to the fraction of a penny; and who would have been the most popular and admired youth in the valley among the maidens of the valley had it not been for their constant, uneasy fear that he might suddenly turn Berserk.

It was this young man whom Scattergood eyed thoughtfully, and, one might say, apprehensively, for Scattergood liked the youth and feared the germs of disaster that lay quiescent in his powerful body.

Pliny Pickett lounged past, stopped, eyed Scattergood, and seated himself on the step.

"Abner Levens 's in town," he said.

"Seen him," answered Scattergood.

"Calc'late Asa'll be in?"

"Bein' 's it's Sattidy night, 'most likely he'll come."

"Hope Abner's feelin' friendly, then," said Pliny with an anticipatory twinkle in his shrewd little gray eyes which gave direct contradiction to his words. "If Abner hain't feelin' jest cheerful them boys'll be wrastlin' all over town and pushin' down houses."

"They hain't never fit yet," said Scattergood.

"Nor won't if Asa has the say of it.... He's full as big as Abner, too. Otherwise they don't resemble twins none."

"Hain't much brotherly feelin' betwixt 'em."

"I hain't clear as to the rights of the matter," said Pliny, "but they hain't nothin' like a will dispute to make bad blood betwixt relatives.... Asa got the best of that argument, anyhow. Don't seem fair, exactly, is my opinion, that Old Man Levens should up and discriminate betwixt them boys like he did--givin' Asa a hog's share."

"Dunno's I'd worry sich a heap about that," said Scattergood, "if they hadn't both got het up about the same gal. Looks to me like one or tother of 'em took up with that gal jest to make mischief.... Seems like Abner was settin' out with her fust."

"Some says both ways. I dunno," said Pliny, impartially. "Anyhow, Abner he lets on public and constant that he's a-goin' to nail Asa's hide to the barn door.... It's one good, healthy hate betwixt them boys."

"And trouble'll come of it.... Wonder which of 'em Mary Ware favors? If she favors either of 'em, and trouble comes, it'll mix her in."

"Hope Abner gits him. Better for her, says I, to take up with a man like Ab, that's a good feller fifty weeks out of the year, and goes on a tear two weeks, than to be married to a cuss like Asa that jest goes along sort of gloomy and still and seekin'. I hain't never heard Asa laugh with no real enjoyment into it yet. He grins and shows his teeth. He's too dum quiet, and always acts like a feller that's afraid you'll find out what he's got in mind."

"Um!..." said Scattergood.

"Mary's about the pertiest girl in Coldriver," said Pliny. "Dunno but what she could handle Abner all right, too. Call to mind the firemen's picnic last year when she went with Abner, and he busted loose on that feller with the three shells and the leetle ball?"

"When the feller had robbed Half-wit Stenens of nigh on to twenty dollars? I call to mind."

"Abner was jest on the p'int of separatin' that feller into chunks and dispersin' the chunks over the county when Mary she steps up and puts her hand en his arm, and says, 'Abner!' ... Jest like that she said it, quiet and gentle, but firm. Abner he let loose of the feller and turned to look at her, and in a minute all the fight went out of his face and his eyes like somebody had drained it off. He kind of blushed and hung his head, and walked away with her.... She didn't tongue-lash him, neither, jest kept a-touchin' his arm so's he wouldn't forgit she was there."

"Um!..." said Scattergood. "Here comes Asa." He lifted himself from his creaking chair and started across the bridge. "If it's a-comin' off," he said to Pliny, "I want to git where I kin git a good view."

In the post office the twin brothers came face to face. Scattergood saw Abner's thin lips twist in a provocative sneer. Abner halted suddenly, at arm's length from his brother, and eyed him from head to foot, and Asa returned an insolent stare.

"You sneakin' hound," said Abner, without heat, as was his way in the beginning, always. "You're lower'n I thought, and I thought you was low." Scattergood took in these words and pondered them. Did they mean some new cause for enmity between the brothers? Suddenly Abner's eyes began to kindle and to blaze. Asa crouched and his teeth showed in a saturnine, crooked smile. No man could look upon him and accuse him of being afraid of Abner or of avoiding the issue.

"I know what you've been up to, you slinkin' varmint ... I know where you was Tuesday." Scattergood took possession of this sentence and placed it in the safety-deposit box of his memory. Where had Asa been Tuesday, he wondered, and what had Asa been doing there?

"I've put up with a heap from you, for you're my own flesh and blood. I hain't never laid a hand on you, though I've threatened it often. But now! by Gawd, I'm goin' to take you apart so's nobody kin put you together ag'in ... you mis'able, cheatin', low-down, crawlin' snake." With that he stepped back a pace and with his open palm struck Asa across the mouth.

Asa licked his lips and continued to smile his crooked, saturnine smile.

"Hain't scarcely room in here," he said, softly.

"Git outside and take off your coat," said Abner, "for I'm goin' to fix you so's nobody kin ever accuse flesh and blood of mine of doin' agin what I've ketched you doin'."

"What's gnawin' you," said Asa, softly, "is that I got the best farm and that I'm a-goin' to git your girl."

There was a stark pause. Abner stiffened, grew tense, as one becomes at the moment of bursting into dynamic action, but he did not stir. Scattergood was surprised, but he was more surprised by Abner's next words. "I hain't goin' to half kill you on account of your lyin' to father, nor on account of her--it's on account of her." The sentence seemed without sense or meaning, but Scattergood placed it with his other collected sentences; he did not perceive its meaning, but he did perceive that the first 'her' and the second 'her' were pronounced so that they became different words, like names, indicating, identifying, different persons. That was Scattergood's notion.

Asa turned on his heel and walked into the square, removing his coat as he went; Abner followed. They faced each other, crouching. Abner's face depicting wrath, Asa's depicting hatred.... Before a blow was struck, a girl, tall, slender, deep-bosomed, fit mate for a man of might, pushed through the circle of spectators. Her face was pale and distressed, but very lovely. Her brown eyes were dark with the emotion of the moment, and a wisp of wavy brown hair lay unnoticed upon her broad forehead.... She walked to Abner's side and touched his arm.

"Abner!" she said, gently.

He turned his blazing eyes upon her. "Not this time" he said. "Go away, Mary." Even in his rage he spoke to her in a voice of reverence.

"Abner!" she repeated.

He turned to his brother. "You get off this time," he said, evenly, "but there will be another time.... Asa, I think I am going to kill you...."

Asa laughed mockingly, and Abner took a threatening step toward him, but Mary touched his arm again. "Abner!" she said once more; and obediently as some well-trained mastiff he followed her through the gaping ring, she still touching his arm, and together they walked slowly up the road.

Two days later, about eight o'clock in the morning, Sheriff Ulysses Watts bustled down the street wearing his official, rather than his common, or meat-wagon, air. He paused, to speak excitedly to Scattergood, who sat as usual on the piazza of his hardware store.

"They've jest found Asa Levens's body," he ejaculated. "A-layin' clost to the road it was, with a bullet through the head. Clear case of murder.... I'm gatherin' a posse to fetch in the murderer."

"Murderer's known, is he?" said Scattergood, leaning forward, and eying the sheriff.

"Abner, of course. Who else would 'a' done it? Hain't he been a-threatenin' right along?"

"Anybody see him fire the shot, Sheriff? Any witnesses?"

"Nary witness. Nothin' but the body a-layin' where it fell."

"What was the manner of this shootin', Sheriff?"

"All I know's what I've told you."

"Gatherin' a posse, Ulysses? Who be you selectin'?"

"Various and sundry," said the sheriff.

"Any objection to deputizin' me?" said Scattergood. "Any notion I might help some?"

"Glad to have you, Scattergood.... Got to hustle. Most likely the murderer's escapin' this minute."

"Um!..." said Scattergood. "Need any catridges or anythin' in the hardware line,

Sheriff? Figgerin' on goin' armed, hain't you?"

"Dunno but what the boys'll need somethin'. You keep open till I gather 'em here."

"I carry the most reliable line of catridges in the state," said Scattergood. "Prices low.... I'll be waitin', Sheriff."

In twenty minutes a dozen citizens of the vicinage gathered at Scattergood's store, each armed with his favorite weapon, rifle or double-barreled shotgun, and each wearing what he fancied to be the air of a dangerous and resolute citizen.

"Calc'late he'll be desprit," said Jed Lewis. "He won't be took without a fight."

It was characteristic of Scattergood that he delayed the setting out of the posse until, by his peculiar methods of salesmanship, he had pressed upon various members lethal merchandise to a value of upward of twenty dollars. This being done, they entered a big picnic wagon with parallel seats and set out for the scene of the crime. Coroner Bogle demanded that the body should be viewed officially before the man-hunt should begin. Scattergood threw the weight of his opinion with the coroner.

The body was found lying beside a narrow path leading from the road through a field to Asa Levens's farmhouse; it lay upon its face, with arms outstretched, very still and very peaceful, with the morning sun shining down upon it, and the robins singing from shadowing trees, and insects buzzing and whirring cheerfully in the fields, and the fields themselves peaceful and beautiful in their golden embellishments, ready for the harvest. Scattergood looked about him at the trappings of the day, and the thought came unbidden that it was a pleasant spot in which to die ... perhaps more pleasant than the dead man deserved.

"Shot from behind." said the sheriff.

"By somebody a-layin' in wait," said Jed Lewis.

"It was murder--cold-blooded murder," said the sheriff.

Scattergood stepped forward as the coroner turned the face up to the light of the sun.

"It was a death by violence," said Scattergood. "It may be murder.... Asa Levens wears, as he lies, the face of a man who troubled God...."

There was none in that little group to comprehend his meaning.

"There was no struggle," said the coroner.

"He never knowed he was shot," said Jed Lewis.

"Be you still a-goin' to arrest Abner Levens?" Scattergood asked.

"To be sure. He done it, didn't he? Who else would 'a' killed Asa?"

"Who else?" said Scattergood, solemnly.

They raised Asa Levens and carried him to his house. Having left him in proper custody, the posse re-entered its picnic van and drove with no small trepidation toward Abner Levens's farm, a mile away. Abner Levens was perceived from a distance, hoeing in a field.

"He's goin' to face it out," said the sheriff; "or maybe he wasn't expectin' Asa to be found yet."

The picnic van stopped beside the field and the armed posse scrambled out, holding its weapons threateningly; but as Abner was armed with nothing more lethal than a hoe there was some appearance of embarrassment among them, and more than one man endeavored to make his shooting iron invisible by dropping it in the long grass.

"Come on," said the sheriff, and in a body the posse advanced across the field toward Abner, who leaned upon his hoe and waited for them. "Abner Levens," said the sheriff, in a voice which was not of the steadiest, "I arrest you for murder."

Abner looked at the sheriff; Abner looked from one to another of the posse in silence. It seemed as if he were not going to speak, but at last he did speak.

"Then Asa Levens is dead," he said.

It was not a question; it was a statement, made with conviction. Scattergood Baines noted that Abner called his brother by name as if desiring to avoid the matter of blood kindred; that he made no denial.

"You know it better than anybody," said the sheriff.

Abner looked past the sheriff, over the uneven fields, with their rock fences, and beyond to the green slopes of the mountains as they upreared distinct, majestic, imposing in their serene permanence against the undimmed summer sky.

"Asa Levens is dead," said Abner, presently. "Now I know that God is not infinite in everything.... His patience is not infinite."

"It's my duty to warn you that anythin' you say kin be used ag'in' you," said the sheriff. "Be you comin' along peaceable?"

"I'm comin' peaceable," said Abner. "If God's satisfied--I be."

Abner Levens was locked in the unreliable jail of Coldriver village, and a watch placed over him. Those who saw him marveled at his demeanor; Scattergood Baines marveled at it, for it was not the demeanor of a man--even of an innocent man-- accused of a crime for which the penalty was death. Abner sat upon the hard bench and looked quietly, even placidly, out at the brightness of day, as it was apparent beyond flimsy iron bars, and his expression was the expression of contentment.

He had not demanded the benefit of legal guidance; he had neither affirmed nor denied his guilt; indeed, he had uttered no word since the door of the jail had closed behind him.

Mary Ware spoke to the young man through the window of the jail in full view of all Coldriver.

"You didn't do it, Abner. I know you didn't do it," she said, so that all might hear, "and if you still want me, Abner, like you said, I'll stick by you through thick and thin."

"Thank ye, Mary," Abner replied. "Now I guess you better go away."

"What shall I do, Abner--to help you?"

"Nothing Mary. Looks like God's took aholt of matters. Better let him finish 'em in his own way."

That was all; neither Mary Ware nor any other could get more out of him, and it was said by many to be a confession of guilt.

"Realizes there hain't no use makin' a defense. Calc'lates on takin' his medicine like a man," said Postmaster Pratt.... There were those in town who voiced the wish that it had been some other than Abner who had killed Asa Levens. "His gun's been shot recent," said the sheriff. It was the final gram of evidence necessary to complete assurance of Abner's guilt.

Mary Ware was observed by many to walk directly from the jail window to Scattergood Baines's hardware store, and there to stop and address Scattergood, who sat barefooted, and therefore in deep thought, before the door of his place of business.

"Mr. Baines," said Mary, "you've helped other folks. Will you help me?"

"Help you how, Mary? What kin I do for you?"

"Abner isn't guilty, Mr. Baines"

"Tell you so?... Abner tell you so?"

"No."

"Um!... 'F he was innocent, wouldn't he deny it, Mary?" He did not permit her to reply, but asked another question. "What makes you say he hain't guilty, Mary?"

"Because I know it," she replied, simply.

"How do you know it, Mary? It's mighty hard to know ***anythin' on earth. How d'you*** know?"

"Because I know," said Mary.

"'Twon't convince no jury."

Mary stood in silence for a moment, and then turned away, not tearful, not despairing.

"Hold your hosses," said Scattergood. "Kin you think of anythin' that might convince a stranger that Abner is innocent?"

Mary considered. "Asa was shot," she said.

Scattergood nodded.

"From behind," said Mary.

Scattergood nodded again.

"Asa never knew who shot him," said Mary, and again Scattergood moved his head. "If Abner had killed Asa," she went on, "he would have done it with his hands. He would have wanted Asa to know who was killing him."

"Might convince them that knows Abner," said Scattergood, "but the jury'll be strangers." He paused, and asked, suddenly, "Why did you let Asa Levens come to court you?"

"Because I hated him," said Mary.

"Um!... Abner say anythin' to you?"

"He said God had taken hold of matters and we'd better let him finish them."

"When God takes holt of human affairs he mostly uses human bein's to do the rough work," said Scattergood.

"Abner's innocent," said Mary, stubbornly.

"Mebby so.... Mebby so."

"Will you help me clear him, Mr. Baines?"

"I'll help you find out the truth, Mary, if that'll keep you satisfied. Calculate I'd like to know the truth myself. Had a look at Asa's face a-layin' there by the road, and it interested me."

"Did you see that?" Mary asked, with sudden excitement.

"What?" asked Scattergood, curiously.

"The mark.... Sometimes it showed plain. It was a mark put on Asa Levens's face as a warning to folks that God mistrusted him."

"When he was dead it was different," said Scattergood, with solemnity. "It said he had r'iled God past endurance."

Mary nodded. She comprehended. "The truth will do," she said, confidently.

"Did Abner mention last Tuesday to you?" Scattergood asked.

"No."

"Where was Asa Levens last Tuesday? Do you know, Mary?"

"No."

"Why did Abner say to Asa yesterday, 'It's not on account of her, it's on account of *her*'?"

"I don't know."

"G'-by, Mary. G'-by." It was so Scattergood always ended a conversation, abruptly, but as one became accustomed to it it was neither abrupt nor discourteous.

"Thank you," said Mary, and she went away obediently.

As the afternoon was stretching toward evening, Scattergood sauntered into Sheriff Ulysses Watts's barn.

"Who's feedin' and waterin' Asa Levens's stock?" he asked.

"Dummed if I didn't clean forgit 'em," confessed the sheriff.

"Any objection if I look after 'em, Sheriff? Any logical objection? Hoss might need exercisin'. Can't never tell. Want I should drive up and do what's needed to be done?"

"Be much 'bleeged," said Sheriff Watts.

Scattergood drove briskly to Asa Levens's farm, watered and fed the stock, and then led out of its stall Asa Levens's favorite driving mare. He hitched it to Asa Levens's buggy and mounted to the seat. "Giddap," he said to the mare, and dropped the reins on her back. She started out of the gate and turned toward town. Scattergood let the reins lie, attempting no guidance. At the next four corners the mare hesitated, slowed, and, feeling no direction from her driver, turned to the left. Scattergood nodded his head.

The mare trotted on, following the slowly lifting mountain road for a matter of two miles, and then turned again down a highway that was little more than a tote road. Half a mile later she stopped with her nose against the fence of a shabby farmhouse, and sagged down, as is the custom of horses when they realize they are at their destination and have a rest of duration before them. Scattergood alighted and fastened her to the fence.

As he swung open the gate a middle-aged man appeared in the door of the house, and over his shoulder Scattergood could see the white face of a woman-- staring.

"Evening Jed," said Scattergood. "Evening Mis' Briggs."

"Howdy, Mr. Baines? Wa'n't expectin' to see you. What fetches you this fur off'n the road?"

"Sort of got here by accident, you might say. Didn't come of my own free will, seems as though. Kind of tired, Jed. Mind if I set a spell?... How's the cannin', Mis' Briggs?"

"Done up thutty quarts to-day, Mr. Baines," said the young woman, who was Jed Briggs's wife, a woman fifteen years his junior, comely, desirable, vivid.

"Um!... Got a hoss out here. Want you should both come and look her over." He raised himself to his feet, and was followed by Jed Briggs and his wife to the fence.

"Likely mare," said Scattergood, blandly.

Startlingly Mrs. Briggs laughed, shrilly, unpleasantly, as a woman laughs in great fear.

"Gawd!" said Jed Briggs, "it's--"

"Yes," said Scattergood, gently. "It's Asa Levens's mare. Was she here last Tuesday?"

"She was here Tuesday, Scattergood Baines," said Jed Briggs. "What's the meanin' of this?"

"I knowed she was somewheres Tuesday," Scattergood said, impersonally. "Didn't know where, but I mistrusted she'd been to that place frequent. Jest got in and give her her head. She brought me.... Asa Levens is dead."

"Dead!" said Jed Briggs in a hushed voice.

"He deserved to die.... He deserved to die.... He deserved to die ..." the young woman repeated shrilly, hysterically.

"Was you in town to lodge Tuesday night, Jed?"

"Yes."

"Asa come every lodge night, Mis' Briggs?"

"He always came--when Jed was here and when Jed was away.... When Jed was here he'd jest set eyin' me and eyin' me ... and when Jed was gone he--he talked...."

"Asa owned the mortgage on the place," said Jed, as if that explained something. Scattergood nodded comprehension.

"Keep up your int'rest, Jed?"

"Year behind. Asa was threatenin' foreclosure."

"Threatened to throw us offn the place ... ag'in and ag'in he threatened--and we'd 'a' starved, 'cause Jed hain't strong. It's me does most of the work.... What we got into this place is all we got on earth ... and he threatened to take it."

"He come Tuesday night," said Scattergood, as a prompter speaks.

"Hush, Lindy," said Jed.

"I calculate you'd best both of you talk," said Scattergood. "You'd better tell me, Jed, jest why you shot Asa Levens."

Lindy Briggs uttered a choking cry and clutched her husband; Jed Briggs stared at Scattergood with hunted eyes.

"It'll be best for you to tell. I'm standin' your friend, Jed Briggs.... Better tell me than the sheriff.... Asa Levens was here Tuesday night...."

"He excused us from payin' our int'rest," said Jed, and then he, too, laughed shrilly. "Let us off our int'rest. Lindy told me when I come home. Couldn't hardly b'lieve my ears." Jed was talking wildly, pitifully. "Lindy was a-layin' on the floor, sobbin', when I come home, and she was afeard to tell me why Asa let us off our int'rest, but I coaxed her, Mr. Baines, and she told me--and so I shot Asa Levens 'cause he wa'n't fit to live."

Scattergood nodded. "Sich things was wrote on Asa's face," he said. "But what about Abner? Wa'n't goin' to let him suffer f'r your act, Jed? What about Abner?"

"Him too.... All of that blood.... I met Abner on the road of a Tuesday when I wa'n't quite myself with all that had happened, and I stopped his hoss and accused his brother to his face.... He listened quiet-like, and then he laughed. That's what

Abner done, he laughed.... When I heard he was arrested f'r the killin', I laughed.... Back in Bible times, if one of a family sinned, God wiped out the whole of the kin...."

Scattergood was thoughtful. "Yes," he said, "Abner would have laughed. That was like Abner.... Now I calc'late you and Mis' Briggs better fix up and drive to town with me.... Don't be afeard. Right'll be done, and there hain't no more sufferin' fallin' to your share, ... You been doin' God's rough work, Jed, and I don't calc'late he figgers to have you punished f'r it...."

Next morning at ten by the clock the coroner with his jury held inquest over the body of Asa Levens, and over that body Jed Briggs and Lindy, his wife, told their story under oath to ears that credited the truth of their words because they knew the man of whom those words were spoken. The jury deliberated briefly. Its verdict was in these words:

"We find that Asa Levens came to his death by act of God, and that there are found no reasons for further investigation into this matter."

And so it stands in the imperishable records of the township; legal authority recognized the right of Deity to utilize a human being for his rougher sort of work.

"I knew it was something like this," Mary Ware said, clinging openly and unashamed to Abner Levens. "It's why he couldn't defend himself."

Abner nodded. "My flesh and blood was guilty. Could I free myself by accusin' the husband of this woman?... I calc'lated God meant to destroy us Levenses, root and branch.... It was his business, not mine."

"I've took note," said Scattergood, "that them that was most strict about mindin' their own business was gen'ally most diligent about doin' God's--all unbeknownst to themselves."

CHAPTER XI
HE INVESTS IN SALVATION

From Scattergood Baines's seat on the piazza of his hardware store he could look across the river and through a side window of the bank. Scattergood was availing himself of this privilege. As a member of the finance committee of the bank Scattergood was naturally interested in that enterprise, so important to the thrifty community, but his interest at the moment was not exactly official. He was regarding, speculatively, the back of young Ovid Nixon, the assistant cashier.

His concern for young Ovid was sartorial. It is true that a shiny alpaca office coat covered the excellent shoulders of the boy, but below that alpaca and under Scattergood's line of vision were trousers--and carefully stretched over a hanger on a closet hook was a coat! There was also a waistcoat, recognized only by the name of vest in Coldriver, and that very morning Scattergood had seen the three, to say nothing of a certain shirt and a necktie of sorts, making brave young Ovid's figure.

Ovid passed Scattergood's store on the way to his work. Baines had regarded him with interest.

"Mornin', Ovid" he said.

"Morning, Mr. Baines."

"Calc'late to be wearin' some new clothes, Ovid? Eh?"

Ovid smiled down at himself, and wagged his head.

"Don't recall seem' jest sich a suit in Coldriver before," said Scattergood. "Never bought 'em at Lafe Atwell's, did you?"

"Got 'em in the city," said Ovid.

"I want to know! Come made that way, Ovid, or was they manufactured special fer you?"

"Best tailor there was," said Ovid.

"Must 'a' come to quite a figger, includin' the shirt and necktie."

"Forty dollars for the suit," Ovid said, proudly, "and it busted a five-dollar bill all to pieces to git the shirt and tie."

Scattergood waggled his head admiringly. "Must be a satisfaction," he said, "to be able to afford sich clothes."

Ovid looked a bit doubtful, but Scattergood's voice was so interested, so bland, that any suspicion of irony was allayed.

"How's your ma?" Scattergood asked.

"Pert," answered Ovid. "Ma's spry. Barrin' a siege of neuralgy in the face off and on, ma hain't complainin' of nothin'."

"Has she took to patronizin' a city tailor, too?" Scattergood asked.

"Mostly," said Ovid, "ma makes her own."

Scattergood nodded.

"Still does sewin' for other folks?"

"Ma enjoys it," said Ovid, defensively. "Says it passes the time."

"Passes consid'able of it, don't it? Passes the time right up till she gits into bed?"

"Ma's industrious."

"It's a handsome rig-out," said Scattergood. "Credit to you; credit to Coldriver; credit to the bank."

Ovid glanced down at his legs to admire them.

"Been spendin' Saturday nights and Sundays out of town for a spell, hain't you? Seems like I hain't seen you around."

"Been takin' the 'three-o'clock' down the line," said Ovid, complacently.

"Girl?" said Scattergood--one might have noticed that it was hopefully.

"Naw.... Fellers. We go to the opery Saturday nights and kind of amuse our-selves Sundays."

"Um!... G'-by, Ovid."

"Good-by, Mr. Baines."

Coldriver had seen tailor-made clothing before, worn by drummers and visi-tors, but it is doubtful if it had ever really experienced one personally adorning one of its own citizens. A few years before it had been currently reported that Jed Lewis was about to have such a suit to be married in, but it turned out that the major part of the sum to be devoted to that purpose actually went as the first payment on a parlor organ and that Lafe Atwell purveyed the wedding garment. This denouement had created a breath of dissatisfaction with Jed, and there were those who argued that organs were more wasteful than clothes, because you could go to church of a Sunday, drop a dime in the collection plate, and hear all the organ music a body needed to hear.

So now Scattergood regarded Ovid speculatively through the window, setting on opposite mental columns Ovid's salary of nine hundred dollars a year and the probable total cost of tailor-made clothes and weekly trips down the line on the "three-o'clock."

Scattergood was interested in every man, woman, and child in Coldriver. Their business was his business. But just now he owned an especial concern for Ovid, because he, and he alone, had placed the boy in the bank after Ovid's graduation from high school--and had watched him, with some pleasure, as he progressed steadily and methodically to a position which Coldriver regarded as one of the finest it was possible for a young man to hold. To be assistant cashier of the Coldriver Savings Bank was to have achieved both social and business success.

Scattergood liked Ovid, had confidence in the boy, and even speculated on the possibility of attaching Ovid to his own enterprises as he had attached young Johnnie Bones, the lawyer. But latterly he had done a deal of thinking. In the first place, there was no need for Mrs. Nixon to continue to take in sewing when Ovid earned nine hundred a year; in the second place, Ovid had been less engrossed in his work and more engrossed by himself and by interests "down the line."

It was Scattergood's opinion that Ovid was sound at bottom, but was suffering from some sort of temporary attack, which would have its run ... if no serious complication set in. Scattergood was watching for symptoms of the complication.

Three weeks later Ovid took the "three-o'clock" down the line of a Saturday afternoon and failed to return Sunday night. Indeed, he did not appear Monday night, nor was there explanatory word from him. Mrs. Nixon could give Scattergood no explanation, and she herself, in the midst of a spell of neuralgia, was distracted.

Scattergood fumbled automatically for his shoe fastenings, but, recalling in time that he was seated in a lady's parlor, restrained his impulse to free his feet from restraint in order that he might clear his thoughts by wriggling his toes.

"Likely," he said, "it's nothin' serious. Then, ag'in, you can't tell.... You do two things, Mis' Nixon: go out to the farm and stay with my wife--Mandy'll be glad to have you ... and keep your mouth shet."

"You'll find him, Mr. Baines?... You'll fetch him back to me?"

"If I figger he's wuth it," said Scattergood.

He went from Mrs. Nixon's to the bank, where the finance committee were gathering to discuss the situation and to discover if Ovid's disappearance were in any manner connected with the movable assets of the institution. There were Deacon Pettybone, Sam Kettleman, the grocer, Lafe Atwell, Marvin Towne--Scattergood made up the full committee.

"How be you?" Scattergood said, as he sat in a chair which uttered its protest at the burden.

"What d'you think?" Towne said. "Got any notions? Noticed anythin' suspicious?"

"Not 'less it's that there dude suit of clothes," said Atwell, with some acidity.

"You put him in here," said Kettleman to Scattergood.

"Calculate I did.... Hain't found no reason to regret it--not yit. Looks to me like the fust move's to kind of go over the books and the cash, hain't it?... You fellers tackle the books and I'll give the vault an overhaulin'."

Scattergood already had made up his mind that if Ovid had allowed any of the bank's funds to cling to him when he went away the shortage would be discoverable in the cash reserve, undoubtedly in a lump sum, and not by an examination of the books. It was his judgment that Ovid was not of a caliber to plan the looting of a bank and skillfully to hide his progress by a falsification of the books. That required an imagination that Ovid lacked. No, Scattergood said to himself, if Ovid had looted he had looted clumsily--and on sudden provocation.... Therefore he chose the vault for his peculiar task.

It is a comparatively easy task to count the cash reserve in the vault of so small a bank. Even a matter of thirty-odd thousand dollars can be checked by one man alone in half an hour, for the small silver is packed away in rolls, each roll containing a stated sum; the larger silver is bagged, each bag bearing a label stating the amount of its contents, and the currency is wrapped in packages containing even sums.... Scattergood went to work. He went over the cash carefully, and totaled the sums he set down on a bit of paper.... He found the amount to be inadequate by exactly three thousand dollars.

"Huh!" said Scattergood to himself. "Ovid hain't no hawg."

One might have thought the young man had dropped in Scattergood's estimation. It would have been as easy to make away with twenty thousand dollars as with three thousand, and the penalty would not have been greater.

"Kind of a childish sum," said Scattergood to himself. "'Tain't wuth bustin' up a life over--not three thousand.... Calc'late Ovid hain't bad --not at a figger of three thousand. Jest a dum fool--him and his tailor-made clothes...."

In the silence of the vault Scattergood removed his shoes and sat on a pile of bagged silver. His pudgy toes worked busily while he reflected upon the sum of three thousand dollars and what the theft of that amount might indicate. "Looked big to Ovid," he said to himself. Then, "Jest a dum young eediot...."

He replaced the cash and, carrying his shoes in his hand, left the vault and closed it behind him. His four fellow committeemen were sweating over the books, but all looked up anxiously as Scattergood appeared. He stood looking at them an instant, as if in doubt.

"What d'you find?" asked Atwell.

"She checks," said Scattergood.

The four drew a breath of relief. Scattergood wished that he might have joined them in the breath, but there was no relief for him. He had joined his fortunes to those of Ovid Nixon--and to those of Ovid's mother; had become *particeps crimi-nis*, and the requirements of the situation rested heavily upon him.

It was past midnight before the laborious four finished their review of the books and joined with Scattergood in giving Ovid a clean bill of health.

"Didn't think Ovid had it in him to steal," said Kettleman.

"Hain't got no business stirrin' us up like this for nothin'," said Atwell, acrimoniously.

"Maybe," suggested Scattergood, "Ovid's come down with a fit of suthin'."

"Hope it's painful," said Lafe, "I'm a-goin' home to bed."

"What'll we do?" asked Deacon Pettybone.

"Nothin'," said Scattergood, "till some doin' is called fur. Calc'late I better slip on my shoes. Might meet my wife." Mandy Scattergood was doing her able best to break Scattergood of his shoeless ways.

"Guess we'll let Ovid git through when he comes back," said Deacon Pettybone, harshly, making use of the mountain term to denote discharge. There no one is ever discharged, no one ever resigns. The single phrase covers both actions--the individual "gets through."

"I always figgered," said Scattergood, urbanely, "that it was allus premature to git ahead of time.... I'm calc'latin' on runnin' down to see what kind of a fit of ailment Ovid's come down with."

Next morning, having in the meantime industriously allowed the rumor to go abroad that Ovid was suddenly ill, Scattergood took the seven-o'clock for points south. He did not know where he was going, but expected to pick up information on that question en route. His method of reaching for it was to take a seat on a trunk in the baggage car.

The railroad, Scattergood's individual property and his greatest step forward in his dream for the development of the Coldriver Valley, was but a year old now. It was twenty-four miles long, but he regarded it with an affection only second to his love for his hardware store--and he dealt with it as an indulgent parent.... Pliny Pickett once stage driver, was now conductor, and wore with ostentation a uniform suitable to the dignity, speaking of "my railroad" largely.

"Hear Ovid Nixon's sick down to town" said Pliny.

"Sich a rumor's come to me."

"Likely at the Mountain House?" ventured Pliny.

"Shouldn't be s'prised."

"That's where he mostly stopped," said Pliny.

"Um!... Wonder what ailment Ovid was most open to git?"

Scattergood and Pliny talked politics for the rest of the journey, and, as usual, Pliny received directions to "talk up" certain matters to his passengers. Pliny was one of Scattergood's main channels to public opinion. At the junction Scattergood changed for the short ride to town, and there he carried his ancient valise up to the Mountain House, where he registered.

"Young feller named Nixon--Ovid Nixon--stoppin' here?" he asked the clerk.

"Checked out Monday night."

"Um!... Monday night, eh? Expect him back? I was calc'latin' on meetin' him here to-day."

"He usually gets in Saturday night.... You might ask Mr. Pillows, over there by the cigar case. He and Nixon hang out together."

Scattergood scrutinized Mr. Pillows and did not like the appearance of that young man; not that he looked especially vicious, but there was a sort of useless, lazy, sponging look to him. Baines set him down as the sort of young man who would play Kelly pool with money his mother earned by doing laundry, and, in addition, catalogued him as a "saphead." He acted accordingly.

Walking lightly across the lobby, he stopped just behind Pillows, and then said, with startling sharpness, "Where's Ovid Nixon?"

The agility with which Mr. Pillows leaped into the air and descended, facing Scattergood, did some little to raise him in the estimation of Coldriver's first citizen. Nor did he pause to study Scattergood. One might have said that he lit in mid-career, at the top of his speed, and was out of the door before Scattergood could extend a pudgy hand to snatch at him. Scattergood grinned.

"Figgered he'd be a mite skittish," he said to the girl behind the cigar counter.

"I thought something sneaking was going on," said the young woman, as if to herself.

Scattergood gave her his attention. She had red hair, and his respect for red hair was a notable characteristic. There was a freckle or two on her nose, her eyes were steady, and her mouth was firm--but she was pretty. Scattergood continued to regard her in silence, and she, not disconcerted, studied him.

"You and me is goin' to eat dinner together this noon," he said, presently.

"Business or pleasure?" Her rejoinder was tart.

"Why?"

"If it's business, we eat. If it's pleasure, you've stopped at the wrong cigar counter."

"I knowed I was goin' to take to you," said Scattergood. "You got capable hair.... This here was to be business."

"Twelve o'clock sharp, then," she said.

He looked at the clock. It lacked half an hour of noon.

"G'-by," he said, and went to a distant corner, where he seated himself and stared out of the window, trying to imagine what he would do if he were Ovid Nixon, and what would make him appropriate three thousand dollars.... At twelve o'clock he lumbered over to the cigar case. "C'm on," he said. "Hain't got no time to waste."

The girl put on her hat and they walked out together.

"What's your name?" Scattergood asked.

"Pansy O'Toole.... You're Scattergood Baines--that's why I'm here.... I don't eat with every man that oozes out of the woods."

Scattergood said nothing. It was a fixed principle of his to let other folks do the talking if they would. If not he talked himself--deviously. Seldom did he ask a direct question regarding any matter of importance, and so strong was habit that it was rare for him to put any query directly. If he wanted to know what time it was he would lead up to the subject by mentioning sun dials, or calendars, or lunar eclipses, and so approach circuitously and by degrees, until his victim was led to exhibit his watch. Pansy did not talk.

"See lots of folks, standin' back of that counter like you do?" he began.

"Lots."

"Um!... From lots of towns?... From Boston?"

"Yes."

"From Tupper Falls?"

"Some."

"From Coldriver?"

"If you want to know if I know Ovid Nixon, why don't you ask right out?"

Scattergood looked at her admiringly.

"I know him," she said.

"Like him?"

"He's a nice boy." Scattergood liked the way she said "nice." It conveyed a fine shade of meaning, and he thought more of Ovid in consequence. "But he's awful young--and green."

"Calc'late he is--calc'late he is."

"He needs somebody to look after him," she said, sharply.

"Thinkin' of undertakin' the work?... Favor undertakin' it?"

She looked at him a moment speculatively. "I might do worse. He'd be decent and kind--and I've got brains. I could make something of him...."

"Um!... Ovid's up and made somethin' of himself."

"What?" She spoke quickly, sharply.

"A thief."

Scattergood glanced sidewise to study the effect of this curt announcement, but her face was expressionless, rather too expressionless.

"That's why you're looking for him?"

"Yes."

"To put him in jail?"

"What would you calc'late on doin' if you was me?"

"Before I did anything," she said, slowly, "I'd make up my mind if he was a thief, or if he just happened to take whatever it was he has taken.... I'd be sure he was bad. If I made up my mind he'd just been green and a fool--well, I'd see to it he never was that kind of a fool again.... But not by jailing him."

"Um!... Three thousand's a lot of money."

"Mr. Baines, I see men and other kinds of men from behind my cigar counter--and the kind of a man Ovid Nixon could be is worth more than that."

"Mebby so.... Mebby so. But if I was investin' in Ovid, I'd want some sort of a guarantee with him. Would you be willin' to furnish the guarantee? And see it was kept good?"

"If you mean what I think you do--yes," she said, steadily. "I'd marry Ovid to-morrow."

"Him bein' a thief?"

"Girls that sell cigars aren't so select," she said, a trifle bitterly.

"Pansy," said Scattergood, and he patted her back with a heavy hand that was, nevertheless, gentle, "if 'twan't for Mandy, that I've up and married already, I calc'late I'd try to cut Ovid out.... But then I've kinder observed that every woman you meet up with, if she's bein' crowded by somethin' hard and mean, strikes you as bein' better 'n any other woman you ever see. I call to mind a number.... Ovid some attached to you, is he?"

"He's never made love to me, if that's what you mean."

"Think you could land him--for his good and yourn?"

"I--why, I think I could," she said.

"Is it a bargain?"

"What?"

"For, and in consideration of one dollar to you in hand paid, and the further consideration of you undertakin' to keep an eye on him till death do you part, I agree to keep him out of jail--and without nobody knowin' he was ever anythin' but honest--and a dum fool."

She held out her hand and Scattergood took it.

"What's got Ovid into this here mess?"

"Bucket shop," she said.

"Um!... They been lettin' him make a mite of money--up to now, eh? So he calc'lated on gittin' rich at one wallop. Kind of led him along, I calc'late, till they got him to swaller hook, line, and sinker ... and then they up and jerked him floppin' on to the bank.... Who owns this here bucket shop?"

"Tim Peaney."

"Perty slick, is he?"

"Slick enough to take care of Ovid and sheep like him--but I can't help thinking he's a sheep himself."

"He got Ovid's three thousand, or Ovid 'u'd 'a' come back Sunday night.... Got to find Ovid--and got to git that money back."

"I've an idea Ovid's right in town. If you're suspicious, and keep your eyes open, you can tell when something's going on. That Pillows man you scared knows, and Peaney acts like the man of mystery in one of the kind of plays we get around here. It's breaking out all over them.... I'll bet they've fleeced Ovid, and now they're hiding him--to save themselves more than him."

"And Ovid's the kind that would let himself be hid," said Scattergood. "Do you and me work together on this job?"

"If I can help--"

"You bet you kin.... We'll jest let Ovid lie hid while we kind of maneuver around Peaney some--commencin' right soon. Peaney ever aspire to take you to dinner?"

"Yes," she said, shortly.

"Git organized to go with him to-night...."

* * * *

It was in the neighborhood of five o'clock when Mr. Peaney came into the Mountain House and stopped at the cigar counter for cigarettes.

"Any more friendly to-day, sister?" he asked.

Pansy smiled and leaned across the case. "The trouble with you," she said, in a low tone, "is that you're a piker."

"Piker--me?"

"Always after small change."

"Just show me some real money once," he said, flamboyantly.

"It would scare you," she said.

"Show me some--you'd see how it would scare me."

"I wonder," she said, musingly, "if you have the nerve?"

"For what?" he said, with quickened interest.

"To go after a wad that I know of?"

"Say," he said, his eyes narrowing, his face assuming a look of cupidity and cunning, "do you know something? If you do, come on out where we can eat and talk. If there's anything in it I'll split with you."

"I know you will," she said, promptly. "Fifty-fifty.... In an hour, at Case's restaurant."

At the hour set Pansy and Mr. Peaney found a corner table in the little restaurant, and when they had ordered Peaney asked, "Well, what you got on your mind?"

"A big farmer from the backwoods--with a trunkful of money. Don't know how he got it. Must have sold the family wood lot, but he's got it with him ... and he came down to invest it."

"No."

"Honest Injun."

"How much?"

"From what he said it's more than ten thousand dollars."

"Lead me to him."

"He'll need some playing with--thinks he's sharp.... But I've been talking to him. Guess he took a liking to me. Wanted to take me to dinner--and he did."

"Say!" exclaimed Mr. Peaney, in admiration, "I had you sized all wrong."

"It'll take nerve," Pansy said.

"It's what I've got most of."

"He's no Ovid Nixon."

"Eh?... What d'you know about Ovid Nixon?"

"I know he was too green to burn and that you and he were together a lot.... Isn't that enough?"

He smiled complacently, seeing a compliment. "He was easy--but he got to be a nuisance."

"Making trouble?"

"No.... Scared."

"I see," she nodded, wisely. "Lost more than he had, was that it? And then helped himself to what he didn't have?"

"I'm not supposed to know where it came from. None of my business."

"Of course not"--her tone was rank flattery. "Wants you to take care of him. Threatens to squeal. I know.... So you've got to hide him out."

"You are a wise one. Where'd you get it?"

"I didn't always sell cigars for a living.... He isn't apt to break loose and spoil this thing, is he?"

"Too scared to show his face.... If we can pull this across he can show it whenever he wants to--I'll be gone."

So Ovid Nixon was here--in town. It was as she had reasoned. If here, he was somewhere in the building Mr. Peaney occupied as a bucket shop.

"It's understood we divide--if I introduce my farmer to you--and show you how to get it."

"You bet, sister."

"Have you any money? Nothing makes people so confident and trustful as the sight of money?"

"I've got it," he said, complacently.

"Then you come to the hotel this evening.... Just do as I say. I'll manage it. In a couple of days--if you have the nerve and do exactly what I say--you can forget

Ovid Nixon and take a long journey."

Two hours later, when Peaney entered the lobby of the Mountain House, he saw a very fat, uncouthly dressed backwoodsman talking to Pansy. She signaled him and he walked over nonchalantly.

"Mr. Baines," said Pansy, "here's the gentleman I was speaking about. He can advise you. He's a broker, and everybody trusts him." She lowered her voice. "He's very rich, himself. Made it in stocks. I guess he knows what's going on right in Mr. Rockefeller's private office.... You couldn't do better than to talk business with him.... Mr. Peaney, Mr. Baines."

"Very glad to meet you, sir," said Peaney, in his grandest manner.

"Much obleeged, and the same to you," said Scattergood, beaming his admiration. "Hear tell you're one of them stock brokers."

"Yes, sir. That's my business."

"Guess you and me had better talk some. I'm a-lookin' for somebody to gimme advice about investin'. I got a sight of money to invest some'eres--a sight of it. Railroad stocks, or suthin'. Calc'late on makin' myself well off."

"I'm not taking any new clients, Mr. Baines. I'm very busy indeed." He glanced at Pansy. "But if you are a friend of Miss O'Toole's possibly I can break my rule.... About how much do you wish to invest?"

"Oh, say fifteen to twenty thousand. Figger on doublin' it up, or mebby better 'n that. Folks does it. I've read about 'em."

"To be sure they do--if they are properly advised. But one has to know the stock market--like a book."

"And Mr. Peaney knows it like a book," said Pansy.

Peaney lowered his voice. "I have agents--men in the offices of great corporations, and they telegraph me secrets. I know when a big stock manipulation is coming off--and my clients profit by it."

"Don't call to mind none, right now, do you?"

Mr. Peaney looked about him cautiously. "I do," he said, in a low voice. "My man in the office of the president of the International Utilities Company wired me to-day that to-morrow they were going to shove the stock up five points."

"Um!... Don't understand. What's that mean?"

"It means, if you invested a thousand dollars on margin and the stock went up five points, you would get your money back, and five thousand dollars besides."

"Say!... I knowed they was money to be made easy.... But I hain't no fool. I don't know you, mister." Scattergood became very cunning. "I don't know this here girl very well--though I kinder took to her at the first. I'm a-goin' cautious. I might git smouged.... What I aim to do is to go careful till I git on to the ropes and know who to trust.... Hain't goin' to put all my money in at the first go-off. No, siree. Goin' to try it first kind of small, and if it shows all right, why, then I'm a-goin' in right up to my neck.... Folks back home would figger I was pretty slick if I come home with a million dollars."

"That's the smart way," Pansy said, with a little grimace at Peaney. "Why don't you try this International Utilities investment, to-morrow--say for a thousand dollars?... If you--come out right, then you'll know you can trust Mr. Peaney, and the next time he has some real information you can jump right in and make a fortune."

"Sounds mighty reasonable. I kin afford to lose a thousand--charge it up to investigatin'.... My, jest think of gainin' five thousand dollars jest by settin' down and takin' it."

"It's the way money is made," said Mr. Peaney.

"How'd I know I'd git the money?" Scattergood asked, with sudden doubt.

"Why, you'd see it," said Pansy, with another grimace at Peaney. "You put your thousand dollars on the counter, and Mr. Peaney puts five thousand right beside it. You see it all the time. If you come out right, you just pick up the money and walk off."

"No!... Say! That's slick, hain't it? Wisht you'd come along when we try, Miss O'Toole. Somehow I'd feel easier in my mind if you was along.... See you early in the mornin'.... Got to git to bed, now. Always aim to be in bed by nine.... G' night."

"Say," expostulated Mr. Peaney, "do you expect me to hand over five thousand to that hick? He might walk off with it."

"He might walk off with the hotel.... I told you you hadn't any nerve.... Why, give that fat man a taste of easy money and you couldn't drive him away. Let him sleep all night with five thousand dollars that came as easy as that, and you couldn't drive him away from your office with a gun.... Besides, I'm here to take care of him ...or are you a quitter?"

"Twenty thousand dollars," Mr. Peaney said to himself. "Then I'll show you how good my nerve is. Bring on your fat man...."

Scattergood was up at his accustomed early hour, and before breakfast had examined Mr. Peaney's premises from front and rear. The bucket shop was in a small wooden building. The ground floor consisted of a large office where was visible the big blackboard upon which stock quotations were posted, and of a back room whose interior was invisible from the street. A corner of the main office had been partitioned off as a private retreat for Mr. Peaney. What was upstairs Scattergood could not tell with accuracy, but he judged it to be a single room or perhaps two small rooms.... It was here, he felt certain, Ovid was secreting himself, and, with a certain grimness, he hoped the young man was not happy in his surroundings.

"I calc'late," he said to himself, "that Ovid, bein' shet up with his own figgerin's and imaginin's, hain't in no jubilant frame of mind.... Meanest punishment you kin give a feller is to lock him in for a spell with himself, callin' himself names...." When the office opened, Scattergood and Pansy were at the door, where Mr. Peaney welcomed them, not without a certain uneasiness at the prospect of intrusting his money to Scattergood.

"Let's git started right off," Scattergood said. "I'd like to tell it to the folks how I gained five thousand dollars in one mornin'--jest doin' nothin' but settin'."

"Very well," said Mr. Peaney. "You buy a thousand shares of International Utilities on a one-point margin.... Sign this order slip."

"And you set out five thousand dollars right where I kinn see it," said Scattergood, with anxious fatuity.

"Certainly.... Certainly."

Mr. Peaney deposited on his desk a bundle of currency which Scattergood counted meticulously, and then laid his own thousand beside it.

"It's as good as yours, right now," said Pansy.

"We'll stay right here in my private room," said Peaney. "We can watch the board from here, and nobody will disturb us."

"I'd kinder like to have folks see me makin' all this money," complained Scattergood, but he acquiesced, and presently quotations commenced to be posted on the board. International Utilities opened at seventy-six. Presently they advanced half a point, lingered, and returned to their original position.

"Kind of slow, hain't it?" Scattergood said, a worried look beginning to appear on his face. "Maybe them folks hain't goin' to do what you said."

Mr. Peaney went out into the back room, and presently the ticker began to click furiously. International Utilities leaped a whole point. In ten minutes they ascended a half point, and at every advance Scattergood figured his profit, and hesitated as to whether or not it would be best to close the transaction then and there, but Pansy cajoled him skillfully, making evident to Mr. Peaney the power of her influence over the old fellow.

Scattergood was the picture of the fatuous countryman. He was childlike in his ignorance and in his delight. He exclaimed, he slapped his thigh, he laughed aloud at each advance. "It's a-comin'. Next time she h'ists, the money's mine.... And 'tain't been two hours. What'll the folks say to that, eh? Me doin' nothin' but settin' here and makin' five thousand dollars in two hours.... Nothin' short of a million's goin' to satisfy me--and when I get that million, Mr. Peaney, I'm a-goin' to show you how much obleeged I be. I'm a-goin' to git you a whole box of them cigars. Pansy knows which ones. They come at a nickel apiece...."

Then ...then International Utilities touched eighty-one. Scattergood slapped Peaney on the back. He laughed. He acted like a boy with a new jackknife.

"It's all mine now, hain't it? Mine? Fair and square? It's my money--every penny of it?"

"It's yours, Mr. Baines. And I congratulate you. I myself have made a matter of fifty thousand dollars."

"Wisht I'd put up every cent I got.... But there'll be other chances, won't they? I kin git in ag'in?"

"Of course. To-morrow. Possibly this afternoon."

"And I kin take this now?" Scattergood had his hands on the six thousand dollars; was handling it greedily.

"It's yours," said Mr. Peaney.

"Calc'lated it was," said Scattergood. "Calc'lated it was.... Now where's Ovid?"

Mr. Peaney stared. Something had happened suddenly to this countryman. He was no longer fatuous, futile. His face was no longer foolish and good-natured; it was; granite--it was the face of a man with force, and the skill to use that force.

"Where's Ovid?" he demanded again.

"Ovid ... Ovid who? I don't know any Ovid."

He became suddenly alarmed and blocked the way to the door. Scattergood's eyes twinkled. "If I was you I wouldn't git in the way to any extent. Feelin' the way I do I sh'u'dn't be s'prised if I got a certain amount of satisfaction out of tramplin' over you."

"Hey, you put that money back ..."

"Mine, hain't it? Gained it lawful, didn't I?"

He walked slowly toward the door, and Mr. Peaney, still barring the way, found himself sitting suddenly in an adjacent corner. Scattergood walked calmly past and made for the back room.

"Stop him!" shouted Mr. Peaney. "Don't let him go in there."

But Scattergood proceeded methodically, leaving no less than three of Mr. Peaney's employees in recumbent postures along his line of march.... Pansy followed him closely, pale, but resolute. He ascended the stairs, and, finding the door at the top fastened from within, he removed it bodily by the application of a calk-studded boot.... Ovid Nixon was disclosed cowering against the wall, pale, terrified.

"Howdy, Ovid?" said Scattergood, as if he had met the young man casually on the street. "How d'you find yourself?"

Ovid remained mute.

"Fetched a friend to see you, Ovid," said Scattergood. "This is her." He pushed Pansy forward. "Find her better comp'ny than you been havin' recent," he said. "She's got suthin' fer you.... When she gits through visitin' with you, I calculate to have a word to say.... Here, Pansy, you kin give this here to Ovid." He counted off three thousand dollars before the young man's staring eyes.

"I--I'm glad I'm found," Ovid said, tremulously. "I was making up my mind to give myself up...."

"What fer?" said Scattergood.

"You know--you know I took three thousand dollars out of the vault."

"Vault don't show nothin' short," said Scattergood, waggling his head. "Counted it myself. Did look for a minute like they was three thousand short, but I kind of put that amount in, and then counted ag'in, and, sure enough, it was all there...."

Ovid stared, took a step forward. "You mean.... What do you mean, Mr. Baines?"

"I'm goin' to step outside of what used to be the door," said Scattergood, "and let Pansy do the explainin'.... What I do after that depends a heap on ... Pansy...."

Scattergood went outside and waited, his eyes on the stairs, but nobody offered to ascend. He could hear the conversation within, but it was only toward the end that it interested him.

"Ovid," said Pansy, "you've been hanging around my counter a good deal--and asking me to dinners, and to go driving on Sunday. What for?"

"Because--because I liked you awful well, Pansy, but now--now that I've done this--"

"If you hadn't done this? If you had made money instead of losing it?"

"I--oh, what's the use of talking about it? I wanted you should marry me, Pansy."

"But you don't want me any more?"

"Nobody'd marry me--knowing what you know."

"Ovid," said Pansy, sharply, "there's nothing wrong with you except that--you haven't enough brains all by yourself. You need to be looked after ...and I'm going to do it."

"Looked after?"

"Ovid Nixon, do you like me well enough to marry me?"

"I--"

"Do you? Yes or no ... quick!"

"Yes."

"Then ask me," said Pansy.

Presently the three emerged into the street from the deserted offices of Mr. Peaney. Scattergood Baines held in his hands two thousand dollars in bills, representing net profit on the transaction. He regarded the money with a frown.

"Somethings got to be done to you to make you fit to tetch," he said to it.

Out of an adjoining store came a young woman in a queer bonnet, with a tambourine in her hand. "Huh!" said Scattergood, and stopped her. "Salvation Army, hain't you?"

"Yes, sir."

"Hold it out," he said, motioning to the tambourine.

She obeyed, and he dropped into it the package of bills, and, looking into her startled, almost frightened eyes, he said: "It come from fools to sharpers.... I calculate nothin' but a leetle salvation'll kill the cussedness in it.... Make it do all the salvagin' it kin...."

Whereupon he passed on, leaving a bewildered woman to stare after him.

Next morning, Scattergood, accompanied by Mr. and Mrs. Ovid Nixon, alighted from the train in Coldriver. Deacon Pettybone happened to be standing on the depot platform.

"Make you acquainted with Mis' Nixon," said Scattergood, with gravity. "She's what Ovid come down with.... Can't blame a young feller for forgittin' work a day or two when he's got him sich a wife.... Deacon, this here girl's performed a service for Coldriver. Increased our population by two--her and Ovid. And, Deacon, Ovid hain't the fust man that ever was made so's he was wuth countin' in the census by marryin' him a wife...."

"Dummed if she hain't got red hair," was the deacon's astonished contribution. It was as near to congratulations as the deacon ever came.

CHAPTER XII
THE SON THAT WAS DEAD

The ox is dressed and hung," said Pliny Pickett, with the air of a man announcing that the country has been saved from destruction.

"Uh!... How much 'd he dress?" asked Scattergood Baines, moving in his especially reinforced armchair until it creaked its protest.

"Eight hunderd and forty-three--accordin' to Newt Patterson's scales."

"Which hain't never been knowed to err on the side of overweight," said Scattergood, dryly.

"The boys has got the oven fixed for roastin' him, and the band gits in on the mornin' train, failin' accidents, and the dec'rations is up in the taown hall--'n' now we kin git ready for a week of stiddy rain."

"They's wuss things than rain," said Scattergood, "though at the minnit I don't call to mind what they be."

"Deacon Pettybone's north mowin' is turned into a baseball grounds, and everybody in town is buyin' buntin' to wrap their harnesses, and Kittleman's fetched in more 'n five bushels of peanuts, and every young un in taown'll be sick with the stummick ache."

"Feelin' extry cheerful this mornin', hain't ye? Kind of more hopeful-like than I call to mind seein' you fer some time."

"Never knowed no big celebration to come off like it was planned, or 'thout somebody gittin' a leg busted, or the big speaker fergittin' what day it was, or suthin'. Seems like the hull weight of this here falls right on to me."

"Responsibility," said Scattergood, with a twinkle in his eye, "is a turrible thing to bear up under. But nothin' hain't happened yit, and folks is dependin' on you, Pliny, to see 't nothin' mars the party."

"It'll rain on to the pe-rade, and the ball game'll bust up in a fight, and pickpockets'll most likely git wind of sich a big gatherin' and come swarmin' in.... Scattergood," he lowered his voice impressively, "it's rumored Mavin Newton's a-comin' back for this here Old Home Week."

"Um!... Mavin Newton.... Um!... Who up and la'nched that rumor?"

"Everybody's a-talkin' it up. Folks says he's sure to come, and then what in tunket'll we do? The sheriff's goin' to be busy handlin' the crowds and the traffic and sich, and he won't have no time fer extry miscreants, seems as though.... Folks is a-comin' from as fur 's Denver, and we don't want no town criminal brought to justice in the middle of it all. Though Mavin's father 'd be glad to see his son ketched, I calc'late."

"Hain't interviewed Mattie Strong as ree-gards her feelin's, have ye?"

"I wonder," said Pliny, with intense interest, "if Mattie's ever heard from him? But she's that close-mouthed."

"'Tain't a common failin' hereabouts," said Scattergood. "How long since Mavin run off?"

"Eight year come November."

"The night before him and Mattie was goin' to be married."

"Uh-huh! Takin' with him that there fund the Congo church raised fer a new organ, and it's took them eight year to raise it over ag'in."

"And in the meantime," said Scattergood, "I calc'late the tunes off of the old organ has riz about as pleasin' to heaven as if 'twas new. Squeaks some, I'm told, but I figger the squeaks gits kind of filtered out, and nothin' but the true meanin' of the tunes ever gits up to Him." Scattergood jerked a pudgy thumb skyward.

"More 'n two hunderd dollars, it was--and Mavin treasurer of the church. Old Man Newton he resigned as elder, and hain't never set foot in church from that day to this."

"Bein' moved," said Scattergood, "more by cantankerousness than grief."

"I'll venture," said Pliny, "that there'll be more'n five hunderd old residents a-comin' back, and where in tunket we're goin' to sleep 'em all the committee don't know."

"Um!... G'-by, Pliny," said Scattergood, suddenly, and Pliny, recognizing the old hardware merchant's customary and inescapable dismissal, got up off the step and cut across diagonally to the post office, where he could air his importance as a committeeman before an assemblage as ready to discuss the events of the week as he was himself.

It was a momentous occasion in the life of Coldriver; a gathering of prodigals and wanderers under home roofs; a week set aside for the return of sons and daughters and grandchildren of Coldriver who had ventured forth into the world to woo fortune and to seek adventure. Preparations had been in the making for months, and the village was resolved that its collateral relatives to the remotest generation should be made aware that Coldriver was not deficient in the necessary "git up and git" to wear down its visitors to the last point of exhaustion. Pliny Pickett, chairman of numerous committees and marshal of the parade, predicted it would "lay over" the Centennial in Philadelphia.

The greased pig was to be greasier; the barbecued ox was to be larger; the band was to be noisier; the speeches were to be longer and more tiresome; the firemen's races and the ball games, and the fat men's race, and the frog race, and the grand ball with its quadrilles and Virginia reels and "Hull's Victory" and "Lady Washington's Reel" and its "Portland Fancy," were all to be just a little superior to anything of the sort ever attempted in the state. Numerous septuagenarians were resorting to St. Jacob's oil and surreptitious prancing in the barn, to "soople" up their legs for the dance. It was to be one of those wholesome, generous, splendid outpourings of neighborliness and good feeling and wonderful simplicity and kindliness, such as one can meet with nowhere but in the remoter mountain communities of old New England, where customs do not grow stale and no innovation mars. If any man would discover the deep meaning of the word "welcome," let him attend such a Home-coming!

Though Coldriver did not realize it, the impetus toward the Home-coming Week had been given by Scattergood Baines. He had seen in it a subsidence of old grudges and the birth of universal better feeling. He had set the idea in motion, and then, by methods of indirection, of which he was a master, he had urged it on to fulfillment.

Scattergood went inside the store and leaned upon the counter, taking no small pleasure in a mental inventory of his heterogeneous stock. He had completed one side, and arrived at the rear, given over to stoves and garden tools, when a customer entered. Scattergood turned.

"Mornin', Mattie," he said. "What kin I help ye to this time?"

"I--I need a tack hammer, Mr. Baines."

"Got three kinds: plain, with claws, and them patent ones that picks up tacks by electricity. I hold by them and kin recommend 'em high."

"I'll take one, then," said Mattie; but after Scattergood wrapped it up and gave her change for her dollar bill, she remained, hesitating, uncertain, embarrassed.

"Was they suthin' besides a tack hammer you wanted, Mattie." Scattergood asked, gently.

"I--No, nothing." Her courage had failed her, and she moved toward the door.

"Mattie!"

She stopped.

"Jest a minute," said Scattergood. "Never walk off with suthin' on your mind. Apt to give ye mental cramps. What was that there tack hammer an excuse for comin' here fer?"

"Is it true that he's coming back, like the talk's goin' around?"

"I calc'late ye mean Mavin. Mean Mavin Newton?"

"Yes," she said, faintly.

"What if he did?" said Scattergood.

"I don't know.... Oh, I don't know."

"Want he should come back?"

"He--If he should come--"

"Uh-huh!" said Scattergood. "Calc'late I kin appreciate your feelin's. Treated you mighty bad, didn't he?"

"He treated himself worse," said Mattie, with a little awakening of sharpness.

"So he done. So he done.... Um!... Eight year he's been gone, and you was twenty when he went, wa'n't ye? Twenty?"

"Yes."

"Hain't never had a feller since?"

She shook her head. "I'm an old maid, Mr. Baines."

"I've heard tell of older," he said, dryly. "Wisht you'd tell me why you let sich a scalawag up and ruin your life fer ye?"

"He wasn't a scalawag--till then ."

"You hain't thinkin' he was accused of suthin' he didn't do?"

"He told me he took the money. He came to see me before he ran away."

"Do tell!" This was news to Scattergood. Neither he nor any other was aware that Mavin Newton had seen or been seen by a soul after the commission of his crime.

"He told me," she repeated, "and he said good-by.... But he never told me why. That's what's been hurtin' me and troublin' me all these years. He didn't tell me why he done it, and I hain't ever been able to figger it out."

"Um!... Why he done it? Never occurred to me."

"It never occurred to anybody. All they saw was that he took their organ money and robbed the church. But why did he do it? Folks don't do them things without reason, Mr. Baines."

"He wouldn't tell you?"

"I asked him--and I asked him to take me along with him. I'd 'a' gone gladly, and folks could 'a' thought what they liked. But he wouldn't tell, and he wouldn't have me, and I hain't heard a word from him from that day to this.... But I've thought and figgered and figgered and thought--and I jest can't see no reason at all."

"Took it to run away with--fer expenses," said Scattergood.

"There wasn't anything to run away from until after *he took it. I* know. Whatever 'twas, it come on him suddin. The night before we was together--and--and he didn't have nothin' on his mind but plans for him and me ... and he was that happy, Mr. Baines!... I wisht I could make out what turned a good man into a thief--all in a minute, as you might say. It's suthin', Mr. Baines, suthin' out of the ordinary, and always I got a feelin' like I got a right to know."

"Yes," said Scattergood, "seems as though you had a right to know."

"Folks is passin' it about that he's comin' home. Is there any truth into it?"

"I calc'late it's jest talk," said Scattergood. "Nobody knows where he is."

"He'll come sometime," she said.

"And you calc'late to keep on waitin' fer him to come?"

"Until I'm dead--and after that, if it's allowed."

"I wisht," said Scattergood, "there was suthin' I could do to mend it all."

"Nobody kin ever do anythin'," she said.... "But if he should venture back, calc'latin' it had all blown over and been forgot!... His father'd see him put in prison--and I--I couldn't bear that, it seems as though."

"There's a bad thing about borrowin' trouble," said Scattergood. "No matter how hard you try, you can't ever pay it back. Wait till he croaks, and then do your worryin'."

"I've got a feelin' he's goin' to come," she said, and turned away wearily. "I thought maybe you'd know. That's why I came in, Mr. Baines."

"G'-by, Mattie. G'-by. Come ag'in when you feel that way, and you needn't to buy no tack hammer for an excuse."

Scattergood slumped down in his chair on the store's piazza, and began pulling his round cheeks as if he had taken up with some new method of massage. It was a sign of inward disturbance. Presently a hand stole downward to the laces of his shoes--a gesture purely automatic--and in a moment, to the accompaniment of a sigh of relief, his broad feet were released from bondage and his liberty-loving toes were wriggling with delight. Any resident of Coldriver passing at that moment could have told you Scattergood Baines was wrestling with some grave difficulty.

"It stands to reason," said he to himself, "that ever'body has a reason for ever'thing, except lunatics, and lunatics think they got a reason. Now, Mavin he wa'n't no lunatic. He wouldn't have stole church money and run off the night before his weddin' jest to exercise his feet. They hain't no reason, as I recall it, why he needed two hunderd dollars. Unless it was to git married on.... And instid of that, it busted up the weddin'. I calc'late that matter wa'n't looked into sharp enough ... and eight years has gone by. Lots of grass grows up to cover old paths in eight year."

A small boy was passing at the moment, giving an imitation of a cowboy pursuing Indians. Scattergood called to him.

"Hey, bub! Scurry around and see if ye kin find Marvin Preston. Uh-huh! 'F ye see him, tell him I'm a-settin' here on the piazza."

The small boy dug his toes into the dust and disappeared up the street. Presently Marvin Preston appeared in answer to the indirect summons.

"How be ye, Marvin? Stock doin' well?"

"Fust class. See the critter they're figgerin' on barbecuin'? He's a sample."

"Um!... Lived here quite a spell, hain't you, Marvin? Quite a spell?"

"Born here, Scattergood."

"Know lots of folks, don't ye? Got acquainted consid'able in town and the surroundin' country?"

"A feller 'u'd be apt to in fifty-five year."

"Call to mind the Meggses that used to live here?"

"Place next to the Newton farm. Recollect 'em well."

"Lived next to Ol' Man Newton, eh? Forgot that." Scattergood had not forgotten it, but quite the contrary. His interest in the Meggses was negligible; his purpose in mentioning them was to approach the Newtons circuitously and by stealth, as he always approached affairs of importance to him.

"Know 'em well? Know 'em as well's you knowed the Newtons?"

"Not by no means. I've knowed Ol' Man Newton better 'n 'most anybody, seems as though."

"Um!... Le's see.... Had a son, didn't he?"

"Run off with the organ money," said Marvin, shortly.

"Remembered suthin' about him. Quite a while back."

"Eight year. Allus recall the date on account of sellin' a Holstein heifer to Avery Sutphin the mornin' follerin' ... fer cash."

"Him that was dep'ty sheriff?"

"That's the feller."

"Um!... Ever git a notion what young Mavin up and stole that money fer?"

"Inborn cussedness, I calc'late."

"Allus seemed to me like Ol' Man Newton might 'a' made restitution of that there money," said Scattergood, tentatively.

"H'm!" Marvin cleared his throat and glanced up the street. "Seein's how it's you, I dunno but what I kin tell you suthin' you hain't heard, nor nobody else. Young Mavin sent that there money back to his father in a letter to be give to the church--and the ol' man burned it. That's what he up and done. Two hunderd good dollars went up in smoke. Said they was crimes that was beyond restitution or forgiveness, and robbin' the House of God was one of 'em."

"Um!... Now, Marvin, I'd be mighty curious to learn if the ol' man got that information from God himself or if it come out of his own head.... No matter, I calc'late. 'Twan't credit with the church young Mavin was after when he sent back the money, and the Lord he knows the money come, if the organ fund never did find it out."

"Guess I'll take a walk down to Spackles's and look over the steer. They tell me he dressed clost to nine hunderd. Hope they contrive to cook him through and through. Never see a barbecued critter yit that was done.... Folks is beginnin' to git here. Guess they won't be a spare bedroom in town that hain't full up."

Scattergood pulled on his shoes and, leaving his store to take care of itself, walked up the road, turned across the mowing which had been metamorphosed into an athletic field, trusted his weight to the temporary bridge across the brook, and scrambled up the bank to the great oven where the steer was to be baked, and where the potato hole was ready to receive twenty bushels of potatoes and the arch was ready to receive the sugar vat in which two thousand ears of corn were to be steamed. Pliny Pickett was in charge, with Ulysses Watts, sheriff, and Coroner Bogle as assistants. They had fired up already, and were sitting blissfully by in the blistering heat, bragging about the sort of meal they were going to purvey, and speculating on whether the imported band would play enough, and how the ball games would come out, and naming over the folks who were expected to arrive from distant parts.

"This here town team hain't what it was ten year ago," said the sheriff. "In them days the boys knowed how to play ball. There was me 'n' Will Pratt and Pliny here 'n' Avery Sutphin, that was sheriff 'fore I was...."

"What ever become of Avery?" Pliny asked.

"Went West. Heard suthin' about him a spell back, but don't call to mind what it was. Wonder if he'll be comin' back with the rest?"

"Dunno. Think there's anythin' in the rumor that Mavin Newton's comin'?" "Hope not," said the sheriff, assuming an official look and feeling of the suspender to which was affixed his badge of office. "Don't want to have no arrestin' to do durin' Old Home Week."

"Calc'late to take him in if he comes?"

"Duty," said Sheriff Watts, "is duty."

"When it hain't a pleasure," said Scattergood. "Recall what place Avery Sutphin went to?"

"Seems like it was Oswego. Some'eres out West like that."

"Wisht all the town 'u'd quit traipsin' over here," said Pliny. "Never see sich curiosity. They needn't to think they're goin' to git a look at the critter while he's a-cookin'. No, siree. Nobody but this here committee sees him till he's took out final, ready fer eatin'."

All that day visitors arrived in town. They drove in, came by train and by stage--and walked. There was no house whose ready hospitality was not taxed to its capacity, and the ladies in charge of the restaurant in Masonic Hall became frantic and sent out hysterical messengers for more food and more help. Every house was dressed in flags and bunting. Even Deacon Pettybone, reputed to be the "nearest" inhabitant of the village, flew one small cotton flag, reputed to have cost fifteen cents, from his front stoop. The bridge was so covered with red, white, and blue as to quite lose its identity as a bridge and to become one of the wonders of the world, to be talked about for a decade. As one looked up the street a similarity of motion, almost machinelike, was apparent. It was an endless shaking of hands as old friend met old friend joyously.

"Bet ye don't know who I be?"

"I'd 'a' know'd you in Chiny. You're Mort Whittaker's wife--her that was Ida Janes. Hair hain't so red as what it was."

"You've took on flesh some, but otherwise--'Member the time you took me to the dance at Tupper Falls--"

"An' we got mired crossin'--"

"An' Sam Kettleman come in a plug hat."

This conversation, or its counterpart, was repeated wherever resident and visitor met. Old days lived again. Ancient men became middle-aged, and middle-aged women became girls. The past was brought to life and lived again. Sometimes it was brought to life a bit tediously, as when old Jethro Hammond, postmaster of Cold-river twenty years ago, made a speech seventy minutes long, which consisted in naming and locating every house that existed in his day, and describing with minute detail who lived in it and what part they played in the affairs of the community. But the audience forgave him, because it knew what a good time he was having.... Houses were invaded by perfect strangers who insisted in pointing out the rooms in which they were born and in which they had been married, and in telling the present proprietors how fortunate they were to live in dwellings thus blessed.

The band arrived and met with universal satisfaction, though Lafe Atwell complained that he hadn't ever see a snare drummer with whiskers. But their coats were red, with gorgeous frogs, and their trousers were sky blue, with gold stripes, and the drum major could whirl his baton in a manner every boy in town would be imitating with the handle of the ancestral broom for months to come.... Through it all Scattergood Baines sat on the piazza and beamed upon the world, and rejoiced in the goodness thereof.

Only one resident took no part in the holiday making, and that was Old Man Newton, who had closed his house, drawn the blinds, and refused to make himself visible while the celebration lasted. He took a savage pleasure in thus making himself conspicuous, knowing well how his conduct would be discussed, and viewing himself as a righteous man suffering for the sins of another.

In the darkness of the evening street Mattie Strong accosted Scattergood that evening, clinging to his arm tremulously.

"Mr. Baines," she whispered, affrightedly, "he's come!"

"Who's come?"

"Mavin Newton--he's here, in town."

Scattergood frowned. "See him?"

"Hain't seen him, but he's here. I kin feel him. I knowed it the minute he come."

"Calc'late I've seen everybody here, and I hain't seen him."

"He's here, jest the same. I'm a-lookin' fer him. Whatever name he come under, or however he looks, I'll know him. I couldn't make no mistake about Mavin."

"Mattie, I hope 'tain't so.... I hope you're mistook."

"I--I don't know whether I hope so or not. I--Oh, Mr. Baines, I'd rather be with him, a-comfortin' him and standin' by him, no matter what he done--"

Scattergood patted her arm. "I calc'late," he said, softly, "that God hain't never invented no institution that beats the love of a good woman.... I'll look around, Mattie.... I'll look around."

It was the next morning, at the ball game, when Mattie spoke to Scattergood again.

"I've seen him," she whispered, and there was a note of happiness in her voice and a look of renewed youth in her eyes. "He's here, like I said."

"Where?"

Mattie lowered her voice farther still. "Look at the band," she said.

"Nobody resembles him there," said Scattergood, after a minute.

"Wait till they stop playin'--and then see if they hain't somebody there that takes holt of the fingers of his right hand, one after the other, and kind of twists 'em.... Look sharp. Mavin he allus done that when he was nervous--allus. I'd know him by it, anywheres."

Scattergood watched. Presently the "piece" ended and the musicians laid down their instruments and eased back in their chairs.

"Look," said Mattie.

The bearded snare drummer was performing a queer antic. It was as if his fingers were screwed into his hand and had become loosened while he drummed. No, he was tightening them so they wouldn't fall off. One finger after another he screwed up, and then went over them again to make certain they were secure.

"I--knowed he'd come," Mattie said, happily.

"Um!... This here's kind of untoward. You keep your mouth shet, Mattie Strong. Don't you go near that feller till I tell you. We don't want a rumpus to spoil this here week."

"But he's here.... He's here."

"So's trouble," said Scattergood, succinctly.

The rest of that day Scattergood busied himself in searching out old friends and neighbors of the Newtons. Nothing seemed to interest him which happened later than eight years before, but no event of that period was too slight or inconsequential to receive his attention and to be filed away in his shrewd old brain. He was looking for the answer to a question, and the answer was piled under the rubbish of eight years of human activities--a hopeless quest to any but Scattergood.

Comedy and tragedy were alike interesting to him. Just as he lost no detail of the old man's conduct when his boy disappeared, so he listened and laughed when Martin Banks recalled to a group how Old Man Newton had fallen under the suspicion of bootlegging and how the town had seethed with the downfall of an elder of the church--and all because the old man had imported two cases, each of a dozen bottles of the Siwash Indian Stomach Bitters recommended to cure his dyspepsia. There had been a moment, said Banks, when the town expected to see Newton shut up in the calaboose under the post office--until the true contents of those cases was revealed.

During the afternoon Scattergood sent six telegrams to as many different cities. Late that night he received replies, and sent one long message to an individual high in office in the state. It was an urgent message, amounting to a command, for in his own commonwealth Scattergood Baines was able to command when the need required.

"It's an off chance," he said to himself, "but it's what might 'a' happened, and if it might 'a' happened, maybe it did happen...."

Wednesday afternoon the band was thrown into consternation, and the town into a paroxysm of excitement and speculation, when Sheriff Watts ascended the platform of the musicians and, placing a heavy hand on the shoulder of the snare drummer, said, loudly, "Mavin Newton, I arrest ye in the name of the law."

Not a soul in that breathless crowd was there who failed to see Mattie Strong point her finger in the face of Scattergood Baines, and to hear her utter the one word, "Shame!" Nor did any fail to see her take her place at the side of the bearded drummer, with her fingers clutching his arm, and walk to the door of the jail under the post office with the prisoner.

Then the word was passed about that the hearing would take place before Justice of the Peace Bender that very evening. So great was the public clamor that the justice agreed to hold court in the town hall instead of in his office; and it was rumored that Johnnie Bones, Scattergood Baines's own lawyer, had been appointed special prosecutor by the Governor of the state.

Opinion ran against Scattergood. It was free and outspoken. Townsfolk and visitors alike felt that Scattergood had done ill in bringing the young man to justice--especially at such a time. He should have let sleeping dogs lie.... And when it heard that Sheriff Watts had carried a subpoena to Mavin Newton's father, compelling his presence as a witness against his own son, there arose a wind of disapproval which quite swept Scattergood from the esteem of the community.

But the town came to the hearing. In the beginning it was a cut-and-dried affair. The facts of the crime were established with dry precision. Then Johnnie Bones called the name of a witness, and the audience stiffened to attention. Even Old Man Newton, sitting with bowed head and scowling brow, lifted his eyes to the face of the young lawyer.

"Avery Sutphin," said Johnnie Bones, and the former sheriff, wearing such a haircut as Coldriver seldom saw within its corporate limits, and clothed in such clothing as it had never seen there, was brought through the door by two strangers of official look. He seated himself in the witness chair.

"You are Avery Sutphin, former sheriff of this town?"

"Yes."

"Where do you reside?"

"In the state penitentiary," said Avery, seeking to hide his face.

"Do you know Mavin Newton?"

"Yes."

"When did you last see him?"

"It was the night of June twelfth, eight year ago."

"Where?"

"In his father's barn."

"What was he doing?"

"Milkin'," said Avery.

"You went to see him?"

"Yes."

"Why?"

"To git some money out of him."

"Did he owe you money?"

"No."

"How much money did you go to get?"

"Two hunderd dollars."

"Did you get it?"

"Yes."

"Do you know what money it was?"

"Church-organ money. He told me."

"Why did he give it to you?"

"I made him."

"How?"

"Lemme tell it my own way--if I got to tell it.... He'd took my girl, and I never liked him, anyhow.... There'd been rumors his old man was bootleggin'. Nothin' to it, of course, and I knowed that. And I needed some money. Bought a beef critter off'n Marvin Preston next day. So I went to Mavin and says I was goin' to arrest his old man because I'd ketched him sellin' liquor, and Mavin he begged me I shouldn't. I told him the old man would git ten year, anyhow."

"What did Mavin say to that?"

"He jest bowed his head and kind of leaned against the stall."

"Then what?"

"I let on I needed money, and told him if he'd gimme two hunderd dollars I'd destroy the evidence and let the old man go. He says he didn't have the money, and I says he had the organ money. He didn't say nothin' for a spell, and then he says, kind of low, and wonderin', 'Which 'u'd be the worst? Which 'u'd be the worst?' Then I says, 'Worst what?' And he says for his father to be ketched for a bootlegger or for him to be a thief.... I jest let him think about it, and didn't say nothin', because I knowed how he looked up to his old man.

"Pretty soon he says: 'I'd be a thief, 'cause I couldn't explain. I'd have to run off--and leave Mattie, that I'm a-goin' to marry to-morrer.... I could pay it back, but that wouldn't do no good.... But for father to be arrested, him an elder, and all, would kill him. I couldn't bear for father to be shamed 'fore all the world or to be thought guilty of sich a thing.... He's wuth a heap more 'n I be, and he won't never do it ag'in.' Then he asks if I'll give a letter to his old man, and I says yes. He walked up and down for maybe a quarter of an hour, talkin' to himself, and kind of fightin' it out, but I knowed what he'd do, right along. At the end he come over and says: 'This here means ruinin' my life and breakin' Mattie's heart ... but I calc'late that's better 'n holdin' father up to scorn and seein' him in jail.... If they was only some other way!' His voice was stiddylike, but he was right pale and his eyes was a-shinin'. I remember how they was a-shinin'. 'I calc'late,' he says, 'that I kin bear it fer father's sake.' Then he says to me, kind of fierce, 'If ever you let on to anybody why I done this, if it's in a hunderd years, I'll come back and kill you.' For a while he kept still again, and then he went in the house and got the money, and wrote a letter to his old man, and I promised to give it to him--but I tore it up."

"What did the letter say?"

"It just said somethin' to the effect that he was willin' to do what he done if his old man would give over breakin' the law and go to livin' upright like he always done, and that he hoped maybe God seen a difference in stealin' on account of the reasons folks had for doin' it--but if God didn't make no difference, why, he'd rather bear it than have it fall on his old man."

"And then?"

"I took the money and come away. And he run away. And that's all."

The town hall was very still. The stillness of it seemed to pierce and hurt.... Then it was broken by a cry, a hoarse cry, wrenched from the soul of a man. "My boy!... My boy!..." Old Elder Newton was on his feet, tottering toward his son, and before his son he sank upon his knees and buried his hard, weathered old face upon Mavin's knees.

Justice of the Peace Bender cleared his throat.

"This here," he said, "looks to me to be suthin' the folks of this town, the friends and neighbors of this here father and son, ought to settle, instid of the law. Maybe it hain't legal, but I dunno who's to interfere.... Folks, what ought to be done to this here boy that done a crime and suffered the consequences of it, jest to save his father from another crime the old man never done a-tall?"

Neither Mavin nor his father heard. The old elder was muttering over and over, "My boy that was dead and is alive again...."

Scattergood arose silently and pointed to the door, and the crowd withdrew silently, withdrew to group about the entrance outside and to wait. They were patient. It was an hour before Elder Newton descended, his son on one side and Mattie Strong on the other.... The band, with a volunteer drummer, lifted its joyous voice, and, looking up, the trio faced a banner upon which Scattergood had caused to be painted, "Welcome Home, Mavin Newton."

Coldriver had taken judicial action and thus voiced its decision.

CHAPTER XIII
HE CRACKS AN OBDURATE NUT

Jason Locker, who was Sam Kettleman's rival in Coldriver's grocery industry, was a trifle too amenable to modern ideas at times. He took notions, as the folks said. Once he went so far as to say that he could do anything in his store that anybody could do in a big city store and make a success of it. He was so progressive that in the Coldriver parade he occupied a position so advanced that it really seemed like two parades.

Old Man Bogle and Deacon Pettybone and Elder Hooper always discussed Locker when politics were exhausted, and their only point of difference was as to when and exactly how Jason would wind up in bankruptcy. They were agreed that he was a bit touched in his head. He was much given to sales. He installed a perfectly unnecessary cash carrier from the counter to a desk where Mrs. Locker made change. He bought a case of olives, which were viewed and tasted (free) by the village loafers, and pronounced spoiled.... In short, there was no newfangled idea which Jason failed to adopt, and in a matter of twenty years the town grew accustomed to him, and tolerated him, and, as a matter of fact, was rather proud of him as a novel lunatic. However, he prospered.

But when, on a certain Monday morning, a strange and unquestionably pretty girl, dressed not according to Coldriver's ideas of current fashions, made her appearance in a space cleared in the middle of the store, and there proceeded to make and dispense tiny cups of a new brand of coffee, the village considered that Jason had gone too far.

It is true that it came in droves to taste the coffee being demonstrated, for it was to be had without money and without price. It came to see what it would not believe without seeing, and regarded the young woman with open suspicion and hostility. It wondered what manner of young woman it could be who would har-um-scarum around the country making coffee for every Tom, Dick, and Harry, and wearing a smile for everybody, and demeaning herself generally in a manner not heretofore observed. It viewed and reviewed her hair, her slippers, her ankles, her frocks, and her ornaments. The women folks, and especially the younger women, held frequent indignation meetings, and declared for the advisability of boycotting Locker unless he removed this menace from their midst.

But when it noticed, not later than the second day of Miss Yvette Hinchbrooke's career in their midst, that young Homer Locker flapped about her like some over-grown insect about a street lamp, it took no pains to conceal its delight and devoutly hoped for the worst.

"Looks like Providence was steppin' in," said Elder Hooper to Deacon Petty-bone. "Dunno's I ever see a more fittin' as *well* as proper follerin' up of sinful care-lessness by sich consequences as might be expected to ensue."

"Uh-huh!... That there name of her'n. Folks differs about the way to say it. I been holdin' out ag'in' many for Wife-ette--that way. Looks like French or suthin' furrin. Others say it's Weev-ette. If 'twan't for seemin' to show interest in the bag-gage, dummed if I wouldn't up and ask her."

"Names don't count," said Old Man Bogle, oracularly. "She hain't to blame for pickin' her name. Her ma gave it to her out of a book, seems as though. Neverthe-less, 'tain't no fit name for a woman, and, so fur's I kin see, she fits her name like Ovid Nixon's tailor pants fits his laigs."

"She's light," said the elder.

"Sh'u'dn't be s'prised," said Old Man Bogle, rolling his eyes, "if she was one of them actoresses. Venture to say she's filled with worldly wisdom, that gal, and that sin and cuttin' up different ways hain't nothin' strange nor unaccustomed to her."

"While I was a-drinkin' down her coffee out of that measly leetle cup," said the deacon, "she was that brazen! Acted like she'd took a fancy to me," he said, with a sprucing back of his old shoulders.

"Got all the wiles of that there woman that danced off the head of John the Bap-tist," said the elder, grimly. "So she dasted even to tempt a deacon of the church."

"She didn't tempt me none," snapped the deacon, "but I lay she was willin'."

"I'll venture," said Old Man Bogle, with a light in his rheumy eyes, "that she hain't no stranger to wearin' tights."

"Shame!" said the elder and the deacon, in a breath. And then, from the deacon, in a tone which might have been a reflection of lofty satisfaction in a virtue, or which might have been something quite different, "I've read of them there tights, Elder, but I kin say with a clear conscience that I hain't never witnessed a pair of 'em."

"My nevvy took me to a show in Boston wunst," said Old Man Bogle, tentatively, but he was silenced immediately and sternly.

"How kin a man combat evil," he demanded, "if he hain't familiar with the wiles of it?"

"He kin set his face to the right," said the elder, "and tread the path."

"You wouldn't b'lieve the things I seen in that show," said Bogle, waggling his head.

"Don't intend to be called on to b'lieve 'em," said the deacon. "Look.... Comin' acrost the bridge. There's Locker's boy and that there Wife-ette, and him lookin' like he'd enjoy divin' down her throat."

"Poor Jason," said the elder, "he's reapin' the whirlwind."

"Kin he be blind?"

"Somebody ought to take Jason off to one side and give him warnin'."

The deacon considered, puckering his thin lips and cocking a hard old eye. "'Tain't fer us to meddle," he said, righteously. "They's a divine plan in ever'thing, and we hain't able to see what's behind all this here. We'll jest set and wait the outcome."

That is what all Coldriver did: it sat and awaited the outcome with ill-restrained enthusiasm, and while it waited it talked. No word or gesture or movement of young Homer Locker and Yvette Hinchbrooke went undiscussed. Nobody in town was unaware of Homer's infatuation for the coffee demonstrator--with the one exception of Homer's father, who was too busy waiting upon the unaccustomed rush of trade to notice anything else.

On the fourth evening of Yvette's stay in Coldriver there was a dance in the town hall. Especial interest immediately, attached to this affair because of the speculations as to whether Homer would be so rash as to invite Yvette as his partner. The village refused to believe the young man would fail them and remain away.

That would be a calamity not easily endured, so it set itself to plan its actions in case she made her appearance. It wondered, how she would dress and how she would behave.

Every girl in the village who possessed clear title to a young man knew exactly how she would deport herself. The night before the dance no less than a score of young men were informed with finality that they were not to dance with the stranger, nor to be seen in her vicinity. Norma Grainger expressed the will of all when she told Will Peasley that if he danced one dance with that coffee girl she would up and go home alone. In the beginning there was no definite concerted action; it was assured, however, that Yvette would have few partners.

Homer did not disappoint his friends. During the first dance he entered the hall with Yvette, and the music all but stopped to stare. Undeniably she was pretty. It was not her prettiness the women resented, however, but her air and her clothes. Actually she wore a dress cut low at the neck, and sleeveless. Coldriver had heard of such garments, and there were those who actually believed them to exist and to be worn by certain women in European society among kings and dukes and other frightfully immoral people. But that one should ever make its appearance in Coldriver, under their very eyes, was a thing so startling, so outrageous, as almost to demand the spontaneous formation of a vigilance committee.

Even yet there was no concerted action, but sentiment was crystallizing. Homer and Yvette danced three dances, and Homer's face began to wear a scowl. No less than five young men approached by him with the purpose of securing them as partners for Yvette declined with brevity.

"What's the matter with you??" he demanded, belligerently. "There hain't no pertier girl nor no better dancer on the floor."

"Mebby so. Hain't noticed. Got all my dances took."

"Me too. My girl she says--"

"She says what?" snapped Homer.

"She says she'll go home if I dance with yourn."

"And I *say,*" said Homer, with set jaw, "*that you fellers is goin' to dance with Yvette, or there's goin' to be more fights in Coldriver 'n Coldriver ever see before. That's* my say."

He announced he would be back after the next dance, and that somebody would dance with Yvette. "The feller that refuses," said he, "goes outside with me."

He went back to Yvette, who, not lacking in shrewdness, sensed something of the situation.

"I wish I hadn't come," she said, uneasily.

"I don't ... if you hain't got no objection to dancin' jest with me."

"It'll look queer if I dance all of them with you."

"Jest ask me, and see if I care," he said, desperately. "It's like I'd want to have it. I couldn't never dance more'n I want to with you. I wisht I could dance all the dances there'll be in your life with you.... Come on. This here's a quadrille."

Pliny Pickett, self-appointed caller of square dances, was arranging the floor. "One more couple wanted to this end," he bellowed. "Here's two couples a-waitin'. Don't hang back. Music's a-waitin'.... Right there. All ready?... Nope. One couple needed in the middle."

Homer and Yvette approached that square where three couples awaited the fourth to complete their set. They took their places, to the manifest embarrassment of the other six. Suddenly Norma Grainger whispered something to her young man and tugged at his arm. He looked sidewise, sheepishly, at Homer, and hung back.

"You come right along," said Norma. "I hain't goin' to have it said of me that I danced in no set with her."

"Nor me," said Marion Towne, also tugging at her escort.

The young men were forced to give way, and, not too proud to cast glances of placating nature at Homer, they fell from their places and walked to the benches around the hall. Yvette and Homer were left standing alone, conspicuous, the center of all eyes.

Homer clenched his fists and glared about him; then--for in his ungainly body there resided something that is essential to manhood, and without which none may be called a gentleman--he offered his arm to Yvette. "I guess we better go," he said, softly. Then squaring his powerful shoulders and glancing about him with a real dignity which Scattergood Baines, sitting in one corner, noted and applauded, he led the girl from the room.

"I'll see you home," he said, formally. "I hain't got nothin' to say."

"It--it's not your fault," she said, tremulously.

"Somebody'll wisht it wa'n't their fault 'fore mornin'," he answered.

"I shouldn't have gone."

"Why? Hain't you as good as any of them, and better? Hain't you the pertiest girl I ever see?... You hain't mad with me, be you?"

"'No.... Not with anybody, I guess. I--I ought to be used to it. I--" She began to cry.

It was a dark spot there on the bridge. Homer was not apt at words, but he could feel and he did feel. It was no mere impulse to comfort a pretty girl that moved him to inclose her with his muscular arms and to press her to him none too gently.

"I kin lick the hull world fer you," he said, huskily, and then he kissed her wet cheek again and again, and repeated his ability to thrash all comers in her cause, and stated his desire to undertake exactly that task for the term of her natural life. "If you was to marry me," he said, "they wouldn't nobody dast trample on you.... You're a-goin' to marry me, hain't you?"

"I--I don't know.... You--you don't know anything about me."

"Calc'late I know enough," he said.

"Your folks wouldn't put up with it."

"Huh!"

There was a silence. Then she said, brokenly: "I must go away. I can't ever go back to the store to-morrow to have everybody staring at me and talking about me.... I want to go away to-night."

"You sha'n't. Nor no other time, neither."

And then, out of the darkness behind, spoke Scattergood Baines's voice. "Hain't calc'latin' to bust the gal, be you?... Jest happened along to say the deacon's been talkin' to your pa about you 'n' her, and your pa's het up consid'able. He's startin' out to look fer you. Lucky I come along, wa'n't it?"

"I'm of age," said Homer, aggressively.

"Lots is," said Scattergood. "'Tain't nothin' to take special pride in.... Homer, I've watched you raised from a colt, hain't I? Be you willin' to kind of leave this here to me a spell? I sort of want to look into things. You go along about your business and leave me talk to Wife-ette here.... Made up your mind you want her?"

"Yes."

"She want you?"

"I--What business is it of yours?" Yvette demanded, angrily. "Who are you?

What are you interfering for?"

"Kind of a habit with me," said Scattergood, "and my wife hain't ever been able to cure me, even puttin' things in my coffee on the sly.... G'-by, Homer. And don't go lickin' nobody. G'-by."

The habit of obedience to Scattergood's customary dismissal was strong in Coldriver. For more than a generation the town had been trained to heed it and to trust its affairs to the old hardware merchant. Homer hesitated, coughed, mumbled good night to Yvette, and slouched away.

"There," said Scattergood, "now you and me kin talk. We'll go up to your room, where nobody kin disturb us." The conventions nor the tongue of gossip was non-existent to Scattergood Baines, and Yvette, not reared in a school where trust in men is easily learned, was shrewd enough to recognize Scattergood's purpose and her own safety.

"I s'pose you're the local Mr. Fix-it," she said, with sarcasm.

"I s'pose," said Scattergood, "that I've knowed Homer sence he was knee high to a mouse's kitten, and I don't know nothin' about you a-tall. I gather you're calc'latin' on marryin' Homer.... Mebby you be and mebby you hain't.... Depends. Come along."

He led the way to the hotel and allowed Yvette to precede him up the stairs to her room, which she unlocked and stood aside for him to enter. He looked about him in the sharp-eyed way characteristic of him, not omitting to include in his survey the toilet articles on the dresser.

"Hain't you perty enough without them?" he asked, indicating the lip stick and rice powder. "Us folks hain't used to 'em, much.... Wunst we give a home-talent play here, and there come a feller from Boston to help out. Mis' Blossom was into it, and he come around to paint her up. She jest give him one look, and says, says she, 'I hain't never painted my face yit, and I don't calc'late to start in now.' ... I got to admit she looked kind of pale and peeked amongst the rest, but she stuck to her principles."

Yvette stared at Scattergood, nonplused for the first time. What did he mean? How was she to take him? His face was serene and there was no glint of humor in his eye.... Yet, somehow, she gathered the idea he was chuckling inwardly and that there resided in him a broad and tender toleration for the little antics and makeshifts of mankind. Possibly he was holding Mrs. Blossom up to her as a model of rectitude; perhaps he was asking her to laugh with him at a foible of one of his own people. She wished she knew which.

"Calc'late on marryin' Homer?" he asked.

"I--"

"Yes or no--quick."

"Yes," she said, lifting her chin bravely.

"Um!... Knowed him four days, hain't you? Think it's long enough? Plenty of time to figger it all out?"

She sat down on the bed, drooping wearily. "I'm tired," she said, "awful tired. I can't stand this life any longer. I've got to have a place to rest."

"Hain't goin' to have Homer used for no sanitorium," said Scattergood.

"I like him," said Yvette.

"'Tain't enough. Up this way folks mostly loves when they git married--or owns adjoinin' timber."

Again she was at a loss. What did he mean? If he would only smile!

"I--I've got a feeling I could trust him," she said, "and he'd be good to me."

"He would," said Scattergood. "I hain't worritin' about his dealin' with you; it's your dealin' with him I'm questionin' into."

"I'd--. He wouldn't be sorry."

"Um!... Nate Weaver, back country a spell, is lookin' fer a wife. Hain't young. Got lots of money, and the right woman could weasel it out of him. Lots of it.... He'd like you fine. Homer won't have much, and if his pa keeps on feelin' like he does, he won't have none.... If you're lookin' fer a restin' place, you might consider Nate. I could fix it." Her eyes flashed. "I haven't come to that yet," she said, sharply, and then began to cry quietly.

"Um!..." Scattergood gripped his pudgy hands together so that each might restrain the other from patting her head comfortly. "Um!... What's your name?"

"My name?"

"Yes.... 'Tain't Wife-ette Hinchbrooke. They hain't no sich name. 'Tain't human.... What's your real one?"

"Eva Hopkins."

"How'd you come to change?"

"A girl's got a right to call herself anything she wants to," she said, defensive-ly.

"Except Mrs. Homer Locker," said Scattergood, dryly. "Now jest come off'n your high boss, and we'll talk. When we git through, we'll do…. Either you'll take the mornin' train out of Coldriver, or you'll stay and well see. Depends on what I hear."

"I could lie," she said.

"Folks don't gen'ally lie to me," said Scattergood, gently. "They found out it didn't pay--and I hain't much give to believin' nothin' but the truth. We deal in it a lot up this here way."

"I hate your people and their dealings."

"Don't wonder at it. I seen what they done to you to-night…. But you don't know 'em like I do. They's times when they act cold and ha'sh and nigh to cruel, but that hain't when they're real. Them times they're jest makin' b'lieve, 'cause they hain't got no idee what they ought to do…. I've knowed 'em these thirty year--right down knowed 'em. Lemme tell you they hain't a finer folks on earth, bar nobody. They don't show much outside, but the insides is right. You kin find more kind-ness and charity and long-sufferin' and tenderness and goodness right here amongst the cantankerous-seemin' of Coldriver 'n you kin find anywheres else on earth…. They're narrer, Eva, and they got sot notions, but they got a power to do kindness, once you git 'em started at it, that hain't to be beat…. I kind of calculate God hain't so disapp'inted with the folks of Coldriver as a stranger might git the idee he is…. Now we'll go ahead."

When Scattergood had done asking questions and receiving answers, he sat silent for a matter of moments. Automatically his hands strayed to the lacing of his shoes, for his pudgy toes itched for freedom to wiggle. He dealt with a prob-lem whose complex elements were human emotions and prejudices, and at such times he found his brain to act more clearly and efficiently with shoes removed. He detected himself, however, in the act of untying the laces, and sat upright with ludicrous suddenness.

"Um!…" he said, in some confusion. "Mandy says I hain't never to do it when wimmin is around. Dunno why…. Now they's some p'ints I got to impress on you."

"Yes, Mr. Baines," said Yvette, who had reached a condition of respect and confidence in Scattergood--as most people did upon meeting him face to face.

"Fust, Homer hain't no sanitorium for weary wimmin. When you kin come and say, meanin' it from your heart, 'I love Homer,' then we'll see."

She nodded acquiescence.

"Second, it won't never and noways be possible fer you and Homer to live here onless the folks takes to you. You got to win yourself a welcome in Coldriver."

"That means," she said, dully, "that I'd better go."

"Huh!... Hain't you got no backbone? You do like you're told. You stay where you be. 'Tain't possible fer you to go back to Locker's store, and that puts you out of a job, don't it?"

"Yes."

"Hard up?"

"I can live a few days--but--"

"Hain't no buts. You kin live as long as I say so. You stay hitched to this here hitchin' post, and I'll 'tend to the money. Jest don't do nothin' but be where you be--and be makin' up your mind if Homer's the boy you kin love and cherish, or if he's nothin' but a sort of shady restin' place.... G'-by."

He got up abruptly and went out. On the bridge he encountered three dark figures, which, upon inspection, resolved themselves into Old Man Bogle, Deacon Pettybone, and Elder Hooper.

"Scattergood," said the elder, "somethin's happened."

"Somethin' 'most allus does."

"This here's special and horrifyin'."

"Havin' to do with what?"

"That coffee gal, that baggage, that hussy!"

"Um!... Sich as?"

"Recall that show Bogle was took to in Boston?"

"Where the wimmin wore tights--that's been on his mind ever since? Calc'late I do. Kind of a high spot in Bogle's life. Come nigh bein' the makin' of him."

"He claims he recognizes this here gal as one of them dancin' wimmin that stood in a row with less on to them than any woman ever ought to have with the lights turned on."

"No!" exclaimed Scattergood.

"Yep!" said all three of them in chorus.

"Stood right in front, as I recall it, a-makin' eyes and kickin' up her heels that immodest you wouldn't b'lieve. Looked right at me, too. I seen her."

"Got your money's wuth, then, didn't ye? Wa-al?"

"Suthin's got to be done."

"Sich as?"

"Riddin' the town of her."

"Go ahead and rid it, then.... G'-by."

"But we want you sh'u'd help us."

"G'-by," said Scattergood again, as he moved off ponderously into the darkness.

The elder moved nearer Bogle and endeavored to peer into his face. "Be you sure she's the same one?" he asked, in a confidential whisper.

"Wa-al--they was about the same heft," said Bogle, "and if this hain't her, it ought to be. I kin b'lieve it, can't I? Got a right to b'lieve it, hain't I? Good fer the town to b'lieve it, hain't it?"

"Calc'late 'tis."

"All right, then. I aim to keep on b'lievin' it."

Next day Homer Locker abandoned his work and with the utmost brazenness hired a rig at the livery and drove to the hotel. A group of notables assembled upon the bridge to watch the event. They saw him emerge from the inn with Yvette, help her into the buggy with great solicitude, and drive away. They did not return until supper time was long past.

"I'm determined to git this settled one way or t'other," said Homer, after a long pause. "Be you goin' to marry me?"

"Why do you want me?" Yvette asked, fixing her eyes on his face. "Is it just because you think I'm pretty?"

He considered. It was a hard question for a young man not adept in the use of words to answer. "'Tain't jest that," he said, finally. "I like you bein' perty. But it's somethin' else. I hain't able to explain it, exceptin' that I want you more'n I ever wanted anythin' in my life."

"Maybe, when I tell you about myself, you won't want me at all."

He paused again, while she studied his face anxiously.

"I dunno.... I--. Tell ye what. I want you like I know you. I'm satisfied. I don't want you to tell me nothin'. I don't want to know nothin'." He turned and looked with clumsy gravity into her eyes, which did not waver. "Besides," he said, "I don't believe you got anythin' discreditable to tell."

"I want to tell you."

"I don't want to hear," he said, simply. "I'd rather take you, jest trustin' you and knowin' in my heart that you're good. Somehow I know it."

She bit her lip, her eyes were moist, and she sat very still for a long time; then she said, softly: "I didn't know men like that lived.... I didn't know."

Then again, after the passage of minutes: "I was going to marry you, Homer, just for a home and a good man and to get peace.... But I sha'n't do it now. I can't come between you and all your folks--and they wouldn't have me."

"You're more to me than everybody else throwed together."

"No, Homer. Before I didn't think I cared.... I do care, Homer. I--I love you. I don't mind saying it now.... I'm going away in the morning."

It was a point they argued all the day, but Yvette was not to be moved, and Homer was in despair. As he drove into the village that evening, glum and unhappy, Yvette said: "Stop at Mr. Baines's, please, Homer. I want to speak to him."

Scattergood was in his accustomed place before his store, shoes on the piazza beside him, and his feet, guiltless of socks, reveling in their liberty.

"Mr. Baines," said Yvette, "I've made up my mind to go away to-morrow."

"Um!... To-morrer, eh? Made up your mind you don't want Homer, have ye? Don't blame ye. He's a mighty humble critter."

"He's the best man in the world," said Yvette, softly, "and I love him ... and that--that's why I'm going. I can't stay and make him miserable."

Scattergood studied her face a moment, and cleared his throat noisily. "Hum!... I swan to man! Goin', be ye?... Mebby that's best.... But they hain't no sich hurry. Be out of a job, won't ye? Uh-huh! Wa-al, you stay till Thursday mornin' and kind of visit with Homer, and say good-by, and then you kin go. Thursday mornin'.... Not a minute before."

"But--"

"Thursday mornin's the time, I said.... G'-by."

Next morning Scattergood was absent. He had taken the early train out of town, as Pliny Pickett reported, on a "whoppin' big deal that come up suddin in the night." It appeared that for once Scattergood had allowed business to distract him wholly from his favorite occupation of meddling in other folks' affairs.... Nobody saw him return, for he drove into town late Wednesday afternoon and went directly to his home.

For forty-eight hours during his absence rumor had spread and increased its girth to astounding dimensions. Old Man Bogle had released his story. He now recollected Yvette perfectly, and when not restrained by the modesty of some person of the opposite sex, he described her costume in the play with minute detail. Hourly he remembered more and more, and the mouth-to-ear repetitions of his tale embellished it with details even Old Man Bogle's imagination could not have encompassed.... Before Wednesday night Yvette had arisen in the estimation of the village to an eminence of evil never before attained by any visitor to Coldriver.

Jason Locker forbade his son his home if ever he were seen in the hussy's company again, and Homer left by the front door.... He announced his purpose of journeying to the South Seas or New York, or some other equally strange and dangerous shore. The town seethed. It had been years since any local sensation approached this high moment.... At half past six Pliny Pickett, Scattergood's right-hand man and general errand boy, was seen to approach Homer on the street and to whisper to him. Pliny always enshrouded his most matter-of-fact errands with voluminous mystery. "Scattergood wants you sh'u'd see him right off," he said, and tiptoed away.

Another sensation occurred that evening. Scattergood Baines went to prayer meeting in the Methodist church. When word of this was passed about, the Baptists and Congos deserted their places of worship in whispering groups and invaded the rival edifice until it was crowded as it had seldom been before. Scattergood in prayer meeting! Scattergood, who had never been inside a church since the day of his arrival in Coldriver, forty years before.... Even Yvette Hinchbrooke and her affairs sank into insignificance.

But the amazing presence of Scattergood in church was as nothing to the epochal fact that, after the prayer and hymn, he was seen slowly to get to his feet. Scattergood Baines was going to lift up his voice in meeting!

"Folks," he said, "I've knowed Coldriver for quite a spell. I've knowed its good and its bad, but the good outweighs the bad by a darn sight." The congregation gasped.

"I run on to a case to-day," he said, and then paused, apparently thinking better of what he was going to say and taking another course. "They's one great way to reach folks's hearts and that's through their sympathy. All of you give up to furrin missions to rescue naked fellers with rings in their noses. That's sympathy, hain't it? Mebby they hain't needin' sympathy and cast-off pants, but that's neither here nor there. You think they do.... Coldriver's great on sympathy, and it's a doggone upstandin' quality." Again the audience sucked in its breath at this approach to the language of everyday life.

"If I was wantin' to stir up your sympathy, I'd tell you about a leetle feller I seen yestiddy. Mebby I will. He wa'n't no naked heathen, and he didn't have no ring into his nose. He was jest a boy. Uh-huh! Calculate he might 'a' been ten year old. Couldn't walk a step. Suthin' ailed his laigs, and he had to lay around in a chair in one of these here kind of cheap horspittles. Alone he was. Didn't have no pa nor ma.... But he had to be looked after by somebody, didn't he? Somebody had to pay them bills."

Scattergood blew his nose gustily. "Mebby he could 'a' been cured if they was money to pay for costly doctorin', but they wa'n't. It took all that could be got jest to pay for his food and keep.... Patient leetle feller, too, and gentlelike and cheerful. Kind of took to him, I did."

He paused, turned slowly, and surveyed the congregation, and frowned at the door of the church. He coughed. He waited. The congregation turned, following his eyes, and saw Mandy, Scattergood's ample-bosomed wife, enter, bearing in her arms the form of a child. She walked to Scattergood's pew and handed the boy to him. Scattergood held the child high, so all could see.

He was a red-haired little fellow, white and thin of face, with pipe-stem legs that dangled pitifully.

"I fetched him along," said Scattergood. "I wisht you'd look him over."

The audience craned its neck, exclaiming, dropping tears. The heart of Coldriver was well protected, it fancied, by an exterior of harshness and suspicion, but Coldriver was wrong. Its heart lay near the surface, easy of access, warm, tender, sympathetic. "This is him," said Scattergood.

He turned his face to the child. "Sonny," he said, kindly, "you hain't got no pa nor ma?" "No, sir," said the little fellow.

"And you live in one of them horspittles?"

"Yes, sir."

"It costs money?"

"Yes, sir."

"How do you git it, sonny? Tell the folks."

"Sister," said the child. "She's awful good to me. When she kin, she stays whole days with me, but she can't stay much on account of havin' to earn money to pay for me. It takes 'most all she earns.... She's had to do kinds of work she don't like, on account of it earnin' more money than nice jobs. We're savin' to have me cured, and then I'm goin' to go to work and keep her. I got it all planned out while I was layin' there."

"Is your sister a bad woman?"

"Nobody dast say that, even if I hain't got legs. I'd grab somethin' and throw it at 'em."

"Was this here sister ever one of them actoresses?"

"Once, when I was sicker 'n usual ... it was awful costly. That time she was in a show, 'cause she got more money there. She got enough to pay for what I needed."

"Wear tights, sonny? Calc'late she wore tights?"

"Sure. She told me. She said to me it wasn't wearin' tights that done harm, and she could be jest as good in tights as wearin' a fur coat if her heart wasn't bad. That's what she said. Yes, sir, she said she wouldn't wear nothin' if it had to be done to git me medicine."

"Um!... What's this here sister's name?"

"Eva Hopkins."

Scattergood turned again toward the door. "Homer," he called, and Homer Locker entered, almost dragging Yvette by the arm.... The congregation heard one sound. It was a glad, childish cry. "Eva!... Eva!... Here I am."

Then it saw Yvette Hinchbrooke wrench free from Homer and run down the aisle to snatch the child from Scattergood's arms into her own.

Scattergood stood erect, looking from face to face in silence. It was a full minute before he spoke.

"There ..." he said. "You kin see the evil of passin' jedgments. You kin see the evil of old coots traffickin' in rumors.... What you've heard the boy tell is all true.... That's the girl you was ready to tar and feather and run out of town.... Now what you think of yourselves?"

It was Deacon Pettybone, blinking a mist from his watery blue eyes, who arose to the moment. "Folks," he said, huskily, "I'm goin' to pass among you directly, carryin' the collection plate. 'Tain't fer furrin missions. It's fer that child yonder--to git them legs fixed.... And standin' here I want to acknowledge to sin in public. I been hard, and lackin' in charity. I been passin' jedgments, contrairy to God's word. I been stiff-backed and obdurate, and I calc'late they's others a-sittin' here that needs prayers for forgiveness.... Now I'm a-comin' with the plate. Them that hain't prepared to give to-night kin whisper to me what they'll give to-morrer--and have no fear of my forgittin' the amounts they pledge.... And I'm askin' forgiveness of the young woman and hopin' she won't hold it ag'in' an old man--when she settles down here amongst us, like I hope she'll do."

"Like she's a-goin' to do," said Jason Locker, with a voice and air of pride. "Why, folks, that there gal is goin' to be my daughter-in-law!"

Scattergood patted Yvette on the back heavily, but jubilantly. "I've diskivered," he said, "that if you can't crack a hick'ry nut with a pad of butter, you better use a hammer.... Sometimes Coldriver's a nut needin' a sledge--but when it cracks it's full of meat."

CHAPTER XIV
HE TREATS AN ATTACK OF LIFE

Scattergood Baines lounged back in his armchair, reinforced by iron cross-pieces to sustain his weight, and basked in the warmth from the Round Oak stove, heated to redness by the clean, dry maple within. He was drowsy. For the time he had ceased even to search for a scheme whereby he could rid his hardware stock of one dozen sixteen-pound sledge hammers acquired by him at a recent auction down in Tupper Falls. His eyes were closed and his soul was at peace.

Somebody rattled the door knob and then rapped on the door. This was so unusual a method of seeking entrance to a hardware store that Scattergood sat up abruptly, blinking.

"Wa-al," he said, tartly, "be you comin' in, or be you goin' to stand out there wagglin' that door knob all day?"

"I'm coming in, Mr. Baines, as soon as I can contrive to open the door," replied a male voice, a voice that appeared incapable of expressing impatience; a gentle voice; the voice of a man who would dream dreams but perform few actions.

"Um!... It's you, hey? What d'you allus carry books under your arm for? How d'you calculate to be able to open doors, with both hands full?"

The knob turned at last, and Nahum Pound, long schoolmaster in the little district school on Hiper Hill, came in hesitatingly, clutching with each arm half a dozen books which struggled to escape with the ingenuity of inanimate objects. Nahum's hair was white; his face was vague--lovably vague.... A man of considerable, if confused, learning, he was.

"Well?" said Scattergood. "Got suthin' on to your mind? Commence unloadin' it before it busts your back."

"It's Sarah," said Nahum, helplessly.

"Um!... Sairy, eh? What's Sairy up to?"

"I don't seem to gather, Mr. Baines. She's--she's difficult. Something seems to be working in her head."

"Twenty-two, hain't she? Twenty-two?... Prob'ly a number of things a-workin' in her head. Got any special symptoms?"

"She--she wants to leave home, Mr. Baines." Nahum said this with mild amazement. His amazement would have been no greater--and not a whit less mild--had his daughter announced her intention to swim from New York to Liverpool, or to marry the chef of the Czar of Russia.

"Um!... Can't say's that's onnatural--so's to require callin' in a doctor. Live five mile from town, don't you? Nearest neighbor nigh on to a mile. Sairy gits to see company only about so often or not so seldom as that, eh?" Scattergood shut his eyes until there appeared at the corners of them a network of little wrinkles. "I'm a-goin' to astonish you, Nahum. This here hain't the first girl that ever come down with the complaint Sairy's got!... They's been sev'ral. Complaint's older 'n you or me.... Dum near as old as Deacon Pettybone. Uh-huh!... She's got a attack of life, Nahum, and the only cure for it ever discovered is to let her live.... Sairy's woke up out of childhood, Nahum. She's jest openin' her eyes. Perty soon she'll be stirrin' around brisk.... When you goin' to drive her in, Nahum? To-morrer?"

"You--you advise letting her do this thing?"

"When you goin' to fetch her in, Nahum?" Scattergood repeated.

"She said she was coming Monday."

"Um!... G'-by, Nahum." This was Scattergood's invariable phrase of dismissal, given to friend or enemy alike. It was characteristic of him that when he was through with a conversation he ended it--and left no doubt in anybody's mind that it was ended. Nahum withdrew apologetically. Scattergood called after him, "Fetch her here--to me," he said, and, automatically, it seemed, reached for the laces of his shoes. A problem had been presented to him which required a deal of solving, and Scattergood could not concentrate with toes imprisoned in leather. He even removed the white woolen socks which Mandy, his wife, compelled him to wear in the winter season. Presently he was twiddling his pudgy toes and concentrating on Sarah Pound. He waggled his head. "After livin' out there," he said to himself, "she'll think Coldriver's livin'--and so 'tis, so 'tis.... More sometimes 'n 'tis others. Calculate this is like to be one of 'em...."

Scattergood was just thinking about dinner on Monday when Nahum Pound brought his daughter Sarah into the store. One glance at Sarah's face taught Scattergood that she was in suspicious, if not defiant, mood. If he had a doubt of the correctness of his observation, Sarah removed it efficiently.

"Scattergood Baines," she said, "if you think you're going to boss me like you do father, and everybody else in this town, you're mistaken. I won't have it.... Understand that, I won't have it."

Scattergood rubbed his chin and puffed out his fat cheeks, and smiled with deceiving mildness. "Sairy," he said, "you needn't to be scairt of my interferin' with you in your goin's and comin's. I'd sooner stick my hand into a kittle of b'ilin' pitch than to meddle with a young woman in your state of mind.... I hain't hankerin' to raise no blisters."

"I won't stay penned up 'way out there in the country another day. I've got a right to live. I've got a right to see folks and to go places, and--to--to live!"

"To be sure.... To be sure. Jest itchin' to kick the top bar off'n the pasture fence. Most certain you got a right to live, and nobody hain't goin' to hender you ... least of all me. But there's jest one observation I'd sort of like to let loose of, and that's this: Your life's a whole lot like one of your arms and legs--easy busted. To be sure, it kin be put in splints and mended up ag'in, but maybe you'll go limpy or knit crooked so's nothin' kin keep the busted place from showin'. Bearin' that in mind, if I was you, I wouldn't be too careless about scramblin' up into places where you was apt to git a fall.... I calc'late, Sairy, that it's better to miss the view than to fall out of the tree...."

"I'm going to see the view if I fall out of every tree I climb," Sarah said, hotly.

"Don't object if I find you a boardin' house?"

"I'm going to board with Grandma Penny that was--Mrs. Spackles."

Scattergood nodded. "G'-by, Sairy.... G'-by, Nahum." He watched father and daughter leave the store with a twinkle in his eyes, not a twinkle of humor, but the twinkle that always came when his interest in life, always keen, was aroused to a point where it tingled. "Calc'late to be kep' busy--more 'n ordinary busy," he offered as an opinion to be digested by the Round Oak stove. Presently he added:

"She's perty ... and bein' perty is kind of a remarkable thing ... bein' perty and young.... Don't seem like God ought to hold folks accountable fer bein' young, nor yet fer bein' good to look at ... but they's times when it seems like He does...." On his way back to the store after dinner, Scattergood stopped at the bank corner, hesitated a moment, and then mounted the stairs to the offices above. A door bearing the legend, "Robert Allen, Attorney at Law," admitted him to a large, bare office, such as one finds in such towns as Coldriver.

"Howdy, Bob?" said Scattergood.

"Good day, Mr. Baines," said the young man behind the desk, who had suddenly pretended to be very much occupied with important matters as his door opened.

"Um!... Busy time, eh? Better come back later."

"No. No, indeed. Take this chair right here, Mr. Baines. What can I do for you?"

"Depends. Uh-huh! Depends.... Calc'late to make a perty good livin', Bob?"

"No complaints."

"Studied it yourself, didn't you--out of books? No college?"

"Yes."

"Hard work, wasn't it? Mighty hard work?"

"It might have been easier," said Bob, wondering what Scattergood was getting at.

"Like to be prosecutin' attorney for this county, Bob?"

Prosecuting attorney! With a salary of twenty-five hundred dollars a year--and the prestige! Bob strove valiantly to maintain a look of dignified interest, but with ill success.

"I--I might consider it. Yes, I would consider it."

"Um!... Figgered you would," said Scattergood, dryly. "Hain't got no help in the office," he observed. "Need some, don't you? Somebody to write letters and sort of look after things, eh?"

"Why--er--I've never thought about it."

"If you was to think about it, you'd calc'late on payin' about six dollars a week, wouldn't you?" Bob swallowed hard. Six dollars a week was a great deal of money to this young man, just embarking on the practice of his profession. "Guess that would be about right," he said.

"Got anybody in mind, Bob? Thinkin' of anybody specific for the place?"

Bob shook his head.

"Um!... Nahum Pound's daughter's boardin' with Grandma Penny, that's now Mis' Spackles. All-fired perty girl, Bob. Don't call to mind no pertier. Sairy's her name.... G'-by, Bob. G'-by."

He walked to the door, but paused. "About that six dollars, Bob--I was figgerin' on payin' that out of my own pocket."

Bob Allen was not accustomed to the oversight of employees--least of all to an employee who was very satisfying to look at, who was winsomely young, whose mere presence distracted his thoughts from that rigorous concentration upon the logical principles of the law.... He did not know what to do with Sarah once he had hired her, and it required so much of his time and brain power to think up something for her to do that it is fortunate his practice was neither large nor arduous. It is no mean tribute to the young man that he kept Sarah so busy with apparently necessary matters that she had no occasion to doubt the authenticity of her employment.

Bob faced a second difficulty, due to his inexperience, and that was that he was at a loss how to comport himself toward Sarah, as to how friendly he should be, and as to how much he should maintain a certain grave dignity and reserve in his dealings with her. This was a matter which need not have troubled him, for Nature has a way of taking into her own keeping the bearing of young men toward young women when the two are thrown much into each other's company. Propinquity is a tremendous force in the life of humanity. It has caused as many love affairs as the kicking of other men's dogs has caused street fights--which numbers into infinity. Consequently, while Bob worried much and selected a number of widely differing attitudes--a thing which caused Sarah some uneasiness and no little speculation as to what sort of disposition her employer possessed--the solution lay not with him at all. It took care of itself.

Scattergood noted the significance of symptoms. He made a mental memorandum of the fact that Bob Allen was seldom to be seen among the post-office loafers; that Bob preferred his office to any other spot; that Bob had ordered a new suit from a city tailor; that Bob wore a constant air of anxiety and excitement, and--most expressive symptom of all for a Coldriver young man--he became interested in residence property, in lots, and in the cost of erecting dwellings.... Scattergood looked in vain for reciprocal symptoms to be shown by Sarah. But Sarah was a woman. What symptoms she exhibited were meaningless even to Scattergood.

"Bob," said Scattergood, one auspicious day, "got any pref'rence for prosecutin' attorneys--married or single?"

"It depends," said Bob, cautiously.

"Um!... How's Sairy behavin', Bob?"

"She's--she's--" Bob became incoherent, and then speechless.

"Calc'late I foller you, Bob.... Git your point of view exact.... About prosecutin' attorneys, Bob, I prefer 'em married."

"Mr. Baines," said Bob, "if I could get Sarah Pound to marry me, I wouldn't give a tinker's dam who was prosecutor."

"Mishandlin' of fact sim'lar to that," said Scattergood, dryly, "has been done nigh on to a billion times.... Any idee how Sairy stands on sich a proposition?"

"She's about equally fond of me and the letter press," said Bob, dolefully.

"Good sign," said Scattergood. Then after a short pause: "Say, Bob, still rent out drivin' bosses at the livery?... G'-by, Bob."

Bob was astonished to find how easy it is to ask a girl to go driving the second time--after you have spent an anxious, dubious, fearsome day screwing up your courage to ask her the first time. He was delighted, too, because he even fancied Sarah now discriminated between him and the letter press--in his favor. Bob came fresh and unsophisticated to the business in hand, which was courtship. Sarah had never before been courted, but she recognized a courtship when she saw it at such close range, and found it delightfully exciting. Bob did his clumsy, earnest, honest best, and Sarah, somewhat to her surprise, became more satisfied with the universe and with her share in its destinies.... In short, matters were progressing as nature intended they should progress, and Scattergood felt almost that they might be trusted to go forward to a satisfactory denouement without his interference.

Then old Solon Beatty died!

This solved one of Bob Allen's problems; it furnished plenty of authentic work for Sarah Pound--for Bob was retained as attorney for old Solon's estate, which he found to be in an amazing state of confusion. Old Solon left behind him, reluctantly, property of divers kinds, and in numerous localities, valued at upward of a hundred thousand dollars, split and invested into as many enterprises and mortgages and savings accounts as there were dollars! This made work. There were papers to sort and list, to file and to schedule--clerical work in abundance. It interfered with the more important business of courtship, but even in this respect it was not without a certain value.

"Who's going to get all this money?" Sarah asked, one morning after she had been listing mortgages until her head ached with the sight of figures and descriptions. "Does Mary Beatty get it all?"

"Not unless we find a will somewhere. Everybody thought Solon's niece--which is Mary Beatty--would get the whole estate. Solon intended it should go that way, and the Lord knows she's worked for him and nursed him and coddled him enough to deserve it. Gave her whole life up to the old codger ... But we can't find a will, and so she won't get but half. The rest goes to Solon's nephew, Farley Curtis ... under the statute of descent and distribution, you know," he finished, learnedly.

"Farley Curtis.... I never heard of him."

"He's never been here--at least not for years. But he'll be along now. We're due to see him soon."

"Correct," said a voice from the door, which had opened silently. In it stood a young man of dress and demeanor not indigenous to Coldriver. "You're due to see Farley Curtis--so you behold him. Look me over carefully. I was due--therefore I arrive." The young man laughed pleasantly, as if he intended his words to be regarded as whimsical, yet, somehow, Bob felt the whimsicality to be surface deep; that Curtis was a young man with much confidence in himself, who felt that if he were due he would inevitably arrive.

"Mr. Allen, I suppose," said Curtis, extending his hand. "I am told you are handling the legal affairs of my late uncle's estate."

Sarah Pound eyed the newcomer, and as the young men shook hands compared them, to Bob Allen's disadvantage. To inexperience any comparison must be to Bob's disadvantage, for Curtis was handsome, dressed with taste, and gifted with a worldly certainty of manner and an undeniable charm. Sarah had never encountered all these attributes in a single individual. She drew on her reading of fiction and knew at once that she was in the presence of that wonderful creature she had seen described so frequently--a gentleman. As for Bob Allen, he was big, rugged, careless of dress, kindly, without pretense of polish.... And besides, to Curtis's advantage there attached to him a certain literary glamour--of heirship--and a mystery due to his sudden appearance out of the great unknown that lay beyond the confines of Coldriver.

"I am in the dark," said Curtis. "All I know is that Uncle Solon is dead. It is proper I should come to you for information, is it not? For instance, there is no harm in asking if there is a will?"

"None has been found," said Bob, not graciously. He had taken a dislike to this stranger instinctively, a dislike which increased at an amazing pace as he noted Curtis's eyes cast admiring glances upon Sarah Pound.

"In which case," said the young man, "I suppose I may regard myself as an interested party."

"Yourself and Miss Beatty are the heirs--so far as has been determined."

"You have searched all my uncle's papers?"

"We have gone through them, but not so thoroughly as to reach a final conclusion. He was a peculiar old man."

"And no will has been found? No--other papers--" Curtis smiled deprecatingly. "It is only natural I should be interested," he said, and smiled at Sarah.

"Was there anything special you wanted to ask?"

"Only if there was a will--or other paper." There was a curious hesitation in Farley Curtis's voice as he spoke the last two words. "I'm glad, of course, there's not.... Thank you. Think I'll stay in town till the thing is settled up. Probably see you often. Pleased to have met you." He included Sarah in the bow with which he took his leave.

For a few days Farley Curtis lived at the Coldriver House, then moved to Grandmother Penny's, where Sarah Pound boarded. Secretly Bob Allen was furious, without apparent cause. He had no reason to draw conclusions, for boarding houses were scarce in Coldriver. What Sarah thought of the event was not so easily discovered.

Bob would naturally have discussed immediately the significance of Farley Curtis's arrival in Coldriver, with Scattergood, for everybody in Coldriver went to Scattergood with whatever important occurrence that befell, but Scattergood was absent on a political mission. When he returned Bob lost no time in laying the matter before him.

"Um!... Calculated he'd turn up. Natural.... Acted kind of anxious, eh? What was it he said about a will--or somethin'?"

Bob repeated Curtis's conversation minutely.

"Um!... That young man didn't suspect--he *knew*," said Scattergood, reaching automatically for his shoes. "What he wanted to know was--has it been found?... Um!... Not a will. Somethin'. Somethin' he's afraid of bein' found.... Hain't the kind of feller I'd like to see spendin' old Solon's money.... Guess you and me'll go through them papers ag'in."

So with minute care Bob and Scattergood examined the documents and memoranda and receipts and accounts of Solon Beatty, but no will, no minute reference to Farley Curtis, was discovered. They went again to Solon's house to question Mary and to rummage there with the hope of falling upon some such hiding place as the queer old man might have chosen as the safe depository of his will. Mary Beatty was not helpful; middle-aged, with wasted youth behind her; she was even resentful that her meticulous housekeeping should be disturbed.

Scattergood and Bob sat down in the parlor, discouraged. It was evident there was no will. Solon had neglected to attend to that matter until it was too late.... Scattergood wiggled his feet uneasily and stared at the motto over the door.

"Solon didn't run much to religion," he observed.

"No," said Mary Beatty.

"Um!... Have a Bible, maybe? One of them big ones?"

"Up in his room, Mr. Baines. It always laid on the table there--unopened."

"Opened it yourself lately, Mary? Been readin' the Scriptures out of that p'tic'lar book?"

"No."

"Um!... Got a kind of a hankerin' to read a verse or two," said Scattergood. "Come on, Bob. You 'n' me'll peruse Solon's Bible some."

The huge Bible with its Dore illustrations lay on the marble-topped table in old Solon's bedroom. Scattergood opened it--found it stiff with lack of use, its pages clinging together as if their gilt edging had never been broken.... Bob leaned over Scattergood while the old man rapidly thumbed the pages.... He brought to light a pressed flower, and shrugged his shoulders. What moment of softness in the life of a hard old man did this flower commemorate?... A letter whose ink was faded to illegibility! Even Solon Beatty had once known the rose-leaf scent of romance.

"Nothing there," said Bob.

"The reason folks seldom find things," said Scattergood, "is that they say 'Nothin' there' before they've half looked.... They might be any quantity of things in this Bible that we hain't overhauled yet." The old man stood a moment frowning down at the book. "Births and deaths," he said to himself. "Births and deaths--and marryin's...." Rapidly he turned to the illumined pages on which were set down the family records of the Beattys. "Um!... Jest sich a place as he'd pick out.... What you make of this, Bob?"

Scattergood loosened a sheet of paper which had been lightly glued to the page. "Hain't got my specs, Bob."

The young lawyer read it, re-read it aloud. "I, Farley Curtis, one of the two legal heirs of Solon Beatty, of Coldriver Township, do hereby acknowledge the receipt of ten thousand dollars, the same to be considered an advance of my share of the said Solon Beatty's estate. For, and in consideration of the said ten thousand dollars I hereby waive all claims to any further participation in the said estate, and agree that I will not, whether the said Solon Beatty dies testate or intestate, make any claim against the said estate, nor upon Mary Beatty, who, by this advance to me, becomes sole heir to the said estate.'"

Bob drew a long breath. Scattergood stared owlishly at Mary Beatty.

"Now, what d'you think of that, eh? Shouldn't be s'prised if that was the identical paper that was weighin' on the mind of young Mr. Curtis. Shouldn't be a mite s'prised if 'twas."

"What is it, Mr. Baines?" asked Mary Beatty. "A will?"

"Wa-al, offhand I'd say it was consid'able better 'n a will. Ya-as.... Wills kin be busted, but this here docyment--I calc'late it would take mighty powerful hammerin' to knock it apart."

"And, Mary," said Bob, "if I were you I shouldn't mention the finding of it."

"Not to a soul," said Scattergood. "We'll take it mighty soft and spry and shet it up in Bob's safe.... Anybody know the combination to it besides you, Bob?"

"Nobody but you, Mr. Baines."

"Oh, me!... To be sure, me."

"And Miss Pound." "Um!... Sairy, eh? Course.... Sairy."

Within twenty-four hours everybody in Coldriver knew a paper of great significance had been discovered affecting the heirs to Solon Beatty's estate, and that the paper was locked in Bob Allen's safe. Bob had not talked; Scattergood certainly had been silent, and Mary Beatty solemnly averred that no word had passed her lips. Yet the fact was there for all to contemplate.... Farley Curtis devoted an entire day to the contemplation of it in his room at Grandmother Penny's.... That evening he invited Sarah Pound to drive with him. She found him a delightful and entertaining companion.

Sunday was still two days away when Bob looked up from his desk to say to Sarah: "This Beatty matter has kept us so busy there hasn't been any time for pleasure. You must be tired out, Miss Pound. Wouldn't you like to start early Sunday and drive over to White Pine for dinner--and come back after the sun goes down? It's a beautiful drive."

"I'm sorry," said Sarah, flushing with a feeling that was akin to guilt, "but I am engaged Sunday."

Bob turned again to his work, cast into sudden gloom, and wondering jealously what was Sarah's engagement. Sarah, not altogether easy in her mind, nor wholly pleased with herself, endeavored to justify herself for being so lightly off with the old and on with the new.... She compared Bob to Farley Curtis, and found the comparison not in Bob's favor. Not that this was exactly a justification, but it was a salve. Sarah was in the shopping period of her life--shopping for a husband, so to speak. She was entitled to the best she could get ... and Bob did not seem to be the best. Farley was sprightly, interesting, with the manners of a more effete world than Coldriver; Bob was awkward, ofttimes silent, lacking polish. Farley was solicitous in small matters that Bob failed utterly to perceive; Farley was always skilled in minute points of decorum, whose very existence was unknown to Bob. In short, Farley was altogether fascinating, while Bob, at best, was commonplace. Yet, not in her objective mind, but deep in her centers of intuition, she was conscious of a hesitancy, conscious of something that urged her toward Bob and warned her against Farley Curtis.

On Sunday Bob saw Sarah drive away with Curtis--and spent a black day of jealousy and heartburning. During the succeeding two weeks he spent many black days and sleepless nights, for Curtis monopolized Sarah's leisure, and Sarah seemed to have thrown discretion to the winds and clothed herself against fear of Coldriver's gossip, for she seemed to give her company almost eagerly to the stranger.... And Coldriver talked.

Bob spoke bitterly of the matter to Scattergood.

"Um!..." grunted Scattergood, "don't seem to recall any statute forbiddin' any young feller to git him any gal he kin. Eh?"

"No. But this Curtis--there's something wrong there. He isn't intending to play fair.... I--He's got some kind of a purpose, Mr. Baines."

"Think so, eh? What kind of a purpose?" Scattergood had his own ideas on this subject, but did not disclose them. It was in his mind that Curtis cultivated Sarah because of Sarah's propinquity of a certain paper which the man had reason to believe was in Bob Allen's safe.

Bob's face was set and stern, granite as the hills among which he had been born and which had become a part of his nature. "If he doesn't play fair ... if he should-- hurt her ... I'd take him apart, Mr. Baines."

"Calc'late you would," said Scattergood, tranquilly, "but there's a law in sich case, made and pervided, callin' that kind of amusement murder ..."

It was not Scattergood's custom to publish his emotions; nevertheless he was worried. He appreciated the state of mind which had brought Sarah to Coldriver- -the spirit of restless, resentful youth, demanding the world for its plaything. He knew Sarah's high temper, her eagerness for adventure.... He knew that thousands of girls before her had been fascinated by well-told tales of the life to be lived out in the world of cities, of wealth, of artificial gayeties ... the lure of travel, of excitement.... And Scattergood did not covet the duty of carrying a woeful story to old Nahum Pound, the gentle schoolmaster.

His uneasiness was not decreased by a bit of unpremeditated eavesdropping that fell in his way the next evening.... Farley Curtis was talking, Sarah Pound was listening--eagerly.

"You can't understand what living is," the man was saying, "How could you? You haven't lived. Here in this backwater you will never live.... You move around in a fog of monotony. Every day the same. But out there.... Everything! Everything you want and can imagine is there for the taking. A beautiful woman can take what she wants--that's what it's all for--for her to help herself to. Life and excitement and pleasure--and love ... they are all out there waiting."

Sarah sighed.

"Did you ever try to imagine Paris, London, Madrid, Rome?" he went on. "You can't do it.... But you can see them. I--I would take you if you would let me ... if things fall out right. I'm poor ...but with this Beatty money I could take you anywhere. It would give us everything we want.... Half of that money belongs to me rightfully, doesn't it?"

"I suppose so."

"But I may not get it."

She was silent.

"There is a paper," he said, "and that paper may stand between you and me--and Paris and Rome and the world...." He paused, and then said, carelessly: "Won't you go with me, Sarah--away from this? Won't you let me take you, to love and to make happy?"

Presently she spoke, so low her voice was scarcely audible to Scattergood. "I don't know.... I don't know," she said.

Scattergood had heard enough. He stole away silently. The time had come to act, if he were going to act ... if no woeful story were to be carried to old Nahum Pound concerning his daughter. He might even be too late.... The lure of great cities and foreign shores might have done its work, and Farley Curtis's eloquence have served its purpose.

In the morning Bob Allen was early at his office. His first act was to open the safe to take out a packet of papers he had been laboring over the afternoon before.... The packet was not where he had placed it the night before. He remembered distinctly how he had shoved it into a certain pigeonhole.... It was not there. He found it in the compartment below.... Bob was not easily startled or frightened, so now he paused and took his memory to account. No.... The fault was not with his memory. He had done exactly as he remembered doing.... Somebody had opened that safe since he closed it; somebody had fingered its contents.... He caught his breath, not at the fear of loss, but in sudden terror of the means by which that loss had been brought about, the person who might have been the instrument.... Furiously he began going over the contents of the safe--money, securities, papers. Everything seemed intact. But one thing remained--the little drawer. He had put off opening that, because he dreaded to open it, for it contained the paper that excluded Farley Curtis from a share in his uncle's estate.... Bob compelled himself to turn the little key, to open the drawer.... It was empty!...

Bob walked slowly to his desk and sat down, his eyes fixed upon the safe as if it fascinated him.... Facts, facts! His soul demanded facts. Those at hand were few, simple. First, the safe had been opened by some one who knew the combination. Three persons existed who might have opened it--or betrayed its combination: Scattergood, himself, Sarah Pound.... Second, he knew he had not opened it nor betrayed the combination. Third, he was equally certain Scattergood had not done so.... Fourth--he groaned!...

Bob comprehended what had happened; why Farley Curtis had wooed so persistently Sarah Pound. It was not out of love nor desire, but for a more sordid purpose ... it was to win her love, to blind her to honor, to make a tool of her, and through her to secure possession of that bit of paper which stood between him and riches.

Presently Sarah Pound entered. Bob could not force himself to look at her; did not speak. She gazed at him curiously, and when she saw the grayness of his face, the lines about his mouth, and eyes that advanced his age by twenty years, she felt a little catch at her heart, a breathlessness, a sudden alarm.

"Miss Pound," he said, in a voice which he himself could not recognize as his own, "you needn't take off your hat.... You--you actually came back here! You were bold enough to come again to this office.... I fancied you would be gone--from Coldriver." His voice broke queerly. "I suppose you realize what you have done--and are satisfied with the price--the price of forfeiting the respect of every honest man and woman you know! That is a great deal to give up. It ought to command a high price--treachery.... I hope you are getting a sufficient return.... It means nothing to you, of course, but--I loved you. I thought about you as a man thinks about the woman he hopes will be his wife ... and his children's mother ... so it--pains--to find you despicable...."

Sarah's little fists clenched, her eyes glinted.

"How dare you?" she cried. "What affair is it of yours what I do?... You're a silly, jealous idiot." With which childish invective she flung out of the office.

In an hour Bob Allen was calmer, and so the more unhappy. His mind cleared, and, being cleared, it directed him to carry his trouble to Scattergood Baines.

"Um!... Gone, eh?" said Scattergood. "Sure it's gone?... Um!..."

"Yes, and Sarah Pound will be gone, too. How dared she come back to my office?... Now she'll go with Curtis."

"Shouldn't be s'prised," said Scattergood, waggling his head. "I heard Farley a-pointin' out to her the dee-sirability of Paris and Rome and sich European p'ints last night.... You calculate Sairy took the paper?"

"What else can I think?"

"To be sure.... Um!... Paris, Rome, London--might be argued into stealin' it myself, if I was a gal. Um!... Ever see a toad ketch flies, Bob? Does it with his tongue. There's toad men, Bob, that goes huntin' wimmin the same way--with their tongues. Su'prisin' the number and quality they ketch, too. What was you plannin' on doin', Bob? Goin' back to your office, wasn't you? And keepin' your mouth shet? Was that the idee? Eh?"

"I don't know what to do, Mr. Baines."

"Didn't figger on droppin' around to Grandma Penny's boardin' house about eight sharp, did you? Eight sharp.... And kind of settin' down quiet on the front porch? Jest settin'? Eh?... G'-by, Bob."

After Bob left the store Scattergood sat half an hour staring at the stove; then he left the store to its own devices and wandered up the street toward Grandmother Penny's. He encountered Sarah Pound as she came out through the gate.

"Howdy, Sairy?" he said, cheerfully. "Havin' consid'able amusement with life--eh?"

"I've been enjoying myself, Mr. Baines," Sarah said, making an effort at coldness and dignity.

"Bet you hain't enjoyin' yourself enough to warrant your doin' a favor for an old feller like me, eh?... This evenin', for instance?"

"I--I'm going away this evening."

"Um!... Goin' away, eh? Alone? Or along with somebody?"

"That's my own affair."

"To be sure.... To be sure, but the train don't leave till nine, does it? Couldn't manage to do me a favor at eight?"

"What is the favor, Mr. Baines?"

"'Tain't much. Sca'cely anythin' a-tall. I calc'late to be a-settin' in Grandma Penny's parlor at eight sharp. I won't keep you waitin' more 'n a second--unless somebody happens to be with me a-talkin' my arm off. If they hain't nobody with me, why, you walk right in. If they is somebody, why, you jest stand outside of the door a second, and they'll be gone. Then you come in. But don't come rompin' in if you hear voices. It's a mite of business, and 'twon't take but a second. Calc'late you kin manage that, eh?"

"Yes," she said, shortly.

"Promise?"

"Yes."

"G'-by, Sairy."

At five minutes before eight Scattergood Baines rapped at Grandmother Penny's door and asked to speak to Farley Curtis, "Tell him it's somethin' p'tic'lar ree-gardin' the Beatty estate," he said, and stepped into the parlor. Farley appeared almost instantly; dapper, his usual courteous, self-possessed self. Scattergood began a peculiar and roundabout conversation after the manner of a man who fears to broach a subject plainly. Farley showed his irritation.

"Mr. Baines," he said, "suppose you get down to business. I'm going away this evening."

"To be sure.... To be sure. It's overlappin' eight now, hain't it?" Scattergood paused, listening. He fancied he heard some one approach and halt just outside the door. He was certain that a chair creaked on the porch outside the window.... He cleared his throat and drew a big yellow envelope from his pocket.

"Calculate I'm ready for business, if you be.... Which d'you calc'late is most desirable--havin' half a loaf, or no bread?"

"What do you mean?"

"You come to Coldriver on business, didn't you? Money business?"

"Why I came is my own affair."

"Certain.... Certain.... But things gets noised about. Things has got noised about concernin' a paper that stands betwixt you and half of the Beatty estate. Heard 'em myself." Scattergood waggled the envelope. "I hain't exactly objectin' to makin' a leetle quick money myself--supposin' it kin be done safe, and the blame, if they is any, throwed somewheres else.... Now, Mr. Curtis, what kind of a course would you foller if that paper we been talkin' about was to fall into the hands of a feller that felt like I do about makin' money?"

"What do you mean?" Farley demanded, moving forward eagerly in his chair.

"Hain't good at guessin', be you?"

"That paper doesn't worry me," said Farley. "Calc'lated on havin' it before you took the train to-night, eh?"

Farley scowled.

"Uh-huh!... Wa-al, I wasn't seein' sich a chance to make a dollar slip by. The way you was figgerin' on gittin' that paper, Mr. Curtis, won't work. I know. Uh-huh! I know, because I got ahead of you. I got that paper myself.... And we kin deal if I kin be made to feel safe.... Most things leaks out through wimmin.... Hain't mixin' any wimmin into this, be you?"

"No."

"Um!... How about Sairy Pound?"

Curtis shrugged his shoulders.

"Calc'latin' on takin' her away with you to-night?"

"Not now," said Farley.

"Seein's how you can't use her to git this paper for you, eh? That it?"

"Yes."

"Calc'lated on marryin' her, didn't you?"

"Fiddlesticks!" said Mr. Curtis, harshly.

"Understand me, I hain't takin' chances.... If this gal's mixed up in this, I don't deal."

"Do I look like a man who would let a silly, backwoods idiot of a girl stand between me and money? I'm through with her. She's no use to me now. You've said that yourself.... She's nothing to me."

"Good.... I got the paper right here, and I'm a-listenin' to your offer for it...."

"Ten thous--" began Farley, but a swift, furious thrusting open of the parlor door interrupted, as Sarah Pound flung herself into the room. For a moment she was speechless with rage.... Shame would come later.... "You contemptible--contemptible--contemptible--" she cried, breathlessly. "It was a thing like you I--I could choose!... I could throw away a man for you!... For a suit of clothes, and man-

ners, and a lying tongue.... I could compare Bob Allen with you--and choose you!...
Oh!..."

"Sairy," said Scattergood.

"But I never would have done it--not that. I'd never have taken that paper....
You know I wouldn't, Mr. Baines. Say you know that...."

"Wa-al," said Scattergood, dryly, "they hain't no tellin' how fur a woman'll go
when she's bein' bamboozled by a scamp--so I kind of insured ag'in' your takin' it
by takin' it myself.... Er--Mr. Curtis, if I was you, I'd sort of slip out soft by the back
door. Bob Allen's a-waitin' for you on the front porch.... There's a train at nine."

Scattergood put a clumsy arm about Sarah, who, the moment her wrathful energy ebbed away, sobbed and sobbed and sobbed with shame and fear.

"Hey, out there," shouted Scattergood, "git a move on you!"

Bob Allen needed no urging. His arm was substituted for Scattergood's, his
breast for Scattergood's--and Sarah made no complaint. "I wouldn't.... I wouldn't....
You thought I did," she murmured.

"I thought that," said Bob, brokenly. "How can you ever forgive me?... I--But I
love you, Sarah. Won't that make up for it?"

"You--believed it," she repeated, and Scattergood grinned.

"Dummed if she hain't managed to put him in the wrong.... You can't beat
wimmin.... She's put him in the wrong."

Scattergood peered at them a moment, saw what filled him with perfect satisfaction, and discreetly withdrew. He went out and sat on the porch and beamed up
at the stars.... He sat there a long, long time, and nobody called him in. He got up,
pressed his nose against the window, and rapped on the glass.

"Everybody forgiv' and fixed up," he called, "so's I kin git to bed with an easy
mind?"

There was no answer. He had not been heard--but what he saw was answer
sufficient for any man.

The Codes Of Hammurabi And Moses
W. W. Davies

QTY

The discovery of the Hammurabi Code is one of the greatest achievements of archaeology, and is of paramount interest, not only to the student of the Bible, but also to all those interested in ancient history...

Religion   **ISBN:** *1-59462-338-4*   **Pages:132**
MSRP $12.95

The Theory of Moral Sentiments
Adam Smith

QTY

This work from 1749. contains original theories of conscience amd moral judgment and it is the foundation for systemof morals.

Philosophy   **ISBN:** *1-59462-777-0*   **Pages:536**
MSRP $19.95

Jessica's First Prayer
Hesba Stretton

QTY

In a screened and secluded corner of one of the many railway-bridges which span the streets of London there could be seen a few years ago, from five o'clock every morning until half past eight, a tidily set-out coffee-stall, consisting of a trestle and board, upon which stood two large tin cans, with a small fire of charcoal burning under each so as to keep the coffee boiling during the early hours of the morning when the work-people were thronging into the city on their way to their daily toil...

Childrens   **ISBN:** *1-59462-373-2*
Pages:84
MSRP $9.95

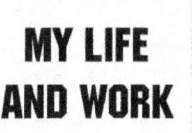

My Life and Work
Henry Ford

QTY

Henry Ford revolutionized the world with his implementation of mass production for the Model T automobile. Gain valuable business insight into his life and work with his own auto-biography... "We have only started on our development of our country we have not as yet, with all our talk of wonderful progress, done more than scratch the surface. The progress has been wonderful enough but..."

Biographies/   **ISBN:** *1-59462-198-5*
Pages:300
MSRP $21.95

The Art of Cross-Examination
Francis Wellman

QTY

I presume it is the experience of every author, after his first book is published upon an important subject, to be almost overwhelmed with a wealth of ideas and illustrations which could readily have been included in his book, and which to his own mind, at least, seem to make a second edition inevitable. Such certainly was the case with me; and when the first edition had reached its sixth impression in five months, I rejoiced to learn that it seemed to my publishers that the book had met with a sufficiently favorable reception to justify a second and considerably enlarged edition. ..

Reference   ISBN: *1-59462-647-2*

Pages:412

MSRP $19.95

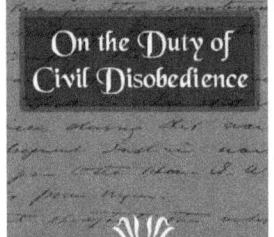

On the Duty of Civil Disobedience
Henry David Thoreau

QTY

Thoreau wrote his famous essay, On the Duty of Civil Disobedience, as a protest against an unjust but popular war and the immoral but popular institution of slave-owning. He did more than write—he declined to pay his taxes, and was hauled off to gaol in consequence. Who can say how much this refusal of his hastened the end of the war and of slavery ?

Law   ISBN: *1-59462-747-9*

Pages:48

MSRP $7.45

Dream Psychology Psychoanalysis for Beginners
Sigmund Freud

QTY

Sigmund Freud, born Sigismund Schlomo Freud (May 6, 1856 - September 23, 1939), was a Jewish-Austrian neurologist and psychiatrist who co-founded the psychoanalytic school of psychology. Freud is best known for his theories of the unconscious mind, especially involving the mechanism of repression; his redefinition of sexual desire as mobile and directed towards a wide variety of objects; and his therapeutic techniques, especially his understanding of transference in the therapeutic relationship and the presumed value of dreams as sources of insight into unconscious desires.

Psychology   ISBN: *1-59462-905-6*

Pages:196

MSRP $15.45

The Miracle of Right Thought
Orison Swett Marden

QTY

Believe with all of your heart that you will do what you were made to do. When the mind has once formed the habit of holding cheerful, happy, prosperous pictures, it will not be easy to form the opposite habit. It does not matter how improbable or how far away this realization may see, or how dark the prospects may be, if we visualize them as best we can, as vividly as possible, hold tenaciously to them and vigorously struggle to attain them, they will gradually become actualized, realized in the life. But a desire, a longing without endeavor, a yearning abandoned or held indifferently will vanish without realization.

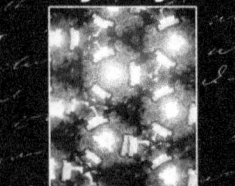

Pages:360

Self Help   ISBN: *1-59462-644-8*

MSRP $25.45

QTY

☐ **The Rosicrucian Cosmo-Conception Mystic Christianity** *by Max Heindel*　ISBN: *1-59462-188-8*　**$38.95**
The Rosicrucian Cosmo-conception is not dogmatic, neither does it appeal to any other authority than the reason of the student. It is: not controversial, but is: sent forth in the, hope that it may help to clear...　New Age/Religion Pages 646

☐ **Abandonment To Divine Providence** *by Jean-Pierre de Caussade*　ISBN: *1-59462-228-0*　**$25.95**
"The Rev. Jean Pierre de Caussade was one of the most remarkable spiritual writers of the Society of Jesus in France in the 18th Century. His death took place at Toulouse in 1751. His works have gone through many editions and have been republished...　Inspirational/Religion Pages 400

☐ **Mental Chemistry** *by Charles Haanel*　ISBN: *1-59462-192-6*　**$23.95**
Mental Chemistry allows the change of material conditions by combining and appropriately utilizing the power of the mind. Much like applied chemistry creates something new and unique out of careful combinations of chemicals the mastery of mental chemistry...　New Age/Business Pages 354

☐ **The Letters of Robert Browning and Elizabeth Barret Barrett 1845-1846 vol II**　ISBN: *1-59462-193-4*　**$35.95**
by Robert Browning and Elizabeth Barrett　Biographies Pages 596

☐ **Gleanings In Genesis (volume I)** *by Arthur W. Pink*　ISBN: *1-59462-130-6*　**$27.45**
Appropriately has Genesis been termed "the seed plot of the Bible" for in it we have, in germ form, almost all of the great doctrines which are afterwards fully developed in the books of Scripture which follow...　Religion/Inspirational Pages 420

☐ **The Master Key** *by L. W. de Laurence*　ISBN: *1-59462-001-6*　**$30.95**
In no branch of human knowledge has there been a more lively increase of the spirit of research during the past few years than in the study of Psychology, Concentration and Mental Discipline. The requests for authentic lessons in Thought Control, Mental Discipline and...　New Age/Business Pages 422

☐ **The Lesser Key Of Solomon Goetia** *by L. W. de Laurence*　ISBN: *1-59462-092-X*　**$9.95**
This translation of the first book of the "Lernegton" which is now for the first time made accessible to students of Talismanic Magic was done, after careful collation and edition, from numerous Ancient Manuscripts in Hebrew, Latin, and French...　New Age/Occult Pages 92

☐ **Rubaiyat Of Omar Khayyam** *by Edward Fitzgerald*　ISBN:*1-59462-332-5*　**$13.95**
Edward Fitzgerald, whom the world has already learned, in spite of his own efforts to remain within the shadow of anonymity, to look upon as one of the rarest poets of the century, was born at Bredfield, in Suffolk, on the 31st of March, 1809. He was the third son of John Purcell...　Music Pages 172

☐ **Ancient Law** *by Henry Maine*　ISBN: *1-59462-128-4*　**$29.95**
The chief object of the following pages is to indicate some of the earliest ideas of mankind, as they are reflected in Ancient Law, and to point out the relation of those ideas to modern thought.　Religiom/History Pages 452

☐ **Far-Away Stories** *by William J. Locke*　ISBN: *1-59462-129-2*　**$19.45**
"Good wine needs no bush, but a collection of mixed vintages does. And this book is just such a collection. Some of the stories I do not want to remain buried for ever in the museum files of dead magazine-numbers an author's not unpardonable vanity..."　Fiction Pages 272

☐ **Life of David Crockett** *by David Crockett*　ISBN: *1-59462-250-7*　**$27.45**
"Colonel David Crockett was one of the most remarkable men of the times in which he lived. Born in humble life, but gifted with a strong will, an indomitable courage, and unremitting perseverance...　Biographies/New Age Pages 424

☐ **Lip-Reading** *by Edward Nitchie*　ISBN: *1-59462-206-X*　**$25.95**
Edward B. Nitchie, founder of the New York School for the Hard of Hearing, now the Nitchie School of Lip-Reading, Inc, wrote "LIP-READING Principles and Practice". The development and perfecting of this meritorious work on lip-reading was an undertaking...　How-to Pages 400

☐ **A Handbook of Suggestive Therapeutics, Applied Hypnotism, Psychic Science**　ISBN: *1-59462-214-0*　**$24.95**
by Henry Munro　Health/New Age/Health/Self-help Pages 376

☐ **A Doll's House: and Two Other Plays** *by Henrik Ibsen*　ISBN: *1-59462-112-8*　**$19.95**
Henrik Ibsen created this classic when in revolutionary 1848 Rome. Introducing some striking concepts in playwriting for the realist genre, this play has been studied the world over.　Fiction/Classics/Plays 308

☐ **The Light of Asia** *by sir Edwin Arnold*　ISBN: *1-59462-204-3*　**$13.95**
In this poetic masterpiece, Edwin Arnold describes the life and teachings of Buddha. The man who was to become known as Buddha to the world was born as Prince Gautama of India but he rejected the worldly riches and abandoned the reigns of power when...　Religion/History/Biographies Pages 170

☐ **The Complete Works of Guy de Maupassant** *by Guy de Maupassant*　ISBN: *1-59462-157-8*　**$16.95**
"For days and days, nights and nights, I had dreamed of that first kiss which was to consecrate our engagement, and I knew not on what spot I should put my lips..."　Fiction/Classics Pages 240

☐ **The Art of Cross-Examination** *by Francis L. Wellman*　ISBN: *1-59462-309-0*　**$26.95**
Written by a renowned trial lawyer, Wellman imparts his experience and uses case studies to explain how to use psychology to extract desired information through questioning.　How-to/Science/Reference Pages 408

☐ **Answered or Unanswered?** *by Louisa Vaughan*　ISBN: *1-59462-248-5*　**$10.95**
Miracles of Faith in China　Religion Pages 112

☐ **The Edinburgh Lectures on Mental Science (1909)** *by Thomas*　ISBN: *1-59462-008-3*　**$11.95**
This book contains the substance of a course of lectures recently given by the writer in the Queen Street Hall, Edinburgh. Its purpose is to indicate the Natural Principles governing the relation between Mental Action and Material Conditions...　New Age/Psychology Pages 148

☐ **Ayesha** *by H. Rider Haggard*　ISBN: *1-59462-301-5*　**$24.95**
Verily and indeed it is the unexpected that happens! Probably if there was one person upon the earth from whom the Editor of this, and of a certain previous history, did not expect to hear again...　Classics Pages 380

☐ **Ayala's Angel** *by Anthony Trollope*　ISBN: *1-59462-352-X*　**$29.95**
The two girls were both pretty, but Lucy who was twenty-one who supposed to be simple and comparatively unattractive, whereas Ayala was credited, as her Bombwhat romantic name might show, with poetic charm and a taste for romance. Ayala when her father died was nineteen...　Fiction Pages 484

☐ **The American Commonwealth** *by James Bryce*　ISBN: *1-59462-286-8*　**$34.45**
An interpretation of American democratic political theory. It examines political mechanics and society from the perspective of Scotsman James Bryce　Politics Pages 572

☐ **Stories of the Pilgrims** *by Margaret P. Pumphrey*　ISBN: *1-59462-116-0*　**$17.95**
This book explores pilgrims religious oppression in England as well as their escape to Holland and eventual crossing to America on the Mayflower, and their early days in New England...　History Pages 268

QTY

The Fasting Cure *by Sinclair Upton*   ISBN: *1-59462-222-1* **$13.95**
In the Cosmopolitan Magazine for May, 1910, and in the Contemporary Review (London) for April, 1910, I published an article dealing with my experiences in fasting. I have written a great many magazine articles, but never one which attracted so much attention... New Age/Self Help/Health Pages 164

Hebrew Astrology *by Sepharial*   ISBN: *1-59462-308-2* **$13.45**
In these days of advanced thinking it is a matter of common observation that we have left many of the old landmarks behind and that we are now pressing forward to greater heights and to a wider horizon than that which represented the mind-content of our progenitors... Astrology Pages 144

Thought Vibration or The Law of Attraction in the Thought World   ISBN: *1-59462-127-6* **$12.95**
by William Walker Atkinson   *Psychology/Religion Pages 144*

Optimism *by Helen Keller*   ISBN: *1-59462-108-X* **$15.95**
Helen Keller was blind, deaf, and mute since 19 months old, yet famously learned how to overcome these handicaps, communicate with the world, and spread her lectures promoting optimism. An inspiring read for everyone... Biographies/Inspirational Pages 84

Sara Crewe *by Frances Burnett*   ISBN: *1-59462-360-0* **$9.45**
In the first place, Miss Minchin lived in London. Her home was a large, dull, tall one, in a large, dull square, where all the houses were alike, and all the sparrows were alike, and where all the door-knockers made the same heavy sound... Childrens/Classic Pages 88

The Autobiography of Benjamin Franklin *by Benjamin Franklin*   ISBN: *1-59462-135-7* **$24.95**
The Autobiography of Benjamin Franklin has probably been more extensively read than any other American historical work, and no other book of its kind has had such ups and downs of fortune. Franklin lived for many years in England, where he was agent... Biographies/History Pages 332

Name	
Email	
Telephone	
Address	
City, State ZIP	

☐ **Credit Card**   ☐ **Check / Money Order**

Credit Card Number	
Expiration Date	
Signature	

Please Mail to: Book Jungle
                   PO Box 2226
                   Champaign, IL 61825
or Fax to: 630-214-0564

ORDERING INFORMATION

web*: www.bookjungle.com*
email*: sales@bookjungle.com*
fax*: 630-214-0564*
mail*: Book Jungle PO Box 2226 Champaign, IL 61825*
or PayPal *to sales@bookjungle.com*

Please contact us for bulk discounts

DIRECT-ORDER TERMS

**20% Discount if You Order
Two or More Books**
Free Domestic Shipping!
Accepted: Master Card, Visa,
Discover, American Express

www.ingramcontent.com/pod-product-compliance
Lightning Source LLC
Chambersburg PA
CBHW080900020726
47502CB00008B/2297